Murder comes to Edendale?

A CJ Gray
Mystery

Murder comes to Edendale?

CJ Meads

ISBN: 979-8-3903-7618-8
Independently Published

DEDICATION

For those I love and cherish.
You know who you are.

MURDER COMES TO EDENDALE?

When local businessman and entrepreneur Oliver Tate's body is found dead on the 4th Green of Edendale Golf Club, CJ Gray, his enigmatic side kick Eden Songe, and his loyal cocker spaniel Oscar, are drawn into an adventure of murder, smuggling, greed, corruption, kidnapping, lust, and romance.

Set around the stunning Golf Club in the picturesque North Yorkshire village of Edendale, the story takes you from the sunny metropolis of Dubai to the glorious Yorkshire Dales.

Prospective Golf Club chairman, Oliver Tate sources the *long missing* Aston Martin DB5 from the 1964 James Bond film Goldfinger, from a wealthy Emirati in Dubai, and sells it to Earl Hargrove, President of the Golf Club, who is prepared to pay over the odds, but will stop at nothing to ensure Tate doesn't become chairman of his beloved club. Once the deal is done, the car is shipped to the UK and is used to smuggle drugs and diamonds.

When things don't go to plan, it starts to get very messy, and people are far from happy with Tate. This includes his glamorous and younger trophy wife, who's latest indiscretion proves too much for her husband, and all hell breaks loose.

The whodunnit story provides an opportunity for everyone to enjoy the escapism, that will keep you guessing until the final twist.

CJ Meads first novel is an easy read, page turning, light hearted romantic whodunnit.

CONTENTS

TODAY   1

PART 1 - EARLIER IN THE SPRING   2

CHAPTER 1 - THE ENCOUNTER   3

CHAPTER 2 - THE MEETING   6

CHAPTER 3 - WAY BACK WHEN   9

CHAPTER 4 – EDENDALE   14

CHAPTER 5 - BRIEF ENCOUNTER   19

CHAPTER 6 - A STROLL IN THE PARK   26

CHAPTER 7 - THE DEAL   33

CHAPTER 8 - THE NOMINATION   36

CHAPTER 9 – THE GLORY   41

CHAPTER 10 - OVERHEAR MANOR   47

CHAPTER 11 - THE MERCHANDISE   52

CHAPTER 12 - THE SON AND HEIR   56

CHAPTER 13 - GGL   60

CHAPTER 14 - RSM CLIFF LEDGER   67

CHAPTER 15 - COMMITTEE MATTERS   78

CHAPTER 16 - THE FIXER   82

CHAPTER 17 - SO NICE TO COME HOME   91

CHAPTER 18 - WHO ARE YOU?   96

CHAPTER 19 - THE LOCAL DEALER   100

CHAPTER 20 - NICE TO SEE YOU AGAIN   103

CHAPTER 21 – YORKSBEY   107

CHAPTER 22 – FELIXSTOWE   115

CHAPTER 23 - THE CONSTABULARY   120

CHAPTER 24 - THE MAN IN THE GRAY SUIT   125

CHAPTER 25 - THE DELIVERY   129

CHAPTER 26 - THE HOOK   135

CHAPTER 27 - PLAYING A ROUND   140

CHAPTER 28 - THE BALLOT   146

CHAPTER 29 - THE LURE   150

CHAPTER 30 - THE FIRST DEMAND   153

CHAPTER 31 - THE STROLL TO THE PUB.   157

CHAPTER 32 - THE SPARE   162

CHAPTER 33 - CHARITY MASQUERADE BALL   166

CHAPTER 34 - THE DANCE   171

CHAPTER 35 - ONE LAST PUSH   176

CHAPTER 36 - THE AUCTION   179

CHAPTER 37 - THE SECOND DEMAND   186

CHAPTER 38 - I LOVE YOU?   188

CHAPTER 39 - THE SLAP   192

CHAPTER 40 - THE BODY   195

PART 2   196

CHAPTER 41 - THE MORNING AFTER   197

CHAPTER 42 - BATMAN'S DEAD   200

CHAPTER 43 - RE-EVALUATION   203

CHAPTER 44 - WELL, WHAT DO WE HAVE?   207

CHAPTER 45 - THE VICTIM   211

CHAPTER 46 - WHAT ABOUT YOU LOT.   215

CHAPTER 47 - A WASTED BALLOT?   221

CHAPTER 48 - SORRY FOR YOUR LOSS….   226

CHAPTER 49 - WHERE WERE YOU LAST NIGHT?   232

CHAPTER 50 - HOW ARE YOU FEELING NOW?   238

CHAPTER 51 - SORRY FOR YOUR LOSS, TOO   246

CHAPTER 52 - POST MORTEM   252

CHAPTER 53 - THE SUSPECTS   256

CHAPTER 54 - WHERE THERE'S A WILL   260

CHAPTER 55 - PRODIGAL SON RETURNS   265

CHAPTER 56 - I'M ARRESTING YOU …   271

CHAPTER 57 - IS THIS REALLY SENSIBLE?   277

CHAPTER 58 - STOP WASTING YOUR TIME   282

CHAPTER 59 - FOLLOW THAT WOMAN   287

CHAPTER 60 - WHAT'S IN THE SAFE?   295

CHAPTER 61 - WHITE AND PARKER   299

CHAPTER 62 - INCRIMINATING EVIDENCE?   304

CHAPTER 63 - DINNER DATES   312

CHAPTER 64 - THE NIGHT OUT   315

CHAPTER 65 - BACK TO MY PLACE   322

CHAPTER 66 - THE MORNING AFTER   325

CHAPTER 67 - WE HAVE A WARRANT   329

CHAPTER 68 - ARE YOU FEELING BETTER?   336

CHAPTER 69 - THE CHASE IS ON   340

CHAPTER 70 - WHERE'S THE CAR?   349

CHAPTER 71 – THE PLAN   357

CHAPTER 72 - WAS THIS HOW IT HAPPENED?   360

CHAPTER 73 - THE EVIDENCE   373

CHAPTER 74 - ALL'S WELL THAT ENDS WELL   380

EPILOGUE   385

EDENDALE GOLF COURSE   391

TODAY

CJ Gray lowered his newspaper, he was relaxing in the high-backed leather arm chair in the restaurant of Edendale Golf Club, overlooking the 18th Green.

What could be the commotion.

'Nancy, what's going on?' CJ enquired.

The pretty young waitress looked flustered, her long brown hair rather dishevelled and falling out of her normal neat bun.

'Oh Mr Gray, you'll never guess, there's a dead body on the 4th Green, they think it might be Oliver Tate.'

'Oh F**k.' I think that's going to mean a change of plan…

CJ Meads

PART 1 - EARLIER IN THE SPRING

CHAPTER 1 - THE ENCOUNTER

The early morning Dubai sun was glistening off the manicured lawns of the sweeping driveway leading to the Montgomerie Golf Club. Jemima Gray's Mini Convertible was speeding, she was late for her first lesson.

She pulled up into the car park. It was full of the usual mixture of Ferrari's, Porsche's, Range Rover's, and other even more luxury cars. Her little car looked rather out of place to the uninitiated, but to the regulars it was readily recognisable.

The doorman opened the large glass door and warmly welcomed Jemima as he always did when she was working as the part time Pro for lady golfers.

'Good morning Miss Jemima.'

'Good morning Rhandi. Sorry can't stop I'm late.'

The stylish woman in her golf attire swept past him and down the stairs two at a time. Even when she was clearly in a hurry, her radiant beauty she had inherited from her mother shone through the pale light of the stairway.

She turned towards the lady's locker room and crashed into a tall dark local man.

'Steady there. Who's died?' he inquisitively asked.

'I'm sorry. I'm just late for a golf lesson.'

He looked lustfully into her deep brown eyes; his steely blue look momentarily took Jemima by surprise. His actions were unusual, but she quickly regained her composure and apologised again before moving swiftly on.

3

'That's odd,' she momentarily thought, what was he doing coming from the lady's locker room, but the moment was gone.

'Hi Charlotte, I'm sorry I'm late.' Jemima greeted the stunning bronzed woman in her thirties who was showing the evidence of vanity cosmetic surgery. Not bad work, but perhaps not quite the best, or really necessary in the circumstances.

'Hello Jemima, that's okay. I've just finished a sweaty workout….in the leisure centre,' replied Charlotte.

The old acquaintances briefly embraced, and air kissed as modern women seem to do, and they slowly walked off aimlessly chatting, preparing for the golf lesson Charlotte had booked earlier with her old school *friend.*

They had both been brought up in Edendale, the sleepy North Yorkshire village, but from rather different sides of the track.

Jemima had reluctantly boarded at St Matilda's School for Young Ladies, as her widowed father was often away on operational duty in the Army with the Royal Engineers. While Charlotte had attended the highly recommended but more main stream local comprehensive, Yorksbey High School.

Charlotte had for some reason always been envious of Jemima, while easy going Jemima had seen through 'Charlie's' falseness from a very early age, but because of her good nature had accepted with good grace, Charlottes ever changing moods that she often displayed.

They had not met for over ten years, not since Jemima had moved to Dubai.

In that time the gold-digging Charlotte had flitted from lover to lover before finally sinking her wonderfully whitened teeth into the older 'bad boy' business man Oliver (Bart) Tate.

Despite of, or because of their age difference, they both had accepted the marriage for totally different but mutually beneficial reasons.

Bart had a glamorous trophy wife, while Charlotte had the money and freedom to undertake the things she had longed for while growing up.

CHAPTER 2 - THE MEETING

Oliver Bartholomew Tate, a.k.a. Bart, sat down at a table on the Montgomerie Golf Club veranda. He was no great fan of the Dubai heat, even in the early part of the spring day he was already sweating profusely.

His weight which his GP had suggested at his recent annual BP clinic, needed a 'little work,' didn't help, but the suggested advice that his diet and alcohol intake could do with moderating, was something Bart assumed was not directed at him, but more the hoi polloi and others with far greater BMI's.

He had contemplated that smaller portions may be worth considering, but reducing one of his favourite bottles of Red or the daily night cap Brandy, was definitely not on.

He didn't in his opinion look bad for his age, and at 55 he was still going to the local leisure centre down by the river, where he swam his usual two lengths of the pool, plus a quick nip around the gym; bike, rower, and treadmill, albeit perhaps not as often as he used too, and definitely not as energetically as he had done previously.

Nonetheless, with his regular medication of Ramipril and Simvastatin, he was at least seeking to reduce his blood pressure and cholesterol levels and trying to stave off the possibility of an early heart attack that a 14 stone 5 ft 8 in male was staring down the barrel of.

'Waiter. Latte and one of those pastries them over there are having.'

One thing though, that Bart did like about Dubai, was that those in service knew their place, and he liked that.

He also understood that there was a hierarchy in the Middle Eastern version of Las Vegas, and being second in the food chain below the local Emiratis was a position he could reluctantly accept.

It also meant that others respected the position he felt he had worked '*bloody hard*' to achieve.

The waiter placed the coffee and the pastry in front of Bart. 'Will there be anything else sir?'

'Nay lad, but I am expecting a colleague to be joining me, it's Mr Saheed Alham. You probably know him, he's big around these parts.'

'Yes Sir, I know of Mr Alham,' said the waiter as he turned and left.

There was one thing though that Bart didn't like, and that was to be kept waiting, and no matter how useful Mr Saheed 'bloody' Alham was, he was currently starting to press his buttons.

Even the sight of that, '*good looking filly*' running down the stairs had only momentarily taken his mind of his increasing frustration.

Presently a tall dark local man suddenly came into view. He was dressed in an expensive dark western style suit and white shirt with matching black shoes.

'Good morning. You must be Mr Oliver Tate. I am Saheed Alham; I am pleased to finally make your acquaintance.'

Bart shook Alham's hand with his usual rock like grip, he was renowned in Yorkshire for his handshake, but this was not the usual response. The athletic Emiratis deep blue glare looked intensely into Bart's rather unassuming hazel piggy eyes, and Bart began to sweat even more.

'Mornin, Mr Alham. Please take a seat.'

Bart was rather pleased the pleasantries were over. He would have to remember not to shake hands with Alham in the future, there were few he had encountered that could match his normal greeting.

'Waiter, a drink for my friend. Saheed what would you like?'

'An Espresso please. Mid fadlak, …. Shukran.'

Alham recognised that in the varied circles he operated, manners made the man, and no matter what his view of the people he dealt with, being polite cost nothing, and he was certainly not fond of those that were disrespectful to others. No matter who they were.

'Well Saheed. Let's get down to finalising business,' said Bart.

CHAPTER 3 - WAY BACK WHEN

Jemima and Charlotte strolled back towards the veranda, the golf lesson was over, much to Jemima's relief, and they were both looking forward to a refreshing cool drink after the mild exertions of the morning,

'There he is,' said Charlotte, pointing towards a table with a slightly short version of Donald Trump, and the good-looking guy Jemima had nearly taken out earlier.

The two men were in the middle of what appeared to be an intense discussion, but as they approached them the conversation ended abruptly... '...so I take it that's a deal Saheed?'

Alham stood up, his expensive western education in Oxford shining through, and money well spent. Bart continued to sit, his South Yorkshire education in Barnsley, was money not so well spent by the local council.

'Well lassies how did that go? Was Jemima Gray as good as they say, she can't be worse than that Ian at the club back home,' Bart enquired.

'Jemima has a slightly different approach to teaching golf, but I still like Ian's intimate way. No disrespect Jem.'

'I didn't realise this was Jemima, I saw you in a hurry earlier,' interrupted Bart.

'Good morning, Mr Tate,' Jemima replied, as she also nodded to Bart's associate, who was actually more good looking than she had first thought, before continuing.

'I fully understand Charlotte, but I think Ian has his work cut out. I am not sure that I could describe you as a natural golfer, but perhaps, more a work in progress.'

Jemima was being her normal polite self; but Charlotte was to be honest, *crap* at golf. It was difficult to understand why she had even bothered to have the lesson, but with punters like her, Jemima wasn't complaining, and it certainly kept her bank balance in the black.

'Me and Saheed here are finished for now, aren't we lad?' said Bart, seeking a response from Alham.

Alham nodded towards Bart and the two women. 'Good day. I'll be in touch Mr Tate,' as he strolled off towards the bar.

As Alham passed Charlotte, was Jemima mistaken or was there the slightest of touches between them? It couldn't have been….could it?

Charlotte sat in the seat vacated by the lithe Emirati, the fragrance of his cologne lingering in the air.

'I'd love a spritzer; would you order one for me darling?'

'Course I will, and for you Jemima?'

Bart undressed Jemima with his eyes as he stood, and went to touch her, but instinctively Jemima moved her hand and quickly sat in the chair next to Charlotte.

'You have your mother's brown eyes, and her elegance.'

Jemima was taken aback by Bart's remark.

'I didn't know you knew my mother.'

'Aye, we goes way back. I met her at college in Leeds, I was on day release when I was an apprentice, chanced my arm, but crashed and burnt. Evelyn Greene only had eyes for one man. CJ Gray…. It's a shame she died so young.'

A knot crept into Jemima's stomach; any mention of the mother she hardly knew, not surprisingly always seemed to have this affect. A pricking in her eye was caught as she swept her hair back as she unconsciously pulled it into a bun, that she adopted whenever playing sport, being active, or cleaning up, especially after her young daughter Emmy and her partner Marcus.

'Aye, Evelyn and CJ were inseparable, like peas in a pod them two,' continued Bart.

Jemima was suddenly miles away, how many times had she tried to get her dad to move on, to find a new woman to love in his life, like Edee. Life was too short to dwell upon the past, but she knew this was an uphill struggle, CJ Gray's love for his wife was eternal.

Luckily, Charlotte broke the moment.

'CJ Gray, now that is *MILF* material…….. *Man*, I'd like to Fuck.'

'Charlotte! That's my dad you're talking about,' said Jemima, in mock horror.

'Yes, I know, but nearly every one of your school friends had a little crush on your dad, …..sorry, Bart darling, I still love you dearly.'

'Dearly, being tut operative word. Love me for me money you do and those gold credit cards I am forever paying off.' Behind Bart's attempt at Yorkshire wit, his eyes told a different story.

He knew their marriage was becoming more of a sham with each passing day. Her indiscretions, while discreet, were becoming more frequent and obvious to him, and while he was prepared to tolerate a lot, one thing was for certain, Lotty Tate wasn't going to get half of his hard-earned fortune. Not while he had breath in his body and definitely not after he was dead.

'Darling how could you say such a thing? You know you're my one and only.'

Charlotte flashed her enormous false eye lashes at Bart, and suddenly all was back to normal. Bart still liked, at least for now, to have this beauty on his arm.

'Okay, Spritzer for you Lotty, and Jem, what would you like?'

'A Diet Coke please, that would be lovely, thank you Mr Tate.'

Bart strolled off towards the bar and the toilets, his bladder was starting to fill with the coffee he had drunk while finalising his latest deal, this time with the very influential Arab. Time to now put the plan into action.

Jemima broke the silence as Charlotte seemed for a moment to have wandered off into a parallel universe.

'So how long have you been back living in Edendale and what has really bought you to Dubai?'

'Sorry, yes, well, I love Dubai - great for winter sun and the hospitality it's right up my street. Lots of eye candy too, nothing wrong in looking is there?'

Jemima thought that 'looking' wasn't all that was on Charlottes mind. She didn't think Oliver Tate could satisfy Charlotte's likely extreme desires in the bedroom department.

'Bart is doing a spot of business and I thought I would pop along, albeit it is a short visit this time, and while I was here I thought I could see if my golf was any better in a warmer climate. Shame it isn't though.'

'Oh, I see, so that is why you are staying here?'

'Yes, we normally stay at the *Atlantis on the Palm*, I love it there, this place isn't really my cup of tea. While Edendale, we have been there since we got married. I convinced him to move there, you more than anyone would know, it's such a wonderful place. Edendale Lane, *Millionaires Row* in a quaint North Yorkshire village, and luckily most people can't afford to live there.'

Bart returned with their drinks now fully relieved after his quick visit to the little boy's room. Perhaps he should have mentioned to the GP his increasing need to go, especially at night, but surely someone of his age didn't need to get a finger up the arse just yet.

'Now them Jem, I think I might be able to put a bit of work your dad's way. You know me and CJ are big pals, go way back,' said Bart.

Jemima knew instinctively her dad and this odious little man were no way friends. The few friends and those close to him always called him James, those that were not included in his inner circle knew him as either CJ or Mr Gray.

Plus, CJ Gray was far more discerning than to be big pals with Mr Oliver Tate.....

CHAPTER 4 – EDENDALE

CJ Gray turned the dark green Land Rover Defender into Edendale Lane off Etongate Road, the main road from Yorksbey. It struggled as he had missed the right gear, the heavy clutch of his aging workhorse was miles away from the modern cars he more often drove.

'Come on old girl, don't let me down now, get me home.'

CJ always felt good when he drove down Edendale Lane, it was the route to home, the place he grew up in and the place he loved.

Edendale was that perfect countryside spot that most people dreamed of living, picture postcard stuff.

He continued down the lane past the entrance of the Golf Club and *Millionaires Row*, on, and under the old stone viaduct of the *Edendale Heritage Railway* down to the large village green, with its modest but beautiful homes and gardens overlooking the stream and duck pond. The village hall was closed, but the local sub post office come shop seemed to be busier than usual. He continued, bearing left onto the five arched stone bridge over the river Eden, with the adjacent *Watermill Arms* pub, looking as invitingly as ever, with a few people even chancing their arm at the outside tables in the spring sunshine.

He presently turned the heavy steering wheel and the Land Rover lurched into Church Lane, past the 12th century *St John's Church* and nearby rectory. The row of Georgian style houses he had grown to appreciate more over the years, were set off by immaculately cut grass verges down both sides of the narrow lane. He loved this place, and the wonderfully pleasant people who lived in the village.

His arms were now showing the evidence of the long drive as he pulled into the drive way of '*Overhear Manor,*' the family home. The tall black wrought iron gates between the high Yorkshire stone walls slowly opened, as the modern electronic operating system recognised the vehicle registration.

He continued up the gravel drive, past the old stable block, which had long since been converted into garages, for his numerous motor vehicles, and he pulled to a halt outside the large oak front doors, overlooking the ornamental pond and fountain with its view of the *Long Drive....* Home, at last.

CJ opened the door, and immediately a golden working cocker spaniel leapt onto his lap.

'Hello boy, have you missed me?'

Oscar started profusely licking CJ's ears and making such a fuss. Like all dogs Oscar's awareness of time was non-existent. CJ had been away one night, but it felt to Oscar as though he had been away an eternity.

Oscar was the most adorable and loving dog and well known to all the locals.

CJ rubbed Oscar's ears and pulled him close. Of all the things in his life, other than Jem and Emmy, he was the one thing that meant most to him, and the feeling was reciprocated. Oscar leapt from the car and CJ followed slamming the door of the faithful vehicle. He might soon have to think about a replacement, but the Land Rover meant too much to him to get rid of it.

He suddenly recollected the times way back when. When he and Eve, spent those long hot summers driving around Cornwall, near their home from home in *Rock*. Wonderful days, happy days, glorious times. Times he missed, but oh such wonderful memories.

Oscar led the way running ahead as always, completely manic as though his master had never seen the delightful vista before, leading him around to the back door, having passed through the ever-changing aromas of the walled cottage garden. The early spring herbs slowly coming into bud, mingling with the spring bulbs and flowers.

CJ pushed open the heavy high gloss black door. 'Hello, Mrs Wembley, I'm home,' he cried out.

The extensive kitchen, bright as a pin as always, with its large island setting off the traditional country style. The smell of fresh bread emanating from the Aga Range intermingling with the aroma of freshly brewed coffee.

Mrs Wembley knew him too well, fresh bread and butter and a cup of cappuccino…heaven.

A short grey-haired woman, approaching retiring age entered the kitchen through the double doors from the Dining Room, her presence lit up the room. The years had been kind to her and despite the fine dining she prepared she had looked after herself and the family well.

'Hello Master James, did you have a good trip?' her slight Yorkshire accent coming through.

Mrs Wembley had been in service at the manor all her working life.

Ms Elizabeth Gray (Aunty Betty) had taken her on as a young school girl looking to earn an honest day's living just as Neil Armstrong had said his immortal words, '*One small step for man, one giant leap for mankind.*'

And so, it had been for a young Jane Browne, but that small step had led her to look after everyone that lived or stayed at Overhear Manor from that day until now.

CJ was so grateful that Aunty Betty had seen the foresight to employ the soon to be Mrs Wembley, without her the Manor would have long passed into a state of abandon and disrepair, but not with Mrs Wembley at the helm.

Mr and Mrs Wembley had *lived in* at the Manor since their marriage, Jim Wembley had moved north from his roots in North West London and had instantly taken a shine to the young Yorkshire lass, and she to him. They were a wonderful loving couple who's love never diminished.

Jim had done the heavy lifting around the manor, gardener, chauffeur, odd job man, butler, and overall dogs' body, and like his beloved wife Jane, had been a godsend to Elizabeth Gray and all the Gray family.

Since he had passed on, the gardening duties had been under taken by the local '*Digging for Victory*' garden services, run by Charlie Dunall, while anything else that would have required Jim's handy skills was now sub contracted as and when required. Unless of course CJ decided it was something he could tackle, but he usually liked to support all local tradesmen seeking an honest living.

'Very good thank you Mrs Wembley, but great to be back. I'll be here for dinner if that's okay,' replied CJ.

'I had assumed as much. You do know Miss Jemima has been trying to get hold of you, she says you have been ignoring her calls.'

'Oh, my phone died on me, and the Land Rover doesn't have any modern charging points.'

CJ considered his peaceful and undisturbed drive home and momentarily wondered; how did we survive before mobile phones? Life used to be so much more relaxing.

'I'll give her a call shortly once my phone is re-charged. Has Edee been in touch?'

Madame Eden Songe was CJ's personal assistant, but realistically she virtually single handily ran Gray Group Ltd (GGL), and the family businesses would not survive without her wonderful work ethic and eye for detail.

'She did call. I think she was worried you hadn't been in touch today, but I said you were in the Land Rover, and she quickly realised your phone had probably run out of power. She also said an Oliver Tate had tried to contact you.'

Mmm, CJ considered what would Bart Tate be after, he only ever wanted things that suited his needs, and they hadn't done business for years. His last dealing with Bart Tate hadn't been that satisfactory and he hadn't expected to hear from him again, or at least any time soon.

But hey ho such is life; he would call Edee later.

'Now then, Mrs Wembley, let's have a coffee and some of that wonderful smelling bread.'

CHAPTER 5 - BRIEF ENCOUNTER

Bart, Charlotte, and Jemima walked back towards the stairs leading to the hotel reception.

'I will leave you both now, I have another lesson shortly,' said Jemima.

Bart was engrossed on his phone and blanked Jemima completely.

'That's fine Jem, been nice to catch up, I think I might go and do some more shopping,' replied Charlotte.

The two women wished each other goodbye, air kissed and parted.

Jemima was pleased to have finally got away, Oliver and Charlotte Tate were not her favourite companions and she somehow doubted she would see Charlotte for another lesson any time soon, and hoped that she did not ever come across Oliver Tate again.

She had tried earlier to call her dad, but the phone had gone to answer phone. She had not left a message but had called Mrs Wembley who had said she would let Master James know she had been in touch when he got home.

Jemima thought to herself, 'I doubt dad will be able to guess who I have seen today.'

What on the other hand did fill her with some joy, was the prospect of the next lesson which would be far more enjoyable than her earlier encounter that day, it was with one of her local friends.....

Charlotte and Bart climbed the stairs to the reception.

'I think I will get a quick shower and then do some more shopping; you don't mind do you Bart darling,' said Charlotte.

'That's alright Lotty, I've got some more business to complete, but try to remember to buy anything in dirhams, not pounds. You always get a better exchange rate that way and for some reason you always get it wrong.'

'Don't be such a tight wad darling. See you later.' Charlotte absently kissed Bart on the cheek and continued up the stairs toward the bedroom suites. She paused at the top to go left towards their room, but then checked Bart wasn't looking and quickly turned right instead.

Bart didn't appear to notice and continued outside to his Mercedes hire car; he seemed preoccupied as he had a bit of business in down town Dubai to conclude while he was still in the Middle East.

Charlotte leant on the door frame of Room 112 in a sexy provocative manner and knocked on the door.

Alham opened the door in his dressing gown and looked longingly into Charlottes blue eyes, his long curvy black hair was wet from the recent shower he had just taken.

'Fancy meeting you so soon.'

'Likewise kind sir, can I be of service?' Charlotte released her hair bun and seductively let down her recently dyed long blonde hair and pouted her high gloss red lips.

Alham's muscular arms pulled her towards him, she gasped at the sudden powerful action. He passionately kissed her while changing his grip caressing her back and neck.

Charlotte's desire was immediately inflamed, and she embraced his firm powerful body while she kissed him fervently in return.

She appreciated the tight muscular feel of a young athletic body. It was so far from what she was used to with Bart, but immediately he was gone from her mind, as Alham stroked her firm surgically enhanced breasts with one hand and her aching woman hood with the other.

She gasped again, 'Steady Tiger!' as she pushed him back onto the Super King-sized bed. Alham was cushioned by the luxurious mattress as he pulled Charlotte on top of him.

His gown fell to one side, and although it hadn't been long since their earlier encounter, his manhood was clearly ready for the impending action, and Charlotte couldn't wait for round two.

The sex had been passionate but also gentle. Charlotte had enjoyed the orgasm; it was a rarity to not have to fake it. Alham certainly knew how to push her buttons and he also appeared to enjoy the encounter as much as she did.

She rolled off him and went to move from the bed, when he caught her arm and pulled her back, kissing her on the neck, she immediately melted once more.

'So, your husband wants the Aston Martin DB5 to also use as a *mule* to smuggle cocaine?'

Alham's question was tender, matter of fact, and not overly searching.

'Yes. I told you, but please don't let Bart know I told you. I think he would be really pissed off, and I don't like it when he's annoyed, he can lose his temper.'

Alham gave a sincere smile. 'Charlie, it's our little secret, but you know that it will be to our mutual benefit.'

Charlotte softened at the Arab's charm, but still slipped off the bed. 'I'm going to have a quick shower.'

She entered the glass walled walk in cubicle and turned on the plunge shower, the warm water poured over her expensively enhanced breasts and recently botoxed forehead, she suddenly felt refreshed and alive.

Unexpectedly Alham's firm body startled her, she pushed out her arms to support herself against the tiled wall. He again caressed her breasts but this time more eagerly, his fingers also toyed with her wet sex, as she gasped in pure delight.

'Fill me big boy,' she cried out in ecstasy.

Alham forced his firm hard throbbing penis into Charlotte from behind, this time it was rougher and more urgent, but she didn't dislike it and moaned in pure pleasure. Charlotte felt another orgasm building deep in her body, his manhood moving faster as he looked to satisfy his and her cravings.

'Yes. Yes,' panted Charlotte, as they both orgasmed.

Unexpectedly there was suddenly a loud knock at the door.

Alham pulled out immediately, and wrapped his luxurious white towelling robe around him and gathered a similar towel to dry his dripping hair.

As he moved to the door he threw the towel over Charlotte's clothes that had previously been urgently strewn over the floor.

He checked the eye hole and put his finger up to his lips at the naked Charlotte who was now also behind the door, looking rather sexy, dripping in water.

'Mr Tate, what a surprise.'

'Ay up cocker. …Opps. sorry Saheed,' Bart said, as he looked beyond Alham's shoulder at the pink golf hat on the floor.

'I am sorry, I can see you're busy. I didn't mean to trouble you when you are in the middle of such important matters! I'll call you later when you are not so busy and preoccupied,' continued Bart.

'Thank you, Mr Tate, that is most kind of you. I trust I can rely on your discretion?'

'No problem, Saheed, you know me always here to oblige.'

Alham closed the door and pulled the smiling Charlotte towards him, kissing her passionately on the lips to stop her laughing out loud.

Jemima was making her way back up to the reception and car park when her path was blocked at the top of the stairs by Oliver Tate.

'Hi, their lass, how's about us spending a bit of one-on-one time together?'

Jemima was taken aback at his directness, but immediately regained her composure.

'Hello their Charlotte,' she called out, looking beyond Bart.

Bart swung around in dismay, worried he'd been caught out by his wife, but there was no one there.

Jemima bound up the remaining steps and passed Bart before he realised.

'I'll be sure to let my dad know about your proposition. Goodbye Mr Tate.'

A sudden shiver went down Bart's back as he realised how this indiscretion might be perceived. He also knew of CJ Gray's tough ex-servicemen reputation, and while he had dealt with and could deal with all types of men, he didn't want or need to cross someone like him unnecessarily, especially as he wanted CJ to do something for him.

He had better get hold of CJ as soon as possible.

Alham closed the door on Charlotte and lent back and sighed while thinking.

'Had it been worth it?'

He had the information he needed, and the sex had been just that, sex. Good sex, very good sex, but still only sex.

He didn't like cheating on his beautiful wife. Their love making was in stark contrast to the animal lust with Charlotte, it was more loving and mutually satisfying.

He hoped that he could trust Oliver Tate to be discreet, he couldn't afford to get on the wrong side of his wife or more importantly her rich influential father.

Alham was well off, but not in the same league as his in-law. He had married above his station when he married the Shiek's daughter, he couldn't afford to let Tate jeopardise anything, no matter what.

Charlotte made her way back to Room 121. She was now more composed, that had been a close call, but it had been worth it.

She was not sure when she would see the handsome athletic Arab again, but when she did she knew it would be worth rekindling their dalliances.

In the meantime, back to her wonderfully wealthy husband.

She pushed the electronic key into the door lock, turned the handle and let herself in.

'Hi there Lotty. Had a good afternoon shoppin?'

She jumped as Bart lay spreadeagled on the bed, his hands down his pants, like most men do, suddenly now watching Rugby League from Headingly on the large LED TV.

'It was okay. I didn't buy anything you'll be pleased to know,' Charlotte informed Bart

'Well, that's a positive if nothing else, Is that a new pink golf hat or the one you had on earlier?' Bart casually enquired.

'No, it's my old one, it's nice isn't it? goes with my top,' Charlotte innocently added.

'It sure does,' Bart replied and thinking. 'It will also help me with my final negotiations with Alham.'

Chapter 6 - A Stroll in the Park

'Come on Boy, let's have a walk before dinner.'

CJ grabbed his gilet, which contained everything for dog walking, ball, pooh bags, and treats. He took Oscars' lead off the hook next to the back door, not that the obedient dog needed a lead, just an old habit from when he had been a mischievous pup, and he slipped it into his pocket.

'See you soon Mrs Wembley.'

'Yes, you two have a good walk, see you later, dinners at 6 pm as usual.'

Meals at Overhear Manor had been at '*regimented*' times for as long as CJ could remember, Aunty Betty had set the trend; Breakfast at 8 am, not that CJ ever had breakfast, a quick slug of fresh orange juice, a couple of multi vitamins and a good cup of coffee, was his starter for the day; Lunch at 12 Noon, only occasionally for CJ; Dinner at 6 pm, the only main regular meal of the day.

CJ though, was not going to alter Mrs Wembley's schedule, it would be more than his life was worth, especially as he liked the routine. It was reminiscent of his army days in the Royal Engineers (RE) and later in the Royal Logistics Corps (RLC), but those days were a thing of the past, although the standards developed over 30 years had formed how he now conducted himself and expected of others.

CJ could be charming; brooding; arrogant; smart; funny; intelligent; all within a few seconds. Which was for some, slightly intimidating, but if he let you into his confidence he could actually be even more infuriating, but also most understanding and caring, while being a truly loyal friend.

One thing though that CJ did aspire to, in himself and others, was tolerance, something he felt was often missing in the modern world of today.

He opened the back door and Oscar charged forward slipping on the tiled floor, seeking the necessary grip as he leapt the threshold and step. CJ walked smartly behind as always trying to keep up, his tall athletic frame as usual ready for action, set off by his short cropped dark hair. He still had a slight feel of the military about him, but in other ways his rugged look made him appear very ordinary and non-descript, which was a style he quite liked to convey.

They both walked through the cottage garden, down the meticulously laid neat brick pathway toward a high stone wall, with conifer trees beyond.

A solid wooden gate blocked their path, Oscar was already their looking back in expectation, straining to be released onto the other side where he knew he could run unchecked.

CJ stopped; he heard the familiar metallic sound of golf driver striking golf ball and the customary shout of '*Fore.*'

'Well Oscar, sounds like someone's drive is not what it should be.'

CJ looked at a small security TV screen fitted into the wall, adjacent to the gate.

He waited until the *Two Ball* moved off from the 10th Tee over the wooden foot bridge to the fairway of the golf course beyond the river.

He touched a screen button and then checked the 9th Green…. all clear.

CJ then keyed in the security code that released the lock of the gate.

He pulled the gate open, and Oscar was away, off to chase rabbits if they were foolish enough to still be around.

The gate on the far side was hidden by the tall conifer trees and the *Half Way House Hut* used during golf tournaments to provide a location for providing snacks, soup, and drinks to keep the corporate player's content.

CJ appeared from behind the hut as if by magic, many a time he had suddenly appeared or disappeared to players who had been concentrating on their putts.

The 9th Hole at Edendale Golf Club was one of its two signature holes.

The land the green was on, had been donated by CJ's father in exchange for right of way to remain across the course for hikers and dog walkers alike.

The land was originally part of the Overhear Manor pasture, previously used for exercising the horses that had been kept in the stable block.

It now had *'Private – Keep Out'* signs but these were more to discourage ramblers from trampling over the green or tee, rather than anything particularly legal in the instruction.

The 9th Tee (Par 3 – 175 yards) was north back over the River Eden. The view from the tee was stunning and much photographed, while the 10th green (Par 5 - 495 yards) was north east, dog legged to the right also back over the river.

As one of the four trustees of the golf club, CJ was fortunately allowed, subject to competitions, to start his round at the 10th Tee which was really convenient for his twice weekly golf excursion. He really enjoyed hitting the tiny ball and the fulfilment it provided when striking a shot as good as any professional.

The Ninth provided a challenge to golfers of all handicaps, but if you are ever short of a golf ball, best go looking when the river is low as there are possibly hundreds in there. All from shots that have ended many a potentially good round.

CJ followed briskly after Oscar as they remained on the east bank of the river. Their path was presently halted by a kissing gate, which CJ pulled to let Oscar through, and he followed.

They were now on the charming River Meadows, a wonderful expanse of open countryside. The path was less trodden here as it led primarily back to Overhear Manor and the golf course, but shortly it converged with the main footpath that started in Edendale at Church Lane, through the Churchyard, over the stone style and onto the two miles or so to the *Town Bridge* in Yorksbey.

The many specimens of old English trees dotted along the route were starting to bud with some of the early summer growers already in broadleaf. They provided rich opportunities for local artists and welcome shade for ramblers in the later summer months.

The shaggy sheep, now overdue a shearing following the long winter months, were grazing spasmodically along the route.

Oscar as usual had his arse up, tail wagging constantly, nose down sniffing out all and sundry like all cockers, checking, stopping, and re-marking his territory from previous walks.

Today CJ had chosen to stroll anti-clockwise along his normal circular walk, going north up the river bank towards the steel cable stayed footbridge that spanned the river, with the footpath leading towards the golf club house on the opposite bank.

The path now at times was narrow and steep as the ground sloped towards the river, but was generally extensively broad and open with wonderful views of the meadow.

CJ presently noticed that a Kingfisher was perched on an overhanging bough, above a deep part of the river. The eagle-eyed bird was intently watching its prey in the calm water below, there was a sudden flash of blue and orange as the bird dived headlong into the cool water.

A couple of seconds later, and the beautiful bird rose serenely back from the depths with its prey firmly clamped in its beak, and landed back on its starting point on the branch.

Nature's cycle was so wonderful but in a blinking of an eye, so brutal for the fish.

CJ was momentarily in another world but was dragged back to life.

'Afternoon. Well actually, nearly evening,' said a woman, with her Labrador, as she greeted CJ warmly, as virtually all dog walkers seem to do.

'Hi there, lovely part of the day now,' responded CJ, smiling.

'Yes wonderful.' she replied.

Oscar and the retriever undertook the normal smelling ritual and having said their proverbial hello's continued on their opposite paths, CJ swiftly following Oscar.

CJ suddenly realised that he ought to call Edee and Jem, and dug into his pocket for his phone.

'Oh Bollocks.'

Having put the phone on charge he had then forgotten to pick it up after savouring his cappuccino. To be honest though, he was rather pleased, he savoured the tranquillity of his twice daily rambles with his best pal and always intentionally put his phone to silent whenever walking.

After about a mile and a half the two companions passed through another kissing gate and into the playing field areas where the local Yorksbey Football and Rugby Clubs played their fixtures. The grass here was well maintained for sport and rather different from the adjacent natural meadow.

Shortly they arrived at the steel bridge and crossed over the river, where it was possibly at its deepest along their route. The water course there turned abruptly right and started to flow faster from there on, as it approached the weir in Yorksbey just before the old *Town Bridge*.

Once on the west side of the river they turned for home on the opposite bank, with the 1st Green (Par 4 - 405 yards) and 2nd Tee (Par 4 - 425 yards) on their immediate right.

Oscar took no notice of the players at various stages of their rounds but continued his incessant sniffing of the undergrowth in a vain attempt to find something challenging.

The sun was lowering in the sky and the golf course looked in wonderful condition in the early evening spring light.

They presently passed the 12th (Par 4 - 415 yards), 11th (Par 4 - 385 Yards) and 10th (Par 5 - 495 Yards) back towards the wooden bridge and the 9th Green (Par 3 - 175 Yards) and home.

Oscar suddenly caught the smell of a pheasant and gave chase, but the wild fowl alluded him and flew off. A quick whistle from CJ and Oscar was back at his side, bum firmly on the finely manicured grass yearning for a treat, which CJ slipped from his pocket and offered it and was immediately whoofed down.

'Come on boy, that was a good walk, but its dinner time now for both of us'

CHAPTER 7 - THE DEAL

Bart's phone rang. He looked at the screen, he needed to get this.

'Hello Barty, old boy, its Earl Hargrove. Just seeking an update on the Aston Martin DB5.'

'Hello *My Lord*. Yes, things are progressing well,' Bart replied at his sycophantic best.

'And it's definitely the original?'

'Of course, you know me, always thorough,' Bart continued in his ingratiating tone.

'Wonderful, and the price as we agreed.'

'Well, there is a slight problem, the Arab is playing hardball and I think he is going to stick to his guns.'…'Now the hard sell,' thought Bart.

'That's a shame but we knew it was likely. So what are we at?' asked Earl Hargrove.

'Well, I think I can get him to agree £6.75m.'

'Could be worse I suppose, and still within the original budget. Well done Barty, I take it 35% upfront, balance on delivery as previously discussed.'

'I'm sorry My Lord,' as Bart resorted to his grovelling manner. 'You know these people, it's now 50% upfront, balance on arrival in the UK. It's the best I can do, but it is the original one from the film that went missing in Florida in 1979.'

'Yes, yes I suppose so. It will when all said and done complete my collection.'

'I think it would be the piece de resistance. Can I conclude the deal My Lord?'

Bart was keen to get this across the line and get back home.

'Yes Barty you can.'

'And My Lord, will you transfer the £3.375m today.'

'Yes, OF COURSE!' Earl Hargrove's manner for the first time changed. A slight annoyance was apparent, he didn't enjoy parting with money at the best of times and £3.375m upfront was a risk, albeit manageable.

He thought Oliver Tate was a man he could usually rely upon, if not he knew someone that could manage him, especially if push came to shove.

'Keep me updated and let me know when the Aston will be in the UK, I can't wait.'

'Shall I see you at the Golf Club on my return?' Bart enquired.

'Mmm.'

The line went dead as Earl Hargrove abruptly ended the call.

'Well, that went better than planned,' Bart thought to himself.

Bart had manipulated it, so he got more than the full cost of the car upfront, so no cash flow issues, and £3.75m in profit to boot once the deal was done. He hadn't lost his touch and an eye for a deal.

A smug smile crept over his rosy face, ...he needed to turn the A/C up.

Earl Hargrove turned to his wife.

'I do despise that toady little man, no sense of style or decorum.'

'David darling, you know that at times you have to deal with the hoi polloi, especially to get the right deal.'

'Yes, Diane, you are right as always, I just don't enjoy having to work with *HIM*.'

Earl Hargrove also had another thing on his mind.

'I need to speak to the Major, can't have that pip squeak being the new chairman of the Golf Club, poor form, but the Major will know how to manipulate that, I am sure.'

Earl Hargrove was concerned about the upcoming club committee election, but a shiny silver Aston Martin DB5 outside Hargrove House would no matter what, put a smile squarely back on his face.

CHAPTER 8 - THE NOMINATION

Major Montgomery had been secretary at Edendale Golf Club for as long as anyone could remember, no one ever contemplated seeking his position, but who would. The man was so efficient, thorough, and trustworthy, that all the members and officials tolerated his slightly pompous manner.

He was the heart of the club, he oiled the wheels, he ensured everything that had to be done, was done and on time, that left everyone else to do the things they all loved. Playing golf as often as possible in glorious surroundings.

The '*Major*' glided around the club and was always on hand if there was an issue, which wasn't often because the Major ran a '*tight ship,*' albeit perhaps with his background a '*tight platoon*' may have been more accurate, but one thing everyone knew, *do not cross the Major*, you would never win.

Many had tried to their misfortune.

The Major was for him though perturbed, in fact very perturbed and not to put to finer point on it down right seething. He looked at the club notice board, what was going on?

The Election of Members this year, as all election years should be a formality, a coronation as was usual, orchestrated by him, yours truly '*Major Mortimer Montgomery*,' formerly of the Queens Own Regiment.

Everything was as normal but for a series of ink scrawls on his pristinely printed schedule.

Under Chairman, not only was the perfectly typed name of Mr Graham Brook JP and his proposer, Earl

Hargrove, and seconder Major Montgomery, but a totally unexpected and thoroughly unwanted name….

……Mr Oliver Tate; proposer Mrs Charlotte Tate; seconder Mr Justin Tate.

'This needed heading off and quickly.' What was the Major to do, he would speak with Earl Hargrove at the earliest convenience.

One thing was certain, Mr Oliver '*Bloody*' Tate, was not going to rock his perfect boat…ship….platoon…whatever….his club.

The Major was momentarily rather flustered, which he sure as hell wasn't going to let happen for long.

No one disrupted the Majors perfect world.

Ian Westbank pushed his golf trolley along the snaking gravel path from the Club House down towards the Driving Range. Next to him was a rather plain 28-year-old woman whose fiancé had suggested she should take up golf so they could spend more time together, doing the other thing he enjoyed in life.

Ian usually appreciated this aspect of being the Club Professional. The chance to get close and personal with a firm young lass, but today Jill Cuthbertson was going to be he felt, a more professional proposition for him.

'Have you played around before Jill?'

Jill's cheeks coloured up at the innuendo

'No Ian, I was hoping you could teach me a few basics and see if I have what it takes.'

Ian would have normally liked how the conversation was developing, but today, he wasn't so sure?

He was pretty sure this arrangement was probably going to develop into a cash cow of lessons, but he doubted she had what it took, either to play golf or provide him with anything more interesting.

He liked to flirt with pretty girls, and he felt that most quite liked the banter, despite what seemed to emanate from social media. The problem he felt was that the small minority of those that objected seemed to make the most noise, but in his experience most young women were more than able at holding their own and understood the modern joking of today. Modern women were usually worldly wise.

He did however recognise that sometimes he may have overstepped the mark. Lads' banter on the golf course didn't always translate to reciprocated acceptance of a sensitive woman, he perhaps needed to consider others slightly more than he had in the past.

His high jinks had led to him parting company with mutual agreement with his last employer and he recognised that he had been very fortunate to get the position as resident *Golf Pro* at Edendale.

They passed under the bridge of the single-track *Heritage Steam Railway* embankment that bisected the golf course. The track having started from the station at Yorksbey forges a meandering path along the dale for twelve miles finally sweeping into the spa town of Etongate and the terminus with the railway line between Leeds and York.

The bridge was one of two that allowed golfers to reach both sides of the course, with the embankment running parallel to the river for a while before turning westward over the beautiful and stunning *Edendale Viaduct* with its nine stunning stone arches.

The railway and its four quaint stations on the route, (*Edendale; Hargrove Halt; Folly Overblow and Cannal*) were renowned for being used as TV and Film locations, and more recently for the film, '*Henry Browns School Days*' and the just released TV series, '*My Beating Heart.*' With everyone hoping it had been popular enough for the commissioning of a second series, especially the local railway enthusiasts and its supporters.

The pair continued down the gravel path until it petered out at the 1st Tee. (Par 4 - 425 yards, slight dog leg right due to the course of the river.)

They veered left and pulled up at the teeing ground of the driving range.

The big hitters could just about drive the river, which Tom the Head Groundsman was not particularly happy about, albeit it was usually Phil the apprentice greenkeeper, who had to get his feet wet or use the waders to retrieve the numerous golf range balls that ended in the shallows. Those with big egos to match their big drives were always striving to drive the river but very few managing what Tiger Woods may well have done more easily in his prime.

'Right then Jill, let's get this lesson started. As with everything in life you will learn that the grip is the most important aspect........Your swing will improve tremendously if you have a tender but firm grip.'

Ian knew who had a thorough understanding of the right grip, that was the provocative and sexual Charlotte Tate. Charlotte knew all the right positions, not it would appear like the dowdy Jill....this was potentially going to be a rather tedious lesson, he just had that feeling.

He couldn't on the other hand wait for Charlotte to get back from Dubai, no doubt wonderfully bronzed…and her arrival would be anything but dull.

CHAPTER 9 – THE GLORY

Alham called Ali into his office of the large warehouse operation in downtown Dubai.

The set up was slick. Ali was a skilled technician; he could replicate almost anything and when it came to cars this was his speciality.

If you wanted a specialist car no matter what its specification, Ali could build it, even the original manufacture would think it was one of their own.

But this project had been a challenge even for Ali.

Alham realised that Ali was worth his weight in gold, well figuratively at least, £3.5m would be quite a lot even for him and his weight, but if you considered how quickly he had transformed the DB5 into the replica of the original complete with authentic Chassis No: DP/216/1, and the 3 Rotating Number Plates; BMT 216A; LU 6789 and 4711-EA-62, this was a near perfect example of James Bond's Aston Martin DB5, used in the 1964 Film Goldfinger.

Everything was included, Replica Machine Guns, popping out from behind the front indicators, Rear Bulletproof Screen, Rear Wheel Tyre Shredders, Oil Slick Delivery System, Rear Smoke Screen, Revolving Number Plates and of course the Ejector Seat.

Any school boy or classic car collectors dream, it would have any aficionado creaming themself.

However, Alham knew, and Oliver Tate knew, this was *NOT* the original stolen from a Florida Airfield in 1997, but to anyone else this was as close to perfection as you could get, and at £3.1m a steal.

If it were the original, it would probably be worth best part of £20m at auction.

'Ali are you nearly done; I have a buyer who is champing at the bit to get the car to the UK.'

'Sure Boss, nearly done, a final polish and QA Check and we should be there.'

Alham could see the pride in the eyes of the small local artisan.

'I just need to do the final clocking of the speedometer, don't want to miss a silly trick like that.'

'As our usual deal, 50% each of the sale value, so $1.25m will be coming your way. 50% now and the balance on the cars arrival in the UK.'

While Alham valued Ali, he didn't get where he was by not being astute when it came to business, but as long as Ali was happy, then he was happy. 'In sha 'Allah,' if God wills.

Bart pulled up and parked the hired Mercedes in one of the vacant visitors' spaces in the car park outside the glass fronted offices of Alham Industries. He was looking forward to this.

The automatic all glass revolving door started to turn as he approached, 'Bloody Hell, it's a bit warm.' Bart entered the reception. 'Blimey that's a bit chilly.' He still found the extremes of Dubai not really to his taste, although he knew his wife loved the early spring and late autumn climate the largest Emirate by population offered.

He still found it quite remarkable that the small port and desert oasis of 50 years ago, now had a population of about 3 million and was a much sort after winter holiday destination.

'I have a meeting with your boss, could you let Mr Alham know I'm here, its Oliver Tate.'

As was Bart's way, once the normal initial formalities were over from the first meeting, he felt that everyone was his best mate and he showed scant regard, or any act of reverence, and Alham's receptionist was even lower down the pecking order than most.

'Good morning Mr Tate, Mr Alham is expecting you; would you like a drink while you wait? please take a seat.' The young Filipina woman was, as would be expected, polite and helpful, and she glossed over Bart's obvious brusqueness.

'No, I'm fine for now,' said Bart.

She picked up the desk phone. 'Mr Alham, Mr Tate is in reception…... certainly'

'Mr Tate would you please come this way; Mr Alham will see you now.'

She walked towards a pair of double doors and Bart followed, and as was his want, his eyes followed the slim rear bottom and shapely legs that glided across the floor, he was however suddenly found wanting though as she stopped and opened the door to let him pass.

'Ah…. Yes. Mmm… Thank you.' His embarrassment though didn't show under his sunburnt complexion, as he passed through the door and walked down the corridor which was adorned with pictures of wonderful and beautiful Classic and Luxury Sports Cars, of every type and make.

Even Bart was seriously impressed, he had definitely made the right call when he had engaged Saheed Alham.

The young receptionist now matched Bart's stride and she suddenly stopped and knocked on one of the oak doors

'Come In.'

She opened the door and gestured for Bart to enter the office.

'Mr Tate, sir,' she announced.

'Good morning Mr Tate, it is so nice to see you again,' said Alham. Even Bart was impressed by the Emiratis falseness.

'Please take a seat,' continued Alham.

'Bart got the distinct impression that Alham knew that Bart was not willing to contemplate another polite greeting handshake, not unless forced, he would have to save the *'show of testosterone'* until the deal was concluded.

'You know its Bart, please,' as he sat in the deep upholstered armchair opposite the large oak panel desk and leather swivel chair to which Alham had now resumed.

'Would you like some more refreshments?' the receptionist enquired of her employer.

'Yes, please bring some coffee, tea and water, thank you.'

'You're looking different today,' Bart continued.

The Emirati was dressed in traditional Muslim robes, a white full length Kandura, with a Ghutrah on his head held in place with a black Agal, all traditional UAE clothing.

'Yes, it is cooler to wear the Kandura, Mr Tate, sorry, Bart,' said Alham, before adding. 'You'll also be pleased to know that the car is looking wonderful, it will be available for collection by the end of the week.'

'That's grand, can we take a look I've been dying to see it, are you okay you look a little …peaky than you did yesterday?'

'Of course. I'm fine, let's go to the workshop and see this classic, you will then fully appreciate it in all its glory, and realise its true value.'

The viewing was more than Bart could have hoped, Earl Hargrove was going to be so pleased, his election as Golf Club Chairman was in the bag. The car was *'Bloody Marvellous,'* more than that, it was perfect, it would fool anyone.

'Alham, just one thing, the price.' Bart was going to enjoy this.

'Sorry, Mr Tate.'

'Well, I think perhaps a little discount might be in order, I mean you wouldn't want any indiscretions becoming public, would you?'

So, this was it, he could trust Oliver Tate's discretion, but only at a price.

'What were you thinking Mr Tate, you do know this car is virtually priceless to some, perhaps you.'

'Look, I like you as you know, but business is business, what about say a three percent discount and if you could ensure that some merchandise was well hidden in the spare tyre, then our deal is sealed.'

Alham was inwardly incensed, but outwardly as cool as always, the deal proposed wasn't really a hardship, the earlier agreement with Ali had meant he was not worse off. Tate's assured discretion though was priceless, and with the knowledge of the drug smuggling he still had a final card that he might play, especially if it became necessary at some point.

Also, now that Tate was in the frame if the drugs were ever found, the car could also be used to smuggle other elicit items.

'Mr Tate, we have a deal if your discretion is definitely assured.'

'I knew you would see it my way, it's a deal.' Bart smiled smugly but forgot too late as Alham crushed Bart's grip.......

CHAPTER 10 - OVERHEAR MANOR

'Hi Pop's, how's things?' Jemima's phone greetings to her father were as varied as her moods. It's funny how a couple of words and you can instantly sense the mood of loved ones.

CJ instantly knew this was possibly going to be a light-hearted chat and his mood was already in easy mode has he sipped his orange juice, in the *Orangery* overlooking the *Play Lawn* at the rear of the house, with Oscar curled up asleep at his side. The early morning dew was glistening on the immaculately manicured lawn, its stripes enhanced by the early spring sunshine.

'Hi Yaa.'

CJ and Jemima while often talking regularly, it could also be days between chats or messages, alternatively there could be a series of intense messaging. They also had an understanding that they both subconsciously recognised, born out of love and mutual respect, where having gone days without contact they could pick up and talk as though they had only just been speaking.

'You'll never guess who I bumped into earlier, go on, go on,' she teased.

'Mmm, let me think,' mused CJ. 'Could it be some obnoxious Yorkshireman, and his Femme Fatale wife.'

'Ah, Dad, you've been talking to Edee,' said a deflated Jemima.

'No, but she did leave a message with Mrs W.'

'You're no fun anymore. Anyhow he says he may have some work he could put your way.'

'I gather so, but that is slightly disconcerting, Bart Tate only thinks of himself, or if it suits his purposes to be involved with others, either way you watch yourself with him Jem.'

'Yes, I have already seen him in action.'

'He hasn't said anything, or done anything to you has he? I'll set Cliff onto him if he has.'

'No, I can handle Oliver Tate, no need for your *fixer*, well not for now.'

'Jem, please steer clear of Bart, he's potentially bad news.'

'Okay dad understood, take care, bye, bye.'

'Bye.'

As with most calls it ended as abruptly as it had started, no frills, no lovey dovey niceties, succinct and to the point, two peas in a pod those two.

Jemima had a feeling that Oliver Tate was up to no good and she didn't want her dad getting involved with anything illegal. Now, she knew CJ Gray could look after himself, but something wasn't right, and she was going to just do a little checking in Dubai. It was easier than from 3,500 miles away, also she wasn't actually disregarding her dad's advice, she was just going to go for a little drive.

Mrs Wembley breezed into the bright and airy room, at this time of year it was a wonderful place to relax, especially at this hour of the day as it faced west, and the sun was not yet shining directly through the extensive glass facades.

CJ was relaxing in one of the three mahogany coloured leather chesterfield sofas; he was miles away wondering about Bart Tate's likely proposition.

'Here you go Master James, your cappuccino.'

He was instantly brought back to Edendale.

'That's great, thank you Mrs W.'

She placed the glass coffee cup on a coaster on the large glass coffee table that was centred between the sofas. A good coffee was one of CJ's indulgences, that, and a nice glass of red. 'Ah, nectar,' but surprisingly the fluid he couldn't live without was the liquid of life, H_2O, a cool glass of water.

Many times, on operational duties it was the only sustenance available for days and had kept him and his comrades alive on more than one occasion. He had learnt very early in life its importance to everyone's wellbeing.

'Keep hydrated and sleep 7 to 8 hours, and you'll be fine.'

Was a saying he advocated to those that chose to listen.

The Orangery was one of the best rooms of *Overhear Manor,* which was a rather grand, late Georgian stone family home that had always been in the Gray family. The two-storey building was located at the edge of the village and comprised colloquially the North and South Wings.

The central entrance stone steps, guarded by two circular columns led to the double oak doors with Oriel window above, that flooded the entrance hall and twin oak staircases with light. The staircases led up to the minstrel gallery on the first floor that provided a view eastward through the oriel window down the *Long Drive* pasture towards the *River Meadows* which was a breath-taking view.

The old servants' quarters, which were now Mrs Wembley's Lounge and Bedroom, separated the two wings on the first floor. The North Wing comprised one of the large Main Bedroom suites with en-suite and walk in dressing room to the front, having a dual aspect also overlooking the 10th Tee, (Par 5 – 495 Yards). To the rear were the other family bedrooms. Jemima's room, when she and Marcus visited, had a dual aspect overlooking the 9th Green (Par 3 – 175 Yards) and the rear view toward the River Bridge and Watermill Arms in the distance. Next door was Emmy's room, they were separated by a family bathroom.

The South Wing was a mirror image of the North, with the Main Guest Room, formally Aunty Betty's suite, to the front and two further guest rooms to the rear.

The Ground Floor was of a similar layout to the First, to the right of the entrance hall was a hallway leading to the North Wing, the dining room was to the front and the kitchen to the rear, with its walk-in pantry and utility room. Built onto the rear was the conservatory/winter garden.

On the opposite side of the hallway was the lounge to the front, with the library to the rear with the orangery built onto the rear of the house, between the two wings was the study.

The *grounds* comprised the stable yard and former stables, now garages to the left, the *play lawn* to the rear, with the *cottage garden* rear and right, the *croquet lawn* was to the front right with a view of the *ornamental pond* and *fountain*.

Overhear Manor had always provided a wonderful environment for children to grow up in and provided the secure happy base and family home that all Gray's returned to at some point during their lives.

CJ finished his coffee and took the cup back to the kitchen, passing under the minstrel gallery, Oscar at his side.

'Thank you Mrs W, I'm off now to the office,' said CJ, as he entered the kitchen.

'I'll see you for dinner Master James?' Mrs Wembley enquired, already knowing the answer.

'Yes, unless something crops up.'

A quick whistle and, 'Come on boy,' and Oscar was again at his side. CJ slipped his dark grey jacket on and took the dog lead from the hook in the kitchen.

'Let's go and see what Edee has to report.'

CHAPTER 11 - THE MERCHANDISE

Alham punched in a speed dial number on his phone, it rang twice, 'Hi, it's me.....yes I am well, I trust you are.....I am looking for that favour we discussed................ yes......Oliver Tate.......okay and you will deliver the package we discussed earlier........yes, as agreed five million dirhams. Thank you... Shukran'

Bart got back into his car and smiled.

That went as he had hoped, he liked it when things went his way.

He dialled a local number.

'Mr White, its Oliver Tate, are we all set?.....good.... yes, I'll be there in about 20 minutes.' The call ended as quickly as it started.

Bart pressed the car's start button and engaged drive and moved off, he just had this last part to complete and then he was off back home to the relative cool of the UK.

Jemima ducked down as she attempted to turn on the ignition of her little mini, she was pretty sure Bart hadn't seen her, mainly because he wasn't particularly expecting her to be outside Alham Industries. Now she had seen Bart go in about an hour ago, and she had no idea what he was doing there but she had in that time took advantage of Google and established that Alham Industries specialised in Automotive Engineering and more especially, the manufacture of luxury replica sports cars.

Once the silver Mercedes was past and moving down the service road adjacent to the Shiek Zayed Road, she pulled out and followed at a reasonable speed, luckily Bart was not that used to Dubai's road system, and was driving rather cautiously and she was easily able to keep up, maintaining a safe discreet distance.

Most visitors to Dubai found the American style interchanges and broad motorways rather intimidating and usually decided it was easier to take one of the abundant taxis that were readily available and relatively cheap. Jemima felt that Bart must have visited Dubai quite often, to be assured enough to drive himself around, and something she had already established from her chat with Charlotte, was that they did visit quite regularly to allow her to get a top up to her tan and mingle with the many TV and Showbiz B and C listers that frequented *The Palm Jumeirah.*

The Mercedes pulled onto the slip road and increased speed to maintain the flow of the traffic on the broad twin carriageway, twelve lane E11 highway that dissected Dubai on its long route between Abu Dhabi in the south, to the far north of the UAE via Sharjah.

Bart kept to the speed limit and Jemima maintained two or three cars between him and her. They continued north over the Dubai Creek Bridge towards City Centre Deira and the International Airport.

Jemima thought it strange that he was going to the airport without Charlotte, but perhaps she was now staying on for a longer holiday, but that was contrary to her earlier discussions.

The Mercedes took the right onto D89 the Airport Road. 'Looks like he is off home,' thought Jemima, but the car passed both Terminal 1 and Terminal 3 turn off's and then took a right onto D62 and then a slip road, before turning again into an area Jemima didn't know, and one that tourists would certainly not frequent.

Jemima now had to slow to ensure Bart didn't notice her, luckily he was more worried about where he was going than what was behind him. He eventually pulled over in front of a substantial lock up garage block with a Red Ferrari parked outside.

Jemima stopped 100 metres or so back so as not to be seen.

Bart got out of his car with a brown leather briefcase, and after having looked all around walked cautiously to the lock up and knocked on the door. Moments later he was inside, and out of sight of Jemima.

'What was this all about,' Jemima contemplated; whatever it was it didn't look kosher.

Ten minutes later Bart emerged weighed down with a large Black Holdall, and no briefcase.

He opened the boot and placed the holdall in, closed the boot and climbed back in the car and gingerly turned it around and headed back the way he had come. Jemima for the second time that day ducked down to hide her face, and then steely followed his return path.

An hour later Jemima pulled into the car park at the *Montgomerie* as Bart parked the Mercedes.

On the route back Bart had again called in at Alham Industries, taking in the Black Holdall, but returned to his car empty handed a short time later. The rest of the journey back to the Hotel Resort and Golf Club was completely uneventful.

'I don't know what just occurred, but it definitely looked shifty,' contemplated Jemima, thinking as to whether she should tell her dad or not.

Alham called Ali into his office for the second time that day,

'Ali can you please take the contents of this bag and place them in the spare tyre of the DB5. Oh, and can you also ensure that these are also discreetly concealed.' He passed him a blue velvet draw string bag.

'I suggest perhaps in the air filter or behind the carburettors may be suitable, or somewhere you feel is more appropriate, and Ali, not a word to anyone.'

Alham felt rather better now that the odds had again potentially turned in his favour.

CHAPTER 12 - THE SON AND HEIR

'What's this all about?' The Major shook the nomination paper wildly in the air.

'What on earth is your father playing at?' he continued as he confronted Justin Tate in the club car park the moment the young man pulled up in his black BMW M4 Coupe and opened the driver's door.

'And good morning to you too Major,' Justin retorted.

'It's not a good morning, answer my bloody question.'

'Major, less profanities please, Dad thinks things could do with modernising around here and he has something to offer, something that would be beneficial to the club.'

Justin Tate wasn't usually this confident and he even surprised himself with this act of bravado, however he was quickly brought down to earth as the Major tore into him even more.

'When Graham Brook is re-elected, you and your family might just find that your membership may come under greater scrutiny than usual, if I was you, I would start looking for a new golf club.'

'Whatever.' And Justin barged past the major towards the club house.

At that moment Ian Westbank was also arriving and he overheard everything. He didn't like what he heard and would have to speak urgently with Charlotte on her return, to head off this potential battle of the titans.

'Hi Justin, are you okay?' Ian enquired.

'I'm fine, The Majors just venting his wrath, doesn't like things not going to his plan.'

'Nothing new there. When are your dad and step mother due back? I gather they are in Dubai,' Ian nonchalantly enquired as they strolled through the glazed double doors into the grand club lobby.

'Not sure, I don't particularly keep tabs on them, and they rarely keep me in any loop.'

Ian was hoping it wasn't long, he was missing the captivating Charlotte's tantalizing ways.

Justin Tate was Bart's only child from his first marriage which had ended in divorce a few years ago, following his steamy affair with Charlotte, who had easily turned Bart's head with her alluring ways. Charlotte had seen the prize for what it was but had played the game magnificently, tempting Bart but shifting the blame towards him for the breakdown of the failing marriage to Carol, who he had married quite young following a short engagement.

The divorce had been on Bart's terms, having manipulated Carol into signing a prenup agreement when they were far from common, she had eventually drifted away, far from satisfied with what she had received as a settlement for her husband's dalliance, but pleased in some ways that she had finally shaken off the over bearing husband that the man she originally loved, had become.

Justin now spent time with both his parents as he loved them for totally different reasons, he adored his mother for her kindness and maternal love, and he loved his father purely for his money, simple as that.

Not that he made it that obvious as he obsequiously agreed with anything his father said or did, and while Justin was no chip off the old block, he was smart enough to know that without his father's money he was nothing. Justin was far more like his mother than his father, that was for sure.

He enjoyed his time at his mother's Duplex Apartment in Etongate, as he was able to associate with his friends and acquaintances enjoying a more hectic lifestyle in what was the thriving town centre.

The time at his father's home on Edendale Lane amongst the plethora of millionaire's houses, gave him chance to relax and unwind from his often-chaotic world of sex drugs and rock n roll.

His recreational habit was at times, bordering on obsession, but he felt it was under control, so the time in Edendale was a regular re-hab, an attempt to keep him on the straight and narrow, ensuring his life was not ended prematurely before it had even got going.

What however was more surprising to him, especially considering her part in his parents' divorce and the breakup of the family unit, was that he actually quite liked his step mother, she wasn't the archetypical step mom. Charlotte, well, she got him, and was sympathetic too him, what he was, and what he had gradually become.

Whether this was born out from her part in his parents' divorce he wasn't sure, but it was more likely to be the fact that he liked Charlotte, he liked her a lot, a *MILF* of the sexiest order. He often considered, when fuelled by drink or cocaine or both, whether he could chance his arm at something more intimate, but his nervous shyness sensibly always got the better of him.

At many a house party at the family home he had felt a spark, the spark everyone gets when your guard is down due to the excesses of life, and when carnal lust overtakes your every thought.

Charlotte occasionally had similar feelings, which she sensibly managed to keep in check for the sake of the family union, there was no way at the moment, a quicky with her attractive stepson was happening, she valued too much the bankroll her husband provided.

Justin parted company with Ian who went off towards the Pro shop and he strolled into the Club House Restaurant as he fancied some breakfast as no one was at home to cater for him, plus he hoped to see Nancy, the new young waitress at the club.

He liked Nancy and she liked him, they were of similar ages and often joked and maybe flirted a little. She wasn't his normal girl, his sexual deviances were at times rather extreme, but that's all that was, sex. He was though still looking for the love of his life but let's be honest he was still too young to be settling down.

'Hi Nancy, can you provide me with something, I fancy something hot.'

'Hi Ya, I'm sure you do Justin, but let's try to keep our minds out of the gutter for now, shall we…'

Chapter 13 - GGL

CJ walked around the side of the house and past the front door overlooking the fountain, as he followed Oscar who had shot ahead towards the garages of the old stable block.

He passed under the stone arch into the stable yard quadrangle and onto the first garage on the left, he pressed a button on the remote in his pocket and the door glided up revealing a dark metallic grey Audi RS6, which was miles away from the Land Rover he had driven only yesterday.

It wasn't that CJ didn't like British cars; he was fond of Aston Martin's just as his father had been. He owned a 2015 Aston Martin DB9, but the Grand Tourer was only used for special drives or occasions, the Audi RS6 on the other hand was his everyday car of choice. Immaculate interior, with every knob and whistle to make driving effortless and with 'Vorsprung Durch Tecknik' German technology at its finest.

He opened the rear off side door and Oscar jumped in and sat down in the middle of the rear seats, with his nose attentively looking forward. CJ closed the door and opened the driver's door and slid into the figure-hugging seat. He pressed the start button and the 600 BHP 4 litre V8 burst into life, its deep growl resonating in the confides of the garage, the door closed with its normal assured clunk, and he clicked his seatbelt into place.

'Right then boy, let's go and do some work!'

CJ selected drive and manoeuvred the executive saloon of choice out of the garage turning sharp right under the stone arch and along the gravel drive towards the gates, which opened automatically as always. He momentarily stopped to check that the road was clear and turned left accelerating into Church Lane and onto towards the river bridge and ultimately Yorksbey.

Madame Eden Songe was busy at her desk in the offices of Gray Group Ltd, which incorporated Gray Global Logistics, Gray Commodities and Gray Enterprises Ltd.

She had as usual been at work since 8 am, as she had been since the first day Elizabeth Gray had employed the young 16-year-old French student who had applied for the position of secretary to the single-minded emancipated English business woman, who at the time owned Gray's Ltd.

Aunty Betty had moulded the bright young girl into the woman she was today, a near mirror image of her, passing on all her best qualities and also some of her more infuriating ones.

The slim, smart, liberated, multilingual, enigmatic beauty with the long ebony hair and a penchant for Jimmy Choo and Christian Louboutin footwear, virtually single handily ran the Gray Group of Companies. Now, while this wasn't strictly true as CJ was now also key to most operations, Eden Songe could effectively run the business without CJ, but he would have to admit he couldn't run the business without her.

She pushed her Reactolite glasses she predominately used for reading onto the top of her head in the way she did when in deep thought. She had taken an instant dislike to Oliver Tate when he had called asking for CJ, there was something about his manner that just rubbed her up the wrong way. She was always polite to everyone, even if they were often obnoxious, her tutor Ms Gray had taught her how to disarm the most insufferable of people, and she had over the years, had to calm many angry and unbearable individuals when they felt things were not as they had hoped, or expected.

Oliver Tate wasn't quite any of those but all of those all in one, and she couldn't quite put her finger on the real issue, but she wasn't particularly looking forward to the prospect of having to deal with him, but somehow knew she would.

CJ, turned right out of Edendale Lane onto Etongate Road the main road into Yorksbey from the west, he passed the 'Welcome to Yorksbey' sign as he crossed over the railway bridge and shortly passed the Heritage Railway Station on the left, the car park just starting to fill up in anticipation of the first of the four train departures due that day at 09.30 am. The Heritage Railway was one of the most popular tourist attractions in the area and was virtually always busy, no matter what the time of year.

He continued on and into Westgate, which leads into the heart of the Market Town, that is mentioned in the Doomsday book of 1086, before turning left into Bank Street.

Oscar licked CJ's ear in anticipation of their arrival at the office, CJ slowed and turned the RS6 into the small rear carpark of Gray Group Ltd and his reserved space next to the metallic blue BMW Z4, there were also a further two spaces for visitor's when they were required.

The two storey GGL offices were sandwiched between the offices of Kipling and Sons Solicitors and Lloyds Bank, with all businesses and shops having their main entrances to the front, facing onto the Market Place where the regular Thursday market was held.

CJ let Oscar out who quickly cocked his leg, before moving swiftly towards the solid black back door of the building. CJ punched in the code on the security keypad secured to the door frame and pushed the heavy door open, allowing Oscar to charge forth.

Oscar dragged Eden from her thoughts, and she spun her high-backed leather chair to greet the dog who immediately jumped onto her lap.

'Hi there Oscar, how are you?' Her accent had softened over the years and was barely noticeable now, unless she felt it suited her womanly wiles or purposes.

'Morning Edee how are you this fine morning?' Was CJ's bright retort.

From their first meeting all those years ago, CJ had always affectionately called her *'Edee'* pronounced *Ee'dee,* unless he was being extremely serious or sincere, when he used her full name for affect.

'Good morning, James, I am okay.' Her answer conveyed her perplexed mood. 'How are you?'

'I'm good,' replied CJ. 'What's up I sense all may not be well at GGL this morning.'

Edee continued to convey her concerns to James about Oliver Tate and that she didn't trust him one little bit.

'I concur, but let's see if or when he calls back what he has to say,' was CJ's calm reply, as he continued into his office with Oscar in tow, who settled into his bed in the corner of the room behind the large teak table and leather swivel arm chair into which CJ settled before lifting the lid of the Dell laptop situated on the centre of the desk.

Shortly afterwards the office phone rang, it was an international call which Edee answered.

'Good morning GGL, Eden Songe speaking, how may I help you?' she said in her immaculate telephone manner.

'Oh, it's you, please hold I'll see if he his available.'

Edee called through. 'Obnoxious Male on Line 2.'

'Okay, put him through,' CJ light-heartedly responded.

'CJ Gray speaking.'

'CJ, it's Bart, Bart Tate. How are you old son? Got some business you might be interested in?'

CJ rolled his eyes, as Edee appeared at the doorway, she lent on the door frame in the casual and sensual manner she had, raising her glasses again onto the top of her head, keen to listen in on the upcoming conversation, and what Tate was after.

The call lasted a while and CJ finally established that Oliver Tate had purchased an Aston Martin DB5 in Dubai, and required it shipping to Edendale.

Tate had come to GGL the company, and CJ the individual, who had the reputation for providing quality personalised service with the utmost discretion, with any worldwide logistic challenge.

If you required *anything* delivering, no matter what, no matter where, no matter when, GGL would organise everything to your satisfaction.

If it was possible, GGL would do it.

'Bart, I think I nearly have all the information to prepare our quotation for you, just a couple of final points, do you want the car Air Freighting or....'

'No, no,' came Bart's urgent response before CJ could complete his question,

'Container to the UK will be fine, and then could you transfer it to a low loader for the final part. There's no urgent delivery date and I would prefer it shipping, to be shall we say, discrete, I don't want a big fuss,' Bart continued.

'Okay, I have all the details, we will prepare your quote with all relevant information, including price, delivery details, import taxes, etc. We'll email your contact in Dubai to finalise any other items, can you get them to confirm the value of the goods and a copy of the invoice with the bill of sale with any non-standard specifications. We'll then do everything else.'

'Yes, sure, but it's a standard 1964 Aston Martin DB5, value £350,000 that's about 2 million Dirhams,' confirmed Bart.

'That's a good price, they have really increased in value in the last couple of years,' added CJ.

'Yes, I've got a good deal.'

Bart paused before continuing.

'Oh, and by the way, did Jemima happen to say anything else to you?' he casually asked.

'Jemima. No not really. Just that you had been your usual self. Bye,' CJ concluded, before Bart could even reply.

'Well, what do you make of that Edee?' asked CJ.

'I still wouldn't trust him, albeit the task seems pretty straight forward, so why us?'

'My thoughts too, but can you please prepare the paper work and quote as usual and check best rates and deals as always, with standard margin. Plus, I think you should add an extra forty five percent for luck,' CJ suggested, 'If we're going to work for Oliver Tate, it might as well be profitable, and Edee, I think we might just need Cliff on a First Class Flight to Dubai shortly.'

CHAPTER 14 - RSM CLIFF LEDGER

Cliff looked down at his vibrating phone, he immediately pressed the button and answered the call.

'Morning Governor. How are you?' he cheerily answered.

'Morning Cliff, I'm good. How are you?' replied CJ.

'You know another day, same shit.' Cliff's response was a hangover from their military days together, where often, that was just how it felt. 'Another day another dollar, what can I do for you today sir?' he added.

'How do you fancy a trip to Dubai………..?

Retired, Regimental Sergeant Major Cliff Ledger MC, formerly of the Royal Engineers and Royal Logistic Corps, knew that if the '*Governor*' called, he was looking for something resolving.

Cliff was CJ's go to *fixer* for anything, especially if it was rather unconventional or even considered slightly outside the law, but often it may just be something very simple but needed his expertise.

Cliff would though, not to put too finer point on it, do anything for the '*Governor.*'

Cliff had throughout his military career, reported to Lt. Colonel CJ Gray DSO, they had both joined the Royal Engineers at the same time and rather surprisingly a bond between them had sprung up, even though he was a mere private, and CJ an inexperienced Lieutenant having graduated from RMA Sandhurst.

The mutual respect for one another was sealed on day one, and was as strong today as it had ever been.

No airs and graces between them, albeit the military codes necessary for command and control were always honoured and fully understood, even to this day.

The main reason for Cliff's undying loyalty was because of an incident when he was a rather reckless and headstrong Lance Corporal, when he was staring down the barrel of a potential Court Marshall.

The Lance Corporal had got mixed up in an unsavoury and illegal deal with some locals while they were posted in Cyprus, and he had been arrested by the Military Police.

Now most officers would wash their hands of a soldier caught in such silly and unnecessary circumstances, what about CJ Gray.

Lance Corporal (LC) Ledger stood to attention in front of Colonel Smythe's desk, the A/C working overtime to keep the summer heat of Cypriot climate to a bearable limit. LC Ledger was sweating despite the A/C he knew what was about to come, drummed out of the army, his career in tatters, no job and no prospects, his life ruined for what, a moments stupid indiscretion and an extra few hundred pounds.

Colonel Smythe looked up from the paper work he had been reading.

'Lance Corporal Ledger, you are aware of the seriousness of the charges before you, if these alleged charges stick it will involve a court martial hearing and if you are found guilty you know the punishment.'

'Sir.' LC Ledger responded.

'Do you have anything further to say Ledger?'

'No Sir, other than to say I am sorry to have dragged the good name of the regiment and your command into disrespect by my foolish actions, I am completely at your mercy.'

The Colonel, looked down at his notes one more time and shook his head, he then looked to his left at the other officer in the room, Captain Gray who was stood at ease.

The Colonel cleared his throat, LC Ledger knew what was coming, or so he thought.

'Lance Corporal Ledger,…… why do judges and officers have this way of dragging out the impending doom……Captain Gray has pleaded your case, his arguments have been very persuasive, he believes you are a good soldier, no more than that, a very good soldier, that you would be a loss to the regiment and the army, he also believes you have the qualities to advance and become an excellent NCO.'

LC Ledger was taken aback, he was stunned, what was happening.

The Colonel continued, 'I am therefore swayed by his reasoning and loyalty towards you, he has clearly, put his career on the line for you, I hope you understand the significance of his actions.'

LC Ledger nodded……

'I therefore dismiss the case, and Ledger no more indiscretions.'

Cliff knew exactly what the 'Governors' action meant, he had put his career on the line for him, he had figuratively saved his life, but for the deed of CJ Gray he would have been finished, a nobody.

He would from that day, always do, anything for the 'Governor.'

Lance Corporal Ledger did show the qualities that Captain Gray had seen, and as their careers progressed in tandem, with their promotions coming at similar times, more often because, and definitely not despite of, as they were always looking out for one another.

CJ Gray also recognised, that his position as a commissioned officer was fully dependant on good NCO's, and loyal troops, but loyalty is a two-way street and he looked after his men as a good leader should always do, and they repaid his loyalty with total respect and devotion. Every soldier in his unit would quite literally volunteer if asked by Lt Colonel Gray.

Because their promotions were instep they remained in the same unit and brigade throughout their careers, which is unusual. Their respect and loyalty honed over 30 years of service to queen and country.

What was slightly strange, was that even though they were true servicemen, they were specialist, they were not the elite killing machine or the fighting infantry in the firing line of the British Army, they were part of the whole Logistics that are needed to keep that fighting machine working, day in, and day out.

Over the years, they had proved their worth at providing the unique engineering know how necessary for modern warfare, plus the required logistics required for the best troops in the world to undertake their job.

They were though, more often than not, like many others in the armed services, the unsung heroes of the modern British Army.

While Lt. Colonel Gray and RSM Ledger had been promoted to the respective high commissioned, and non-commissioned ranks, within the Brigade, and they served as such for a while, their specialist expertise was renowned, and they actually more often ended up doing specialist section work, usually undertaken by a Major and a Sergeant.

If there was a logistics job that hadn't been done before, Lt. Col. Gray and RSM Ledger were likely to be in the frame.

They like all soldiers though, also spent quite a lot of time based in the UK and then away on operational duty which could be anywhere in the four corners of the world.

Their military service was varied, and due to their specialist skills often took them on specific operations, which could be very routine or extremely dangerous, but the operation that nearly proved fatal, but also of significant importance, was in Afghanistan.

While in Helmand Province there was a shout for the routine recovery of a forward reconnaissance team who were providing eyes on the ground for RAF Tornado Bomber strikes on an insurgent camp in Afghanistan. The Section to be picked up comprised a lieutenant (observer/ radio operator) and three soldiers, who provided the armed escort, one of which was a corporal.

Lt Col. Gray and RSM Ledger having been advised of the routine nature of the sortie, decided to take the Mastiff Armoured Vehicle, and left the other members of the team to relax in camp as they had just come back from a rather hectic tour in the north of the province.

The outbound journey was as expected, and LCG dozed while RSML drove the 6-wheel drive patrol vehicle. As they approached the small town of Masammadabad, things seemed strange, and rather quiet. RSML stirred LCG.

'Somethings not right,' he advised his superior.

The two soldiers were suddenly on high alert, and while they were not front-line soldiers, they were experienced enough to sense when things weren't right. and also how to take care of themselves, unless of course, the odds were totally against them.

LCG took to the radio,

'Oscar Bravo 1,4, come in this is Oscar Bravo 1,9, over.'

'Oscar Bravo 1,9, receiving, over.'

'Oscar Bravo 1,4, we are approaching the village is everything okay? things seem very quiet, over.'

'Oscar Bravo 1,9, all is okay we are in the Market Square, it's the building with the green door, over.'

'Oscar Bravo 1,4, understood, will be with you shortly, out.'

LCG turned to RSML.

'Are we just over cautious RSM?' asked LCG.

'Maybe,' came the uncertain reply...

They were just pulling into the village square when an almighty explosion ripped apart the building with the green door.

All hell suddenly broke loose, there was heavy gun fire all around, and further hand grenade explosions rocked the small square.

'Oscar Zero, come in this is Oscar Bravo 1,9, we are under heavy attack, request immediate air support, Heading 32 03358, 64 38333 over.'

'Oscar Bravo 1,9, roger.'

'Oscar Bravo 1,9, this is Oscar Zero, inbound due 10 minutes, over.'

'Oscar Zero, understood, Oscar Bravo 1,9, out.'

'Well, RSML, looks like we need to get those boys out PDQ, you provide covering fire and I'll go and see if I can get them,' LCG said, concerned the air support may not get there soon enough.

LCG ran weaving towards the damaged building.

RSML provided heavy machine gun fire from the top of the vehicle to try and keep the insurgents pinned down as best he could.

LCG bust into the building and quickly assessed the situation, all four injured and bleeding.

'Shit.'

Luckily three soldiers were just about able to walk with support. They had a combination of slight head and arm injuries and some minor leg injuries, and the corporal fortunately looked the least hurt.

'Corporal can you help me support these two? I'll have to come back for the Lieutenant he looks like he may not make it,' said LCG.

The Lieutenants right foot was missing, and he was unconscious with a significant bleeding head wound, it didn't look good.

'Sir let's do this,' the corporal responded resolutely.

The youngest soldier, barely out of school looked into LCG's eyes.

'Are we going to make it sir?' he hopefully enquired of his superior, but clearly fearing the worst.

LCG smiled back at the frightened soldier. 'That's what I'm here for lad.' But even he knew the odds were strongly against it.

The four of them linked arms, LCG taking the majority of the weight of the two squaddies that were hurt the most, the corporal supporting the other side of the worst injured.

They kept as close to the buildings, looking to get the most cover they offered.

RSML firing the Heavy Machine Gun incessantly at where the incoming fire was coming from. He was taking a lot of flak but luckily the vehicles armour was just about providing protection, but for how long?

LCG somehow got the three injured back to the Mastiff and ushered them inside.

'Corporal, take care of these guys and patch them up as best you can, I'll be back shortly. All being well.'

'RSM are you okay? Keep those Bastards heads down as much as possible'

'I'm doing the best I can, Governor,' said RSML dryly.

LCG, again took a weaving route back to get the lieutenant, but this time he went around the back of the buildings, and he came under less fire, as he had hoped. As he went to go through the broken green door, a burst of incoming fire made him dive for cover, and he picked up a flesh wound to his midriff, which stung like crazy, luckily though not life threatening, just bloody painful.

The Lieutenant looked in a bad way.

'Sorry old chap this is going to hurt you far more than me, but it's the only way,' LCG advised the delirious soldier.

LCG pulled him up, and put him into a fireman's lift, the Lieutenant groaned in agony.

'Come on fellow let's get you home.'

LGC jogged as quickly as he could, but the deadweight of the officer was making life extremely difficult, he was weaving though as best he could, as enemy gunfire peppered his path.

He turned a corner, expecting to see the Mastiff ahead, but he came face to face with an insurgent Taliban, his rifle aimed at his head,

'Fuck.'

LCG stopped in his tracks.

'Sorry old chap, but this looks like the end of the road for us,' LCG informed his injured companion. 'It's not quite been our day, has it?' he wryly commented, as he winked knowingly at his adversary.

The Taliban smiled broadly in return; his yellow teeth heightened by the bright sun of the Afghan desert; he knew he had outwitted his enemy.

'Time to die American Infidel.'

The Afghan started to pull the trigger of his rifle.

CJ smiled weakly in recognition of the hopelessness of the situation.

But the Phut Phut sound from the silencer of RSML's pistol filled the air.

The insurgents brains, and deep red blood sprayed across the wall of the adjacent building.

'Not today old son. And by the way, we're British Infidels,' RSML advised the dead prostrate rebel.

'Thanks Cliff, ...but how come you took so long?' A relieved LCG dryly joked.

'Got here as quick as I could sir. Oh, and by the way, you've got a drop of blood on your cheek,' he retorted. 'It's not a look that suits you,' he sardonically added. 'Come on, let's get out of here while we can.'

They moved as swiftly as possible, RSML now providing cover with his light machine gun, killing a further insurgent that sort to stop them.

The incoming fire was now getting even heavier, as RSML had given up the use of the Heavy Machine gun, which had previously provided good covering fire.

Suddenly, there was a roar of an RAF Tornado as it swept in overhead, and two explosions on the Taliban emplacements shook the ground, as the aircraft's payload hit the intended target.

'Remind me to seek out and thank the pilot and co-pilot if we get out of this alive,' LCG earnestly advised his friend. 'We definitely owe them one.'

The men soon got back to the Mastiff, RSML took up his place again with the heavy machine gun, taking shots at where the isolated gunfire was now coming from.

LCG started the engine of the Mastiff, and they set off as rapidly as the armoured vehicle could accelerate, and sort to maintain the 60-mph top speed, to get them out of the area of ground fire as soon as possible.

RSML was still taking the odd incoming round, but the armour held, and he valiantly kept the heavy machine gun pumping out 12 mm bullets, until they were away from the combat area.

Fortunately for all of them, the remainder of the trip to base went as had been originally planned. Just another routine sortie.

Luckily, with good hospital care, all four of the wounded soldiers recovered, and despite losing a foot, the Lieutenant with a suitable prosthetic, also made as good a recovery as was possible.

All four of them were forever thankful, that on the fateful day, Lt.Col. Gray and RSM Ledger were the men sent with the task to pick them up.

As a result of their bravery in the face of heavy enemy fire and overwhelming odds, the two comrades were rightly awarded medals. The Distinguished Service Order (DSC) for Lt.Col. CJ Gray, and the Military Cross (MC) for RSM Cliff Ledger.

From that eventful day, Lt. Col. CJ Gray was forever in the debt of RSM Cliff Ledger for saving his life, and he would no matter what, always do anything for the 'Fixer'

CHAPTER 15 - COMMITTEE MATTERS

Earl Hargrove swirled his expensive vintage cognac in the large bowl brandy glass, as he sat in the high-backed leather arm chair in the golf club lounge bar, he was far from happy, and contemplating.

'Well Major what are we to do?' he asked.

The Major was of a similar mind, both men were adamant that Oliver Tate would not be the next Chairman, but how to ensure he wasn't, and that their man remained in office.

They had been mulling things over since the nomination had been posted on the notice board.

Bart had already been canvasing support from all and sundry, he had made his intentions clear. He had made lavish promises both of a business type to curry favour with members, and where necessary of a potential brown envelope variety. Bart was pulling out all the stops to become the next Chairman of Edendale Golf Club and it was evident he would do almost anything to get the votes necessary to win the ballot.

'He's been doing everything to get the necessary votes and he's not even back in the country yet, My Lord, but it's not clear whether members are truly on his side or just playing lip service to the awful little man.'

'I know, it's a difficult position Major, I have spoken to many members and while several support his campaign, there are similar numbers who are in our camp.'

'Because of the unprecedented contentious issue of their being two formal candidates nominated before the AGM, this will have to go to a written ballot, rather than the normal show of hands normally adopted, and I am not sure whether I will be able to influence the invigilators,' the Major continued.

Earl Hargrove polished of the last of his cognac and beckoned the young waitress over and continued. 'I think we need to ensure that the vote goes our way Major, do what you have too, and I mean do anything, let's be clear Oliver Tate will not be the next Chairman, I will stake my life on it….. Ah Nancy, another Louis Treis please.'

Earl Hargrove had spoken, and the Major knew what was required, albeit he didn't like the idea of the *ultimate* option, but hopefully that wouldn't be necessary.

Edee had finalised the price for the Quotation requested by Bart, and had emailed it to him in Dubai, it was an inflated price as agreed with CJ, but they were offering a personalised service, the best service. Bart didn't need to consider anything, all he needed to do was bank transfer the value of the proforma invoice to the GGL account and the Aston Martin DB5 would be delivered to his home in 10 days' time.

This included; transfer to secure container, road haulage to Jebel Ali Port, (the world's 9th busiest port and by far the biggest and busiest in the Middle-East), 8 days shipping by container ship to the UK's busiest container port, Felixstowe in Suffolk, 6100 miles via The Gulf, Arabian Sea, Gulf of Aden, Red Sea, Suez Canal, Mediterranean Sea, Atlantic Ocean, English Channel and North Sea, including customs clearance, and transfer to specialist individual covered car transporter, for the road trip to Edendale. Plus VAT and Import Duty.

The value of the VAT, and Import Duty was based upon the value of the vehicle, but the VAT could be claimed back, and Bart knew this, and while the value was quite high on the documents, it was not as high as the true value, but was declared by Alham Industries, in the *sales invoice*.

'How Much!' Bart thought, but realised he was slightly over a barrel. He knew CJ Gray would inflate the price, but would also not ask too many questions, he dialled the GGL offices.

Edee started to answer as usual.

'Good morning.' But before she could get any further with the greeting Bart interrupted.

'Hi there, is CJ there Love?'

'Hello Mr Tate,' her voice changing in an instance. 'I'm afraid he is not here at the moment. Can I be of service?' she falsely enquired.

'I doubt it, I've received the quotation, which seems a bit on the high side, I was looking for some discount from CJ,' Bart continued.

'The quote is very competitive for the service we provide Mr Tate,' added Edee.

'Yes, yes I'm sure it is, and you would say that, wouldn't you,' he said smugly.

'Mr Tate, I understand. Look I shouldn't do this, and please don't tell Mr Gray, I'll get into so much trouble,' she lied, 'but how about I give you a two percent discount,' Edee offered, knowing she had more to give, and wanted Tate to feel he was calling the shots. Plus,

James had given her free reign to conclude deals as he always did.

'Let's say five percent,' Bart countered.

Edee was now in the play mode that many customers wanted to enter.

'Shall we say two and a half percent,' she suggested.

'Three percent and we have a deal,' said a confident Bart in reply.

'Mr Tate, you do drive a hard bargain,' Edee lied. 'You have a deal. I'll re-submit the invoice with the agreed value and once you transfer the money we'll get straight on with shipping the goods.'

'Thanks darling. I won't say owt to CJ. You have my word. Just our little secret.' Bart thought he had one over, on the French beauty, but little did he know, that was far from the case.

'Bye. Bye.' He slyly concluded.

'Goodbye Mr. Tate,' said Edee, thankful the horse trade was over, but it resulted in a nice little earner with a good return for GGL.

Bart smirked at his own ability to do a good deal.

'At least I got the best discount possible,' he thought.

At that moment the revised invoice came through by email, he printed it out and signed the quotation and transferred the amount to GGL bank account. At last, he could now get home to the UK.

'Lotty, get your bags packed.' He shouted to Charlotte in the other room of their suite. 'We're going home.'

CHAPTER 16 - THE FIXER

The Boeing 777-300 touched down at Dubai International Airport, 15 minutes ahead of schedule, the 3,500-mile, 7-hour 30-minute flight from the UK had been uneventful, and Cliff had been thankful for the First-Class seat Edee had booked him, with all that entailed, including the class leading inflight entertainment. The ICE system offered by Emirates was as good as any and he liked flying with them.

This was to be a quick trip and the opportunity to lay down properly and sleep on this night flight was very much appreciated, not that he wouldn't have slept in economy. He had learnt during his time in the military to sleep anywhere, under any conditions, his life had at times depended upon this resourceful knack. He had also during the flight taken the opportunity to reflect on his discussion with the Governor and his view of what needed to be done in Dubai and the plan, and he was ready to implement things as requested by the boss.

As the plane taxied towards Terminal 3, there was the usual announcement by the chief steward. 'Welcome to Dubai, where the temperature is 31 degrees centigrade, local time is 08:15, we trust you have enjoyed the flight with Emirates and we wish you an enjoyable stay in Dubai, or alternatively a pleasant onward journey, good morning.' Followed shortly after by the captain's announcement, 'Cabin Crew, doors to manual and cross-check.'

Once the plane had docked on its stand and the seat belt sign was extinguished, Cliff took his holdall from the overhead locker, he was used to travelling light, and as he moved towards the exit he nodded and smiled at the female flight attendants.

'Thank you,' he said gratefully, as he moved on towards the Arrivals Hall.

The airport was not particularly busy at that time of day and as he started down the long escalator he was as always, impressed by the cool air-conditioned feel of the large cathedral like white marble clad arrivals hall, so different from the older often dingy and claustrophobic feel of many UK and European airports.

The many security desks and extensive Smart Gates were also in contrast to UK arrivals. He breezed through the security checks with visa stamping and as he had no hold baggage to collect was clear of customs with nothing to declare within 30 minutes of landing, oh so different again than in the UK.

As he passed through the automatic exit doors he was as always on high alert, his senses in overdrive and while not expecting any particular issues in such a safe city, he was always aware of people around him, it was again a throwback to his military training, something both he and the *Governor* had in common.

As he passed the Costa Coffee Bar he suddenly saw who he was looking for, the *Governor's* daughter Jemima, who was to meet him, she was smiling broadly at her father's oldest colleague and friend, and he returned her warm smile.

The briefest of hugs was all they allowed themselves so as to not seek to offend any locals, as public displays of affection and kissing in Dubai and Islamic countries is illegal, something many western visitors have apparently forgotten or often don't seem to know, and

Cliff didn't want to draw any attention to himself, not with what was planned.

'Hi Cliff, how are you? You look well,' Jemima enquired.

'I am fine but not as well as you look,' he replied.

'How are Emmy and Marcus?' Cliff asked.

'Emmy's good, she's at school as usual and Marcus is Marcus, He's fine, but he's on another business trip, he is in Saudi for the next few days.'

They continued chatting about general things as they made their way to the car park where she had left her Mini.

As they exited the Bi-Parting glazed sliding doors, the heat and the humidity hit Cliff, and even though he was used to the extremes of middle east weather, the transition from the air-conditioned airport terminal was a significant contrast to the intense outside environment.

'Thanks for acting as taxi driver, I'm sure the *Governor* has told you enough of the plan and I hope it's not too much of a disposition, but I hope to be on the flight back home at 08:20 tomorrow,' said Cliff.

'He has and it's fine, and after you get things sorted you can sleep at ours tonight before an early 4:15 am start tomorrow,' responded Jemima, not envying him the early departure.

'So, let's go and see this lock up, and what we think is occurring,' said Cliff, as Jemima drove out of the Multi-storey car park and on towards the lock up garage she had last seen during Oliver Tate's visit.

They shortly pulled up where Jemima had parked previously, the Red Ferrari was also parked as before in front of the dusty unassuming building.

'Right, I hope this is going to be quick, but if I'm not out in 15 minutes, call the local police and let the Governor know, because it might be bad,' Cliff evenly told Jemima.

She nodded; she also knew the score.

Cliff got out of the vehicle, holdall slung over his shoulder and sauntered to the lock up, the early morning sun already making things quiet hot.

Cliff banged on the door, shortly he heard several bolts and locks being unlocked, a well-dressed local man in western suit, cautiously part opened the steel door, recognising that Cliff wasn't local, he answered in perfect English with a strong Arabian accent. 'Yes, what do you want?' he enquired.

'Sorry to trouble you, but is this your car?' Cliff asked.

'Yes, it is, what is it too you?'

'It's that a car just swerved out in front of me, and it looked like it may have caught your wing mirror, I thought I should let you know.'

'Let me look, thank you for letting me know,' he genuinely answered. 'It looks okay.'

The two of them looked for the potential damage, albeit Cliff already knew there wasn't any, but he had now established what he wanted to know.

Who the owner of the Super Car was and more importantly the person he had come to see.

Cliff looked towards Jemima and raised his eyebrow and offered the slightest of nods, she nodded back.

'All good then, now for a deal,' he thought.

'Excuse me,' Cliff nonchalantly enquired. 'I'm Cliff Ledger, a close friend of mine Mr Oliver Tate said you could provide good quality merchandise, I was hoping you could please help me out, I am looking for 5,000 US Dollars' worth of cocaine,' he said, gambling on the response.

The Arab looked potentially rather concerned.

'Can I trust you? Tate was not supposed to let others know of our dealings,' the Arab replied.

Cliff answered sincerely, 'He knows that I am a man of honour, like you are Mr...'

He hopefully proposed, seeking a positive response to this next gamble.

'...White,' the Arab replied. 'Mr White.'

'Of course.' Cliff smiled knowingly.

'Let's go in and see what we can find you Mr Ledger.' Mr White, gestured to Cliff to go into the lockup.

The two men had instantly established an acknowledged understanding, and recognition that they were both men of the world and were not to be messed with, mutual respect without any further word's having to be spoken.

Inside the lock up garage was a neat but small air-conditioned office, with large desk and swivel chair, and a number of filing cabinets around the plain white painted walls. The lock up on review by Cliff, was very, very, secure, and not surprisingly, considering the contents that were held there, large quantities of cash and drugs.

Cliff took out a neat bundle of cash from his holdall and placed it on the desk in front of Mr White.

'Do I need to count it?' asked Mr White.

'No,' replied Cliff evenly.

Mr White turned and took a sealed brown package from the safe behind him and placed it on the desk next to the money.

'Do I need to check it?' enquired Cliff.

'No,' confirmed Mr White in a similar tone.

They briefly shook hands, both knowing that a testosterone contest was unnecessary and unworthy of them both.

'Thank you,' concluded Cliff and put the brown package in his holdall.

'Shukran,' replied Mr White.

Cliff left the cool of the lock up for the rapidly rising temperature of the bright outside and heard the numerous locks being re-engaged and strolled towards a relieved looking Jemima in the Mini.

Cliff got in and Jemima started the car.

'All go to plan?' she enquired.

'Of course,' replied a cool looking Cliff. 'Yes and the Governors thoughts have been confirmed.'

The following 30-minute journey to Alham Industries was uneventful, although the 12 lane highways as usual were very busy, but Jemima was used to the traffic and weaved in and out as required taking the often-intimidating roads and complicated interchanges in her stride.

As they pulled up Cliff spoke sincerely.

'Jemima, if you don't mind, I think it would be better if you again didn't come in, I know the *Governor* wants you to be involved as little as possible with this little foray, as it may get, shall we say, complicated and not without risk.'

Jemima nodded and acknowledged the request. She had learnt from a very early age if her father said do this, he meant, *do this*, and no questions asked.

'I'll go for a coffee at the Mall of The Emirates, it's not far, just give me a call when you are done,' she suggested.

'Good idea,' Cliff agreed, as he got out of the car and strolled over to the glazed entrance with the holdall on his shoulder.

'Good morning,' Cliff smiled at the receptionist, who smiled in return. 'I have a meeting with Mr Alham and Ali, I'm Cliff Ledger of GGL.'

'Ah, Mr Ledger, you are expected, please follow me.' The receptionist led Cliff to Alham's office.

Following the briefest of introductions to Alham, Ali took Cliff to the factory to get on with the necessary business of arranging transfer of the goods.

The two of them got on immediately, both recognising that they had the requisite qualities for the roles they undertook.

'The articulated lorry and container are already here as planned; you just need to verify the car is as expected and to your satisfaction and we can then sign the already prepared paperwork necessary for the export from the UAE and import to the UK,' Ali advised.

Ali then led Cliff over to the gleaming silver DB5.

'Well, what do you think?' The proud engineer asked.

'It's a classic, and it looks in great shape for the year,' teased Cliff. He was pretty sure from the photos he had seen in the office corridors that this wasn't what the paperwork implied, but a wonderfully, constructed replica of the one in the original James Bond film Goldfinger.

Cliff meticulously looked over the car to check for any issues, but he knew there wouldn't be any, he checked everything, underneath the car, under the bonnet and in the boot. He even took out the spare wheel to check everything was in order, and having momentarily distracted Ali, he also slipped a package from his holdall under the spare wheel, before replacing it in the boot and covering it with the boot floor. All sorted.

Cliff took numerous photos and forwarded them to all parties concerned.

He finally turned to Ali and said, 'It's a wonderful example of craftsmanship,' as he nodded.

Ali understanding that Cliff knew what he already knew.

'Right then let's get the paperwork signed and emailed to all parties concerned and get the car into the container,' instructed Cliff.

The articulated lorry with the container reversed up to the loading bay. GGL had sub contracted this to a local road haulage company that CJ had used on numerous times in Dubai and trusted them explicitly.

Ali, then drove the car into the large steel box which was to be the DB5 home for the next week or so.

The doors were closed, sealed, and padlocked, the two car keys and the padlock keys were passed to Cliff. The Container was secured and sealed and ready to depart.

Cliff gave the lorry driver his final instructions and his copy of the paperwork and sent him on his way.

Cliff warmly thanked his hosts for their hospitality, including Alham, who had finally re-joined them to check that everything was okay and had gone as planned, and following the shaking of hands, he bode them a fond farewell, waving as he left.

He punched in Jemima's phone number on his phone and let her know that he was ready to be picked up, and more than satisfied with the way things had transpired, it was as expected. He now just needed to let the Governor know things were progressing as intended.

CHAPTER 17 - SO NICE TO COME HOME

Following the meeting at Alham Industries, Cliff called CJ to give him an update on the day's events.

'Okay Cliff, that is understood, I think we know what is going down, thanks for going out to check things, let me know when you get back in the UK, I would like you to review things once the container gets to Felixstowe.'

'No problem Governor, bye for now.'

'Bye Cliff,' and CJ ended the call.

CJ turned to Edee in the office. 'Right then Edee, I think we probably need to let our friends in blue know, what we are doing, just in case things go pear shaped at some point, as there is still something that is niggling me, that I can't quite fathom.'

'I think you're right, but once Cliff is back and the DB5 in the UK, we can verify everything is as we suspect. Meanwhile, shall I call DI Smith and let him know what we are doing, you know how you two don't always see eye to eye,' suggested Edee.

'Good idea.'

DI Simon Smith, and his own sidekick, DS John Jones, were local CID officers, and had previous dealings with CJ and Edee, where they had helped the two detectives with providing evidence that helped solve a local crime involving several targeted burglaries of business premises at the Langham Arch Industrial Estate, to the east of Yorksbey.

Now DI Smith, a cross between Barnaby and Morse, respected CJ, and especially his military record, but they were at times, too similar in their manner, and they tended to rub each other up the wrong way, so it often required Edee, and the easy-going sergeant, a combination of Troy and Lewis, to act as the 'go betweens.'

Edee called DI Smith, and with her normal charm conveyed to him what GGL was doing for Oliver Tate, and once Smith was aware of Tate's involvement in this dubious deal, he was more than content to go along with things, albeit he recognised that CJ's plan was not without some jeopardy.

Smith had long suspected that Tate was not beyond doing things illegally, but they had been unable to pin anything on him, and he had slipped the local constabulary's net on more than one occasion.

Smith was also pleased to renew the relationship, especially as Edee was involved, as he had always admired her charm and easy-going manner, plus he trusted her integrity slightly more than CJ Gray's.

'Okay Edee, please keep me updated, and once the car arrives in the UK, please let me know. In the meantime, I'll advise HMRC of what we are doing, I think they would be pleased, to finally get some firm evidence on Tate's dubious finances.'

'Oh, and Edee, are you free next Friday, I have a pair of tickets for the Ed Sheeran concert in Leeds, I thought you might like to go.'

'Oh, that is a nice offer,' Edee lied. As while she admired the DI's policing skills, she was less keen on him as a potential suitor. 'Unfortunately, I already have something on,' she said innocently.

'Okay, never mind,' replied Smith, albeit rather disappointed. 'Perhaps we can do something another time.'

'Perhaps,' teased Edee and ended the call.

CJ looked over at his friend fully aware of what had been conveyed, and smiled. 'So, what have *you* got planned for next Friday young lady?' he asked.

'Wouldn't you like to know,' replied Edee returning the smile.

Bart pulled up and parked his new Bentley Continental GT in the Golf Club car park, he was pleased to be back in the UK. The spring sunshine and temperature much more to his liking, to that which he had been recently witnessing in Dubai. Charlotte though, was not so pleased but she looked wonderfully tanned in the front passenger seat, and was looking forward to showing off her bronzed body to her plethora of admirers.

Bart considered that cars which were good enough for Premier League Footballers, were also good enough for him, as he opened the boot and took out his expensive TaylorMade clubs, heaving them onto his shoulder. He wasn't however going to do this for long, as he preferred to play when he could use a Golf Buggy, or if not, he alternatively had a caddy, more often than not, his son Justin.

Charlotte kissed him on the cheek, 'Enjoy your round darling, I'm going to have some lunch in the restaurant, I'll see you later.'

'Aye, I've got some glad handing to do today, but if you get a chance to influence any members into voting for me, do what you can,' he suggestively asked.

Bart made his way to the 1st Tee (405 yards - Par 4) having changed his shoes in the Locker Room and taking charge of the Buggy. His companions for today's Four Ball were three influential members who he felt could assist his cause, he also felt they held significant sway with a number of other members.

The other three were already on the Tee waiting patiently for the final player and were idly taking practice swings.

'Morning all, sorry I'm a little bit late. Charlotte took her time powdering her nose,' Bart offered; the others all smiled knowingly. 'Let's get going shall we. What are we playing for today, shall we say £50 a hole?'

Charlotte sashayed into the bar, her high heels tapping rhythmically on the tiled floor, she looked quite stunning in a deep blue mini dress which highlighted her totally tanned complexion. Every male member turned their head in appreciation, the few female heads there, also turned jealously in pure hope that they could look so eye catching.

'Hi Jarvis, could I have my normal Spritzer and a table for lunch please?' she seductively asked the silver haired steward.

Jarvis had been in charge of Hospitality at the club for the past 20 years and everyone liked him. He had a wonderful way of making you feel welcome to the Bar and Restaurant, no matter who you were, but he always had an eye for a beautiful lady, albeit his romancing days were perhaps long behind him.

'Of course Charlotte, would you like your usual table in the bay window?' he replied already knowing the answer. 'Will you be dining alone, or do you have company today?'

Charlotte was a regular diner at the club, albeit she was a regular diner at all the best local restaurants, one thing Charlotte didn't do was cooking, she much preferred to be waited upon, and loved fine dining.

'I'm expecting Justin to join me, if he remembers.'

'Very good, and how was your visit to Dubai?' Jarvis continued. 'You look quite wonderful and so tanned.'

'Oh, thank you, it was all over too quick, but I had an enjoyable and extremely satisfying time,' she added, smiling.

Bart's round though, was not going too well, but he was not too concerned about the scores. Today was not about the winning, that would be for another day, today was about ensuring that he could rely on three more votes and the votes they could nurture on his behalf.

He was under no illusion; his task was difficult but not impossible, and he knew enough tricks and incentives to secure the required votes to take the prize.

His biggest challenge was however, getting Earl Hargrove on board, and that was a huge challenge under normal circumstances, but perhaps not when an apparent original DB5 from the film Goldfinger, was his trump card.

He smiled at his own conniving way, despite just missing the easiest of three-foot puts.

CHAPTER 18 - WHO ARE YOU?

Jemima picked up Cliff from Alham Industries and they made their way south along the Shiekh Zayed Road for a few miles before turning off onto the D61 Hessa Street sweeping under the motorway and then passing the Jebal Ali Racecourse on the right, before bearing right onto the D72 Al Asayel Street which led to some of the nicest residential areas of Jumeirah District of Dubai.

After the next interchange they turned right at the next traffic lights into Street 1 of Meadows 8, they momentarily paused at the security gate that are common to all residential areas. Jemima waved to Samael, the security guard on duty, who waved back while opening the yellow barrier. They continued on their way over the next roundabout and then pulled up on the left in front of the garages to Villa 8.

The pair of them didn't appear to notice the *Red Ferrari* following that turned right at the end of Street 1, into Street 4, or the driver as he watched Cliff and Jemima go into the villa.

Marcus, Jemima, and Emmy had lived at the two storey, five-bedroom villa for the last couple of years and while the rather uninspiring view to the front was very much like other residential villas of the style, the rear offered a wonderful vista of the lake beyond with views towards Jumeriah Lake Towers and the Dubai Marina in the far distance.

While Dubai may not be everyone's home of choice, Marcus and Jemima had made this modern city their home and they enjoyed the lifestyle it offered including the villa with its large living areas, its sumptuous garden and swimming pool. It provided a safe and secure home in which to bring up their wonderful daughter and the city provided first class facilities for everything they needed or required.

Cliff thanked Jemima for being his taxi service for the day, as they sat around the large kitchen island of the open plan ground floor living area, drinking coffee, and reflecting on the day's events.

'Cliff, please make yourself at home as usual, you're in the rear guest bedroom where you stayed last time you were here. I've booked you a taxi for 4:45 am which should give you plenty of time to get to the airport for your flight,' said Jemima. 'I'm now going to pick up Emmy from school, I'll see you later, but you might want an early night,' she added as she left Cliff to mull over the day's events and his trip home.

The Red Ferrari remained parked at the end of the road when she left and was still there later when she returned but there were now two occupants who seemed to be ready, willing, and able for a long wait.

Cliff's taxi arrived as scheduled the next morning and the driver rang his mobile to advise he was outside.

Cliff left a note for Jemima on the breakfast bar thanking her for her usual hospitality and made his way outside, reviewing the tranquillity of the dark but warm early morning.

The taxi set off and the two occupants remained silent for the journey other than the driver asking if it was Terminal 3 Emirates they were going to, to which Cliff confirmed it was.

The Red Ferrari followed and kept a discreet distance behind all the way to the airport, and as the taxi pulled into the drop off zone for departures it also pulled in about twenty yards back, and a tall local man in a dark grey suit got out of the passenger door and collected a small carryon wheelie luggage case from under the bonnet of the Ferrari.

The man in the grey suit (*'MITGS'*) started to pull it behind him and discreetly followed Cliff into the departure's hall, maintaining a reasonable distance behind him, far enough away to ensure he was not readily observed, but close enough to not to lose him in the crowds. He maintained this discrete distance all the way through the smart gates, security checks and up the long escalators to the shopping mall and finally to the departures gate B-17 which led to the Boeing 777-300 due to depart for Stansted at 08:20 expected at Stansted 12:10 local time.

The first-class travel as the outbound journey was very pleasant, Cliff this time taking the opportunity to watch a couple of recent released movies and to enjoy the meals and one or two drinks as he wasn't driving at the end of his journey.

As always Cliff was aware of those around him, but due to the confides of the plane, he relaxed and enjoyed the flight.

On arrival in the UK Cliff went through all the paraphernalia that goes with arriving at UK airports, and despite having no hold luggage, it still took him the best part of an hour to get through Passport Control and eventually to the taxi rank outside.

He quickly got into the car and asked the driver to take him home to the sleepy Suffolk village of Long Melford, about 31 miles away.

The *'MITGS'* hailed the next taxi and said the renowned words to the driver.

'Follow that cab.' Which he did, while maintaining the similar discreet distance to that which the Ferrari had done in Dubai.

On arriving at Long Melford Cliff eventually unlocked his front door and checked the surrounding village green and street before entering.

The *'MITGS'* taxi pulled up 100 metres back on the other side of the green. He pressed a speed dial number on his phone and typed the following message.

'CL arrived Long Melford, will keep you updated.' Before pressing send.

The *'MITGS'* then checked in, and ordered room service at *The Black Lion. The* homely 15th Century Inn, on the corner of Church Walk and Westgate Street, that overlooked the green and with a very good view of Cliff's home and his front door.

He then called Avis, and ordered an Audi A5 hire car, at £70 a day, with a minimum hire of 11 days, more than sufficient he thought, to conclude his intended business in the UK.

CHAPTER 19 - THE LOCAL DEALER

Peter Parker was a small-time drug dealer, and heavy, well known in Barnsley. He was seeking to grow his 'empire,' and having worked previously for characters of a dubious nature, that included Oliver Tate, while doing some rather unlawful deals, and also providing protection to local small-time businesses, had established that if he sunk all his ill-gotten gains into a bigger package of white powder, he might just be able to achieve his next goal.

Parker though, was like many of his kind, a bully. He felt his working out at the gym, provided him with a physique that would intimidate or frighten most people he came into contact with, but when the chips were down, he had a yellow streak as long as Dorothy's path to the Emerald City. He also had many tramp stamps that he believed emphasised his tough look, but the misspelling of 'Death or Glory' to 'Deth or Gory' on his fore arm, wasn't his finest work or a great look.

However, being just 5 foot 9 inches and 12 stone, he also needed to rely upon carrying other tools, to ensure that those he wanted to intimidate, understood his menace, and that he would ultimately always carry out any threats he uttered.

He had a criminal record, mainly from when he was younger for burglary, and two counts of ABH, but he had eventually understood, that it was better to keep out of the way of the 'boys in blue,' and steer clear of prison, if you wanted to get any further up the pecking order of life. The other misdemeanours he had committed had gone under the radar of the local police, if not the other local criminals, and his reputation for being uncompromising, was well known, and most people avoided Peter Parker if at all possible.

So, when Bart had made contact asking if he could raise £500k, he nearly choked on his Big Mac, but having regained his composure had said he could. Albeit realistically, he doubted that this was the case. However, he didn't want Tate to feel he was not where he wanted to be, or be embarrassed at saying he couldn't.

So having liquidated most of his available assets and pooled all his cash, he had raised £395k, not a bad haul considering, but not quite enough to get to the total required. He could perhaps sell the BMW M5 which might just get him where he needed to be, but how would he get around without his pride and joy, so not really an option, and not really necessary, not just yet.

On the back of this predicament, he had bluffed Bart into allowing him to only front fifty percent of the total, on the basis he would provide the balance on delivery of the goods, and he felt that once he was 'around the table', his tools would allow the final negotiations to be smoothly completed to his satisfaction, and with the right persuasion, everyone's agreement.

'Pete old son,' Bart began the telephone conversation. 'I'm expecting the merchandise to be in the country next week. When and where shall we conclude our business?'

'I was thinking it should perhaps be on my home ground,' replied Parker.

'I was actually thinking at my place may be more sensible, don't you agree Peter,' countered Bart.

'Mmm, okay, let's say next Thursday, at 1pm. How does that sound?'

'Okay, that's fine, so at my place 1pm Thursday, oh, and Peter, make sure you have *all* the money,' said Bart, as he ended the call.

Parker was mulling over the options, but he felt that despite his potential minor cash flow issues, he was still in the right place to conclude matters to his satisfaction.

CHAPTER 20 - NICE TO SEE YOU AGAIN

Charlotte looked at her watch again for the umpteenth time, it wasn't like Justin to not show for a free lunch, but the thought of food was now fast fading from her consciousness, especially as she had just seen Ian Westbank wave at her on his walk back towards the pro shop. She smiled back at him, choosing to not draw attention to her actions, and discreetly nodded her head to the left and winked at him. Ian realising what was on offer smiled broadly at her and subtly nodded.

Justin had definitely lost his opportunity, but new opportunities were now opening up for Charlotte. She strolled over to Jarvis at the bar and asked him to put the several drinks she had consumed, onto her husband's account and asked him to put a generous tip on the bill for himself. She smiled and left, with Jarvis also smiling while tilting his head slightly and admiring her wonderful leg action as she left the room.

Charlotte walked down the stairs towards the exit and the course, she knew that in her heels she was looking rather conspicuous as her attire wasn't really suitable for a round of golf, but then again, she wasn't looking to play around of that type, she just hoped she didn't bump into anyone else, especially not Bart.

As she emerged from the doors at the bottom of the stairway, the spring sunshine momentarily blinded her, but as she regained her vision the beauty of the golf course hit her, the expanse of perfectly cut grass of the fairways and manicured greens along with the established trees lining the fairways couldn't be bettered anywhere, the sound of bird song, completing the picture.

A firm pair of hands suddenly embraced her, and she turned to see who it was, as he kissed her passionately, she responded immediately, but then pulled away in case there were any onlookers she had potentially missed.

'Ian, be careful, anyone could be watching,' she exclaimed.

'No chance, I'd already checked, you look stunning as usual, and what a wonderful tan. Oh, I've missed your worldly charms and your beauty,' Ian countered.

'Well thank you Mr Westbank, I've also missed you, but we have to be discreet, I can't afford for Bart to suspect anything, you know what he's like.'

'I do, but anyone that doesn't look after you like they should, deserves to lose you, especially to someone like me, that thinks your marvellous.'

Charlotte smiled while coyly looking down and blushed slightly at the compliment.

'Have you time for some one-on-one tuition, Mr Golf Professional? she asked. 'But not here it's too risky.'

'I'm sorry Charlotte, I can't leave the club until later I have a lesson booked in twenty minutes.'

'Well, let's go to your office and see what we can put in your diary,' said Charlotte, with a twinkle in her eye and leading him by the hand towards the locker room area and Ian's office. Ian followed like a love-struck puppy dog, willing to do anything his mistress required.

There was no one about, so Ian took out a bunch of keys from his pocket and unlocked the door and started to open it as Charlotte pushed him into the office and immediately closed the door behind them, while in one complete movement grabbing him around the neck and kissing him passionately. With one eye on the window to check they weren't overlooked she started to caress Ian with one hand and lifted her perfect bottom onto the edge of the table, both of them caught up in the urgency of the moment.

With the dexterity of a polecat, Charlotte twisted the operating rod of the vertical blinds in the window with one hand, and removed her tiniest of thongs with the other, and all while still urgently kissing Ian on the lips.

Ian was clearly aroused and had already undone his pink golf trousers which had dropped to the floor along with his black Calvin Klein boxer shorts which quickly followed.

He caressed Charlotte's breasts with one hand and her perfect Brazilian waxed labia with the other, she was instantly aroused and kissed him more passionately, while now stroking his erect manhood.

Ian broke away from the kiss and licked Charlotte's left ear lobe, avoiding the large hoop earring while whispering, 'I've missed this Charlotte, you are truly the sexiest female I know.'

'I know,' she replied. 'Now fulfil me.'

Ian pulled Charlotte towards him, his hands firmly around her tight sexy bottom, and he entered her hot wet pussy. She groaned in delight, while wrapping her long legs around him and draping her arms around his neck, kissing him ardently on the mouth, her tongue searching for his, which she instantly found.

Ian had been desperate for a release since Charlotte had been away, and it wasn't long before his gentle thrusts became quicker and more urgent, he was soon on the edge of an orgasm.

'Easy big boy, I need this as much as you,' Charlotte whispered, but the feel of this sexy femme fatale was too much for the virile young man and his orgasm erupted like an almighty explosion in her.

Charlotte, slightly disappointed, kissed him gently and added. 'Well, you can try again later, perhaps you will then be in a little more control.'

She smiled and pulled a tissue from the box on the corner of the table and wiped her lady garden, and delicately pulled her thong back into place and straightened her dress which had ridden up quite high during their sexy exploits.

Ian also quickly dressed himself and suddenly looked far more composed, albeit with a rather brighter colour to his cheeks than normal.

'Thank you Charlotte. I do love you; I have missed you.'

'And I've missed it and love it too,' came Charlotte's honest reply.

'You know I would do anything for you,' said Ian earnestly.

'I will hold you to that,' as she smiled, blew him a kiss, and slipped sexily out of the door.

'I'll call you later,' she said, without looking back. 'And you might want to wipe the lipstick from your lips, it's not a good look.'

CHAPTER 21 – YORKSBEY

Work at GGL had been rather mundane and business like that morning, CJ looked at his watch and called out to Edee in the next office.

'Fancy a stroll down by the river, Oscar could do with a quick walk around the block, then perhaps a quick bite to eat at the Swan and Talbot?'

Edee initially hesitated. 'Go on then, it's been a bit quiet today and a break from these four walls would be welcome,' she nonchalantly replied, but to be honest she was really pleased CJ had offered.

It had been a while since they had been out together, other than work, and she really liked his company, and if truth be known she would like to spend more time away from work with him.

Edee knew though that CJ Gray was rather a closed book to her subtle advances, and despite the encouragement of Jemima he was nothing but the perfect gentleman, and Edee would actually quite like him not to be so perfect, but all she could do was keep trying and encouraged him.

CJ uncrossed his fingers, and smiled inwardly as he was not quite sure if Edee liked him.

He knew she liked him as a work partner and as a friend, that was obvious, but would she like him as a closer *friend.* She was only ever the perfect lady, and he loved her for that, but he would like her at times to be, perhaps, more of a woman towards him, and while Jemima had said that Edee 'really' liked him, he wasn't quite so sure.

He struggled these days to judge women's subtle ways, he knew how Eve had been, it was always natural and instinctive, they both knew how they felt without even saying anything.

They seemed to know what each other thought and were often thinking exactly the same thing at the same time, but with Edee, she was so cosmopolitan, and assured. He struggled to read her ways at times, and it frustrated him completely as his life didn't work like that, but all he could do was to keep trying.

'Come on then Oscar let's go for a walk with our favourite lady,' said CJ, as he slipped his jacket on. Oscar was up and bouncing in an instance, rushing in and out between CJ and Edee's offices.

Edee slipped on her black leather bomber jacket that complimented her simple white blouse and black ski pants, plus black Jimmy Choo killer heels, she also took off her reading glasses and put on a pair of large dark sun glasses, ready for the spring sun which was shining brightly outside.

'Come on then, I like walking out with my two-favourite boys,' said Edee, making her way to the front door, leading out onto the Market Square.

CJ and Oscar followed Edee, Oscar instinctively at heel, not requiring a lead, albeit as always it was in CJ's pocket just in case of any emergency, with Oscar occasionally looking up to CJ for reassurance and confirmation that all was good in the world.

As Edee locked the front door and turned left towards *The Black Bull Inn*, they saw Bart going into the solicitors next door, Edee was pleased that he didn't see them as she knew that a needless and unwelcome conversation would otherwise ensue.

Having avoided Bart, they strolled on towards *The Shambles*, a pedestrian street where there is a series of small shops interlaced with small cafés and coffee shops, with tables and chairs full of local shoppers enjoying the spring sunshine while resting and taking on refreshments.

Oscar occasionally stopped for a stroke from those that knew him and CJ well from their regular daily lunchtime walks.

They continued on, turning left into Cross Street with more independent shops of all types, Yorksbey, being a quaint local market town of about 10,000 inhabitants, that serviced the local community and villages in the area, with all its local attractions.

As they crossed the road preparing to turn into the High Street, Edee suddenly pulled CJ out of the way of a car going rather quicker than the 20-mph speed limit, now imposed around the town, and linked arms with him.

'That was close. Thanks Edee.'

CJ liked the feel of Edee on his arm, and hoped she would leave them linked together, which she did, as she also like the feel of being arm in arm with the rugged man of her dreams.

They continued on towards the Town Bridge that crosses the river Eden, and they passed down the footpath to the right and onto the riverside walk. The river weir was in moderate swell and flowing quite fast, they continued down turning left under the first of the six arches, that made up the stone bridge with its origins in the 13ᵗʰ Century, which had been re-built in the 17ᵗʰ Century.

The two of them walked mostly in silence, content in each other's company, mainly because they were rather unsure as to how to start up a conversation that didn't involve work. Oscar though, now unshackled from the traffic was walking on ahead as was his want, nose down tail up wagging profusely as usual, sniffing virtually everything in sight.

They passed the empty Bandstand, that was used most Sundays by the local silver band, which overlooked the grassy river bank where there were plenty of families sitting on the benches with children feeding the ducks and wild birds, that congregated there, despite the signs asking them not too, and they continued walking back up in a loop towards the High Street again.

'Shall we have some lunch here at the café by the river?' CJ asked. 'It's such a lovely day it would be good to sit outside and watch the world go by,' he continued.

'Yes, that would be nice,' replied Edee, as they sat down at one of the wooden tables with integral benches, situated in the lawned garden of the café.

Having placed their order of BLT baguettes and chips with a diet coke and a glass of Sauvignon Blanc they were finally forced to enter into conversation to break up the silence.

'So, we know Bart is up to no good, it just a matter of getting the right proof to help Smith and Jones finally nab him,' started Edee.

'Yes, but we also need to get enough evidence to implement all those involved, which is still a challenged,' replied CJ.

'True, but we are moving in the right direction, Cliff's trip confirmed your initial thoughts, we just need to get the other conspirators to show their hands,' continued Edee.

'And that's not quite as easy as it sounds, but I have some thoughts on that,' countered CJ.

Just then the waitress called out, 'Number 6,' in a cheery voice.

'Over here,' called out CJ, and the young waitress placed the tray with their order on the table and handed out the fare. 'Enjoy,' said the waitress obligatorily.

'Thank you,' said Edee and CJ together. 'Cheers,' they continued, chinked glasses, and tucked into their lunch.

They were enjoying the spring day and their *lunch date* and presently CJ asked, 'Go on then, what have you got planned for next Friday?' as he was curious as to what her secret plans were.

Edee finished her mouthful of fresh bread and BLT then wiped the drip of mayonnaise from her lips with the paper napkin.

'You mean you've forgotten,' replied Edee, smiling broadly at him.

CJ looked back blankly; he had clearly forgotten any earlier conversation.

'It's the *'Captains Charity Masquerade Ball'* at the golf club, how could you forget that,' she teased.

'Crikey, I had, so who are you going as Edee?' he enquired casually, as he had previously tried in vain to get Edee to let him know what costume or character she planned to go as.

111

'That's for me to know and you to find out on Friday night, what about you?'

CJ thought, two can play that game.

'That's for me to know, and you to also find out on the night,' he said laughing.

'Touché,' she replied.

Oscar who had been lying down under the table like the good dog he was, suddenly raised his head up at the frivolity, and CJ offered him the last morsels of the baguette and he leapt up and sat to attention and lifted his paw in anticipation.

'Good boy, you wait there with Edee, while I go and pay the bill.' With that CJ wandered into the café leaving the pair enjoying the sunshine of the splendid spring day.

Shortly CJ came out of the café to see that Edee and Oscar were already waiting on the narrow path of the lane leading back to the High Street, and they all marched off together up the slope back towards the town.

As they turned right to re-join the bustling high street, CJ collided into a stunning blonde woman in a tight blue dress and killer heels, he instinctively grabbed her, so she didn't fall.

'Oh, I am sorry, please forgive me,' apologised CJ automatically. 'Are you okay?'

'I am now I know it's you,' came the reply. It was Charlotte Tate, looking wonderfully bronzed.

'You can take me out any time CJ Gray,' she continued, flirting profusely with CJ.

'Hi Charlotte, long time no see. Are you sure you're okay?' CJ asked evenly.

'I'll live, luckily for you,' continued the smiling Charlotte, raising her eyebrow, and completely ignoring Edee.

Charlotte though, suddenly realised Oscar was sat down, bolt upright and still, nose in the air.

'Hi Oscar, you are your usual obedient self, always sitting politely,' she said while affectionately rubbing his ear.

'Just going to get my car,' continued Charlotte, 'I've been doing a bit of shopping in town. I trust you will be bidding for me at the Charity Auction at the *Ball* next Friday?' she teased CJ, flashing her large false eyelashes at him and winking.

Edee rolled her eyes in mock boredom at Charlottes exaggerated flirting, and she linked arms with CJ, and said dryly.

'I doubt it Charlotte, but I'm sure there will be lots of your admirers that will.' As she pulled CJ away from a situation she knew he was far from comfortable with.

'Goodbye then, see you next Friday CJ.' Charlotte winked again and walked off towards the *Wilderness Car Park* and her Audi TT.

'Bye,' replied CJ rather coyly, thankful the encounter was finally over.

'Thanks Edee, you're a life saver,' said CJ, as he gently kissed her on the cheek.

'You're welcome. Oh, and by the way, why did Oscar sit bolt upright like that, it's not usual for him is it?' she asked.

'It's quite normal actually, when he meets Charlotte,' said CJ smiling. 'It's his dog training coming to fruition, I guess she's carrying some *magic white powder* for her social pleasure,' he added, as the three of them continued, walking back to the office.

CHAPTER 22 – FELIXSTOWE

The '*MITGS*' started the Audi A5, selected drive, and slowly pulled away from outside The Black Lion, he kept a reasonable distance from the powerful *Kawasaki Ninja H2* motor bike, as they set off on the A134 towards Bury St Edmunds.

He didn't want to get too far from the bike as he knew if it set off in anger, he would be unlikely to keep up, however he had a good idea where it was probably heading.

He was correct, eight days had passed since Cliff had been in Dubai, and the container was now at the port in Felixstowe, and he had to arrange collection. but first he had to pick up the car transporter that was to carry the DB5 to Edendale.

Cliff looked in his right rear mirror and smiled, he was coming up to a series of sweeping bends on the road, he dropped down several gears and opened the throttle fully and the super bike launched ahead like a rocket, he was doing over 140 mph within seconds, the A5 was not going to keep up.

When Cliff looked again in the mirror there was nothing in sight, good he thought, as he was fast approaching the tiny hamlet of Bridge Steet, he was still exceeding 120 mph as he entered the village. He slammed on the brakes and leant the bike over as he turned a sharp right into Bridge Street Road, before accelerating hard again back up to 100 mph on the tiny back roads towards Lavenham.

He looked again in the mirror, still nothing, so he gently slowed down to just over the legal limit of 60 mph, for his onward journey towards Felixstowe.

The '*MITGS*' reacted fast, but not fast enough, the A5 was quickish for a car, but no match for the high-powered bike he sought to catch, he accelerated up to 100 mph, but on these roads that was pushing it, he slowed slightly through a tiny hamlet but no sign of the bike and shortly he was behind a Ford Mondeo doing only 55 mph as they approached the village of Alpheton.

'Damn it,' he knew he had lost the bike and also that the rider was now on to him, he would have to be rather more discreet from now on, but first he had to find him.

The '*MITGS*' realised one option was to possibly go to the port and stake it out in the hope he would pick up the trail again, but that was unlikely, or alternatively he could travel north to Edendale and as he expected the merchandises final destination.

Cliff collected the enclosed car transporter from Classic Car Transport Service, a specialist firm that Edee had organised, based in Felixstowe. He stored his bike on the trailer and set off for the port.

He called CJ with an update, 'Hi Governor, how are you today?'

'I'm fine Cliff, how are you?' replied CJ, knowing what the next reply would be.

'Another day same shit,' was Cliff's stock reply. 'Just called to give you an update, I lost our *man in the grey suit* from Dubai, he couldn't quite keep up,' added Cliff dryly.

CJ smiled, understanding the significance of Cliff's response.

'He was never likely too, what's the top speed of that bike of yours, must be circa 200 mph.'

'Just a bit more, but yeah about that,' Cliff added.

'He might try and find you again, but he won't know what to look for now, so I expect him to come to Edendale to try and pick up the trail, but keep your eyes peeled and let me know if he shows up again.'

'Okay Governor, once I've picked up the DB5 I expect to be up north later this afternoon, I'll let you know if anything changes from our plan,'

'Great. Bye Cliff,'

'Bye,' and Cliff ended the call.

The container had arrived as scheduled on the large container ship and had been off loaded, and transferred to the *Yallore Logistics* warehouse within the port, having subsequently cleared the regulatory customs checks.

Cliff drove up to the main gate of the warehouse, and stopped at the security barrier.

'Morning, I have a delivery to collect, I'm Cliff Ledger of GGL, I was asked to contact Richard Winters on arrival.'

'Morning,' the security guard replied. 'Yes that's fine, follow the road around to the left, the container will be at the rear loading bay. I'll get Richard to meet you there.'

'Thanks pal,' said Cliff, as he drove on after the barrier was raised, he slowly pulled up, as a man in a high viz jacket waved him down. Cliff stopped and lowered the window.

'Morning you must be Cliff,' said the man. 'Richard Winters, pleased to meet you.'

'Morning Richard, pleased to meet you too. Where should I park up?'

'Over there on the left, the blue container is yours, by the loading ramp.'

Cliff parked the transporter and got out, shaking hands warmly with Richard.

'Let's get the car off loaded, and on your way. How's CJ? I haven't seen him for a while, although we regularly do business, but it's mostly Edee I deal with on a day-to-day basis. She's wonderful isn't she?' said Richard complimentary.

'He's fine, you know the Governor, and yes, Edee is, simply the best.'

They checked the security seals, and then unlocked the container.

'Everything go okay with customs clearance?' Cliff enquired.

'Yes, went like a dream. No hassle, and all the paperwork signed off. How did CJ manage that?' asked Richard inquisitively.

'You know, friend of a friend,' answered Cliff. 'It always oils the wheels of logistics,' as he smiled at Richard.

'I'll ask no more.' Richard was used to accepting things on face value when dealing with CJ Gray, least said, soonest mended, he thought.

The DB5 started first time, and Cliff carefully reversed it out of the container, and down the loading ramp.

'That's a smart looking car,' added Richard. 'If you don't mind me saying though, it looks worth rather more than £350k.'

Cliff smiled and said nothing more than, 'Maybe. Let's get it off loaded and onto the transporter, I've got a 220-mile trip ahead of me.'

CHAPTER 23 - THE CONSTABULARY

DI Simon Smith and DS John Jones were in discussion in their office in the Police Station in Yorksbey.

The station had on a number of occasions, been scheduled to close as part of the normal cost cutting exercises undertaken by North Yorkshire Police Force, but had somehow managed to always get a reprieve, which suited both of the only CID detectives based there.

They reported to DCI Peel, at the Police HQ in Northallerton, but other than his routine visits to the station, and DI Smith occasionally going to HQ, he let the two detectives get on with their jobs. He knew they were both good sound officers, despite Smith being a bit awkward at times, but nothing he couldn't put up with or tolerate, plus they got results, which kept him, and his superiors satisfied.

'…but sir, I think we should check out Peter Parker a bit more, the nick at Barnsley, has said he's up to no good, he's liquidating lots of his assets, and he's a known accomplice of Oliver Tate,' said Jones, looking for his superiors support.

'Look Jones, we are up to our necks in unsolved cases, just look at the number of files in your *In Tray*. If we don't get those reduced, yours, and my balls, are in for a mauling by Peel, and we don't want that do we?'

'Yes. No. I know that, but with this shipment from Dubai due to arrive here shortly, shouldn't we provide a bit more support to CJ and Edee,' Jones continued.

John Jones had a good friendship with the two local logistics experts, and he liked working with them, and while he knew they could look after themselves, he still felt some extra support wouldn't go amiss, and he just felt Parker was involved somehow, and by all accounts was a wrong'un.

'Jones, how many more times, we know what's occurring, they'll keep us updated. We'll react to things as they develop,' replied Smith. 'Look I also like working with Edee, and to a lesser extent CJ Gray, but come on let's get some current police work sorted first, we'll deal with Tate later.'

With that the matter was currently closed, Jones knew his boss too well to keep pushing, and when all said and done, DI Smith was a good detective and a sound boss, not everyone in the force had such a good working relationship with their superior.

However, he didn't like not helping out his friends. He might just do a little digging into Parker, and Tate on the side while also trying to reduce the plethora of files on his desk.

Suddenly the office phone rang.

'Yorksbey CID, DI Smith speaking. How can I help you?'

'Hi Simon. How are you?' Smith's heart suddenly skipped as it was the delightful Eden Songe.

'Hi Edee. I am well. How are you? me and Jones were just talking about you and Gray.'

'Really, were you now,' Edee teased. 'It's actually… *Jones and I…*, and I am fine, thank you.'

'What, oh yes, sure,' said a momentarily flustered Smith.

'I just thought I would give you an update as I promised,' continued Edee.

'Oh, that's good, what have you to report,' enquired Smith, his composure restored.

'The shipment is on route from Felixstowe, due in Edendale later this afternoon, all going as planned.'

'That's fine, I take it customs clearance went as planned, HMRC are aware of things as you know.'

'All went as scheduled, thanks for your help,' said Edee with gratitude, in her subtle endearing manner.

'Pleased we could be of service,' replied Smith, enjoying the conversation with Edee. 'I take it you will just keep us informed as agreed. Oh, and by the way, I don't suppose your plans for Friday have fallen through have they?' he hopefully enquired.

'I'm sorry Simon, they haven't. Perhaps another time,' she playfully teased.

'That would be nice,' said Smith hopefully, 'keep in touch then, bye, bye, bye.'

'Goodbye Simon,' said Edee evenly ending the call.

'See, it's all going as scheduled Jones, nothing to worry about, well not for now.....'

Edee dialled Oliver Tate's mobile number.

'Oliver Tate, who's calling.' Came the abrupt answer

'Ah, Mr Tate it's GGL here,' said Edee politely. 'Just a quick courtesy call to let you know the DB5 is in the UK, and we are still planning to deliver the vehicle tomorrow morning if that is fine with you.'

'That will be great, thanks love. Do you know what time?'

'It will probably be mid to late morning, assuming the delivery address hasn't changed, any issues, and we will give you a call.'

'Great and deliver it to my home address, as previously planned love.'

'Thank you Mr Tate, you have a good day now,' lied Edee. 'Goodbye.'

'Uh. Bye then,' replied Bart, as the line went dead.

Well, that's all positive, thought Bart, I had better give Earl Hargrove a call, and give him the news.

Bart scrolled down his recent calls, and pressed a saved number.

After several rings Earl Hargrove finally answered.

'Hargrove speaking.'

'Ah, My Lord, it's Oliver Tate, just to let you know the DB5 has arrived in the UK.'

'Excellent, when will you be delivering it?

'Just need you to transfer the balance amount of £3.375m, and we can deliver in a couple of days.'

'What do you mean Barty, it's balance on delivery as agreed.' Came the stern response.

'My Lord, if you recall our telephone conversation when we agreed the final price, the Arab insisted on balance on arrival in the UK,' said Bart deferentially.

'Tate, don't fuck me about, I've already paid you £3.375m upfront, you'll get the balance when the car is sat outside Hargrove House and not before, do I make myself clear.'

'Now you look here, a deal's a deal, you'll get your car when you pay the balance, so get the money transferred pronto,' Bart insisted, he was not going to be pissed about by anyone, not even small-time nobility.

'Tate, deliver the bloody car and you will get your money, you have my word, don't mess with me.' With that the line went dead.

'That could have gone better,' thought Bart. 'Ah well, his loss, I'll let him stew, I will have the car tomorrow and currently I'm up on the deal by £375k, and £3.375m still to come.'

While he had no desire to antagonise Earl Hargrove, he was pretty sure he could off load the DB5 elsewhere if needed, but he would smooth talk Earl Hargrove once the car was in his hands. He felt confident all was still going as planned, plus he had the little issue of the cocaine to move on.

Bart, again scrolled down the names on his phone and pressed *Spiderman,* he liked that, Peter Parker, Spiderman as he laughed at his own joke.

'Peter old son, it's Bart.'

'Hi Bart, everything okay.'

'It's fine, just checking everything is still okay for Thursday at 1pm.'

'Yep, as agreed, I'll see you then, must go, got a customer wanting a few wraps.'

With that Parker abruptly ended the call.

Bart was thinking, just how rude everyone was today, and all he had for them was positive news, very strange, but hey ho, he would soon be better off once the deals were concluded. He could then concentrate on the upcoming election, and his new position as chairman of the golf club.

CHAPTER 24 - THE MAN IN THE GRAY SUIT

'*TMITGS*' drove slowly down Edendale Lane until he came upon Tate House, the black A5 not out of place driving along this much sort after area. He briefly came to a halt, and did an immediate recce of the gates, house, and adjacent road, and then continued driving into Edendale.

He carried on driving through the delightful village, and momentarily slowed, as he noticed the quaint local pub the Watermill Arms, it looked like it may be a possible place to stay if they did rooms, he would have to check out the website.

He continued over the bridge, and turned into Church Lane and again slowed, as he passed Overhear Manor, the address of CJ Gray, director of GGL as recorded on the *Companies House* website. He again did a quick recce, and realised it wasn't the easiest place to go unnoticed as he tried to monitor movements, he might have to stay at the local inn, that may just give him a reasonable place to base his final activities in the UK.

So, he drove a little further, before turning around and making his way back to the Watermill Arms. He pulled into the car park, which was quiet as it was still not quite the busy lunch time period.

He checked the pubs website on his iPhone, which he found did rooms, not dissimilar to the Black Lion at Long Melford, he smiled and thought that he might have to start doing reviews of Good British Pubs, if he stayed any longer in the UK.

He got out of the car, opened the boot, and took out his pull along luggage, he then locked everything, and having checked all around, as he tended to, he walked into the main entrance of the cosy pub.

As he walked in he saw on the notice board the following, *Edendale Golf Club Captain's Masquerade Ball,* before he continued onto the bar.

Ted Malone the cheery and well-liked publican, was behind the bar, polishing glasses before the lunchtime rush started.

'Good morning sir, I'm afraid we don't start serving until twelve noon, but your welcome to sit down and have a coffee or something similar,' he said cordially.

'Good morning. Thank you, I was wondering if you had any rooms, for four days,' replied *TMITGS*.

'Of course sir, they are £95 for a double, or £110 for a King Size, which would you prefer?'

'I'll take the King Size please. Oh, I note on the notice board the Golf Club Ball. What's that all about.'

'Swanky do that is, fancy dress, by invitation only. It's one of the highlights of the social calendar,' replied Ted. 'I managed to get an invitation this year, tickets are like rocking horse shit. Pardon my French.'

'Your French?' asked *TMITGS* inquisitively.

'Sorry, I can see you're not from around here. I meant pardon me for swearing,' apologised Ted.

'Ah, I see. So, a room for four nights and I'll pay now, cash if that is okay.'

'Certainly sir, and if you need anything just ask me or any of the staff, we are here to make your stay as welcoming as possible. Could you please fill in the guest register, what name is it?'

'White….. Mr. White.'

Earl Hargrove was not happy, in fact he was far from happy, Oliver Tate was now becoming a real problem.

He did, however, recognise that once the car was in Bart's hands, he would negotiate the transfer of the money. He had played many games over the years, and when you are talking £3.375m, that does a lot of talking.

No, the real issue remained the position of chairman. Now, he hoped that the deal with the car, and the election could be inextricably linked, and he was confident that money always won the day. Especially with people like Oliver Tate, and with a bit of negotiation he could get Bart to withdraw, and if he didn't, well, he would make sure the outcome still suited him completely.

Mr White was settled in his pleasant bedroom he had negotiated with the publican. This was a rear facing room which gave him a direct view, albeit quite away off, of Overhear Manor, but with a pair of binoculars he could just make out part of what appeared to be a quadrangle, with either stables, or garages on three sides. He also got a view of the upstairs rear of the manor, plus partial views of the driveway and gardens. It wasn't perfect, but the best he could do under the circumstances, and if the merchandise turned up there, he would definitely know about it.

Having lost Cliff Ledger earlier, he had decided that he was better placed driving North ahead of him, as he would be slower, especially if he was to bring the merchandise by road. He was therefore confident that he was in the area before him, and he also felt that it wouldn't be delivered direct to Oliver Tate, albeit that was still possible, but something he would have to deal with if it arose.

Mr White had also done some checking on the Charity Ball, and felt that it might be to his advantage if he attended. He had delicately persuaded Ted to open up about the locals, especially Oliver Tate and CJ Gray, and he was confident they would be going to the gala event, however, getting a ticket might prove problematic, but definitely not beyond his acquired skills.

He looked up and thought, 'Hello, what's this then?' as he raised the binoculars to his eyes. 'Ah, a delivery.'

CHAPTER 25 - THE DELIVERY

The car transporter turned into Edendale Lane, the journey north from Felixstowe had been uneventful, other than the temporary stop over at Overhear Manor. It slowly drove along seeking out the required address passing the numerous beautiful homes that had slowly been built along the lane during the late 20th Century, and some more recently.

Each one individually built to high architectural standards, representing the styles of the day they were built. Many were of a similar design representing the feel for houses that were valued well over a million pounds, with some ranging to two or three times that, and the odd one or two, far more. Edendale Lane was a much sort after area if you had the wealth and desire to live there.

The houses all had something in common, being built on the west side of the lane with the advantage of an elevated position and an uninterrupted outlook overlooking Edendale Golf Course. Including the Heritage Railway, and the River Eden in the dale below, with extended views on towards Yorksbey.

As with most properties of value what was important was, location, location, location, and the location here was near perfect.

The transporter pulled into the driveway of *'Tate House'* and stopped in front of the high security gate common to most of the properties along *'Millionaires Row,'* the owners expected privacy along this much sort after post code.

Cliff had to open the vehicle door to reach the key pad and pressed the call button.

Eventually an evocative sounding woman answered.

'Hello, can I help you?'

Cliff, suddenly in his element, attempted to turn on his southern English charm and felt an opportunity to flirt was in order.

'Good morning, madam, I have a delivery for a Mr Oliver Tate, this is GGL, Gray's Global Logistics.'

'Oh, wonderful, he will be pleased…. Bart darling the car has arrived….come on up.'

There was a long buzz and the gate started to roll slowly sideways, allowing the vehicle to ascend the curved slightly inclined driveway leading up to a modern, but by comparison with the other homes, modest designer-built home with large expanses of feature glazing and glass balustrades to the first-floor balconies.

It comprised a mere 6 bedrooms, 5 bathrooms, 3 reception rooms, study, dining room, extensive kitchen and breakfast area, utility room, conservatory with separate annex and garage block, and was home to Oliver and Charlotte Tate.

Cliff continued along the driveway and finally pulled up outside the large glazed front door, where there were now three smiling people standing, all obviously eager to see the prize he had on board.

Bart was there, arm in arm with his wife and while Charlotte and Justin's smiles were slowly ebbing, Bart's was still beaming with his own self-importance.

'Good morning, sir, special delivery for Mr Tate,' Cliff said, smiling and eyeing up Charlotte while talking to Bart, recognising a stunning woman when he saw one.

'Great, let's get it off loaded and into the garage,' said Bart enthusiastically.

Charlotte returned Cliff's grin with one of her own renowned smiles, recognising a bit of rough when she saw it.

Cliff presently reversed the car down the ramps from the curtained sided vehicle and presented the gleaming silver Aston Martin DB5 to Bart.

'Great looking car sir, you must be very pleased, it's a classic,' beamed Cliff.

'That's not the fucking car I bought!' Bart furiously shouted at Cliff.

'Maybe so sir. But it's the one I've delivered,' Cliff retorted, evenly.

'On who's fucking instructions?' Bart continued, his rage growing with every second.

'That would be....... CJ Gray sir.'

Charlotte and Justin struggled to hide their laughter, their shoulders lifting, but they just managed to keep their growing amusement to a smirk.

'But it's not the right fucking car,' continued Bart.

'But Mr Tate, the car is as the paperwork you agreed and that was emailed to you.'

'I know what's on the bloody paperwork.' Bart's blood pressure was rising dramatically, his face an incandescent red.

'Shall I get Mr Gray or the office on the phone sir,' Cliff calmly enquired. He was also revelling in Bart's increasing displeasure at a situation which had the potential to grow legs at a great rate of knots.

'Damn right you fucking will, and right away, I want to know what's going down here.'

Cliff punched in the speed dial number for the office on his phone and handed it to Bart.

'Good morn.....'

Before Edee could get a further word out Bart was down her throat in an instance.

'Get me CJ Gray, now,' demanded Bart.

'I'm afraid Mr Gray is not here at the moment,' Edee lied; he was however sat opposite her, listening on the other phone.

'Well, I don't want to speak to his French floozy,' Bart spat out.

CJ's smile changed in an instant, if Bart didn't wind his neck in pretty quick, he would be regretting every further word.

Edee could see CJ was extremely unhappy, but she could handle this, she shook her head slowly at CJ and raised her hand gently to soothe him.

Edee continued in her calm and collected manner.

'Mr Tate, I'm sure we can resolve this amicably to everyone's satisfaction.'

'Where the fucks my car and my dru...,' Bart stopped himself just in time.

'Mr Tate, it would appear you're rather dissatisfied with the delivered merchandised, that is not good. I suggest we contact Alham Industries as a matter of urgency to resolve any potential issue,' Edee continued, revelling in Bart's growing displeasure.

'What, no, no, I'll contact Alham, but you let CJ '*bloody*' Gray know, if he's had anything to do with this almighty cock up, he'd better watch his back. No bastard crosses Oliver Tate and gets away with it.'

'I'll be sure to pass on your message Mr Tate, you have a nice day, and sir. I suggest you calm down, you wouldn't want to have a coronary, and leave a young widow now. Would you?' concluded Edee sarcastically.

Bart ended the call and threw the phone back at Cliff, who had from the one-sided conversation established what was going down.

He smiled and asked. 'Shall I continue with the delivery, or shall I return the vehicle to the supplier. Sir?'

'Just leave it and fuck off.'

'Certainly sir, your wish is my command. Oh, and sir,' Cliff lowered his voice, so Bart had to get closer to hear. 'Don't ever talk to me, or Edee like that ever again,' he menacingly whispered, and he punched him hard in the midriff. 'Otherwise, you are a dead man, do I make myself clear.'

Bart doubled up in agony and collapsed on the floor.

'Did I make myself clear?' Cliff evenly repeated.

'Yes, yes, perfectly clear.' Bart coughed, suddenly realising that the delivery driver was rather more than just a delivery man, and not someone to cross.

Cliff made the car transporter safe, smiled at Charlotte and Justin who knew not to get involved in the skirmish, but who had gone to Bart to check he was okay.

Charlotte winked at Cliff while helping Bart to his feet and said in a rather reluctant tone. 'I think you had better leave before we call the police.'

'Good day, Madam, Sir,' said Cliff, as he passed the paperwork and two car keys to Bart, who snatched them from his hands.

'Thank you too,' said Cliff mockingly and he got into the vehicle smiling, returning Charlottes wink, and drove off down the drive towards Edendale Lane.

CHAPTER 26 - THE HOOK

Edee settled the phone onto its cradle and looked over the top of her glasses at CJ.

'Well, that went as we expected, what now James?' She looked into his deep brown eyes.

'I think we have to let time take a hand, but we need to keep an eye on Bart Tate. Edee, please check that Cliff is okay and ask him to make arrangements to return the transporter, and then ask him to set up a stake out of Bart,' said CJ, as he returned the look and smiled, thinking just how stunning she always appeared.

'As we have a little time to kill, how about a round of golf to help us ponder our next steps?' asked CJ.

'I'd like that, but what about work?' Edee replied.

'That can wait, occasionally being the boss has its perks,' said a smiling CJ.

Bart stormed back into the house having made sure the DB5 was securely in place and locked in the garage block. He proceeded to his study and considered locking away the two sets of car keys safely in his safe, but stopped, suddenly deep in thought.

He proceeded to call Alham, the number immediately went to answer machine

'Alham, it's Oliver Tate, please call me urgently. What's going on? Where's my car and my merchandise?'

Bart hung up, still getting more frustrated by the minute.

Outside the study door Justin was listening intently.

Bart looked at his watch, late morning in the UK, mid-afternoon in Dubai.

He dialled the Alham Industries office number in his phone, two rings and the young Filipino receptionist answered.

'Alham Industries. How may I help you?'

'It's Oliver Tate. Can I speak with Mr Alham? Its urgent.'

'I'm sorry Mr Tate, but Mr Alham is not here, he's on route to the UK as we speak.'

'What, oh okay,' continued Bart. He was curious as to why he was already due in the UK, but somehow slightly reassured that he could get a chance to see him face to face.

'Okay, pass a message on to him and get him to call Oliver Tate urgently, it's about the car and the merchandise.'

'Certainly Mr Ta......' Bart cut her off before she could even finish.

'Fuck, fuck,' said Bart out loud, his annoyance continuing to fester.

Bart mulled over his immediate options and decided he would confront Alham when he knew where he was, but first he needed to check if the drugs were in the spare tyre.

Justin timidly knocked on the study door and cautiously entered.

'Dad is everything okay?' he enquired, clearly knowing the answer.

Bart tried to sound calm and composed.

'No, not really son, that is not the car I bought, I need to know what's happened. Can you do me a favour. I may have to leave urgently, can you keep an eye on Charlotte and let me know if, or when she goes anywhere and if she meets up with anyone, especially an Arab.'

'Of course Dad, you can rely on me.'

Justin as always sort to please his overbearing father, but he was rather curious as to the reason behind the question. He would seek to find out more from his stunning step mother.

Bart walked purposely towards the kitchen and picked up a large carving knife from the block on the black marble topped island. Charlotte was idly drinking coffee, listening to the radio while checking her Facebook account, she looked up as she attempted false concern with her unmoving botoxed forehead

'Bart darling, are you okay now? Do you want me to do anything?'

Bart had finally regained his composure, albeit he was still inwardly mad as hell.

'No Lotty, not at the moment, but I don't like being made a fool of. Someone is going to pay for what's happening and I don't care who,' said Bart, as he shook the long-bladed knife intimidatingly in the air

He continued to open the back door and slammed it shut behind him, before striding towards the garage block where he momentarily stopped to unlock the garage and then the DB5 boot.

'Well, am I being taken for a fool, or a complete fool?'

He raised the boot floor that hid the spare wheel and stabbed the knife into the tyre wall, the air violently expelled with a bang and a fine plume of white powder blew out with the air. He withdrew the knife and licked the tip which had residue of powder on the end, he smiled.

'Just a fool then.'

At least he could now get the money he had planned for the cocaine, and he was still up on the deal even without the right car, but another £3.375m was not going to slip through his fingers, not without a fight.

Justin took care to make sure he wasn't seen as he discretely watched Bart through the garage window and smiled knowingly. He suddenly realised that he might just have a new cheap dealer to hand, and a new supply of cocaine.

Bart closed the boot slightly reassured, when his phone rang, he looked at the ID, but it came up as unknown, he cautiously answered the call.

'Hello, who's this?'

'Mr Tate. Its Alham, I have just got your voicemail.'

Bart was suddenly in confrontation mode.

'Alham, what the bloody hell is going on. Where's my car I bought; you've delivered a plain old DB5 not the replica I saw in Dubai.' Bart's voice was crackling with animosity.

'What do you mean Mr Tate, your car left here in the container sealed by the engineer Ali, I have kept my side of the bargain.' Alham sounded similarly as perturbed as Bart, what was going down?

'I hope you aren't playing games with me Mr Tate.'

'Me playing games? I've paid you £3m for my perfect replica and what have I got, a piece of 1964 shit worth £300k, you or your engineer hadn't better be messing me about.' Bart's blood pressure was again rising dramatically.

'You'd better get this sorted, and quick; my buyer is expecting that car on his drive tomorrow and if it isn't, you're a dead man,' threatened Bart.

'Mr Tate, I don't take kindly to your idle threats, I suggest you work with me to resolve this unfortunate situation, I will contact *your* delivery agents and find out what's gone wrong, but let's be clear, you organised the shipment not me.'

Alham was wildly thinking what was happening and more importantly, where were the diamonds.

'I'll look to be on the next flight available to the UK; you have my word, this will get sorted, trust me.'

'Next flight?' Bart curiously asked. 'Your receptionist said you were already travelling here.'

'Lei must have got things muddled, but I'll hopefully be there ASAP,' and Alham hung up.

Both men were wildly contemplating what was going down, but they both thought the same thing. CJ Gray was right in the mix.

Chapter 27 - Playing a Round

Mr White had observed the delivery of the DB5 from his vantage point.

He had established from his earlier recce that the Tate's next-door neighbours were fortunately away, and he had easily circumnavigated their low-level security measures and had climbed a tree overlooking the Tate's property that gave him a perfect view of the delivery.

'Well, that was interesting,' he thought, having observed all the outside activity, he now needed to decide how to deal with the developing situation, it wasn't going quite as he had originally planned, but nothing beyond his expertise to resolve. He just wanted Tate out of the way so he could retrieve his package.

The dark grey Audi RS6 and the blue BMW Z4 pulled up and parked in the golf club car park. Oscar and both the two drivers got out, both of them now looked more suitably dressed for a round of golf. CJ in his usual all black attire, similar to how the former South African golfer Gary Player used to look, while Edee had adopted her familiar all-red outfit, of golf top and short skirt, embraced by most lady golfers of her stature, complemented with red visor and her hair tied in a neat pony tail.

They collected their golf bags and trolleys from the boots of their respective cars and made their way towards the locker rooms to change their shoes, Edee, not quite looking ready for the first tee shot, especially while she was still wearing her matching red soled stiletto heeled Jimmy Choo shoes.

As they made their way across the comparatively quiet car park, Earl Hargrove approached them.

'Good afternoon, CJ, Madame Songe, and of course Oscar,' he warmly welcomed them. Oscar rolled on his back expecting a tummy rub, but the Earl ignored him, as he usually did.

'Good afternoon My Lord,' they both replied, smiling.

'Sorry to interrupt you CJ, but do you have a couple of minutes,' Earl Hargrove continued haughtily.

'Certainly My Lord. What is it?' asked CJ, intrigued by the request.

'I was hoping you could help me with a little problem I have, comes by the name of Tate. Oliver Tate.'

'I am sure that if we can, we will,' answered a smiling CJ.

The three of them plus Oscar continued walking towards the club house in earnest conversation but nodding as they went. They appeared to have already struck some form of accord.

As the two golfers reached the entrance to the locker area they acknowledged Earl Hargrove, nodding towards him, he smiled and said, 'I think that might just work, thank you for your suggestion CJ. You are as always, someone who considers things from a slightly different perspective.'

'I'm pleased to be of service.'

Without further ado, Earl Hargrove left them and wandered off to find the Major, he suddenly felt more at ease than he had done for quite a while.

Having changed into their golf shoes, CJ and Edee made their way down the gravel path from the club house under the railway bridge, pushing their golf trolleys towards the 1st Tee (Par 4 – 405 yards) Oscar keeping to heel, as even though the club like other elite and prestigious clubs, allowed dogs on the course and also in the club, CJ was mindful of him being on his best behaviour, which he always was.

The two golfers had eventually after many previous rounds of golf and much debate, established they would play off the same tees when playing together. They therefore agreed as usual to play off the yellow tees, and while red tees were still provided for higher handicapped ladies and those that preferred to use them, most women were now encouraged, and often preferred, to use the same tees as the men.

Edee had consciously taken up golf again having previously played when she was younger, encouraged by her then regular partner Elizabeth Gray, she had though, after her mentors passing played rather less, until more recently when she saw it as a wonderful opportunity to be out and about with CJ Gray.

Being the gentleman he was, CJ as always offered to allow Edee to tee off first, which she again declined, and so CJ tossed a coin to decide.

'Heads,' called Edee. The coin landed on tails.

'My honour then Madame Songe but you can still tee off first,' said CJ playfully.

Edee placed her tee and ball and took a couple of smooth practice swings with her driver. She addressed the ball, and ping, the ball went straight as an arrow down the fairway about 220 yards, just missing the fairway bunker on the left, a near perfect shot.

'You've been on the driving range again, haven't you?' said CJ admiringly but inquisitively enquired.

'Might have had the odd practice,' Edee replied, laughing, so that it made CJ's heart fill with pride, just like when he had originally taught Jemima the basics and seen her develop.

'I think we might have to review your handicap if you keep hitting them like that,' added CJ, as he placed his own ball on a tee, and having earlier warmed up with some stretches he addressed the ball without any further practice swings, and hit a pretty good drive, not quite as straight as Edee's, but an extra 25 yards further, and just rolling onto the left fringe of the fairway.

'Good shot, have you also been on the driving range?' asked Edee, smiling wryly.

'No, not me. I've not got the time, just the usual First Tee luck,' replied CJ, also smiling.

Both of them having been better golfers in their youth, playing then off single figures, were now playing to a similar standard with handicaps of 12 and 13 respectfully, however, neither of them was a match for Jemima, who played off scratch and was a golf professional in Dubai.

'So, loser pays for the drinks as usual,' said CJ, 'and match play today?'

'Agreed.' They both placed their clubs in their bags and strolled off down the fairway enjoying the spring afternoon, with Oscar leading, tail wagging as normal on point.

Edee took a 5 wood for her second shot and came up 50 yards short of the green on the right.

CJ took a 5 iron and hit another decent shot, and landed his ball on the fringe of the green on the left, just missing one of the greenside bunkers.

Both were well placed to potentially make pars, but now an all-important part of the hole, the final approach.

Edee took out her pitching wedge and with Oscar looking on attentively, hit a delicate chip shot that pitched on the fringe and rolled gently to within a foot of the pin.

'Brilliant shot,' came CJ's retort. 'Well done.' With Oscar also letting out a short approving bark.

Edee smiled acknowledging the compliments.

They walked up to the green. 'Well, what do you make of how Earl Hargrove reacted to you suggestion?' asked Edee.

'I think it gives him a way out of things if he needs that option, but I think we will have to see how things pan out, a long way to go yet,' replied CJ, as he removed his golf glove and pulled his putter out of his bag and removed its cover.

'Well, you've got a certain par, net birdie, Madame Songe, I need this to win the hole,' he continued and reviewed the line of the putt as he approached the ball, and as with all his shots, never taking a practice swing.

'In or out,' asked Edee, holding the flag stick.

'Out please.' CJ went through his normal minimal putting routine, composed himself, checked the line and gently swung the club, but he had misjudged the speed of the green and it ran past to the right by about 2 feet.

'Bollocks.'

'That to half the hole and leave us even,' toyed Edee, not offering to let him have the shot.

CJ took the shot quickly, as his usual style and immediately regretted it, as it lipped out.

'Double bollocks,' said CJ, as Edee laughed out loud.

'Less haste, more accuracy Mr Gray,' she teased, as she cheekily tapped her own ball into the hole.

'One up to me I believe fine sir.'

As they picked up their golf balls and made their way to the 2nd (Par 4 – 425 yards), Oscar looked up at his master as much as to say, 'What the hell was that dad!'

CHAPTER 28 - THE BALLOT

Earl Hargrove having discussed issues and possible options with CJ Gray, definitely felt more content than he had for a while, and with more of a spring in his step he went into the clubhouse.

In the foyer he bumped into the steward.

'Ah, Jarvis, how are you? Have you seen The Major? I fancy a word with him,' he grandly asked.

'No, My Lord, I haven't seen him for a while, but he may well be in the Bar.'

'Thank you. If you do see him though, please let him know I am looking for him and I will be in the Lounge Bar.' With that Earl Hargrove strolled off.

'Ah, there you are Major,' exclaimed Earl Hargrove as he marched into the Lounge and sat down next to him. 'Just been discussing a few things with CJ Gray and the beautiful French lass that works with him. Is everything set up for the secret ballot?'

The Major, momentarily taken aback, immediately regained his composure.

'Yes My Lord, all is ready.'

'When will voting be allowed and when is the ballot closing? Ah, Nancy my usual please,' said Earl Hargrove as he beckoned the young waitress across, 'and whatever the Major would like. Oh, and put it on my tab. Thank you,'

'Certainly My Lord, and for you Major?' the young waitress asked.

'I'm okay, nothing for me, thank you Nancy,' replied the Major.

'The voting starts at 10 am tomorrow and closes at 10 am the following day. Only registered ballot papers and those signed with membership numbers will be accepted. The Ballott Box will be on show and locked and sealed in the Foyer.'

'And the counting, when will that be done?' Earl Hargrove continued inquisitively.

'Counting will occur immediately after the ballot closes and will be conducted in the Restaurant supervised by me with two adjudicators.'

'Who are they Major?'

'I've asked the local solicitor Mr Kipling Snr and a member of the local constabulary, DI Smith. I thought if I can't influence the vote, I had best make sure that neither could Tate.'

'Quite right,' added Earl Hargrove. 'Sounds like everything is in hand Major, I hope you have been doing some more canvassing, I've now been in touch with every member.'

'Yes, so have I. It's still difficult to call,' said the Major worryingly. Just as the waitress placed Earl Hargroves glass of Louis Treis on the table between the two men.

'Anything else My Lord?' she enquired.

'No, that's fine thank you. I agree, while I think our man is in the driving seat, this will be close, and you know my views on the outcome,' added Earl Hargrove earnestly.

'Oh, I do that, I do that,' replied the Major. Not wanting to contemplate the thought of a Tate victory.

'Well, this to make us even,' said CJ, as he eyed up his putt on the 18th Green. Edee had holed out a pretty impressive 18-footer, so from being in a position to win the round, he was now seeking to draw. Oh, the variances of golf, they can change things in a moment.

The round had been engrossing, nip and tuck at times. CJ had pulled back the error on the first and at one point had established a 3-hole lead but a series of poor shots on the back 9 had been his downfall.

While he was leading he had teased Edee slightly, but she had taken it in her normal easy-going manner, just happy to be out enjoying the spring weather with her boys.

The boot now though, and for the last three holes, had definitely been on the other foot, and what goes round comes round, and it was now for Edee to be the one teasing in good humour.

The 12-foot putt was doable, but tricky, the 18th Green contours were notorious for ending many a good round with golfers either tiring or getting too cocky at the death.

CJ unusually took slightly longer than normal in assessing the putt, his competitive edge from his youth still evident, he had been hoping to putt to win, but now a putt to half.

He struck the ball with confidence, it had the right speed, it had the right line, it looked just about perfect, it was just about to drop, when it stopped, right on the edge of the hole.

'Well,' said Edee, slightly mockingly. '*You're no better than that*, but what a putt and what around. Well played, but hard luck,' as she offered her hand to CJ which he shook while removing his cap and kissed her warmly on the cheek.

'Well played, Eden Songe, I definitely think we need to review your handicap though,' he said smiling broadly. 'A most enjoyable afternoon though. Thank you.'

'Can't get much closer than that. I thought you had me,' added Edee. Hoping for just that.

'Perhaps next time,' replied CJ, as they put their putters in their respective golf bags and strolled off pushing their trolleys towards the club house, Oscar leading the way as always.

Once off the course CJ switched on his mobile to check for any calls, Edee did the same, such is the way with modern life, the best part of 4 hours without a phone can feel like a lifetime to some.

'A message from Alham not surprisingly, asking me to call him,' said CJ.

'Snap, me too,' said Edee, smiling. 'I think it was inevitable after what has happened,' she continued.

'Now who's best placed to ring him, you with your subtle womanly ways, or me with my direct abrupt manner.... mmm, let me think?' added CJ, seeking Edee's reply.

'I think he can wait,' she added smiling. 'It's your round, I deserve that drink, let's not ruin a wonderful afternoon. Well not just yet.'

To which Oscar gave a quick bark, acknowledging the good time they had all had.

CHAPTER 29 - THE LURE

CJ and Edee decided that it might be better to try to defuse the situation and let Edee call Alham back, but they both knew that the die was set, and things now had to play out regardless of the impending phone call. It was also not a call that should be overheard,

They were enjoying the drinks on the veranda overlooking the 18th Green that CJ had bought as his forfeit, and with the sun moving below the yard arm, CJ finally suggested, 'Fancy dinner at Overhear Manor, Madame Songe? Mrs W will have cooked enough for the village as usual,' he joked. 'Plus, you can make the call in private from there.'

Edee was pleased that CJ had offered, it had been a while since he had invited her to the family home. She had previously enjoyed living their when Elizabeth Gray was alive, but not long after Aunty Betty's passing she had moved out and now leased her own apartment overlooking the river, and while she liked her seclusion and privacy, she at times missed the happy feel of the Gray family home.

'That would be nice, thank you,' she said smiling, and the two of them finished their drinks and made their way to their cars. Oscar seemed to sense that all three of them were going to spend the evening together and was bouncing around with his tail wagging ten to the dozen.

On the short drive back to Overhear Manor, CJ just noticed a powerful motor bike discreetly parked back from the road and hidden from most unobservant passer-by's, Cliff was obviously keeping tabs on Bart as requested, he would call him later for an update.

The Audi and the BMW pulled into the stable yard, CJ parked the RS6 in its garage and Edee parked her car in the area allocated for guests and visitors.

Oscar, having been let out of the car, shot off towards the back door seeking out Mrs Wembley and his dinner, while Edee sidled up to James and linked arms.

'Thanks for a nice afternoon,' she said. 'I really enjoyed it.'

'So did I, except for you winning though. Come on let's see what delight Mrs W has conjured up for dinner.' With that they walked off after Oscar.

The phone call was going more or less as CJ and Edee had expected.

'Mr Alham, I understand your concern,' continued Edee, 'but it was your engineer Ali that supervised the DB5 being sealed in the container, so I am at a loss as to what's happened.'

'But why isn't it the vehicle what Mr Tate was expecting?' Alham stated yet again.

'Mr Alham we are going over the same ground again,' said Edee, as calmly as possible. 'GGL delivered the vehicle identified on the paperwork and documents, I don't know what else you can expect us to do, we can't perform magic and change cars, now can we?'

'No, I suppose not,' admitted Alham reluctantly. 'I will I suppose have to come to the UK to sort this out, as Mr Tate is far from happy, I just don't understand what has happened,' he added, sounding a mixture of anger and despondency at the same time, if that was possible.

'Neither do I,' added Edee, sounding as sympathetic as she could under the circumstances. 'Please let us know if we can be of any further assistance, and when you get to the UK please get in contact if you require any further help. By the way, I assume that Mr Tate has paid you in full, as your agreement?'

'Thank you. I will, and yes we have been paid in full, it's just that...' But Alham suddenly trailed off what he was about to say, realising the incriminating nature of what he could have said.

'Sorry Mr Alham is there anything else?' asked Edee curiously, but already sure of the reply.

'No, I'll be in touch if, or when I get to the UK, goodbye.'

'Goodbye Mr Alham, you have a nice day now,' Edee concluded, rather condescendingly.

'Well, you handled that very well Edee, you are so good at deflating potential explosive situations,' said CJ, complimenting her. 'I am not sure I would have been able to do that.'

'We all use our talents to the best of our abilities,' replied Edee. 'It will be interesting to see how Tate reacts and what happens next, especially if Alham arrives in the UK.'

'It sure will, but at the moment things are developing as we expected,' said CJ, before adding. 'I think it's time we got changed out of these golf clothes and had some dinner.'

CHAPTER 30 - THE FIRST DEMAND

Mr White looked on as Justin and Charlotte left in the BMW M4, he had been waiting for the opportunity to check over the DB5 for his merchandise and now that Bart was alone in the house he had his opportunity.

Cliff also saw them leave and as per CJ's instructions didn't follow but remained incognito watching the property, and to see if Bart left.

Mr White dropped over the tall fence from his vantage point in the neighbour's tree, he didn't want to be in the UK longer than necessary, the sooner this was done the better.

He had checked out that there was no CCTV and he now only had to consider any security alarm for the property, but with Tate still at home it was unlikely to be armed.

He checked the rear door and found it unlocked, he pushed it open and went into the utility room that led into the kitchen, he quietly drew a Glock 19 from its shoulder holster and held it conventionally just in case there was any trouble. He continued slowly not knowing the layout of the house and listened for the sound of Tate which he soon heard emanating from a room off the hallway.

Mr White slowly pushed open the door and saw Tate sitting at a desk in the study with his back to him, looking out of the window.

'Ah. Mr Tate it is good to see you again,' he said, making Bart nearly jump out of his skin.

'What the fuck!' exclaimed Bart, as he shot around in his leather swivel chair. 'Oh, it's you, what the fuck are you doing in my house, how did you get in?'

'Just a quick visit Mr Tate, and through the back door,' said Mr White smiling.

'I have come for something that belongs to me,' he added, now in a rather threatening way that Bart knew not to provoke further.

'There's no need for the gun,' added Bart. 'If there something that's yours you can have it, whatever it is.'

'That is reassuring and very wise of you Mr Tate, we wouldn't want any accidents now, would we?'

'Let's go to the garage shall we, there is something of mine in the DB5.' Mr White encouraged Bart to stand, who didn't need further persuasion, and he got up and started walking promptly towards the garage, beads of sweat appearing on his brow.

'I suggest you also bring the car keys; I wouldn't want to damage such an expensive car unnecessarily,' added Mr White sarcastically as he holstered the revolver.

With that they made their way to the garage and the DB5.

Bart unlocked the car and pulled the bonnet catch as requested by Mr White.

'What are you looking for?' asked Bart inquisitively.

'Never you mind,' said Mr White, lifting the bonnet and putting the stay in place.

He then felt behind the triple set of HD8 Carburettors and smiled as he pulled out a blue velvet bag.

His smile though, quickly faded, as he felt the weight of the bag, it was empty.

He looked at Bart menacingly and again pulled the Glock from its holster and aimed it directly at Bart's head. 'Where are they?' he calmly asked Bart.

'I don't know what you're talking about,' answered Bart. Looking extremely worried, the beads of sweat building on his forehead and now also dripping down the middle of his back.

'Where are they?' Mr White repeated. More intimidatingly. 'I won't ask again.'

'I don't know what you're talking about.'

'You are either very stupid or very cunning,' added Mr White. Clearly in no mood to be messed with.

'I want my diamonds and I want them within 24 hours,' said Mr White menacingly. I suggest if you took them, you let me have them back, if you didn't take them, then I suggest you find them quickly, and let me have them.'

Bart's mind was going ten to the dozen, 'What the fuck was happening?' he thought.

'You have 24 hours; I am not someone to be messed with.' Mr White fired the pistol, missing Bart's head by millimetres. 'Do I make myself clear?'

Bart nodded meekly and said, 'Yes, perfectly clear,' in a very shallow voice.

'You might also want to change your trousers,' said Mr White, smiling at the wet patch now forming in Bart's crotch, and with that he turned and left the garage, as Bart fell to the ground in pure relief, head in his hands.

Outside, Cliffs attention was aroused. Was that a gunshot he heard, he wasn't sure, but it sounded like perhaps a 9 mm calibre, but where did it come from.

Just then the gate to Tate House slid open and out strolled someone Cliff knew, and he wasn't totally surprised, it was his earlier shadow, and he didn't look too happy as he kept looking at the empty velvet bag in his hand, shaking his head.

Cliff remained hidden taking a series of photos of the visitor with his digital camera with telephoto lens. His pursuer went to the neighbour's house, and shortly after, the black A5 Cliff had previously lost in Suffolk, drove out and turned right towards Edendale. Cliff fired off the camera with a series of more photos. He had better give CJ and Edee an update.

CHAPTER 31 - THE STROLL TO THE PUB.

CJ heard the tapping of Edee's heels on the wooden floor of the Minstrel Gallery and came out of the Study as she started walking down the left-hand staircase from the Guest Wing.

As he looked up he thought she looked beautiful as always, she had changed back into the skinny fit jeans with the black tank top she had been wearing earlier, and she held her bomber jacket over her shoulder. Oscar charged up to greet her and then led her back down the stairs.

'Shower okay?' asked CJ, adding, 'I take it you found the towels?'

'Yes, fine thanks,' replied Edee, as she joined him at the bottom of the stairs.

'Just in time,' said CJ, 'Mrs W is just serving up.'

He breathed in the fragrance of her expensive French perfume, not only did she look good she smelt so good too.

Mrs Wembley as always had prepared a wonderful but simple meal, she also attempted to play cupid and declined to eat with CJ and Edee, saying she had a meeting at the Women's Guild in the village.

CJ and Edee both saw through her plan, and despite asking her to stay and eat with them she graciously served up the food in the dining room and left the two of them with Oscar at CJ's feet.

'I'll not be late,' she said, and with that left the room.

'Bye, Mrs Wembley,' they both said together. 'See you later.'

'Well, this is good,' said Edee, tucking into the wonderfully prepared meal.

'As always,' added CJ. Before then going quiet, as he was as usual lost for words when left in Edee's sole company away from work.

They continued eating in silence, both still appreciating each other's company and the food, both feverishly contemplating what to say next, but not wanting to ruin the moment with some inane or senseless comment.

They looked slightly odd, the two of them at the large dining table that seated twelve, but could be extended for another six if needed. This room like most of the others in Overhear Manor had been originally decorated and furnished by Elizabeth Gray, who had a wonderful eye for what looked just right, using only the best quality materials and often characteristic antique furniture.

CJ had chosen a nice Malbec from the cellar, which was going down very well as an accompaniment to the meal.

As was the case with most meals at the Manor, it was over rather quickly, not surprisingly as if you concentrate on eating rather than talking, the meal is soon concluded.

'Well, that was splendid, thank you Mrs W,' exclaimed CJ as he looked up at Edee who was wiping her mouth with her linen napkin. 'Fancy a short walk to the pub? Oscar won't say no,' he continued.

'Yes, that would be nice,' replied Edee, appreciating the suggestion.

They cleared the table and took the tableware and cutlery through to the kitchen and put them in the dishwasher, Oscar seeking to lick the plates that were momentarily on the kitchen side before being told to stop.

CJ picked a jacket off the hooks in the kitchen and slung it over his shoulder, Edee slipped her bomber jacket on and the three of them ventured forth, CJ opened the back door and Oscar charged out as usual, slipping on the tiled floor as he leapt the threshold and step.

'He'll never learn,' commented CJ, as Edee laughed, and they followed briskly after the energetic dog.

Having checked the security cameras and seen that no one was on the 9th Green or 10th Tee, the three of them suddenly appeared from behind the Half Way House Hut and turned left towards the bridge and the pub.

'It's a lovely spring evening,' stated Edee, linking arms with CJ. ' What a lovely way to end a perfect day,' she added.

'Mmm, wonderful,' said CJ. Lost in his own thoughts, as the three of them walked into the sunset, as usual in silence. The walk to the pub took no more than 5 minutes, and as they crossed the stone bridge over the river towards the Watermill Arms they realised that the beer garden was packed as it was such a glorious evening.

Suddenly a black Audi A5 pulled rather sharply into the carpark, the driver staring at the pair of them before parking and getting out of the car.

'Edee, I'm not so sure this was a good idea,' said CJ. Eyeing up all the locals enjoying their drinks and food, all the tables were taken in the beer garden and on the terrace overlooking the river.

'I thought you might say that.'

Edee knew CJ well enough to understand he was not a fan of crowds, and he preferred quiet, more intimate social gatherings, this noisy throng was definitely not his cup of tea.

As they walked past the beer garden they saw Nancy having a drink with Justin.

'Hello Mr Gray, lovely evening,' said Nancy brightly.

'Hi Nancy. Hi, it sure is. I gather you're not working today at the club,' replied CJ.

'No, I've managed to get tonight off, so I thought I would have a quiet drink and a meal with Justin, but it's slightly busier than we thought it would be.'

'Well, you couldn't have asked for a better evening, enjoy yourselves. See you later,'

Justin nodded, smiling at CJ and Edee, as Nancy and he both said, 'Goodbye.'

'Bye,' said Edee, and then she quietly whispered to CJ as they walked on, 'Do you know Justin?'

'No, not really, but I've seen him about at the golf club.'

'Come on, let's continue in a loop back along the river to home and we can have a nightcap at the Manor and sit out on the rear terrace,' added Edee, as the three of them walked on through the carpark towards the rear gate, leading to the riverbank.

The driver of the A5 was nonchalantly walking back to the pub when Oscar sat down immediately in front of the man, his nose in the air.

'Hello, you're a fine-looking dog,' said the man, rubbing Oscar's ear, 'and so obedient.'

'Good evening,' said CJ, nodding towards the man. 'Come on boy.' Oscar immediately carried on walking with CJ and Edee.

'Good evening, Mr Gray,' said the man, as he continued walking towards the pub, where he stopped to talk with Peter Parker, who was unexpectedly leaning on the wall next to the entrance to the pub.

'Do you know him?' asked Edee, curiously looking back over her shoulder.

'Never met him before,' said CJ smiling.

'And what about Oscar, do you think he smelt drugs on him?' asked Edee.

'Maybe, but I think it might have also been something else he recognised,' added CJ knowingly, as the three of them made their way back to Overhear Manor and their nightcap.

CHAPTER 32 - THE SPARE

Bart felt better, the shower and change of clothes had worked wonders, he had finally regained his composure, but what the fuck was Mr White on about, but he didn't have time for that just now, Peter Parker was due, albeit later than planned.

Bart threw his soiled trousers into the linen basket and made his way downstairs when he heard the gate buzzer sound, he continued and pressed the intercom.

'Hello,' said Bart, sounding still rather annoyed.

'Hi Bart, it's me Peter, sorry I'm a bit late, I got held up,' said Parker jovially.

'That's a fucking understatement, you were due here hours ago.'

'Yes, as I said I'm sorry about that, I got detained, but I'm here now and with what you enjoy most.'

Bart pressed the security gate button.

Parker drove slowly up the driveway and parked his BMW outside the front door and got out relishing the fine spring evening and what was instore.

Bart opened the front door and walked out to meet Parker, closing it after him.

'Have you got the money?' asked Bart pointedly.

'What the fuck's up with you, get out of the wrong side of someone else's bed did you?'

'Never you mind, but I've had better days, now where's the fucking money?' spat Bart.

'It's in the boot,' said Parker, as he moved to the rear of his car, and he took a blue holdall out of the boot. 'Where's the merchandise?'

'It's in the garage, come on,' said Bart as he led Parker to the garage block.

Bart opened the side door and went inside leading Parker.

'Nice motor, Bart!'

'Mmm, could be a whole lot fucking better,' said Bart, as he opened the boot of the silver DB5, and lifted the boot floor to reveal the spare wheel and tyre.

'Well,' said Parker.

'Well what.'

'Where the fuck are the drugs?' asked Parker, starting to grow impatient.

'There in the fucking tyre, where do you fucking think they are,' exclaimed Bart, adding, 'How did you think I would get them past customs you idiot. Just walk through with them?'

'Don't call me a fucking idiot,' shouted Parker.

'Well don't fucking act like one then,' said Bart, also losing his patience.

'So, what are you telling me?' Parker asked irritably.

'Give me the money and take the wheel, I can't get the bloody tyre off the rim,' said an annoyed Bart.

'Are all the drugs there?'

'Of course they bloody are, don't you trust me?' quizzed Bart, really getting annoyed now. 'I supervised the packing myself in Dubai.'

'Yes, yes of course I do,' said Parker, trying to calm things down a little as he passed Bart the holdall.

'Is the money all here?' Bart asked, opening the zip, and looking into the bag, full of a mixture of used notes and looking up at Parker, who moved his right arm to his back and gently held the grip of his Glock, which was nestled in the waistband of his trousers.

'Of course it's all there, don't you trust me?' asked Parker nonchalantly, knowing that it wasn't, his grip on the revolver tightening.

'Yes. Yes of course I do,' said Bart, adding to himself. 'Not really, but I also know where you live.'

Parker relieved, gently let his grip of the gun ease, pleased that he hadn't had to resort to the ultimate show of force.

'Right, I've got the money you take the drugs, but let me have the wheel back once you have the tyre off, my client would really like a spare wheel,' continued Bart, looking to get things concluded before Charlotte and Justin came home.

'Okay,' said Parker, lifting the spare wheel and rolling it out of the garage towards his car.

'Thanks Bart,' said Parker, offering his hand, which Bart reluctantly took, he had no reason not to, albeit he felt it unnecessary and the two of them were suddenly engaged in the latest strength battle of the males.

Both instantly gripping the others hand, seeking to gain an advantage, they both knew what was in store as they had done this before, and because of that, they ended the unnecessary duel even quicker than they would normally both have done.

'I hope it brings you the rewards you strive for.' said Bart poetically, smiling and pleased this part of the plan was concluded. He had the balance of the £500k, and with it a tidy little profit, plus he had off loaded the most dangerous part of his scheme, and also a grateful Parker to boot.

Parker put the spare wheel in the boot of his M5 and got into the car.

'I'm sure it will be most rewarding.' With that he closed the door and drove off down the driveway.

Bart turned on his heels with the holdall, thinking he should put it in the safe, but then decided to put it in the boot of the DB5.

Cliff having watched the BMW M5 arrive, now saw it depart from his discreet hiding position. He had already taken a series of photos of the encounter between Bart and his visitor, he now had to send those plus the earlier photos he had taken, to CJ and Edee ASAP, as he was sure the boys in blue would welcome the incriminating nature of their content.

No sooner had the BMW departed towards Yorksbey, when Justin's BMW M4 came into view from the other direction, though Charlotte, wasn't now in the passenger seat, but another woman Cliff didn't recognise. So he fired off a further number of photos as the car pulled into the gateway.

Justin opened the window and punched in the security code into the keypad, and the security gate opened, allowing him to drive up to Tate House with his mysterious female guest.

CHAPTER 33 - CHARITY MASQUERADE BALL

CJ was only really there this year because Edee had asked him to come, the Golf Club Captain's Charity Ball, had been a must attend annual event for the past 35 years, CJ could still vividly remember the first one, which he and Eve had graced as young lovers all those years ago. Since her death though, CJ had only occasionally attended, usually if Jemima asked him, but since she had left for Dubai he had attended rarely, if at all.

It was however, always a very well attended and supported event with invited guests only, with the highlight being the charity auction of the attending ladies to the highest bidder, and each woman was then at the winner's beck and call for an evening of their choice. It was however accepted that this was traditionally a dinner at Oak Hall Luxury Resort, the 5-star Hotel and Michelin star restaurant just four miles from Yorksbey. Now usually this was where husbands had bid for their wives but were forced to pay more than they hoped, as many local wealthy business men were not beyond a little sport to boost the coffers of the local charities chosen for the evening, by continually raising the bids. It was usually good honest fun with many laughs on route with much jostling and frivolity.

This didn't mean that over the years some new relationships weren't established, and similarly, some previously happy marriages being abruptly ended.

CJ had won the apple of his eye that first year, his Batman had won his femme fatale adversary, the sexy Cat Woman.

The resulting sensual encounter had resulted in the best thing that had ever happened to the pair, the birth of their wonderful daughter 9 months later.

The ball was an extravagant fancy dress dance with everyone in masquerade masks, now most people and their characters were easy to recognise, but some were more difficult, and some only became known once the results of the Charity Auction were formally announced on the Golf Club Notice Board the next day.

James Bond, OO7 licence to kill, entered the Restaurant that had been transformed for the evening, he stood in full character, and surveyed the room, looking predominately for his partner for the evening. He looked resplendent in his white tuxedo and black tie. His partner had been very mysterious about her character in the same way he had, he was curious as to whether it would be obvious or whether she was going to really go to town and leave him guessing all night. He knew however, that even with a mask on he was easily recognisable, he couldn't hide his stature and the name was also a potential give away. He also knew that she was expecting him to ensure he was the highest bidder for her services at the auction.

He recognised some easy tells, Earl and Countess Hargrove were clearly Julius Ceasar and Cleopatra, Graham Brook and his wife were Lord Nelson and Lady Hamilton. He was also pretty sure the resident golf pro was Indiana Jones, and the Major was unsurprisingly a Major, a role he adopted every year.

The room was filling with every old and new character that could now be found on the plethora of streaming movie channels now available, some extremely authentic some rather predictable, but overall, a good turn out as usual, the event should be an enjoyable evening.

James Bond heard a commotion and turned towards the foyer, making a grand entrance were *Batman* and *Cat Woman,* he was pretty sure who these two were, and the sight of the two characters suddenly transported him back to his first ball, and to what a wonderful, glorious night it had been.

He smiled and took a glass of champagne from the tray Goldilocks was holding,

'Thank you.' He was also pretty sure who it was, but not sure that was her real hair, she smiled back, but before he could ask anything more, a further gasp went up as another *Cat Woman* entered the room, OO7 smiled, this had all the potential for ending up in a cat fight, that was for sure.

The two Cat Women were very alike but also very different to the keen-eyed connoisseur. Both in full length zip, skin tight outfits, one in satin black leather, the other in shiny PVC, one in Christian Louboutin killer stiletto shoes, the other in thigh high PVC stiletto boots, one whose ample enhanced breasts were struggling to be contained in the tight sexy outfit, the others modest but ample breasts adding to her sensual model curves, one with a flowing expensive long black wig, the other with her ebony hair tied in a neat bun, both with similar traditional cat woman masks with tiny pointed ears, one in shiny black PVC, the other in soft black leather, and finally one in leather gloves and spiky long claws, the other in opened fingered, elbow length shiny black PVC gloves and manicured finger nails.

The tantalising looks they both agreed upon and had in common was the heavy reliance on black eye shadow and mascara, plus the deep red lip gloss that accentuated the unnaturally filled lips of one and the luscious sensual lips of the other.

James Bond was intrigued, but seriously favoured the one he knew was his partner for the evening.

Cat Woman 1 (CW1) sashayed over towards OO7 on her towering heels, she slid one of her long talon like claws down his cheek and slipped her body close to the secret agent, she leant in and whispered provocatively.

'Is that a *Glock* in your pocket or are you just pleased to see me?' before she continued, 'You look purrrfect in you outfit OO7, but I think you would prefer to be out of it with me, you do know if you want to die for some more pussy, just seek me out later and I'm all yours.'

James Bond struggled for a quick retort, and finally as his brain re-engaged, he said, 'Surely you know OO7 only uses a *Walther ppk*.' But the sexy Cat Woman was gone.

'Wow, now that was unexpected,' OO7 thought to himself. He sighed and immediately took a large gulp of his champagne to regain his composure.

Before he was able to seek out his partner for the evening he was approached from behind, and a pair of beautifully manicured fingers in shiny black PVC gloves covered his eyes.

'Guess who?' Came the whispered provocative question from behind, her breath making him shiver in expectation.

'Let me think, I can only guess its Cat Woman,' replied OO7.

'How did you know?'

'The gloves were rather a giveaway and your expensive perfume, I would know that any day of the week, you smell divine as always, albeit your outfit is rather risqué.'

Cat Woman 2 (CW2) was pleased with the response and released her grip on the secret agents eyes and linked arms with him. 'Time I think for a Vodka Martini, shaken, not stirred OO7, if my memory serves me well,' as the pair strolled off towards the bar, both with broad smiles on their faces.

CHAPTER 34 - THE DANCE

The evening was going well, much alcohol was consumed, dancing was virtually continuous except for a Luxury Buffet part way through the evening. All the ladies were sharing their time with many of the men and seeking to curry favour in preparation of the auction, while trying to guess the names of the not so obvious characters.

CW1 had left Batman to his own devices very early in the evening, he was more than content to be drinking with many of his business associates and courting favour as he attempted to obtain votes for the upcoming election.

There were at times some heated debates in the bar, and the Major had walked away a number of times in disgust at Batman's point of view and his contentious opinions.

CW1 had danced extensively with Indiana Jones, and they seemed to be enjoying each other's company, but part way through the evening a tall lithe *Lawrence of Arabia (LoA)* caught her eye and she seemed to be revelling in the attention the athletic 'Arabian' was giving her. Indiana Jones though, struggled to maintain his composure and at times looked like he might well turn into the Hulk, the envy he was conveying.

CW1 led *LoA* out of one of the open Bi-Folded doors onto the veranda next to where the dance floor was at its most congested, and they went unnoticed apart from one pair of eyes, as she hastily pulled him down the stone steps towards the path leading to the 1st Tee.

Once at the bottom of the steps she quickly pulled him into the darkness below the veranda.

LoA stopped and pulled her back to him, kissing the back of her neck, while firmly caressing her heaving breasts though the skin tight cat suit.

CW1 moaned in delight. He continued to caress her breasts and gently lowered the front zip to allow him to feel the warmth of her firm tanned skin, his firm grip made her groan with even greater pleasure.

He instantly started to pull the other end of the zip which reached up to her lower back. Many dance partners that evening, had teased her with the prospect of a similar manoeuvre, but she had repeatedly discouraged them with a strong word of advice or a playful tap. The only other person who had looked to receive a favourable response to his flirtation was Indiana Jones, who had the look of a man who had been there before.

LoA continued to pull the zip forward until her hot wet sex was exposed, he urgently fingered her, stimulating her enjoyment, and slowly building her to a climax. *CW1* was now sighing gently with every fresh encouragement, if he didn't penetrate her soon she would come regardless. He parted his Bisht to reveal his hard throbbing weapon, which he forcibly pushed into Cat Woman from the rear, she had been waiting a while for this sensation again and was not disappointed. His firm rhythmic movements increasing until she was groaning in pure pleasure, her pussy throbbing as the climax built within her.

They both climaxed as the *LoA* pushed hard while continuing to urgently stroke her aching clitoris.

She turned and passionately kissed him on the lips, her tongue seeking out his in pure pleasure.

She quickly zipped up her cat suit, tidied her long wig, tenderly kissed him again and said. 'Thank you that was wonderful, although you do look a little different tonight.'

'Shukran,' he replied. 'So, do you.'

'Wait here for a few minutes before coming back up to dance, and I will see you again, won't I?' she continued.

He nodded with a smirk on his face and a twinkle in his eye.

She quickly checked that there was no one about and promptly walked up the steps, her heels gently tapping on the cold flagstones.

She turned back into the Club House nearly bumping into Spiderman.

'Sorry,' he said, as he eyed up what he liked.

CW1 quickly turned to ensure the coast was still clear and moved on, giving Spiderman one of her stunning alluring smiles.

CW1 deftly made her way back into the dance room via the ladies' room, and crept up on Indiana Jones, and discreetly touched his hand with her leather gloved hand and claws. He jumped slightly but turned and smiled at her. 'I was wondering where you had got too, I was missing you.'

'I have just been powdering my face, if you know what I mean.' *CW1,* wiped the residue of the fine white powder from her nose, she was unquestionably now on an even greater high than before.

'You will be bidding for me won't you Indiana, as agreed?'

'Of course, you know I will, I am not missing this opportunity to be out with you legitimately, plus it's for charity.' He cracked his whip, and he inconspicuously caressed her firm tight rear. 'You look stunning this evening, any chance of something later?'

'If you play your cards right, I will see what I can do.' She winked suggestively and glided off towards Batman in the bar.

James Bond and *CW2* had also danced on numerous occasions through the evening, but the lithe woman had been much in demand, and as was her manner, she was polite and courteous to all that asked for the pleasure of a dance. Many of the older members wives gave her a sideways glance as their spouses plucked up the courage to ask the Femme Fatale character for her hand in a dance, but she looked at ease with most of the characters and most encounters were light hearted and enjoyed by both the dancers, and she always politely returned her dance partners to any potentially jealous wives.

There were a couple of odd exceptions, Indiana Jones was discretely told to move on when he had attempted to pull the rear zip of her cat suit. A more embarrassed young Del Boy was also told to raise his hands from her curvaceous bottom which was highlighted by the skin tight catsuit.

Her dance with Marilyn Monroe, did raise one or two eyebrows from the committee members, but they both shrugged off the stares for what they were.

She had also enjoyed the dance with *Lawrence of Arabia,* who had maintained a discrete silence throughout their waltz, she was however pretty sure who he was, but not totally certain.

As the highlight of the evening was approaching she sidled over to James Bond, and linked arms as the lights were switched on in preparation for the auction, and she whispered. 'I trust you will be bidding for my honour as agreed OO7.'

She was just starting to show the early effects of the considerable amount of alcohol she had consumed.

'Of course Cat Woman, I wouldn't trust anyone else with you in an outfit like that, your honour will be safe with me.'

She gently kissed him on the cheek, and she moved away to join the other ladies in preparation for the cat walk and auction.

James Bond felt more relaxed than at any time he had known for a considerable while, and he thought that maybe he was now able to move on to the next stage of his personal life.

CHAPTER 35 - ONE LAST PUSH

The Major was in the Foyer keeping an eye on the Ballot Box and seeing who was voting, and more importantly those that hadn't.

Not all the members were at the Ball, there were two hundred invited guests there and while most men attending were members it wasn't all of them, as there were guests from other clubs and old friends of the club also in attendance.

Similarly of the women attending there were far fewer members, many were wives and partners who tolerated their other halves passion for ruining a good walk, while many encouraged it as it meant they could get rid of them for at least a good four hours at a time.

Therefore, the Major had established that of those there this evening, there were probably only at best 130 eligible members who could vote for the chairman, leaving about 280 not even there. Notwithstanding this, getting to even some of the 130 or so members before they were starting to be affected by the influence of alcohol was seen as potentially a good move.

The Major being the Major had already done a thorough check on the members over the last week or so, and while he couldn't be sure that everyone was being truthful during his interrogations, he felt he was a good judge of character and knew when people were lying. So having spoken to every eligible member he reckoned the vote was 'bloody' close, in fact too bloody close for his liking.

Many of the members, about 65%, had chosen to vote by post, and all postal votes were already in, having had to be at the club before personal voting had even started earlier that day

By his reckoning most of those attending had also already voted, having wanted to get it out of the way before the evening got into full swing, but there were still some stragglers that hadn't, and every vote was likely to count.

He felt these were the ones that were seeking to get free drinks all night from the two candidates in exchange for their vote, would it work? he was not sure, so he was caught between keeping an eye on the Ballot Box, and definitely catching up with them, or mingling in the bar areas and trying to influence them there. He did dislike dilemmas.

'Ah Michael, how are you and your good lady, wonderful outfit,' he lied, as a prospective voter approached him. 'Can Graham rely on your vote? You know he is the best candidate.'

'I'm not sure,' came the reply. 'Perhaps Oliver Tate would bring some new ideas to the club.'

The Major was dumbfounded, how could this buffoon think such a thing.

'Michael,' said the Major fawningly. 'You know Graham has done so many good things and he only thinks of the members interests, not like Tate, the man only thinks of himself and what's in it for him,' added the Major.

'I'm still not convinced,' was the response.

'Michael, you do know that you would make a great Club Captain,' enticed the Major. 'But I can only influence that, if I can be assured of where your vote goes.'

'Oh, alright then, I suppose you're right.'

'That's the idea, you know it makes sense,' said the Major sycophantically, as he put his arm around Michael and ensured he put his cross in the right box before watching him post his voting paper in the black ballot box.

'Not a chance of him being captain, just the wrong sort all together, but another tick in the right box, that's all that matters,' thought the Major as he looked for the next prey of his assault, before he finally decided to go on the offensive in the bar.

CHAPTER 36 - THE AUCTION

Local TV celebrity Barney Bridger, conducted the auction with a mixture of wit, drama, and hype, providing an acceptable balance for this local event. Historically, bids had slowly increased to the current average winning bid of circa £500, providing the chosen charities with about £50,000, a reasonable and welcome addition to their coffers.

Of the hundred or so female guests, some felt the ignominy of this tirade beneath them, or any other woman for that matter, some feminists also didn't see that the benefit to the charities was something they could square away with their beliefs, but even with these no shows, the event was still well supported. This year there were also more lesbians bidding, which up until even quite recently would have been frowned upon by most of the guests, but as with most things now, Britain and the golf club was more tolerant and accepting of change.

Bidding was quick and brisk, which was very fortunate, otherwise the event would have potentially taken hours.

Barney was his usual self, wringing the most out of the enthusiastic and vocal audience and even when bidding was perhaps, not going as well as it could, he always managed to get an extra few pounds from someone.

It was clear, as usual that the bids were often artificially raised by boisterous men suffering from the effects of one too many shots, their bravado often questioned, when there was a sudden realisation they might be lumbered paying for a woman they had no real eye on.

More often than not though, the husband of the woman in questioned saved their blushes and bank balance, by out bidding and winning the prize, accompanied by the great cheers of the relieved bidders' friends, and drinking colleagues.

The auction continued in the similar manner as in previous years, with the bids nicely totting up with the odd bid that might just break the current record.

Julius Caesar, finally secured the arm of Cleopatra, having had to bid £1100, a new record. Just slightly more than last year, but something he felt was only right, as when all was said and done, it was going to a worthy cause.

The auction was heading for its conclusion, and the two stunning alto egos on offer were about to come under the hammer.

James Bond's suddenly felt a need to raise his awareness, he didn't want to cock this up, Cat Woman was relying on him.

'Gentleman, possibly the highlight of the evening, I know it is for me, please show your appreciation for the magnificent *Cat Women*.'

The two alto egos both sashayed along the improvised cat walk, and now stood at opposite ends, posing provocatively, hamming up the moment to the joy of the younger male guests, and some of the older ones. There was much wolf whistling and cheering in progress and Barney was momentarily struggling to keep the audience in check. The women struck up various different poses in an attempt to find who was likely to be worth the most and secure the prize for winner of the evenings highest bid.

'Gentleman, the first of two lots for the beautiful Cat Women, the first is….'

Just at that moment OO7's elbow was accidently nudged.

'Sorry.' An elderly member apologised.

'Sorry, that's okay,' replied James Bond.

'…….what am I bid?' Barney enquired.

£200, came a bid from someone behind OO7, that he couldn't see.

'Excuse me,' enquired OO7 to the man next to him. 'Which Cat Woman are we bidding on?'

'I think it's that fine figure of a woman in the Black PVC,' said the member next to him, who was much the worst for wear.

'300,' '400,' the bids came thick and fast from two bidders that the secret agent couldn't spy.

'Oh no,' thought OO7. 'This is a disaster.'

The bidding rattled along in unprecedented style, both Cat Women smiling provocatively, this bid was surely going to break the record, but who was bidding? They must surely know that James Bond was supposed to secure this lot. With the bid at £1900 Barney enquired.

'Indiana your bid, do I see, £2000?'

A shake of the head indicated that even Indiana Jones pockets had limits and were not that deep to secure the honour of the wonderful Cat Woman.

'Going once, going twice… gentlemen your last chance or Lawrence of Arabia takes the prize.'

'What!' OO7 was suddenly shaken, he couldn't let Lawrence of Arabia steal the prize… his best friend.

'Two thousand pounds,' he cried out. His deep voice echoing across the room.

'We have a new bidder. James Bond has shown his appreciation for the fine lady on my right.'

James suddenly realised his error; he had bid on the erotic cat woman in the leather outfit.

'Oh Shit!'

He looked around in desperation for *LoA* to save his blushes.

He then looked towards the sensual cat woman in the skin tight PVC, and shrugged his shoulders and attempted a wry smile, and he mouthed, 'Sorry.'

CW2 initially looked quizzical but suddenly smiled broadly, and shaking her head while looking at OO7, she mouthed. 'Idiot.' In realisation of the unfolding events.

She then turned to *CW1* who was clearly in the limelight and was like the proverbial cat that had got the cream, her perfectly white teeth shining in the dazzling lights.

'… gentlemen any more offers, going once, going twice, sold to James Bond, for a record £2,000, congratulations OO7.'

'Gentlemen the last lot of the evening, *Cat Woman 2*, what am I bid?'

After the drama of the last auction there was still a buzz going around the room, but with most partners now paired up there were few prospective bidders left.

James Bond could no longer bid, as it was customary that once you had secured your prize, no matter what the circumstances, you couldn't bid again. So, he was helpless to save his friend and he was fully aware of at least three potential suitors, they included Batman, Indiana Jones, and Lawrence of Arabia.

OO7 knew that *CW2* would not want at least one of them to win the auction for her.

A £200 opening bid quickly followed by others, it was rising quickly, and *LoA* had just out bid *Batman* at £900. The previous broad smile on *CW1* was slowly waning, her envy was clear, and the new found intention of *LoA* was not to her particular liking,

Batman raised the stakes, '£1000.'

CW2 understanding that the proceeds were for charity, played to the baying crowd despite her loathing for the superhero bidding, she just hoped that perhaps Lawrence of Arabia, whoever he was, would be victorious and her saviour.

Barney sort to encourage *LoA*, but he shook his head, *CW2* suddenly realising it was now or never, she smiled broadly at him and winked seductively.

Batman meanwhile seemed to be suddenly preoccupied, *Spiderman* was whispering in his ear, he looked over and there was a very authentic looking policeman in the doorway, *Batman's* carefree and light hearted manner was suddenly transformed as he walked out of the room with *Spiderman*.

CW2's charm fortunately seemed to have won the day, as *LoA* called out, '£1100.'

Barney tried in vain to get any more, as the other bidder was now thoroughly engrossed in other matters.

James Bond struggled to hide his rising envy, he had hoped to win the hand of *CW2* and while he was pleased Batman was not triumphant, he was still somewhat heart broken.

'Sold for £1100 to Lawrence of Arabia….. that concludes the auction My Lord, Ladies and Gentlemen, I have also just been advised by the Major, that it looks like we have raised £53,550, beating last year's total, thank you for your generosity, give yourselves a huge round of applause.'

The applause launched forth and continued for quite some while, but eventually Barney added. 'Would any couples who have not done so, please make their way to the Lobby for the formal photographs that will be in the '*Charity Ball Album,*' which will be on sale for Christmas, all proceeds to charity as usual.'

Lawrence of Arabia strolled over towards his prize, who was smiling graciously, he bowed and took the PVC gloved hand in his, and politely kissed it, *CW2* courteously nodded her approval.

James Bond admired their graciousness, but his heart was bursting.

CW1 though glided over towards him, the biggest of smiles on her bright red glossy lips.

'Well OO7, I wasn't sure you would take me up on my earlier invitation.' She again stroked his face and kissed him firmly on the cheek, leaving a perfect impression of her voluptuously filled lips. 'I'm looking forward to our night out,' she added flashing her long false eyelashes. 'I think we could just make the perfect couple.'

James knew that despite everything, he had to go with the flow and treat the prospective liaison with the required sense of occasion it deserved, it was when all said and done, for a charity, so he smiled kindly and accepted the arm of *CW1*.

'You do know it was a mistake, I bid on the wrong Cat Woman,' he finally stated.

'Really, I can't believe that for a minute,' *CW1* said mockingly and smiling broadly.

'Come on big boy, let's get our photos taken, I think as highest bidders we will make this year's front cover and also the next edition of the *Yorksbey News*.'

He accepted her arm and they moseyed towards the lobby, *CW1* teetering on her high heels, again looking like she was the cat that most definitely had got the cream.

CHAPTER 37 - THE SECOND DEMAND

Following Spiderman's quiet word with Batman, the two of them walked out of the restaurant and the growing excitement of the last bid, and onto the quiet of the veranda.

'What's this all about? I don't like being dragged out here when I'm out with my wife, enjoying myself,' said Batman.

'Perhaps you should bloody well tell me? What it's all about?'

'What! You're talking in riddles.'

'Riddles am I, well let me fucking tell you something for nothing.'

'Don't take that fucking tone with me you twat.'

'I'll take whatever fucking tone I fucking like, you shit.'

'Oh fuck off and leave me alone.'

'Don't fucking walk away from me, you fat bastard, I gave you £500k and what do I get in return, one bag of top-quality merchandise and the rest is fucking worthless powder.'

'What, I don't know what you're talking about, I checked the goods myself, it must be there.'

'Well, I can assure you it isn't, and I want my cocaine.'

'Keep your voice down, anyone could hear.'

'To be fucking honest, I don't give a shit who fucking hears.'

'I don't know what you're talking about!'

'You are either very stupid, or very cunning, but I want my cocaine, or money or both. If you fucking took it you better let me have it back, if you didn't take it, then I suggest you find it fucking quick, and let me have it.'

'I didn't take it, it's in the tyre.'

'Sort it and sort it quick, I am not someone to be messed with, do I make myself clear,' said Spiderman, with menace.

'Oh, and by the way, your trollope of a wife has just shagged Lawrence of Arabia, the lucky bastard.'

With that they parted company, neither of them very happy.

Just inside the restaurant, Goldilocks was over hearing everything.

CHAPTER 38 - I LOVE YOU?

CW2 sauntered over to James Bond, who was still being monopolised by *CW1,* albeit the photographs had been taken, and the local reporter had his scoop, which would make interesting reading when the next weekly addition was out the following Friday.

CW1 was also enjoying seeing OO7 squirm, she had her claws into the man she had fantasised about since she was a girl.

CW2 if she admitted it, was extremely jealous of *CW1*, though she wasn't going to give her the pleasure of letting her know it, she had really hoped that James Bond would win her, and take her on a romantic evening meal, something she had dreamed of for quite some while.

'I think you may have out stayed your welcome Cat Woman; I think Batman is seeking you out,' teased *CW2* as she approached.

CW1 looked around hoping that Batman was not about, she needed to keep him well and truly onside, and while flirting with OO7 was fun, she knew that it was unlikely to lead anywhere. Batman on the other hand was definitely a necessary evil.

'I will leave him in your capable hands for now Cat Woman, but I suggest you take more care of him.' *CW1* flashed her eyelashes one last time and sashayed off, working her tight ass to the limit. Off in search of other more appreciating conquests.

'Well, that didn't go as planned?' *CW2* looked annoyed, her statement more of a question.

'I'm so sorry Cat Woman, what a fool I have been.' OO7 bowed his head in mock shame.

'Too right you are.' *CW2's* grimace broke into a broad smile. 'You'll have to tell me the full story over another Vodka Martini.'

'Am I forgiven?' he hopefully enquired.

'Of course you are, how could I be mad at you, I love you too much, and let's be honest, I have the enigmatic Lawrence of Arabia for my dinner date, you on the other hand have the flirtatious Cat Woman to contend with. I know who got the best deal.'

She linked arms as she so often had that evening and they strolled off to the bar. 'Oh….and by the way, you have lipstick on your cheek. It's not a look that suits you.'

OO7 suddenly considered her statement….'love you too much?'….did she mean it, or was she just making small talk, or perhaps just the cocktails taking affect he thought, as he wiped the lip gloss away.

The pair whiled away the rest of the evening, occasionally drinking, often dancing, and sometimes unbelievably, chatting. James Bond couldn't remember when he had last enjoyed himself so much with a woman, and when he had been this happy.

The dancing had been a mixture of fast jives and slow intimate smooches, which they both seemed to enjoy. He loved to feel of her firm lithe body beneath the shiny black cat suit, her arms wrapped around his neck, her head nestling into his, their bodies in an intimate embrace.

She occasionally looked up into his eyes and he looked down and they both smiled contentedly, words weren't required, they just both felt good together.

Eventually the last waltz struck up and they both knew the evening was drawing to a close, but how would they now conclude such a wonderful night. They both knew the next few moments would be key to their long-term relationship, and neither of them wanted to get this wrong, their respect for each other immeasurable.

James Bond chucked *CW2* gently under the chin, she looked up again, her eyes glowing with passion, they instinctively kissed. Initially gently to make sure they both knew where this was leading, and then more passionately like two young lovers both knowing, but both hesitant at potentially misreading the signs, and getting it wrong.

The kissed developed, it had been so long since he had kissed a woman ardently, she felt wonderful.

CW2 also felt inflamed she was in heaven, the man of her dreams finally kissing her passionately the way she had imagined for so long, their tongues entwining as the two of them released the many years of unrequited love.

Eventually they parted lips, he gently held her hand and led her towards the hotel bedroom suites of the golf club, though she momentarily slipped on her high heels, and he caught her.

'Oops,' she said, starting to seriously show the effects of mixing cocktails and champagne. 'I think I may have had one too many,' she continued.

'I think we need to get you to bed,' suggested OO7. He gently held her close, and they both slowly made their way to her room.

'Your key Cat Woman?'

She provocatively pulled it from her cleavage and attempted to insert it in the door lock, but failed miserably. 'Oh dear,' she sleepily sighed.

James Bond took the key from her, and unlocked the door and gracefully picked her up and carried her into the room, closing the door with his foot. Fortunately, she had sensibly left a bedside light on earlier in the evening.

He gently laid her onto the bed, and the moment her head hit the pillow she was fast asleep.

OO7 unzipped the long thigh-high boots and pulled them from her legs, placing them neatly on the arm of a chair. He gallantly pulled the bedspread over her beautiful latex covered body as she murmured.

'Come to bed James, I do love you.'

He proudly smiled and gently removed her mask and admired her radiant beauty.

'And I love you too,' he said, as he gently kissed the top of her head.

He placed the key on the bedside table and quickly scrawled a note…

'Thank you for a purrfect evening. x OO7.

ps I'll see you at breakfast?'

He left quietly, switching off the light while closing the door, and wondered what might just have been.

CHAPTER 39 - THE SLAP

Batman was seeking out *CW1*, he looked incandescent,

'Have you seen my wife?' he asked a number of people, but all of them shook their heads or answered, 'No.'

With the dance coming to a close, most revellers were making their way out towards the exit, and home, or the coaches taking them to the local hotels, and most people were none too interested in Batman or his wife.

'You're no good are you,' he said on numerous occasions to people who were well past caring, as his beady eyes sort out its target.

Suddenly he saw her, cosily talking with Indiana Jones.

'There you are, where have you been?' he demanded to know.

'What's up darling?' she coyly said to Batman, taking her hand off Indiana Jones shoulder and flashing her long eye lashes at the superhero, expecting as usual for his displeasure to instantly melt, but for once it didn't work.

'I'll tell you what's up, you fucking cow. You've embarrassed me once too often.'

'Sorry darling, I don't know what you are talking about,' said *CW1* timidly, wondering what was going on.

'Spiderman has just informed me you've just shagged, *Lawrence of a fucking Arabia,*' said Batman as he slapped her hard around the face and shouted, 'You fucking tart.'

In an instant Indiana Jones was flailing punches towards Batman, who was giving as good as he got, the two of them trading blows and insults like there was no tomorrow.

Eventually the two of them were separated, both still looking to keep the fight going, despite three men on each side holding them in check. Spiderman had also come across to see what the commotion was about, and was smirking at the two of them and *CW1*.

'You fucking bastard, what sort of c**t hits a woman, you're a fucking dead man,' Indiana Jones said angrily.

'What the fucks it to you anyhow, I'll do what I want to my wife,' countered Bart completely incandescent with rage.

CW1 had regained some of her composure, but a bruise was fast appearing on her cheek.

She was mad, so mad, but what to do, remain composed, or go for it.

She decided to go for it.

'Well, you can tell Spiderman, he's a lying bastard. It wasn't me; it was that other Cat Woman shagging the Arab. Look who he bid for in the auction,' *CW1* shouted at Batman for everyone to hear, before adding with venom. 'And I'm now going to take you for all the money you have, you tiny little prick. No one does that to me and gets away with it, you're as good as dead.'

'What?' Batman suddenly realising he might have got things all wrong, but recognising he had to bluff it out.

'You can fucking try, but you'll get nothing more than the prenup you signed. You fucking whore,' he shouted. 'You'll get nothing more out of me.'

'Maybe, we'll see, but you're going down, I have witnesses here to your assault on me,' said *CW1*, finally, more reassured and composed, with Indiana Jones comforting her with an ice pack that had been brought from the bar.

Eventually, the warring parties separated and went they own ways, and the Major and Jarvis encouraged everyone to either leave or go to their rooms, the nights eventful entertainment was definitely over…………..

CHAPTER 40 - THE BODY

CJ Gray lowered his newspaper, he was relaxing in the high-backed leather arm chair in the Restaurant of Edendale Golf Club overlooking the 18th Green.

What could be the commotion.

'Nancy, what's going on,' CJ enquired.

The pretty young waitress looked flustered, her long brown hair rather dishevelled and falling out of her normal neat bun.

'Oh, Mr Gray, you'll never guess, there's a dead body on the 4th Green, they think it might be Oliver Tate.'

'Oh Fuck.' I think that's going to mean a change of plan......

CJ Meads

PART 2

CHAPTER 41 - THE MORNING AFTER

Edee's sleep had been disturbed, her vivid dreams were mixed with the real events of the previous evening until she was unsure what was real and what was fantasy. Her body had seemed at times in the still of night, to explode in euphoria at the exotic fantasies and when she finally woke, she was in the foetal position her hands between her thighs, her sex suddenly felt warm and wet.

Her eyes opened, suddenly awake, she looked around in the twilight, but she was alone and still fully clothed.

Had she kissed James, passionately as she thought and hoped, or not?

Had she made passionate love? She was virtually convinced she hadn't and hoped not, she wanted to remember forever that day, as it actually happened, not as a drunken sexual encounter.

CJ was still in the Restaurant of the Golf Club, it was now 8.45 am, he was trying to relax reading the Newspaper having unusually had some breakfast. When he had a few drinks, it was one of the few times he needed something so early, to settle his stomach, he was now slowly drinking his second cappuccino of the morning, but his mind was now racing with the recent news and also from last night's events.

A young waitress came over to clear away the used tableware and cutlery.

'Good morning Goldilocks, are you okay? I trust you had a good evening and avoided the three bears.'

She smiled. 'Yes I had a good evening, despite having to work most of the night, it was shall we say different.'

'Very good, that's a pretty earing you have there,' CJ continued.

'Earing?' commented the young waitress, she instinctively touched her ear lobe with her hand. 'Yes, it's unusual isn't it. A treasured present from my late mother.'

The waitress continued to tidy the table, as CJ's attention was suddenly drawn to the faltering clip clop of stiletto heels entering the tiled floor of the restaurant.

Edee was pulling a small black wheeled carryon case behind her.

She was wearing black thigh-high boots over skinny fit jeans, a white vest top with a red leather bomber jacket, to complete the outfit she had large sun glasses. Her hair was tied in a tight bun on the top of her head, and her lip gloss was a neutral tone to reflect her mood. She looked extremely fragile.

Edee stopped at the lectern just inside the room and smiled weakly at the waiter who turned and pointed at CJ. She nodded, which she immediately regretted and left her case just inside the door, before she gingerly continued her path towards CJ.

Despite her obvious weariness from the previous night's excesses, he felt she still looked her usual charming self.

CJ didn't stand as being great friends, they had long passed on the usual politeness and etiquette, he smiled and greeted her. 'Good Morning Edee, you look a little worse for wear.'

She tentatively sat down in the chair opposite him. 'Good Morning James, yes, I feel rather *tired.*' The usual euphemism for hungover. 'I could murder an Americano and a couple of paracetamol.'

'I hope I didn't make a fool of myself last night,' she continued. 'To be honest I don't recall that much after the auction, or how I got to bed.'

CJ knew, but Edee's statement left him pondering what his enigmatic friend did remember of last night and where their relationship was heading, if at all, but the latest news meant all that would have to wait.

CHAPTER 42 - BATMAN'S DEAD

DI Smiths mobile rang, it was Jones. Strange he was calling so early.

'Mornin sir, sorry to trouble you so early, but Batman's dead.'

'Sorry?'

'Batman's dead.'

'Jones, while I value being kept informed of the latest blockbuster movie news, it's not particularly on the top of my to do list this morning.'

'Sorry sir. Not, The Batman. A Batman.'

'What! You're still not making much sense Jones. Have I woken in a parallel universe?'

'No sir.'

'No sir what?'

'No sir. You haven't woken in a parallel universe.'

'To be honest Jones, I didn't think I had, it was a rhetorical question.'

'Ah, I see.'

'You see what?'

'I see that it's a rhetorical question.'

'Yes, so?'

'So, what.'

'Jones, could you cut to the chase? Life is too short for this.'

'Yes sir.'

'Yes sir what?'

'Yes sir, I can cut to the chase.'

'Well *bloody* do so. Now.'

Smith was clearly getting to the end of his metaphorical tether, but he felt that if he ventured down that route, the already unnecessarily lengthy conversation would only get even longer.

'Sorry, sir.'

'I know your sorry Jones, but pray tell me, succinctly why you called? Now.'

'Ah, Batman's dead on the 4th Green at Edendale Golf Club,' said Jones. Now quite pleased with his summing up of the situation considering how the conversation had started.

'What?'

'Batman's dead on the 4th Green at Edendale Golf Club.'

'I know what you said Jones, but it still makes no sense to me.'

'Sorry sir. It's quite clear really.'

'Oh, I wish it were, I wish it were,' said Smith, feeling a session with a psychiatrist was called for.

'For clarity sir. Uniform received a 9 9 9 call early this morning, from the Head Groundsman of Edendale Golf Club, advising that a man in his mid-fifties in a Batman outfit had been found unconscious on the 4th Green. PC Perfect of Yorksbey attended within about fifteen minutes and on her arrival she found that the man was actually dead. Forensics and CID were called immediately, and that's why I am calling you now.'

'Bravo Jones, that's more like it. Now why couldn't you have started like that? It would have saved us both a lot of heartache.'

'But I did.'

'You did what?'

'Start like that.'

'Jones, stop. Please stop. I was, believe it or not, already going to the Golf Club, I will be there in about fifteen minutes, please make sure everything is cordoned off and nothing is touched or moved.'

With that Smith ended the call.

'Well, that's just added to our already significant workload, who would be a copper,' he thought.

Fifteen minutes later, Smith pulled up in his unmarked Vauxhall Insignia and parked in the golf club car park, it was still early but there were more vehicles there than he expected under the circumstances. He saw Jones unmarked Astra and the marked Fiesta patrol car of PC Perfect, he also recognised the forensic teams van and the car of the local pathologist Dr Steven Stephens.

As he got out of his car, Jones came walking over.

'Sorry about earlier, sir, I hope I didn't confuse you too much?' Jones enquired, not wanting to get on his bosses back so early in the day.

Smith though had eventually seen the funny side of the conversation and was now just keen to get on with the job in hand.

'It's fine, don't worry, what have we got?' Smith asked, putting the young sergeant at ease.

'Well forensics and pathology will need to confirm things, but it appears that the death is suspicious and you're not going to believe this, but it looks like Oliver Tate.'

'What, oh no, that's just what we needed,' replied Smith.

'Well at least the job I had planned for this morning isn't so urgent now. Tate's no longer going to be the next Chairman of Edendale Golf Club.'

CHAPTER 43 - RE-EVALUATION

Edee's head felt awful, her stomach didn't feel much better, she felt fragile to say the least, but the second black coffee and the paracetamol were slowly starting to have a positive effect.

The news that CJ had told her had shocked her to the core, despite her loathing for Oliver Tate she had no desire to see him dead, but dead he apparently was, but the full circumstances were not yet known.

The club restaurant was now full of many of last night's guests who had stayed at the golf club's hotel, which had a modest thirty double rooms in the 4-star facilities, and they were now having breakfast.

The room had been returned back to its usual layout after last night's ball, with the table and chair arrangement normally used for dining throughout the day.

There was much discrete discussion going on at the various tables, with lots of blank looks, and many guests looking and feeling like Edee, very much the worse for wear, following the vast amounts of alcohol consumed, but no one it would appear at present, knew the true circumstances surrounding Oliver Tate's death.

The local police were outside, and the golf course had been shut and many of the outside and inside areas were cordoned off with blue and white *Police Do Not Cross* tape, there was also a small team in disposable white hazmat type suits that kept walking between the 4th Green and their van in the car park, with many heads continually turning in the restaurant as they passed by the windows.

The Major had not long since made an announcement to everyone, that the police had asked him to make, stating that the body of a 55-year-old man had been found on the golf course, and requesting that no one should leave the building until the local police had spoken to them all. This was initially to get everyone's name so that they could be interviewed at some point, most likely later, and to eliminate them from the ongoing enquiries, or as the Major jokingly put it, 'make sure you've got an alibi.'

At this there was much consternation amongst the guests as suddenly people were speculating as to the nature of the death.

There was also much speculation about who the man might be, as this hadn't been formally announced, but the rumours were rife, as a number of the staff had blabbed what they had heard from Tom the Head Groundsman, who had found the body.

It was therefore the widely held belief of many that the dead man was prospective chairman Oliver Tate, but many were still completely in the dark as to whom it was, and there were rumours that it might even be Earl Hargrove, and before the Major had made his announcement it might also have been him. The other rumour was that it was the other prospective chairman, Graham Brook JP.

'Well James, what does that do to our plans?' Edee enquired, rather wearily, her sunglasses still on her head and looking rather out of place in the restaurant, but making her look even more like a film star than usual.

'I've been pondering that Edee,' replied CJ, as he finished his second coffee. 'It will possibly need a minor re-think, but I'm not sure the overall strategy will change much, but if as we suspect the main protagonist of our sting is dead, I guess we will have to adjust things slightly if we want to snare the others involved,' he continued.

'That's just what I was thinking, but do you think we can still get the evidence the police will need?' said Edee, rubbing her aching brow with her wonderfully manicured fingers.

'Perhaps, I might also have some information that Smith and Jones may find interesting for their new investigation, but I need you to do a little digging first. I don't want to set the hare running unnecessarily,' answered CJ quizzically.

'Well are you going to let me in on your titbit or is it also a secret to me?' asked Edee cheekily.

'I'll tell you what, once we are let out of here, we'll make a couple of calls and I'll let you in on my theory,' said CJ tantalisingly.

CJ's mind, however, was still racing, one minute about the death of Bart, the next about what a wonderful evening he had had, but he was unsure if Edee had remembered everything, and one thing he didn't want to do was cock things up, and make a fool of himself.

Perhaps he would also have to let their relationship simmer along for now, until he was confident that Edee definitely felt the same way he felt about her.

'Why was life so problematic,' he thought.

Just then a uniform police officer came into the room looking very conspicuous, it was the local *bobby,* PC Patricia Perfect, who stood at the lectern talking to Jarvis who pointed towards CJ and Edee. The PC nodded and took off her hat and walked over to the pair of them.

'Good morning, Mr Gray, Madame Songe,' said the constable solemnly and also rather unnecessarily.

'Good morning constable,' said CJ, going along with the official nature of the conversation, which would normally not have occurred as the three of them knew one another very well, but due to the situation he didn't want to undermine the officer in her duty, especially considering the circumstances.

'Sorry to trouble you,' she continued. 'But DI Smith has asked if you would join him outside, he has one or two questions for you both.'

The whole restaurant turned as one and were looking at the three of them, listening intently and many making two plus two equal five

'Certainly constable,' they both said, as they arose from their chairs and followed the constable out of the room. Edee's thigh boot heels clicking noisily as they left, with many, if not all of the men admiringly following her rear.

Chapter 44 - Well, what do we have?

Jones led Smith from the car park, past the club house and down the gravel path that led towards the 1st Tee and the adjacent 4th Green. They walked under the railway bridge, with Smith looking intently at everything he felt might help the investigation, observing things that the average man or woman in the street wouldn't even consider. His twenty odd years in the service had given him a good eye for detail, but he wasn't silly enough to think he knew everything, that premise he left to the fools that thought they did.

Jones was reading from his notes in his notebook, like all good coppers he recognised that notes were essential to his job, you couldn't rely solely on your memory for anything.

'Well, what do we have?' enquired Smith evenly.

'Uniform received a 9 9 9 call early this morning from the Head Groundsman Tom Gardener of Edendale Golf Club, advising that a man in his mid-fifties in a Batman outfit had been found unconscious on the 4th Green. PC Perfect of Yorksbey, attended within about fifteen minutes and on her arrival she found that the man was actually dead.'

'I think I got that bit before Jones,' Smith said, rather ironically.

'Yes, sir,' said Jones, rather defensively and continued. 'The dead man, though not yet officially identified, but we all know him, is Oliver Tate.'

'Cause of death?' asked Smith.

'Single gunshot to the mouth, looks like close range to me, but I'm not an expert,' added Jones.

'Time of death?'

'Subject to post mortem, but Dr Stephens says between midnight and 3 am, based upon his initial assessment.'

'Weapon?' asked Smith.

'Subject to PM verification, but a revolver, a Glock,' said Jones confidently.

'How can you be so sure Jones?' asked Smith questionably.

'Well, it's our first bit of good news and potentially a big lead, it was in Tate's right hand.'

'What, so its Suicide?' asked Smith incredulously.

'Possibly sir, but I'm not so sure, I think it may be murder, but made to look like suicide.'

Smith's brain was suddenly in over drive, murder, or suicide, it made things so much more difficult to investigate if there was some doubt, they would have to treat this information carefully, plus how to release it to the family and general public.

'Oh fuck, not only a bloody death, but not sure of the circumstances, Peel is going to want answers and quickly,' said Smith irritably.

'Let's have a look at the crime scene and the body, plus I need to chat with Stephens pronto,' he added, as they walked towards the 4th Green the early morning sun glistening off the dew on the grass.

A tent had been erected over the body which was virtually in the middle of the green. Smith and Jones were offered Hazmat suits, overshoes, and masks by a member of the forensic team, and as they put them on Dr Stephens came out of the tent and walked towards them.

'Morning, Dr Stephens, what have we got then?' Smith got straight to the point; pleasantries were not really the order of the day in such circumstances.

'Good morning, DI Smith. Well, I am sure DS Jones has given you the initial synopsis,' replied Stephens, also, in a business-like manner. 'And to be honest until I complete the Post Mortem, I am reluctant to say too much,' he continued.

'Understood, but I would like your take on whether its suicide or murder,' asked Smith inquisitively.

'That, I'm afraid is your job, DI Smith, I can only give you facts based upon my examination,' came the curt reply.

'I know the formal line Steven,' said Smith, in a more conciliatory tone. 'I'm not going to hold you to anything, but I need to set this investigation off in the right direction, and it would help a lot if I had a good steer on the cause of death.'

'Okay, but don't hold me to this, but it looks like suicide on initial inspection, the gun in the hand, the position of the body, it all leads you to make that assessment,' Stephens said evenly.

'But, I sense a but coming on,' said Smith, raising an eyebrow.

'You're right, I think it may be murder, but I will know for certain once I have concluded my PM, which I will try and get done ASAP.'

Smith looked down at the dew on the grass, and his wet overshoes, and contemplated.

'Right, let's have a look at the body to see if we can form an opinion based on what we can see,' he added, as he tentatively walked with Jones and Stephens to the tent. Currently he wasn't quite sure how to progress this investigation.

CHAPTER 45 - THE VICTIM

Ian Westbank, pulled up to the gate of Tate House in his Ford Focus ST, he lowered the window and pressed the call button on the keypad.

After a short while a familiar but groggy voice emanated from the speaker.

'Yes, what is it.'

'Hi Charlotte, it's me Ian, just checking how you are this morning,' he said in a cheery voice.

Last night's events had meant that with a bit of luck, his relationship with Charlotte might be on a rather more frequent basis than it had been to date. Currently their relationship had been kept very incognito, so as to not spook Bart, so any encounters were very private and discrete, which to be honest he didn't like. He really liked Charlotte and he would love nothing better than to be seen out and about with the stunning woman, plus more regular and intimate liaisons would have a distinct advantage.

Bart and Charlotte had definitely hit the buffers, the relationship was over, no one hits their wife like that in public.

Charlotte had been very clear last night….. ' *I'm going to take you for all the money you have you, tiny little prick. No one does that to me and gets away with it, you're as good as dead.' …….' you're going down, I have witnesses here to your assault on me,' ……..* with what had happened he now just had to look after her and nurture her affections.

'Oh, Ian it's you, come on up, the front doors open.' With that the intercom went dead and the gate started opening.

Ian parked his car outside the front door, the only other car in the driveway was Charlotte's Audi TT.

He knew Bart was not going to be there, not after last night's events.

He opened the front door and sauntered into the hallway calling out, 'Hi, anyone at home?'

'I'm in the kitchen,' came the reply.

Ian checked as he went that there was no one else around and walked in to the kitchen, Charlotte was sat on a high stool at the breakfast bar with her back to him, in a black silk dressing gown and matching black kitten heel slippers, her long golden locks trailing down her back, she was cradling a mug of coffee in both hands and looking aimlessly in the far distance out in the garden.

'Hi Charlotte, how are you this morning? That was some night. Aye.'

She turned towards him, and his gasped, her right cheek had a whopping blue and yellow bruise where she had been hit. She looked dreadful, her perfect mascara of the previous evening had been ruined by the tears she had been weeping all night, she looked more like a zombie and nothing like the glamorous woman she normally conveyed.

'Oh Charlotte, darling,' said Ian, as he rushed towards her and gently wrapped his arms around her. He kissed her gently on the head and continued. 'I will look after you, that bastard won't get away with this.'

'Thanks Ian, that means a lot, I feel so humiliated,' she said, as tears started to fall again from her red bloodshot eyes.

'I hope you didn't mind me not staying last night,' Ian said, adding. 'I didn't feel it would look right, not after what had happened.'

'No, I think it was for the best, luckily Bart didn't come home either, I don't know what I would have done if he had though.'

'Do you know where he slept last night?' asked Ian inquisitively.

'I don't know for certain, and I don't care,' replied Charlotte.

Ian suddenly feeling concerned for her, worryingly asked, 'Do you need to see a doctor, or go to A and E, with that cheek?'

'No, it looks worse than it is, I think it will be fine, I keep putting ice on it and I've taken some pain killers,' replied Charlotte, seeking to put a brave face on things.

'It will though, take me hours to put some make up on to cover up the discoloration.' With that she picked up the large sun glasses that were on the breakfast bar and put them on, which fortunately covered most of the bruise, and made her look more like the usual Charlotte.

'Is Justin here, I didn't see his car outside?' asked Ian, struggling to re-evaluate things.

'No, he didn't come home either last night, it's just me here,' said Charlotte, starting to slowly look and sound a little more like her normal self.

'Ian, please make yourself at home, I'm going to have a shower and get dressed, I doubt that Bart will be coming home anytime soon,' Charlotte said, pretty positively.

'No, I don't think he will,' replied Ian, just as surely.

CHAPTER 46 - WHAT ABOUT YOU LOT.

Smith and Jones were walking back towards the club house, they had reviewed the body and the scene of the *crime,* and had disposed of their Hazmat suits and accessories, Smith was also trying to evaluate things and make his initial assessment. Peel would want something sooner rather than later, it was how he was, his superiors would also be putting him under pressure once they got wind of it, plus the media would be poking their nose around pretty soon.

Gone were the days when it would take hours or perhaps days for the press or TV to get wind of an issue, now with social media, an incident could make national news within minutes of it hitting Twitter or Facebook, the media had people dedicated to just reviewing such eventualities.

Smith though, was pretty sure it was murder, why would a shit like Tate take his own life, especially with what he was currently involved with. No, people like Tate, didn't do the world any favours and take their own lives, but someone, the killer, wanted them to think it was suicide, and not murder, and if that was the case then perhaps for now, they had to go along with that.

Smith knew he had probably 24 hours before he needed to say anything definite to the media, he could hide behind the PM investigation not being completed, at least initially, but he would still have to talk with Peel and agree on the initial statement and to get their ducks in some sort of row for the potential media frenzy.

'Well Jones, we are damned if we do and damned if we don't, do you agree?' asked Smith.

'You mean showing our hand too soon on whether its suicide or murder?' replied Jones

'Yes.'

'I think for now we can only go with what we are being shown and have seen,' stated Jones assuredly.

'Agreed, so for now its suicide as far as everyone is concerned, but you and I know different, *right*.' Smith said, finally in his own mind making the call.

'Right,' agreed Jones.

Smith continued thinking, and then added, 'What is rather strange is that he didn't have a mobile phone on him, that might have been useful.'

'Yes, it is odd, but not many places to put a phone on a Batman suit,' replied Jones paradoxically.

'Anyway, let's first have this quick chat with Gray and Edee, and then we need to start getting around to considering how we interview any potential suspects, without letting them know it's a murder investigation. Plus, we need to speak to the next of kin and get a formal ID on the body.'

Murder investigations were so complicated, thought Smith, albeit revelling in the thought of solving what lay ahead.

The two of them walked under the railway bridge and back up the path towards the club house. PC Perfect was walking towards them, having collected CJ and Edee as she'd been asked. Smith couldn't help but notice that Edee seemed to be walking rather gingerly, but still looked rather stunning in her thigh-high boots and sun glasses.

The dilemma he had though was, did he trust them, and did he let them into his and Jones confidence on the matter at hand.

'Morning Edee, Gray,' said DI Smith.

'Good morning DI Smith, DS Jones,' said CJ and Edee together, both mindful still of the official nature of the impending conversation.

'Thank you Perfect, that will be all for now. Could you please ensure you get the names and details of all the guests and the staff, plus anything they think may be of use to our enquiry and then they are free to go,' Smith said with authority.

'Yes sir,' replied the constable.

'Oh, and Perfect, please be discrete about any details you offer, as for now, the death is being treated as suspicious, I'll give you some further advice on what you can say shortly.'

'Edee, you look a little worse for wear, did you have too much to drink last night?' asked Smith curiously, as she had knocked him back on his invitation.

'Yes, I'm feeling a little tired and fragile this morning, how was the concert?' she replied, also suddenly remembering his earlier invite.

'Good, thank you, you missed a really good night, I think you would have enjoyed it, ……anyhow, back to business.'

'Suspicious?' said CJ enquiringly. with a wry smile.

'I was just asking how Edee was,' said Smith rather irritably.

'No,' said CJ, smiling even more that his question had been misconstrued. 'You said the death was suspicious.'

'Oh, yes....' said Smith, realising his mistake and continuing quickly, '....suspicious death.'

Why was it that Gray got to him?

'You two both know that Tate *was* involved in something dodgy, and you are involved with his current, shall we call it misdemeanour.'

'Was!' said CJ and Edee, together.

'I'm pretty sure the rumour mill has been going ten to the dozen this morning and you will have already heard things,' continued Smith.

'Well, I can advise that the body is Oliver Tate, but I would appreciate it if you kept any information we give you to yourselves.'

'Of course,' CJ and Edee replied together, nodding.

'And, because of your involvement in the ongoing *sting* operation, I thought I should let you know our current thoughts, just in case you have any information that may help with our enquires surrounding the death.'

'That's very good of you Simon,' said Edee, trying to keep things on an even and friendly level, as she felt CJ as usual, was maybe just starting to slightly tease Smith.

'You're welcome Edee,' said Smith, smiling at her and giving CJ a sideways glance. 'And for your ears only, we are currently treating this as a suicide,' added Smith.

'Suicide! Now that is a surprise, and if you want my opinion, highly unlikely,' replied CJ firmly.

'Tate's not the sort of guy to take his own life,' CJ added.

'I agree,' Edee said, backing CJ up.

'We concur,' said Jones, also supporting the two friends.

'It's pretty clear to us that the murderer wants us to think it's a suicide, so for the time being we are going along with this,' added Smith, seeking to regain influence of the conversation.

'Now as I said, if you can think of anything that could help us with our enquiries we would really welcome firm evidence, but if you can think of anything, no matter how insignificant, please let either me or Jones know.'

'Jones or I,' corrected Edee, not for the first time, smiling at Smith.

'What. Oh yes, sure,' said Smith, annoyed he'd got it wrong yet again with Edee. He must check up on that, such a schoolboy error to keep making.

'Have you had a chance to look at the photos I sent you yesterday?' asked Edee. 'They might be nothing to do with the murder, but I think that they do need checking out, if only to rule the people in or out of your enquiries.'

'I haven't yet, how about you sir?' answered Jones, 'I've been too busy.'

'No, me too. When you say they, who do you mean?'

'Well one of them is our friend from Dubai. The other we don't know, but you guy's probably do, he looks a rum'un and the other photo just shows Justin and Nancy arriving together at Tate House,' said Edee, clarifying matters.

'Thanks, we'll put them on our list to interview,' said Smith, as Jones made a note in his book.

'Do you mind if we just wander down to the scene of the crime, we won't get too near, but I wouldn't mind just getting a feel of things or if there is anything we might notice.' asked CJ politely. 'We'll keep a reasonable distance and not go trashing the site,' he promptly added.

'Okay,' said Smith. 'But please, don't get too near forensics or Dr Stephens, they are very difficult people to work with, and I don't want them upset.'

'Understood,' said CJ. With that the two pairs parted, going their separate ways.

'James, I think I'll stop here on the path, the heels of these boots are not really suitable for walking on grass.'

Which suddenly made CJ consider something, and he looked around at the adjacent teeing ground of the 1st Hole and stooped to momentarily take a closer look, before walking on towards the 4th Green and the crime scene.

'No worries Edee, I'll not be long.'

CHAPTER 47 - A WASTED BALLOT?

Smith and Jones walked into the club house lobby and were greeted by the Major and local solicitor Mr Kipling Snr.

'DI Smith, are you planning to join us for the counting of the ballot papers? The voting has now ended,' asked the Major, in his normal officious tone.

'To be honest Major, I have rather more important things on my mind, and in particular a suspicious death on your golf course.'

'Oh, yes of course,' the Major said, rather apologetically. 'It's just that we were hoping to announce the new chairman this morning, but I guess it will have to wait.'

'I don't think announcing the new chairman will be an issue, but if you and Mr Kipling would complete the vote counting without me and let me know the result of the ballot, that would be good,' said Smith invitingly.

'Without you?' questioned the Major, 'but won't we need two independent invigilators to verify the result.'

'Not today, I don't think Oliver Tate will be querying the result,' continued Smith evenly. Looking keenly at the Major for any give away indicators.

'So, the rumours are true,' the Major said, rather red faced.

'Let's just say for now, Graham Brook will still be your chairman, no matter what the ballot result, I'll let you know more once the body has been formally identified and the next of kin advised,' added Smith.

'Oh,' said the Major and Mr Kipling Snr together, as they stared at one another, rather lost for words.

Smith and Jones, continued to the restaurant and sought out PC Perfect who was still systematically taking peoples details, before advising them that they were free to leave.

Smith advised her to complete the task and then ensure the crime scene and golf club remained secure until Dr Stephens and Forensics had completed their work, and they were now going to seek out the next of kin.

'Well Jones what is your initial take on things, how many suspects do you think we might have?' asked Smith quietly, as they made their way out of the club house to the car park.

'Considering when it occurred and where, I am guessing there are about 218 people who could have done, it plus one,' replied Jones, quite positively.

'And what makes you so certain of the number, it's quite high and precise.'

'Well, there were 200 guests here last night for the *Charity Ball* and 18 staff on duty, that's pretty accurate and I think it's likely to be one of them or if not, the killer is the extra one, but I just have a feeling the killer was likely to have been at the Ball.'

'I have also checked the CCTV, albeit it only covers the entrance and the car park, I get the feeling that because of where we are the club doesn't feel it's necessary to have anything more extensive, but what's quite odd is that there is no file for last night or this morning, the system had been switched off. Now whether that was deliberate or pure coincidence, I don't know,' said Jones.

'That's strange it might have given us a clue as to somebody wandering around at the time of the murder, but not much we can do about that now,' Smith said, rather grudgingly.

'No sir, as you say one less piece of potential evidence though.'

'Okay, understood, so now we should really contact the next of kin, I assume you've done the leg work already Jones.'

'Yes sir. The wife is Mrs Charlotte Tate, his second wife, well known around the golf club, quite stunning apparently, and has a bit of a reputation for liking other men. She's a lot younger than Tate. The only son is Justin Tate, aged twenty, lives with his father and stepmother, but also spends time at his mothers' apartment in Etongate, the divorced Carol Tate,' said Jones, before adding.

'I have also checked the guest register for last night, Justin Tate didn't stop at the club, and I don't as yet know where he was or is. Oliver Tate had booked a double room for the night at the club, Room 23, but I have checked and there was no one in the room earlier and it also looked like no one had slept in the bed, so from what I can gather Charlotte didn't stop there either.'

'So where did she stay the night?' asked Smith inquisitively.

'I guess at the family home at Tate House on Edendale Lane, its actually not far, less than a couple of hundred yards from here, one thing though, sir.'

'Yes, Jones.'

'The two of them, Mr Tate, and Mrs Tate, argued last night, lots of witnesses. Tate slapped her after accusing her of adultery, and in the aftermath the club pro, Ian Westbank came to blows with Tate. After they were parted, well both Westbank and Charlotte both made death threats of a sort towards Tate.'

'Oh, that could be rather incriminating,' said Smith, considering this latest news and where that might lead the investigation, before adding, 'Well, I think we had better pay a visit to Tate House.'

Meanwhile, the Major and Mr Kipling Snr, had moved to the restaurant and opened the sealed black ballot box and removed the new ballot papers, there weren't that many, but they were checked for authenticity. They were then added to the more significant pile of postal ballot papers.

The Major went through them putting them onto one of two piles, either voting for Graham Brook or Oliver Tate. Mr Kipling Snr scrutinised every paper as he did it, verifying the member and their membership number.

Once the two piles were complete, the Major counted the votes in each pile and recorded them, Mr Kipling Snr repeated the process until they were both satisfied that they had a true record of the ballot.

'Well, that is a surprise,' said the Major.

'Perhaps, but all I can do is verify the result Major, I am not privy to any of the information regarding the members preferences or friendships or how they had said they may vote.'

'No, but I can assure you it's still a shock.'

'I will record the vote and advise DI Smith. You Major, can do what you want with the information:

Graham Brook 195; Oliver Tate 198. Oliver Tate would have been elected Chairman based upon the ballot,' stated Mr Kipling Snr with authority.

'Mmm, I will await DI Smith's confirmation of the death of Tate before I formally advise the members of the result, but more importantly is that Graham Brook will remain as Chairman of Edendale Golf Club for the next two years,' said the Major, quite relieved at how things had panned out.

'In the meantime, I think I can give Earl Hargrove the…. '*Good News*,' said the Major smiling to himself.

He was very pleased. *His Club* was very much, back under normal control.

CHAPTER 48 - SORRY FOR YOUR LOSS....

Di Smith pressed the call button on the intercom of the security gate to Tate House, the walk hadn't taken long, no more than two or three minutes as Jones had said, as it wasn't that far from the golf club.

After a minute or so the speaker came to life with the sound of a young woman who sounded rather upset.

'Hello, can I help you?'

'Yes, It's Yorksbey Police, can we come in?'

'Crikey, that was quick. Come on up.' Came the reply as the buzzer sounded and the gate started to open.

Smith and Jones looked at one another, '..that was quick...' They both said together, unsure what the woman had meant.

The two walked up the gently sloping driveway to the house, admiring the immaculately cut lawn with its perfect stripes, they both thought that could only be cut by a professional, they didn't imagine Oliver Tate ever having cut his own lawn.

Jones pressed the door bell, and immediately they were welcomed by a stunning blonde woman wearing large dark designer sun glasses, she was wearing an expensive cashmere sweater and skinny fit jeans with black stiletto shoes.

'DI Smith and DS Jones,' said Smith, as the two officers showed their warrant cards. 'May we come in? We have some rather sad news.'

'What do you mean?' asked Charlotte. 'Are you telling me I can't press GBH charges against my husband.'

'I'm sorry, Mrs Tate, I take it is Mrs Tate, we are not here about any charges,' said Smith rather confused.

'Yes of course I'm Mrs Tate, and why not? just look at my cheek.' Charlotte took off her sunglasses and revealed the large bruise.

'Wow,' said Jones, shocked at the extent of the injury. 'That's not very good, have you seen a doctor?'

'No, I probably ought too though, will you need evidence of the full extent when you charge Bart.'

Smith finally had a grasp of the situation and sort to get the conversation back where he wanted it.

'I'm sorry Mrs Tate, I have some other, sad news. It's not about any assault at the *Ball* last night, it's your husband. He's been found dead,' said Smith, pausing before adding. 'I'm sorry for your loss.' Realising that the normal police response to this type of situation was totally inappropriate in the circumstances, but it would be interesting to now see how Charlotte responded.

'Oh, does that mean I can't press charges?' replied Charlotte, looking rather crestfallen.

'Well, a dead man can't stand trial now can he Mrs Tate?' said Smith rhetorically.

'No, I suppose not,' said Charlotte, now coming to terms with the topic of the police officer's conversation.

Just then Ian Westbank, joined them and put his hand gently on Charlottes shoulder.

'Is everything okay Charlotte?' he asked sounding rather concerned.

'Ian, it's Bart, he's dead,' said Charlotte, without any real feeling.

'Oh,' said Ian, unsure what further to say.

'And you are sir,' asked Smith

'Sorry, I'm Ian Westbank, a friend of Charlottes, I'm the Golf pro at the club.'

'Please come on through,' said Charlotte, leading them all into the Lounge. 'Please take a seat.'

They sat on opposite luxury white sofas, between them a huge glass coffee table, in what was a very large modern lounge with expensive modern artwork on the walls.

'Mrs Tate, would you like a Family Liaison Officer to stay with you, I will allocate PC Patricia Perfect in case you need any assistance at this difficult time,' added Smith, as sympathetically as he could, considering he could see that Charlotte appeared rather indifferent to the tragic news, and handed her a card with the details.

'No, I think I will manage, but I would like someone to speak to Justin, I'm not sure I could tell him about the news in the circumstances.'

'Of course,' replied Smith. 'Do you know where he is?'

'No, he didn't stop here last night, he more than likely went to his mothers in Etongate, he often stops there, but I guess he could have stopped at the golf club or even a local hotel as he was at the charity ball.'

'So, how did he die?' asked Ian, adding rather directly. 'Was he killed?'

'Any reason you ask that?' asked Jones.

'No.....it's just, it's out of the blue,' said Ian rather sheepishly,

'I'm afraid we are treating the death as suspicious, at least until the results of the Post Mortem are known,' added Smith evenly, looking for any reaction from either Charlotte or Ian.

'So, suicide….,' said Charlotte. At which the two officers looked up at her. '…or murder,' she quickly added, mindful of how what she said might sound.

'If you lot think its suspicious, it surely has to be one or the other!' added Ian, wanting to support Charlotte.

'As I said, until the PM is complete we are keeping an open mind, but you are correct, the death is not from natural causes,' said Smith.

'Well, I can't believe the bastard killed himself,' stated Ian.

'What makes you say that?' asked Jones.

'It would have done us all a favour, if he had,' replied Ian, regretting it once he'd said it.

'Would it now,' added Smith. 'We gather you made certain threats last night, following Mr Tate hitting Mrs Tate.'

'That was in the heat of the moment, lots of things were said, by lots of people. If you had seen him slap your wife I think you would have looked to protect her,' said Ian defensively.

'But it wasn't your wife, was it sir?' said Jones inquisitively.

'No,' said Ian rather quietly.

'Mrs Tate, we do need to formally identify the body, would it be something you would be prepared to do?' asked Smith, back in sympathetic mode.

'Yes of course, if it's necessary,' said Charlotte, seeming rather indifferent to the task.

'Thank you. Oh, and regarding last night, do you recall if your husband had a phone with him?' asked Smith casually.

'I assume so,' said Charlotte, not really taking much notice. 'He always had it with him, why do you ask?'

'We thought it strange, as there wasn't one on the body,' said Smith, looking deeply at Charlotte and then Ian, but both didn't offer any meaningful response.

'We may need to ask you some further questions once the PM is complete, purely as a precautionary matter and to establish any facts that may be outstanding, I trust that will be okay?' asked Smith nonchalantly.

'Yes, of course,' said both Charlotte and Ian.

'One thing though, where were you both between midnight and 3 am this morning?' asked Smith.

'I was here…,' said Charlotte, '…we, were both here,' added Charlotte quickly. To which Ian swiftly looked at her and said, 'Yes, we were here, having walked home from the Ball at about 1.30 am, once the evenings events had finished.'

'And you were here together until we arrived?' asked Jones.

'Yes,' said Charlotte quickly, and Ian nodded sheepishly.

'Thank you, we'll be in touch about when the body will be ready for identification,' said Smith. 'Once again, we are sorry for your loss. Oh, and we'll look to contact Justin, and we'll let ourselves out.' With that the officers left the two *friends* in silence in the lounge and made their way out.

'Why did you say that?' asked Ian once the policemen had left. 'Do you have something to hide?'

'Well, did you have an alibi?' said Charlotte, tersely, before adding matter-of-factly. 'Because, we both have now, don't we.' And she winked at Ian.

'Oh, yes,' said Ian, grateful at least for now, of Charlottes quick thinking.

CHAPTER 49 - WHERE WERE YOU LAST NIGHT?

Smith and Jones, walked back down the driveway, contemplating what they had learnt if anything from the encounter. As they approached the security gate it automatically opened letting them out into Edendale Lane and as they turned left back to the golf club the gate slowly closed behind them.

'She's quite a stunner, isn't she sir? exclaimed Jones.

'She sure is,' said Smith absentmindedly, as he pondered the case in his mind.

'Do you think either Charlotte or Westbank could have killed Tate?' asked Jones, breaking Smith's thought pattern.

'Mmm….It's possible, we will need to start our list of potential suspects, with means, motive, and opportunity. At the moment those two have motive and maybe opportunity, but did they own or have the apparent means, that is part of the dilemma,' replied Smith, not sure where the required leads and evidence were to come from in this investigation.

'Do you think they are lovers?' asked Jones.

'Quite possibly,' said Smith, before adding, 'but I'm not sure they were, last night….'

They walked on in silence, both lost in their thoughts about what they had seen and heard at Tate House, and shortly as they turned into the golf club car park they noticed that quite a number of the cars that were there earlier had now gone. The owners being guests for the night were now pleased to get away and home after lasts nights ball.

PC Perfect was now patrolling the gateway deterring any would be golfers from entering, well at least until the crime scene investigation had been concluded.

'Sir. I have taken all the guests details. No one was particularly forthcoming with anything that might be useful, but I will forward the list to you and DS Jones by email and log them onto the system. Any change on the status of the death?' said Perfect, seeking guidance.

'Thanks, Perfect, that's good work, no change at present, I'll let you know once the PM results are in. Once forensics are done we can also decide what further needs doing here, but keep watch for now, I'll get another uniform to assist you.'

'I have obtained a list of the other guests that didn't stop the night from Major Montgomery, the club secretary, I will also send you a copy of that,' said Perfect, pleased with her initiative.

'Well done, good thinking Perfect,' said Smith appreciatively.

'Thanks, Pat,' added Jones smiling. He liked Pat, and he was pleased she was impressing the boss, it wouldn't go amiss when it was appraisal time.

'The Major, also said he had some news and would like a word when you got back, sir.'

'Okay, very good,' said Smith, as he and Jones walked on towards the club house, leaving Perfect to the mundane work of a uniform police officer.

'I think we need to try and find Justin Tate, if only to let him know what's happened, I think a visit to his mother's wouldn't go amiss either. It would also be good to eliminate an ex-wife from our enquiries, if we can,' said Smith. With that the Major exited from the club house along with Earl Hargrove.

'Now then,' said Smith, quietly. 'Watch yourself now Jones, nobility, do you know Earl Hargrove?' as the four of them came together under the glazed entrance canopy.

'Good morning, Earl Hargrove, Major, this is DS Jones,' said Smith officially, despite having met Earl Hargrove on many previous occasions.

'Morning DI Smith, DS Jones,' said Earl Hargrove, in his normal slightly pompous manner. The Major nodding to the two officers.

'Rum do, eh, we need to get this resolved pretty damn quick.'

'Yes My Lord, I think we would also like to get things resolved, but we do have a suspicious death on our hands, and I am sure you will appreciate that we need to do things thoroughly,' added Smith in a firm but even manner.

'Yes, yes, of course, didn't mean anything, you know.'

'Of course My Lord' said Smith. Pleased he had regained some authority, but he knew that Earl Hargrove would be onto the Chief Constable PDQ, looking to get this all wrapped up and the club reopened, more unnecessary pressure he could do without.

'PC Perfect, said you wanted to see us Major.'

'Yes, thought I had better let you have the result of the ballot as you asked,' said the Major glumly. 'Graham Brook 195; Oliver Tate 198.'

Jones made a quick note of the result in his book.

'So, Oliver Tate would have been the next Chairman,' said Smith, staring at the Major and Earl Hargrove. 'Not the result either of you would have liked.'

Smith letting the statement hang there and slowly sink in.

Eventually Smith added inquisitively, 'Did either of you have an inkling of the result?' again, looking deeply at the two club officials.

The Major looked down at his shoes and said, 'No,' rather guiltily, while the Earl said authoritatively, 'No, and to be honest while we knew it was close, we fully expected Brook to win, didn't we Major?'

'Well, it looks like you two got the result you were after then!' said Smith, contemplating further potential motives for the murder.

'Anything else?' said Smith, eager to get on with the case.

'Just one thing, DI Smith,' added the Major. 'Tate's car could do with it moving, it's the Bentley over there, he parked it in rather a stupid position. As soon as its convenient could you move it…..please,'

'I'll check with forensics to see if they have found any car keys on the body,' said Jones, making a note in his book.

'No need, I have them here. All the guests were asked to leave their cars keys with the car park attendant last night, we knew it was going to be busy and we might need to move some cars around, you know how things are, didn't want anyone getting breathalysed,' joked the Major, as he passed the electronic fob to Jones.

'Oh, that's handy,' said Smith, considering the implications,

'The keys were eventually left with the night porter until they were finally collected by the owners,' added the Major matter of factually.

'Once forensics have completed their checks we'll look to get it moved Major,' said Jones positively.

'Oh, and one more thing, could you please tell me where you both were between midnight and 3 am this morning?' asked Smith directly.

'What are you implying Smith?' Earl Hargrove said indignantly.

'We are just seeking to eliminate as many people as possible from our enquiries, this is a suspicious death when all said and done,' said Smith calmly, not wishing to annoy Earl Hargrove any more than necessary.

'Oh, yes, of course, I was in bed by 12:30 with my wife, prior to that I was in the bar, everyone saw me say good night, I woke this morning about 8ish. Will you want to speak with the countess? But I trust that won't be necessary,' said the Earl firmly.

'Thank you, no that won't be necessary.' said Smith. 'And you Major?'

'I was checking all was settled down after the big to do with Tate and Charlotte, you must have heard about that. Then I went to bed about quarter to two or there abouts and woke for breakfast about 7:30am.'

'Can anyone collaborate that Major?' asked Smith directly.

'No, I don't think they can,' said the Major self-consciously.

'But I can vouch for the Major,' said Earl Hargrove with authority.

'Yes, I'm sure you can,' said Smith sceptically before adding. 'And yes, we are aware of a little set too between the Tate's.'

CHAPTER 50 - HOW ARE YOU FEELING NOW?

CJ wasn't long at the crime scene. He purposely kept out of everyone's way, and having established what he wanted, and also having had a quick chat with Dr Stephens who had known Elizabeth Gray very well, he made his way back to Edee, who was sat down on the bench adjacent to the 1st Tee, looking rather forlorn.

She got up delicately as he approached.

'Everything okay James?'

'Yes, I think so,' as he took one parting look at the 4th Green and the 1st Tee.

'How are you now?' he asked Edee caringly.

'Slowly getting there, I think I might need a nap though when I get home.'

'Yes, that's a good idea, let's get your case and I'll drop you off, good job you're not driving,' said CJ. 'If you were stopped, I think you would still be way over the limit,' he added showing concern for his *friend.*

'I think your probably right, I did drink rather a lot of alcohol last night, but hopefully all the local police are here so I wouldn't have got stopped,' she feebly joked.

They turned around and started walking back under the railway bridge up towards the club house

'I enjoyed last night,' said Edee, hoping to get CJ to confirm the things she was struggling to recall. 'Well, the things I remember,' she added, smiling meekly, her fingers touching CJ's, seeking reassurance.

'I also enjoyed last night, you were great company,' said CJ, torn between what he could or should say, but gently linking fingers, liking the touch, but not knowing fully how to respond to Edee's intimate gesture.

As they reached the club house they saw Earl Hargrove, The Major, DI Smith, and DS Jones, who were concluding an earnest conversation under the entrance canopy, before the two police officers walked off towards their respective cars.

Earl Hargrove and the Major walked towards them, and CJ and Edee awkwardly let go of one another's fingers, unsure as to how their sign of affection would or could be construed.

'Rum business, ay, what,' said Earl Hargrove, in his normal manner.

'Good morning My Lord, Major,' said both CJ and Edee together.

'Oh, yes, sorry, Good Morning,' replied Earl Hargrove, not really apologetically.

'Good morning CJ, Madame Songe,' said the Major, rather more politely.

'Yes it is a strange carry on,' added CJ.

'CJ, I just wanted to know if there had been any change to our plan?' Earl Hargrove asked inquisitively.

'Not at the moment,' said CJ evenly.

'Fine, good, great,' added Earl Hargrove, unsure what to say next.

'*The Ball* went really well last night didn't it,' said Edee, breaking the pause in the conversation. 'I gather the club raised a record amount of money for charity.'

'Yes, a wonderful evening as usual, you both looked marvellous in your outfits,' added Earl Hargrove, in a complimentary manner. 'It all helped with the fund raising especially having two Cat Women in the auction, what say you CJ?'

'Yes, My Lord,' said CJ, rather embarrassed, recognising that his error had resulted in the record bid. 'I always look to aid local charities,' he added more assuredly. 'You and the countess also looked resplendent.'

Edee again broke the silence.

'So, what was the outcome of the ballot, Major?' she asked directly. The Major was initially thrown at not being able to read the question, Edee's eyes being hidden by her large dark sunglasses.

'Well a bit of a shock really, not that it matters now, but Brook got 195, and Tate got 198.'

'So, the events of *last night* have worked in your favour then gentlemen,' added CJ evenly, pleased he was no longer the focus of attention and looking for a reaction.

'Yes, and you're not the first to mention that,' replied the Major, rather forcefully.

'Just stating the obvious, and what most other people will be saying,' said CJ, in a lighter tone, seeking to diffuse the conversation.

'Yes, I suppose so,' added the Major, acknowledging the point.

'Well, the good thing is the club carries on as usual, so I'm pleased with that,' said CJ, lightening the mood even further. 'I'm not sure the club would have benefited with Tate as chairman.'

'Quite right,' said the Major, pleased that CJ was firmly on their side.

'If you don't mind, we would like to get off, Edee is not feeling quite her normal self,' added CJ, before mouthing, 'She had a bit too much to drink last night.'

At which both Earl Hargrove and the Major both smiled fondly at Edee.

CJ and Edee left the two club officials, and went looking for her suitcase in the restaurant, which was now empty of guests, where they met Jarvis.

'Hello CJ, Edee. Oh, you don't look too good, do you?' said Jarvis, looking longingly at Edee, as he had long admired her charm and sophistication.

'Hi,' said CJ and Edee together.

Before Edee added, rather mockingly, 'No, I'm still a little fragile Jarvis, thanks for noticing.'

'Oh Edee, I'm sorry, I meant no offense, you still look stunning as always, it's just I can see that you're perhaps not feeling 100% this morning,' replied Jarvis, seeking to get back on the right side of her.

'It's fine Jarvis, it's my own fault, I shouldn't mix drinks, and not in such large quantities,' she added, smiling meekly.

'Have to say, you looked stunning last night, always love a cat fight,' added Jarvis, teasing Edee, but torn between which Cat Woman he had fancied the most.

'Have you seen my carry on case?' asked Edee, looking to get home as soon as possible.

'Oh, I think Nancy moved it earlier, it was in the way, ah there it is,' said Jarvis, pointing to it.

'Merci, thanks Jarvis, goodbye, au revoir.'

'See you later Jarvis,' said CJ.

'Yes, bye. Take care you two,' said Jarvis, rather jealous of CJ, as the two friends left the restaurant.

On their way out of the club they bumped into PC Perfect.

'Hi Pat, how are things going now?' Edee asked, cheerily to her friend.

'Well, were nearly there I think, the Forensics guys are finishing up, and the body has been taken to the mortuary, I also hope to get finished up soon,' replied Perfect.

'Any more news?' Edee asked inquisitively, but in a light manner, hoping she might just get the young police woman to say something she perhaps shouldn't.

'No, the death is still being treated as suspicious, but we all have our own thoughts on it,' added Perfect.

'Oh, do you?' asked Edee again leaving the question hanging.

'Yes, while it looks like suicide, I can't believe that…….' Perfect stopped, suddenly realising she may just have said too much.

'Oh, please don't say anything, please,' implored Perfect, recognising the implications of what she had said and how it could possibly be perceived.

'Pat, don't you worry, CJ and I would never say anything, we always treat our conversations as confidential,' Edee said, smiling reassuringly.

'Oh, thanks Edee, you're a pal, I knew I could trust you, as you're both such nice people,' said Perfect, breathing a sigh of relief.

With that, they parted going their separate ways.

'What do you make of that?' Edee asked, as they got to CJ's car. He had brought the Aston Martin DB9 especially for the occasion, he thought it added the right touch in the circumstances.

'No more than we probably already thought, or knew,' replied CJ. 'But I think you and I should perhaps consider all the things we know, especially as they seem to be coming more and more intwined,' he added, as he graciously opened the passenger door for Edee and took her case and put it in the boot of the car.

As he closed the door, he noticed that a forensics officer was looking over Bart's Bentley for any evidence, so he wandered over and casually looked in the open boot.

'That's odd,' he thought as he walked slowly backed to his own car, where he noticed that Tom the Head Groundsman was walking towards him.

'Morning Tom, how are you? I haven't seen you for a while,' CJ said light-heartedly.

'Morning CJ, it has been a while, hasn't it? I'm fine, how are you? Never expected to find a dead body on my course, that's definitely a first for me,' Tom said smiling.

'I'm good thank you. Yes, it is rather strange. Could I just ask you something?' added CJ, in a perplexed manner.

'Of course, fire away.'

'Now this may seem strange, but this morning did you find any golf balls on the 1st Fairway at about 160 to 170 yards from the tee?'

'Now it's funny you should ask that, but yes I did, they were range balls though, how did you know?' asked Tom rather surprised.

'I just had an inkling. Thanks Tom, you take care now,' said CJ, as he continued back to his car.

'Yes, Goodbye CJ. See you later,' said a rather bewildered Tom.

As CJ got into the car Edee asked, 'Did you notice anything of interest James?'

'Not particularly. Just that there was no, five iron in Bart's set of clubs, which seems a little odd in the circumstances.'

'Mmm, do you think it's relevant,' asked Edee, contemplating the fact.

'Possibly,' said CJ. 'Possibly.'

The 3-mile drive to Edee's apartment in Yorksbey took little time at all. During the brief journey however, CJ was thinking how to say goodbye when he dropped her off, he felt a little like a school boy on a first date.

Edee, meanwhile, lent her head back on the headrest and closed her eyes, she was in a great need of further sleep.

He pulled up outside the 3-storey apartment block, overlooking the river, Edee's flat was one on the roof top, with a wonderful view of the weir.

He turned towards her, thinking as always how lovely she looked.

'Thanks again for last night,' said Edee, opening her eyes and looking towards CJ, hoping for a positive sign.

'Yes, it was wonderful,' replied CJ, but unable to read her eyes because of the sun glasses.

Edee touched his hand on the gear lever and kissed him gently on the cheek.

As CJ went to kiss her on the lips, Edee inadvertently turned away, unaware of CJ's intention.

'I'll get your case from the boot then,' said CJ quickly, unsure of what to do next, as the pair both got out of the car.

The boot lid opened, and CJ lifted the case out and offered it to Edee.

'Thanks again, I really enjoyed last night,' said CJ, as he embraced her around her shoulders. Edee's arms wrapped around his body as she nestled her head into his neck, she felt all happy and content.

CJ kissed her on the top of her head and said, 'You take care, go and have a good sleep and I'll see you Monday, if not before.' Before kissing her on the cheek as they separated.

'Yes, you take care too, I'll see you Monday,' replied Edee, also feeling just a little like a young school girl again.

With that CJ got back in the car, they both waved and smiled, and he sped off, back again to Overhear Manor.

CHAPTER 51 - SORRY FOR YOUR LOSS, TOO

Smith and Jones drove the twelve miles to Etongate, the fashionable Victorian spa town, often voted the 'happiest place to live' in Britain, popular for its large gardens and parks next to the town centre. They pulled up in the car park of the contemporary apartment building where Carol Tate, the former wife of Oliver Tate lived. In the car parking space for apartment 62 was a BMW M4, the car registered to Justin Tate, that Jones had checked on the *ANPR* system.

'Well looks like we might kill two birds with one stone Jones,' said Smith, as the two of them walked towards the entrance lobby of the stylish building.

Jones pressed the call button for apartment 62, after a short wait, what sounded like a middle-aged woman answered.

'Hello, can I help you.'

'Good morning, it's Yorksbey Police, we would like to speak to Justin Tate if he's in.'

'Oh, you had better come up.'

The call ended and the door lock buzzer sounded, and Jones pulled the door open, letting Smith go in first and then he followed.

Jones pressed the lift call button, and the lift door opened immediately, they both stepped into the lift, Jones then pressed the 6th Floor button and the doors closed behind the officers, the two of them stood in silence, looking at the ceiling or floor, like most people seem to do in lifts.

Once at the top of the building they walked along the broad well-lit corridor and stopped outside apartment

62, of the recently refurbished building in the centre of Etongate, which provided good access to all the local amenities and facilities.

Jones again pressed the door bell, and immediately a woman in her mid-fifties with wavy shoulder length platinum grey dyed hair opened the door.

The years had been neither kind or unkind to Carol Tate, she wore the lines of her age reasonably well and unlike many women of her age chose to always apply makeup and looked like a woman who cared about her appearance, no matter what the time of day or occasion.

'Hello, I'm DI Smith and this is DS Jones of Yorksbey CID.' Both officers showing their warrant cards. 'May we please come in; I take it your Carol Tate.'

'Hello, yes I'm Carol Tate, please come in, what do you want with my boy Justin?'

Justin was in the lounge, laying down on the sofa, but sat up as the police officers walked into the room.

'Mum, it's okay, I can answer for myself,' said Justin, not wanting to appear a Mummies boy to the police.

'Hello, are you Justin Tate?' asked Smith solemnly, and rather unnecessarily.

'Yes. What is it?' replied Justin, looking rather worried about being question by two policemen, detectives at that.

'I'm sorry Justin, we have some sad news. Your father was found dead earlier this morning at Edendale Golf Club. I'm sorry for your loss.'

Before Justin could take in the news, Carol spoke up.

'First bit of good news I've heard in ages,' she said, seemingly very pleased at the statement.

'Mum, that's Dad their talking about,' said Justin, slightly more concerned, but not exactly how you would expect a loving son to react.

'What happened, did he have a heart attack? Silly bastard never did look after himself,' said Carol, showing no sign of considering Justin's feelings.

'Mum. Please,' said Justin, now trying to show some sorrow.

'Sorry, would you prefer us to call you Carol or Mrs Tate?' asked Smith. Trying to bring the conversation back into the normal realms of decorum.

'Carol, I suppose, though I've never got around to changing my name after the divorce.'

'Carol, we are treating the death as suspicious at this stage,' added Smith evenly, looking again for any indications from the supposed grieving family.

'So, someone's done us all a favour and killed him,' said Carol, with feeling, before adding. 'Good riddance,' for good measure.

'I'm sorry Carol, Justin, I can't elaborate until after the Post Mortem, which may not be concluded until tomorrow. We will however let you know the findings as soon as possible,' continued Smith, struggling to remember when a death he had reported had been received so coldly by the family, except perhaps for earlier with Charlotte.

'Would you like a Family Liaison Officer to stay with you? I have allocated an officer in case you need any assistance at this difficult time,' added Smith, again as sympathetically as he could, considering he already knew the likely answer to this normal police procedure.

'Not on my account, think I'll manage, he never helped me while he was alive, I'm not going to miss him now he's dead,' said Carol, still venting her anger at her former husband.

'No, I think that I'll also be okay, but perhaps a contact, in case I think of any questions later,' added Justin, directly.

'So, if it wasn't natural causes, how did he die?' continued Justin, now showing a little more concern.

'Unfortunately, as I've already said, until the Post Mortem is complete we aren't able to comment further, I hope you understand,' said Jones, handing a card to Justin with the details he requested.

'Well Justin, at least you'll finally get what I was owed, from the tight-fisted sod,' said Carol. 'He did me up like a kipper on the divorce settlement, after he'd been shagging that bimbo Charlotte.'

'Mum, please don't talk like that about Charlotte, she's okay. She's only ever been supportive to me considering the circumstances,' said Justin, defending his step mother.

'Of cause she has, got him wrapped around her little finger, well did have. She'd better watch out, knowing Bart, he'll probably leave her bugger all in the *Will*. Well would do if its anything like me,' said Carol, as she stormed out of the lounge into the kitchen, adding, as she went, 'Anyone for a cuppa?'

'No thank you,' said the two officers in unison.

'Before we go, just a couple of things,' said Smith. 'Your step mother, Charlotte, has agreed to identify the body, I take it you have no objections.'

To which Justin shook his head. 'And to assist us we may need to ask you both some further questions once the PM is complete, purely as a precautionary matter and to establish any facts that may be outstanding, I trust that will be okay?' asked Smith dispassionately.

'Of course.' Justin said, but looking slightly concerned at the prospect, before adding, 'Is there anything else?'

'Yes,' added Smith. 'Where were you both between midnight and 3 am this morning?'

' I was here…' shouted Carol, from the kitchen, before adding quickly '…We, were both here.'

To which Justin quickly added, 'Yes, we were here. I drove home about 1:15 am as the ball was ending.'

'And you were here together until we arrived?' asked Jones.

'Yes,' said Justin.

'Very good,' said Smith. 'Just one more thing Justin, did you see the altercation between your father and step mother at the ball.'

'Altercation,' asked Justin, looking rather bemused.

'Well, if you didn't see it, then I think we'll leave it there for now,' said Smith decisively.

'Thank you for your time, we'll be going, and again I'm sorry for your loss.' And the two officers left the mother and son in silence.

'Why did you say that Mum?' asked Justin once the police officers had left. 'Do you have something to hide?'

'Well, I don't, that's for certain, but I wasn't so sure about you son. Not with the time you got in this morning, so I thought I would make sure that there's no reason for the law to start looking at you. Especially if your dad's been murdered,' said Carol, looking out for her only son, and herself, with what was likely to be bequeathed to Justin in his Father's *Will*.

'Oh, yes,' said Justin, grateful at least for now of his mum's quick thinking.

Chapter 52 - Post Mortem

DS Jones, put down the phone in the CID office at Yorksbey Police Station and he turned to his superior.

'Sir. Dr Stephens has asked if we could go and view the body of Oliver Tate, he has some information he feels may be important to our investigations.'

'That sounds intriguing,' said Smith. 'I wonder what he has found. Come on then I guess we should do this as soon as possible; I envisage Peel will be seeking an update today and I would at least like to know which way this investigation is leading.'

With that the two officers left and headed off for Northallerton, and about 40 minutes later they entered the Pathology Lab and found Dr Stephens compiling his initial report.

'Good morning, Dr Stephens, how are you today?' Smith said adding, 'What nuggets have you got for us?'

'Good morning, DI Smith, DS Jones, I'm okay thank you,' replied Stephens, in a directly. ' I thought it would be better for you to hear my initial take on things, because I think you may want to ask some questions, and maybe look again at the body.'

'That sounds ominous,' said Smith, wondering what the pathologist was to convey.

'Right, I'll get down to it, feel free to interrupt if you like, but I will just crack on. The cause of death is not from a gunshot wound as we firs……'

'Pardon. Not from a gunshot wound,' said Smith rather alarmed.

'When I said ask questions, I didn't think you were going to stop me on the first sentence,' added Stephens sarcastically.

'Sorry,' said Smith. 'It's just that you did sort of surprise us there.'

'Yes, I'm sure I did. Let me perhaps give you a quick synopsis and then you ask questions,' added Stephens, with a twinkle in his eye as he smiled and winked at Jones.

The pathologist continued directly.

'The cause of death was not a gunshot wound but was perhaps staged to look like it. Death was caused by a blunt force trauma to the right side of the head, resulting in subarachnoid and intracerebral hematoma. The gunshot to the mouth was fired after the death, but most likely within an hour. If you noticed at the scene of the death, there was little blood around or near where the victim was found. We found the bullet a 9 mm round beneath the victim's head in the grass, again with little blood in the area, showing that the victim was already dead when the gun shot was fired. The gun, a Glock 19, found in the victim's right hand was the weapon that fired the shot, only the victims finger prints were on the gun,' said Stephens. Who paused expecting Smith or Jones to say something, which they did.

'So, it was murder?' Smith asked directly.

'I didn't say that,' said Stephens, adding, 'Death was caused by *a blunt force trauma to the right side of the head*, the question really is what caused the blunt head trauma?'

'You don't know?' asked Jones.

'Well, you have been to the crime scene, it was on the 4th Green and no evidence of a blunt instrument was there,' added Stephens dryly.

'I can't see a slip and a fall onto grass causing the injury.'

'So, we are looking for something that caused a blunt head trauma,' asked Jones. 'Do you have *any* idea what caused the trauma?'

'Not really,' said Stephens, before adding, 'There is some small white paint residue to the right side of the head where the trauma occurred, but it was clearly something solid and hard.'

'Anything else,' asked Smith, expecting something else from Stephens look.

'If you look closely at the left temple, you will see a small trauma, again caused by a hard object, most likely metal but I can't be certain. It didn't cause the death, but occurred just before.'

'Mmm, so he could have been hit with something smaller initially, say a cosh or something similar and then after with a larger item,' Smith said, hypothesising.

'It's possible, but without something to compare with the trauma it's difficult to be certain.'

'So do we need to undertake a wider inspection of the murder scene to see if we can find the murder weapon?' asked Jones.

'We should really, but I think that is likely to be like looking for a needle in a haystack,' added Smith, thinking what to do next.

'Is there anything else Dr Stephens?' asked Smith.

'Not really, I will complete my initial report and issue it shortly, but you have the headlines.'

'Thanks for nothing Doc,' said Smith mockingly. 'I was hoping we might be a bit closer to solving this case, but we are certainly not at the moment.'

'Most likely murder, caused by a blunt object, but made to look like a suicide with a gunshot to the mouth.'

'Jones, I think we have our work cut out here,' continued Smith, looking and sounding rather perplexed.

CHAPTER 53 - THE SUSPECTS

Smith and Jones had returned to their office in Yorksbey and were reviewing the large white board containing their initial thoughts, including photographs, names, possible weapons, and the standard criteria in murder investigations; means, motive and opportunity.

There initial brain dump of ideas were all on the board and they were in the process of re-evaluating and seeking to put the information into some type of order and seeking to eliminate things to allow them to focus on the meaningful items.

The significant issue was that it didn't look straight forward, if anything, anything but straight forward. A real conundrum.

'Well Jones, who have we got in the frame?' said Smith, looking for his subordinate to try to put the plethora of information into some type of structure for him.

'To be honest we have a number of possible suspects, but none that truly stand out, and having reviewed the photos sent to us by Edee, those that recently visited Tate are clearly on the list plus the others you and I, had initially discussed.'

'Yes, the two visitors with form have to be at the top of the list,' added Smith. 'Just because they are definitely capable of doing such a crime.'

'Mr White has the international pedigree, he has the means, I'm pretty sure of that, but what is his motive, does he have one? but like all of them he has opportunity, a golf course at the dead of night and he was in the UK at the time.' said Smith.

'Peter Parker who visited Tate, has been verified by Barnsley Nick as a drug dealer and local heavy, who has had previous dealings with Tate. He's also got a record, so definitely the means. Already established as having opportunity and his motive could be linked to the drug smuggling, but what is that actual link?' said Jones.

'The Wife, Charlotte Tate, certainly, has a motive, following the fracas at the ball, plus she would be most likely to benefit from Tate's demise. We need to check Tate's *Will*, but she has an alibi regarding opportunity, and as for means, does she have a gun to stage the suicide? Unlikely, but possible I suppose,' added Smith, concerned this discussion wasn't possibly helping matters.

'The wife's lover, Ian Westbank, again has a motive following his fight with Tate and his threats, but has the same alibi as Charlotte and again does he have access to a gun? Or are the two of them in it together as they could be lovers?'

'We also have Justin Tate, the son, again likely to benefit from Tate's *Will*. So, a clear motive, has an apparent alibi in his mother though, but I'm not really convinced about that,' said Smith, scratching his chin, an old nervous habit he had when under pressure.

'Does he have a gun? Again, possibly but unlikely, but I think we need to check on that. Could be that either he or Charlotte could have used a gun actually owned by Tate himself. I wouldn't put it past him to own a gun,' said Smith, sensing things might be getting slightly clearer.

'Carol Tate has a motive in that she feels wronged by Tate in her divorce settlement. I can see her believing that she can manipulate her son, especially if he was the major beneficiary of the *Will*. But means, I definitely can't see that, neither really the opportunity, unless she was in it with her son,' said Jones, sensing another suspect was possibly moving on the list.

'Then we have the issue of the ballot for the Golf Club Chairman, neither the secretary, Major Montgomery nor the president, Earl Hargrove wanted Tate as the new chairman. Also, the ballot hadn't gone their way, which puts them both on the list regards motive, and a strong motive based upon their desire to not have Tate as chairman of their beloved club. Opportunity is evident. Means is still a potential issue, but I am sure they both have experience of using guns, the issue would be whose gun,' said Smith, suddenly thinking.

'What is it sir?' asked Jones, seeing that Smith had suddenly had an idea.

'What if Tate already had his own gun on him, if he did and it was his, then everyone has means, at least to stage the suicide,' Smith said with conviction.

'The issue then is what caused the trauma, but that could be anything. So, we need to find the murder weapon, that now looks like a priority, without it we are potentially lost,' added Smith, feeling slightly more confident in one regard but in need of finding an elusive murder weapon.

'Which is good sir, in some respects, but it now means they all have potential means. So, our suspect numbers could be back at eight, which is not so good, is it?'

'No Jones, it isn't,' as Smith suddenly went quiet.

'Sir, what are you thinking now,' asked Jones, with Smith seeming to have a light bulb moment.

'There is someone else that could have done it, someone involved with Tate.'

'Who are you thinking of sir?' asked Jones, perplexed by his boss's new line of thought.

'CJ Gray,' said Smith firmly.

'Surely not sir, he's been trying to help us convict Tate. Why would he murder him?'

'Maybe not intentionally. We know that Tate hasn't received the intended car. What if he confronted Gray, accused him, and threatened him. Gray isn't someone to let Tate threaten him. They may have had an argument and Gray lost his temper and it was possibly an accident, manslaughter.'

'But sir, not CJ, he wouldn't try to cover things up, he's not like that,' said Jones, defending his friend.

'Maybe. Maybe not. All I'm saying he needs to be on the list, at least until we can eliminate him from our enquiries,' added Smith. He himself not sure, but realising his theory did have legs, the list of suspects was at least nine.

The two detectives were suddenly silent in deep thought, thinking where the investigation was leading and who realistically was the major suspect.

'Well, we have a number of things we need to check out. I trust you have them all written down Jones.'

'You know me sir, where do you want to start.'

CHAPTER 54 - WHERE THERE'S A WILL

Monday morning 7:55 am and Edee pulled into the car park of GGL, and too her surprise CJ's Audi RS6 was already in the car park. 'Wow,' she thought. 'Now this is unusual, James must have things on his mind.' She wondered, were those things, personal or business.

She got out of the BMW Z4 and made her way to the rear entrance of GGL. Edee was back to her more conservative working outfit, a dark grey slim fitting trouser suit, but still with Christian Louboutin Shoes, she tapped in the security code on the door entry system and opened it, to be instantly welcomed by Oscar, who did his usual I haven't seen you for ages routine, finally rolling on his back seeking a belly rub.

'Well good morning Oscar, I've missed you too!'

'Morning Edee, I hope you are feeling better,' came the greeting from CJ calling from his office.

'Much better thank you James, I trust you are also well this morning,' she replied cheerily.

'Not bad, but I've been thinking of about Tate's death and how we conclude the sting. The more I think about it the more I'm thinking the two things must be linked.'

Straight down to business, thought Edee, realising why CJ was in so early.

'Are you sure they are linked and it's not just a coincidence?' asked Edee, as she wandered into CJ's office and sat in the chair opposite him. Oscar jumped immediately onto her lap encouraging an ear rub from Edee, who swiftly obliged.

CJ thought she looked like her normal bubbly self; not like how he left her the other morning. He was however still considering how to approach their kiss at the ball and whether Edee remembered it or actually meant it, albeit he was pretty sure he knew the answer.

'Edee, anything is possible in life, and I'm not completely convinced, but that's why I could do with you doing a few searches and making some discrete enquires that really need your subtle ways.'

Edee looked CJ in the eye and yearned for a sign to confirm if they kissed passionately at the ball, she was so sure they had, it had been wonderful, but she had been so drunk, and her dreams seemed to mix with reality.

'So, you require my expertise?' she said before provocatively adding, 'Is there anything else you require of me?'

'Mmm, possibly, but if you could do these few things first that would be good,' replied CJ. Who realised too late that perhaps he had missed the opportunity to say something further.

'How about a cappuccino first though?' asked Edee, 'and maybe a Danish pastry, I'm just going to go to the coffee shop on the corner.'

'That sounds like the perfect way to get us going,' said CJ, but thinking of other things he would like to do to start the day.

'Right, I'll be back shortly.'

With that, Edee got up, and wandered off to the front door and out into the market place. CJ trying to look at his computer screen and continuing to type, but having to look up and admire her grace and coolness.

Edee closed the front door to the office and immediately bumped into Mr Kipling Snr.

'Good morning, Bonjour Mr Kipling, how are you today?'

'Good morning, Madame Songe, I'm fine, how are you?'

'I'm very well, thank you. This is most fortunate, I wanted to see you. Have you got a couple of minutes? I've would like to ask you something, in confidence.'

'Ah, Madame Songe, you have me intrigued. Okay, come on in.' Mr Kipling Snr led Edee into the Solicitors office next door.

Edee had known Mr Kipling Snr since she had started working in Yorksbey 25 years ago, and Mr Kipling Snr had known Elizabeth Gray far longer than that, they had both established their businesses at about the same time in the mid-sixties.

The two of them went into Mr Kipling Snr's office, an archetypical solicitor's office, wooden panelled walls, with bookcase containing numerous legal books, thick Axminster carpet, large desk with leather insert, and leather upholstery wooden chairs.

'Please take a seat,' said Mr Kipling Snr. 'Would you like a drink?'

'No, I'm okay, I'm just on my way to the coffee shop, I'm getting some coffee's and breakfast, so I'll pass if that's okay.'

'That's fine, now then, what is it that you are after?'

'Mr Kipling, I hope you don't mind me asking, and please let me know if I am speaking out of turn, plus I realise you may not feel able to answer my questions fully, so, I'll word it so you possibly can.'

'I was already intrigued; I am now even more interested. Pray continue.'

'GGL have imported something for Oliver Tate, I'll not elaborate further if you don't mind, and we are liaising with the police on a few matters regarding the shipment, and to be honest, they may also question you at some point about what I am going to ask.'

'Mmm, that sounds ominous, Madame Songe,' said Mr Kipling Snr. smiling with a twinkle in his eye, he had always had a soft spot for Edee.

'Okay, here goes,' said Edee, taking a deep breath.

'Last week Oliver Tate came to see you.'

'Yes, he did.'

'Mr Kipling, it was a statement, not a question.'

'I know, but I thought I would get things off to a positive start,' he laughed, and Edee smiled acknowledging the spirit in which the old lawyer was playing along.

'Now if the next statements I make are true, you don't have to say anything. Is that okay? but if any are wrong, please say, right. That way I don't think the honesty, discretion and integrity of being a solicitor will be compromised,' continued Edee.

'Madame Songe, you are being mischievous today, but okay, I think I understand.'

Edee continued with her direct questions.

'Did Tate see you about changing his *Will*?'

Mr Kipling smiled, but said nothing.

'Was Mrs Tate to be removed as a beneficiary?'

Silence

'Did Justin Tate benefit further from the proposals?'

Silence

'Were there any other significant changes proposed to the *Will*?'

Silence

'Has a new will been signed and completed?'

'Right,' said Mr Kipling Snr. now looking rather earnest, the smile gone from his face.

'Mr Kipling, you have been as always, most helpful and kind. Merci, thank you for your help,' said Edee, most sincerely.

'Madame Songe, I have said nothing incriminating, and I thank you for your candour and understanding of my position. Is there anything else?'

'No thank you.'

'Okay, then I'll send you my bill in the post,' said the wise sage seriously, momentarily reverting to kind.

'Oh,' said Edee, looking rather surprised and crestfallen, before Mr Kipling burst into laughter.

'Mr Kipling, you are, a one, mon amie. Merci, thank you again,' said Edee, standing and walking around the desk, before kissing the solicitor on both cheeks.

'You're welcome,' said Mr Kipling Snr. blushing as he stood and opened the door to his office and led Edee to the front door.

'I hope the information assists you,' said the wise old solicitor.

'It verifies what we have been thinking. Au revoir, Mr Kipling.'

'Good day, Madame Songe.'

CHAPTER 55 - PRODIGAL SON RETURNS

Justin inserted his key in the lock of the front door and went to open it at exactly the same time as Charlotte opened the door.

'Justin, are you okay, have the police been in touch?' asked Charlotte, faking her sincerity.

'Yes Charlotte they have, are you okay,' replied Justin, in similar mock insincerity.

'I'm okay, my cheek is still a little sore though.'

'Your cheek's sore?' Justin said quizzically, but he quickly saw the bruise as soon as Charlotte removed her sunglasses.

'Yes, your dad hit me.'

'He did that?'

'Your dad slapped me, the bastard!'

'But why?'

'He accused me of sleeping with *Lawrence of Arabia* at the ball, but it wasn't me it was that French floozy of CJ Gray, you know, Eden Songe.'

'Oh,' said Justin, suddenly realising that Charlottes cheek, however sore, didn't quite match his father's death as the most serious item of the day.

'Come on in, would you like a coffee? I've just made one.'

'That would be good,' said Justin, following her into the kitchen.

'So, what did the police say to you?'

'I'm guessing the same as you. Suspicious death,' Justin said, letting the statement hang in the air.

'Yes, they didn't say any more to me either, but who would want to murder him?'

'You think the same as me then, that Dad wouldn't kill himself.'

'No way.'

'So, who would kill him and why?' asked Justin, saying what Charlotte was also thinking.

'Now that's the million-dollar question, but based upon your dad's past dealings, he has crossed quite a few people, and just considering recent events the number who wouldn't care if he was dead could be a lot.'

'I guess so,' added Justin, before asking. 'Charlotte it wasn't you. Was it?'

'Justin, how could you think such a thing,' said Charlotte, mustering all the fake indignity she could. 'No, it wasn't. Justin, there are many things that I am, but a murderer is not one of them.'

With that, the two of them embraced, consoling one another in the way they thought reasonable considering the circumstances, but both thinking how insincere they each were and looked.

Suddenly the gate alarm sounded and the two parted.

'I'll get it,' said Charlotte, walking off to the hallway and the intercom, where she pressed the button.

'Hello, can I help you?' asked Charlotte.

'Good morning Mrs Tate, it's DI Smith again, could you please spare us a few moments.'

'Oh, yes of course, come on up.' With that, she pressed the button to open the gate.

Shortly, DI Smith and DS Jones, were sat in the lounge opposite Charlotte and Justin.

'Sorry to trouble you both again, and I would like to thank you for identifying the body Mrs Tate, which must have been quite traumatic,' said Smith, using all the skill he had learnt over the years to sound sincere. 'I'm sure the pathologist also advised you that the body won't unfortunately be released until the investigation is concluded.'

'It needed doing and it was possibly easier for me rather than Justin,' Charlotte said quietly, before adding. 'Has the Post Mortem established the cause of death?'

'While the Post Mortem was not fully conclusive, we are now considering the death as a possible murder,' Smith said, before adding. 'We therefore have a few further questions that we hope you may be able to help us with.'

'So, definitely not suicide?' asked Charlotte. Which made Justin look at her rather suspiciously.

'As I said, we are considering it as a possible murder Mrs Tate,' repeated Smith, before continuing. 'Did Mr Tate own a firearm of any sort?'

'He had a shotgun, for when he went clay pigeon and grouse shooting, it's in the locked cabinet in his study,' said Charlotte.

'Did he own a hand gun of any description?' asked Jones. Looking initially at Charlotte and then Justin.

'Not that I'm aware of, Justin do you know any different?'

They all looked at Justin, who suddenly looked very uncomfortable and blushed.

'Well, I can't get him into trouble now can I,' he said, before adding. 'I have seen a hand gun in his safe.'

'Ah, do you know what type of firearm? and do either of you have access to the safe?'

'It's a Glock I think, but I don't know the safe combination, do you Charlotte?'

'Bart never trusted me with that, the safe was definitely his and no one else's.'

'We are looking for a weapon involved with the death, so I hope you don't mind but I will bring in the experts to gain access to the safe, if only to eliminate it from our enquiries. Will I need to get a warrant, or will you provide permission Mrs Tate?'

'A warrant won't be necessary, we will cooperate with you with whatever is required to resolve matters,' said Charlotte, again, calling on her acting ability to fake sincerity.

'Thank you, that is most helpful. Justin, do you know what type of Glock?' asked Smith.

'What type? Dad just said it was a Glock, are there different types?' replied Justin, looking rather blank at the question.

'Never mind, but another thing. Do either of you know of anyone that might wish to kill Mr Tate,' asked Smith, expecting a list as long as his arm to the question but being taken fully by surprise by the answer.

'No, no one that springs to mind,' said Charlotte. 'What about you Justin?'

'No, not really, but if I think of anyone, I'll let you know, but dad was well liked. He had lots of friends,' added Justin, struggling to hide the lie, and again colouring up slightly.

'Mmm, well thank you for your honesty,' said Smith with incredulity. 'Mrs Tate, I assume Mr Tate had a computer, we would like to take it to review its contents, it may be helpful to our investigation, would that also be okay?'

'Yes, he used a laptop, it's in the study, I'm afraid I don't know the password, Bart was most secretive about such things.'

'I'm pretty sure our Techie nerds will solve his password pretty quickly, if one of you could show me to the study that would be good,' said Jones, pulling out an evidence bag from his coat pocket. Charlotte led Jones to the study while Smith continued chatting to Justin.

'On another matter, where is the Aston Martin that GGL imported for him?' Smith asked, realising his other line of enquiry was going nowhere.

'It's in the garage. Why, is it important?' asked Justin, looking rather concerned.

'It may be linked to the death, we aren't sure, if you could just keep it secure for the time being.'

At that moment Jones and Charlotte came back into the lounge, Jones carrying the laptop.

'Now, it's funny you should mention the car, but you have just reminded me, the delivery driver punched Bart when he delivered it, and threatened to kill him,' said Charlotte, suddenly looking all alarmed. 'Isn't that right Justin, you saw him too.'

'That's right he did,' said Justin, backing up his step mother.

'Oh,' said Smith, caught out by this new information. 'What was the circumstances that led to this, threat?'

'Bart was not happy with something with the delivery and phoned GGL to voice his concern, and was looking to get the matter resolved amicably, but the driver went a bit mad and hit Bart in the stomach, then said he'd kill him. We threatened to call the police, so he left straight away. I didn't think any more of it to be honest, well not until now,' said Charlotte, thriving in the possible misdirection.

'Is that what happened Justin?' asked Smith directly.

'Much of a muchness, he did hurt dad when he hit him and he threaten him, that's for sure.'

'Thank you both for your time, you have been most helpful,' lied Smith.

'I think we will have to question the driver about the threats, if there is anything else you think of, please let us know, in the meantime I'll arrange for our specialist to open the safe.'

CHAPTER 56 - I'M ARRESTING YOU ...

Back in GGL's offices, Edee had been busy following up on the leads CJ had suggested.

'Well done Edee, I never cease to be amazed by your feminine charm, you could lure anything from anyone,' said CJ, after she had come off the phone to the Barnsley Registrar.

Edee momentarily savoured the compliment.

'Well, definitely if they are male,' added CJ, smiling. 'I think a more difficult challenge could be a grumpy female spinster with no sense of humour,' he added.

'I think the Governor, may have a point,' said Cliff, who had earlier joined them in the office. 'I have to agree, you do have a way with dealing with men,' Cliff added, pulling on the thread, initially picked at by CJ.

'Mr Gray, Mr Ledger, I don't think you fully understand my skills,' said Edee, frowning and looking over her glasses at the two of them.

'Madame Songe, I think we do, and you have been very resourceful today, confirming things with the information you have secured,' said CJ, continuing to tease his resourceful friend. 'As usual, you have obtained things us mere mortals would struggle to acquire, what say you boy.'

At which, Oscar suddenly started jumping and dashing around, before finally jumping on Edee's lap and licking her face.'

'That's not fair James, using Oscar as the foil for your fun.'

'He's just showing how we all feel and how we appreciate you and your efforts.'

At which the three of them burst out laughing.

The moment was broken as the front door bell rang and Edee answered the intercom.

'Good morning, can I help you,' Edee said in a light hearted manner.

'Morning, its DI Smith and DS Jones.'

'Oh, come on in,' said Edee, sensing that the visit was official and pressing the door release button.

The two officers entered and looked quite serious, but were immediately confronted by the boisterous Oscar, who made a beeline for Jones, realising he was the more fun loving of the two guests. Oscar bowled into Jones legs and sort an ear rub as he looked up at the smiling officer, who duly obliged.

'You're a good dog aren't you boy,' said Jones, who was clearly enjoying the dog's attention.

'Sorry to trouble you Edee, Gray, we are just following up on a few things relating to the ongoing enquiry surrounding Oliver Tate's death, could we have a moment in private,' said Smith, as he looked towards Cliff and making it obvious that whatever they had to say wasn't for anyone else to hear.

'Of course DI Smith, come through to my office, Edee, please join us. Cliff, could you follow up that item we discussed,' replied CJ.

'Certainly Governor,' said Cliff, realising there wasn't anything, but that he should withdraw gracefully. 'I'll do that right away.'

The four of them went into CJ's office, swiftly followed by Oscar who went immediately to his basket in the corner and laid down.

'Please take a seat gentlemen, Edee,' said CJ, as he sat at his desk, gesturing to the four leather chairs positioned around a small coffee table in the middle of his office. 'Would you like a drink?' he asked politely.

'No thank you,' the two officers said together, with what seemed like their stock answer to the request for refreshments.

'Well, how's the investigation going. Any promising leads?' asked CJ evenly, before adding. 'Edee's been very resourceful, following up on something that might benefit you,'

'Oh, that sounds interesting, what's that Edee?' asked Smith, smiling at Edee looking for a positive response.

'When CJ and I were out walking last week,' started Edee. Which clearly didn't go down too well with Smith as his face suddenly looked like a bee had stung it before she added. 'We noticed that Oliver Tate went next door to see the solicitors.'

'Go on,' said Smith, suddenly more interested.

'Well, I think that perhaps you should have a talk with Mr Kipling Snr, as we thought that perhaps Tate was discussing his *Will*,' said Edee enticingly, 'and depending on whether there were any changes, it might just provide a motive for murder.'

'Ah, that is possible Edee, well done,' said Smith. 'Jones make a note for us to discuss with Mr Kipling Snr about changes to Tate's *Will*.'

'Yes sir.'

'We thought that either Charlotte or Justin were likely to be those most likely affected, so something for you to consider,' said Edee, smiling at Smith.

'Talking of Charlotte and Justin, we have just been to see them, and they have made a serious allegation,' Smith said gravely.

'Oh, said Edee.' Suddenly looking rather concerned as she turned to look at CJ, who remained completely impassive.

'Could you tell us who the driver was that delivered the DB5 to Tate,' said Jones, with his notebook at the ready.

'Of course we could,' said CJ calmly, as the room went quiet.

'Well, can you then,' said Smith firmly. While thinking. 'Why does Gray always have to be so awkward.'

'Can I ask why that information is relevant to your enquiry?' asked CJ, now looking directly at Smith, who broke eye contact, before replying.

'Charlotte and Justin Tate have both stated that the driver punched Tate, after Tate had spoken on the phone to this office,' said Jones, referring to his notebook.

'Oh, did he?' said Edee, struggling not to smile and lifting her hand to her mouth to hide the growing smirk, before adding honestly. 'That's probably because Tate was obnoxious, disrespectful and extremely rude to me on the phone.'

'That might well be the case, but that does not entitle the driver to punch Tate, and then threaten to kill him,' said Smith, now looking steely at CJ.

'I'm sure it's something and nothing,' added Edee, trying to placate Smith and calm a situation that could potentially get out of hand.

'So, as we asked nicely, can you please tell us who the driver was?' said Smith resolutely.

'Of course, but I can vouch for the driver,' said CJ, not liking having to give out the information in such circumstances. 'It was my former RSM, Cliff Ledger.'

'Would that be the *'Cliff'* in the other office,' Smith said, rather sarcastically.

'Yes, it would,' said CJ, regretting having to inform on his old friend to the police.

'Thank you, we will need to ask Mr Ledger some questions,' said Smith, as he and Jones rose from their seats.

'Simon, I'm sure that Cliff hasn't anything to do with Tate's death,' said Edee. Trying to sound convincing, but not quite achieving the desired effect.

'Smith wouldn't your efforts be better spent questioning Charlotte, I think she has a far stronger motive than Cliff,' added CJ, in a forceful manner.

'Maybe,' said Smith, as he walked out of CJ's office and confronted Cliff who was photocopying next door in the main office.

'Cliff Ledger, I'm arresting you on suspicion of the murder of Oliver Tate, "*You do not have to say anything. But it may harm your defence if you do not mention when questioned something which you later rely on in court. Anything you do say may be given in evidence.*" Do you understand?'

'Smith, don't be silly, Cliff wouldn't do that,' said CJ, but thinking to himself, 'Not unless I asked him too.'

'Gray, stay out of this. Mr Ledger, I take it you will come quietly to the station to answer our questions,' continued Smith, in a forthright and official manner.

'It's all right Governor,' said Cliff quite light-heartedly, 'I'm sure that this is just a silly mistake by the inspector, and we can sort things out without embarrassing him, too much.'

'Come this way please,' said Jones, holding Cliff by the arm as he escorted him out of the office to the police car parked outside.

'Okay Cliff, if you need a solicitor, just get in touch, but I'm sure this is just a wild goose chase, I'll get it sorted,' said CJ, clearly in no mood to be messed with, and as always, CJ would do anything for his *fixer.*

CHAPTER 57 - IS THIS REALLY SENSIBLE?

The interview room at Yorksbey Police Station was like most built in that era, a small plain room with no windows, painted a white that had faded over the years. In the centre of the room was a sturdy wooden table with four uncomfortable wooden chairs, two on either side, on the table was the conventional tape-recording machine that was still used as Yorksbey was still a way off going digital. High on the wall were two CCTV cameras used by others, to monitor interviews, as necessary.

The room today was starting to feel a little oppressive due to the lack of natural ventilation for the three people sat in the room, especially as the interview had commenced and the normal initial formalities were out of the way.

DI Smith was however starting to have some doubts about the merits of arresting Ledger. Jones had already asked of him. 'Is this interview really sensible?' as he had established that Ledger had been an exemplary soldier with a distinguished career in the Royal Engineers and the Royal Logistics Corps, who now worked for GGL and for his previous superior officer, Lt.Col.CJ Gray.

As Smith looked at Ledger across the table, he saw a man that was more than capable of killing, but more than likely only on the orders of his superiors, Smith's years in the service had taught him to recognise people and their traits. Ledger was definitely someone you would not cross, but he sat there relaxed and calm and possibly revelling in the situation, this was unlikely to be the man who had committed the murder, but reluctantly Smith had to now see the interview through to a conclusion.

'Cliff, do you mind if I call you Cliff?' asked Smith, seeking to find a way to get the most out of Ledger.

'My friends call me Cliff,' he said, looking steely at Smith, with a slight smile on his face. 'Everyone else calls me Mr Ledger.'

Smith recognised the significance of Cliff's remark and continued.

'Mr Ledger, for the tape, would you please confirm that you have freely decided to not have a solicitor present at this interview.'

'That's correct.'

'Charlotte and Justin Tate have alleged, that while delivering an Aston Martin DB5 to Oliver Tate, you punched him and threatened to kill him,' said Smith in a matter-of-fact manner.

'Have they now,' said Cliff, smiling even more.

'This is a serious matter Mr Ledger,' said Smith. 'Did you punch Tate and threaten to kill him?'

'No,' said Cliff, suddenly deadly serious.

'No, you didn't punch him?'

'Yes.'

'Yes, you did punch him?' asked Smith, feeling that Ledger had the same way of getting to him that Gray did.

'I certainly punched Oliver Tate,' said Cliff. 'No one talks to me, or Edee like that and gets away with it. Tate, was totally out of order, his manner and conduct were outrageous, he was obnoxious, disrespectful, and extremely rude to Edee and it was totally unnecessary, so I gave him a little tap.'

278

'Thank goodness we have that cleared up. So, you did punch Tate, but did you threaten to kill him? We have two witnesses that say you did,' said Smith, trying to get the interview back on track.

'Well, I'm afraid they are mistaken,' said Cliff assuredly.

'So, they didn't hear you threaten to kill Tate?' asked Jones, seeking to support his boss.

'No.'

'So, did you, or did you not, threaten to kill Tate?'

'Yes.'

'Yes,' said Smith, suddenly wondering what he was hearing,

'The two witnesses couldn't have heard what I said, because I whispered in Mr Tate's ear when he was on the ground,' said Cliff. Rather too calmly for Smith's liking.

'So, what did you say?' asked Smith, raising his eyebrows, realising that Ledger had definitely worked too long with CJ Gray.

'I said, *"Don't ever talk to me, or Edee like that ever again,"* which they could have heard, before I punched him. I then however whispered, *"Otherwise you are a dead man, do I make myself clear."* Now you can read into that what you both like, but I didn't actually technically threaten to kill him, but I admit I did threaten him, albeit he did over step the mark, don't you agree?' stated Cliff succinctly.

Smith rubbed his chin with his hand, before continuing.

'Mr Ledger, did you kill Oliver Tate?'

'No, I didn't.'

Smith considered things, and decided to try another tack, as it was becoming obvious where this interview was going.

'Where were you between midnight and 3 am on Friday night, and the early hours of Saturday morning?'

'I was at Overhear Manor, in Edendale.'

'Can anyone corroborate that?' asked Jones, who saw that his boss needed time to consider things.

'Of course they can,' said Cliff matter-of-factly.

'Could you please tell us who?'

'Mrs Wembley, she works for CJ Gray and lives in at the Manor. She and I spent the evening watching TV before retiring at about 1 am. I woke about 7 am, I'm sure Mrs Wembley will verify things.'

'But what about while Mrs Wembley was asleep?' asked Smith, thinking on his feet.

'What about it?' asked Cliff.

'Well, you could have sneaked out of the house across the golf course and killed Tate,' said Smith, suddenly on a roll.

'I possibly could have, so could lots of others based upon that hypothesis, but I didn't as I was asleep, and I'm sure that the high security CCTV cameras around Overhear Manor will verify that I didn't leave the Manor on the night Tate died,' added Cliff, with a rather sardonic smile on his face.

Just then, there was a knock on the door, and in walked PC Perfect.

'Yes Perfect, what is it? Can't you see we are in the middle of an important interview,' said Smith, rather too forcibly than was required.

'I'm sorry to trouble you sir,' apologised Perfect, 'but I thought you would want to know this. There's a Mrs Wembley in reception, she says she has some information that may assist you with your enquiries.'

At which Smith put his head in his hands, as he recognised that the line of enquiry with Cliff Ledger had hit a dead end.

CHAPTER 58 - STOP WASTING YOUR TIME

CJ and Edee sat outside Yorksbey Police station in the Audi RS6, having brought Mrs Wembley to provide Cliff with his alibi for the night of Tate's death, they were both really annoyed that DI Smith had arrested Cliff. What was he thinking?

'I can't believe with all the other suspects; Simon would believe Charlotte and Justin and arrest Cliff. Okay he had to ask the question, but arrest him, that's totally out of order,' said Edee, struggling to contain her displeasure.

'I agree, but I can only assume he's under pressure to resolve matters quickly,' added CJ.

As they spoke, Cliff and Mrs Wembley emerged from the police station, they were both smiling, and they walked over to the car and got in.

'All sorted Mrs Wembley?' CJ asked.

'Yes, Master James, all sorted. DI Smith looked rather sheepish by the time we had finished, but too his credit he at least apologised to Cliff for arresting him.'

'Other than them wasting all our time, it was quite amusing,' said Cliff, smiling.

CJ started the car, and they pulled out of the car park into Boston Road and drove towards the river bridge and the town centre.

'Thanks Mrs W, sorry to put you out this morning,' CJ continued.

'That's okay, always here to help friends of the family.'

'Cliff, I'm afraid it's straight back to work. I would like you to do me a favour and go back on surveillance, this time on Charlotte Tate, if that's okay? I'm off to London, got a bit of business to settle, which I think you'll agree with.'

'No problem, Governor, do you think she's now a prime suspect?'

'I think she's involved; I just can't establish to what extent though,' CJ replied, as he turned the Audi left into Market Place.

'Cliff, I'll drop you and Edee off at the office so you can collect your bike, then I'll take Mrs W back to Overhear Manor, before heading off to London. You all okay with that?' he asked, as he turned right into Bank Street and pulled up at the rear of GGL.

Back in the police station, the two detectives were both looking rather despondent, Ledger clearly wasn't their man, they were now back to the original list of suspects.

'Well sir, what do you want me to do now?' asked Jones, trying not to say, 'I tried to warn you.'

'Have the Tech Lads got into the laptop and found anything of note?' asked Smith.

'Password was pretty straight forward, "*The.K1ss*" it's a famous sculpture in the Tate Modern, quite original I guess for Tate, and obviously better than *Bart1234*,' said Jones smiling. 'But no, nothing, not at the moment, but they are going through everything systematically, you know how they are. They said it would probably be another couple of days before they would have their report,' said Jones, hopeful that they might find a useful lead on the computer.

'Okay, let me know when the report comes in. Could you also follow up on Edee's lead about the *Will* with

Mr Kipling Snr. and then check on the contents of Tate's safe and his gun,' said Smith, before adding. 'After that I think we should check on whether White and Parker have alibi's, they are both capable of doing the crime, that's for certain.'

'Okay sir, I'll get right onto it. What about also looking further at the crime scene for the object that inflicted the killer blow?' asked Jones, sensing finding the murder weapon was possibly key to events.

'I'll speak to Peel, and see if we can have some more uniform officers allocated to the enquiry and undertake another search of the area. I'm surprised he hasn't been on wanting an update following the Post Mortem report,' Smith said, dreading having to speak to his superior.

Half an hour later and Smith was still agonising on how to approach Peel about having more uniform officers to search the crime scene, he knew it was likely to be a tall order. Finally, he grasped the nettle and dialled Peel's mobile, after two rings Peel answered.

'Yes, Smith, what is it? I'm on my way to see you, I'll be there shortly.'

'Oh, I think it will wait then sir. I'll put the kettle on.' With that the line went dead, but from the sound of Peel's mood, Smith was even less confident about getting more resources.

'Peel's on his way, and he doesn't sound in a good mood.'

'That doesn't bode well,' replied Jones, who now looked even more dejected than he had been earlier.

Twenty minutes later Peel arrived at the station with a face like thunder, and stormed into the CID office, and without any pleasantries got straight down to business.

'Well, I've read the PM report, I think we can treat this as a straight forward case of suicide,' said Peel, looking straight at Smith.

'Sorry sir, surely you can't be serious,' said Smith with disbelief.

'Look Smith, Tate's a nasty bit of work. Sorry. W*as* a nasty bit of work, that's got away with numerous crimes, and you've all been trying to get him bang to rights for years.'

'I know that sir, but you must have read the initial PM report and my initial findings, while it's been staged managed to look like a suicide, it's obviously a murder.'

'Smith let's be clear, no one cares about Tate's death, whether it was suicide or murder. Well, no one of any note, I'm not even sure his son liked him that much, and from what I gather went on at the Captain's Charity Ball, his wife will probably be quite pleased he's dead.'

'Is that a good enough reason to not find out the true circumstances and catch the perpetrator.'

'I think you have lots of other things you could be doing, and if the case just quietly petered out you wouldn't get any pressure from me,' Peel said quietly, in a reassuring manner.

'But sir...'

'Look Smith, I'm giving you away out here, the Chief Constable is happy for this to fade away, do I make myself clear.' said Peel, this time more forcefully.

'You mean that Earl Hargrove has been onto him and has asked for a favour, doesn't want his precious golf club in the news or any bad press.'

'Smith, believe what you want, but stop wasting your time on this case, you'll let it drop if you know what's good for you, and unless you can provide a clear-cut case and a killer by the end of the week, the case is closed. Do I make myself clear?' concluded Peel. Who didn't wait for an answer and marched out leaving the two detectives looking at each other speechless.

Eventually Jones found the courage to say sardonically.

'I take it we haven't got any more resources to look for the murder weapon.'

'No, we certainly haven't Jones, and it looks like certain people don't want this case investigating any further.'

'So, shall I just pack up the file now?' asked Jones glumly.

'No, not yet, you heard Peel, we have until the end of the week, so until then we keep going and trying to find the murderer, so we don't have much time,' Smith said resolutely.

'If that's the case we could really do with some extra help though,' said Jones. Who glanced quizzically at his boss, with a knowing look.

'Do you think I should give CJ and Edee a call?'

'You could think that Jones, but I couldn't possibly comment,' added Smith smiling.

With that Jones, picked up his phone and made a call.

CHAPTER 59 - FOLLOW THAT WOMAN

Cliff was back doing what he didn't particularly enjoy, but had got used to it during his army days and to be honest he was pretty good at it. That was why CJ trusted him to do anything that required being resilient and observant. Cliff would however have preferred Charlotte to be out and about more, it would at least have given him the opportunity to be more active. Being in one place for so long was really boring.

Activity today at Tate House had been pretty mundane, a delivery by Royal Mail and another by Evri had been the highlight of the day so far. But then the security gate started to move, and the Black BMW M4 pulled out of the driveway, Justin was driving and the blonde Charlotte still wearing sunglasses, was in the passenger seat. He quickly messaged Edee and then pulled on his helmet while starting the bike, which roared into life.

The BMW turned left towards Yorksbey, and Cliff followed, keeping quite a distance between him and the car, so as not to be particularly noticed, but not too far so he would lose them.

They presently turned right onto Etongate Road still going towards Town, they crossed the railway bridge and then the car indicated left and pulled into the Heritage Railway Station Carpark.

Cliff slowed, and he also turned left into the carpark, to see Charlotte in a bright red rain coat, get out of the car and walk off towards the ticket office. The BMW didn't stay, but pulled out of the carpark and turned right, back the way it had come.

Cliff quickly parked up in the car park but was now caught in a dilemma. He had not previously had chance to check out the carpark payment method, albeit it did look like a pay and display car park, he therefore took the gamble and parked near where the cycles were chained to security railings. He switched off and quickly pulled the bike onto its stand, and then put a security chain in place.

He suddenly realised he looked rather conspicuous in his bike leathers and carrying his crash helmet, but he couldn't do much else now and had to go with it.

A train was preparing to leave at Platform 1, the one closest to him and the ticket office. He walked quickly now, realising that it looked like the train was about to go. Doors were being slammed shut by passengers and by the guard. He was now desperately seeking Charlotte, and fortunately she was very conspicuous in her red coat, as she emerged from the ticket office. The guard opened the door to a first-class carriage and gestured her forward, closing the door after her, and smiling politely.

Cliff realised he was not going to have time to buy a ticket from the office, so just hopped over the barrier and onto the platform as the guard blew his whistle and waved his flag while the train whistle also blew. He opened the rearmost door of the train and stepped into a 2nd Class carriage and quickly slammed the door shut behind him.

The carriages jolted as the train took up the strain, and then slowly pulled out of the station in a cloud of steam, with smoke puffing out of the funnel, as the Standard Class 4MT locomotive gently built-up speed.

Cliff quickly considered what to do and realised he really needed to get a little closer to Charlotte. The carriage was fortunately an open style and he looked towards the front of the train. Luckily, the carriage wasn't particularly busy, so he made the decision to walk forward to seek out Charlotte and a better vantage point to monitor her potential movements.

The train slowly built-up speed, under the railway bridge of Etongate Road and on towards the embankment that split the golf course in two. Cliff moved quickly through two further 2nd class carriages until he could see the 1st Class carriage ahead. He decided to take the last window seat on the left looking forward, so he could easily observe the platforms of the upcoming stations. Fortunately, there was no-one in any of the last four seats, the closest people to him were two rows further behind, a family of four, clearly enjoying their day out on the popular steam railway.

The train passed through the majestic golf course, and it soon started crossing the wonderful stone viaduct, the jewel in the crown on the railway, which stood high above Edendale village and the river below. Cliff looked out over the dale, admiring the beautiful site of the rolling countryside and snaking river below.

The train whistle blew, and the train suddenly slowed. Edendale Station was very close to Yorksbey, and while all the four stations on the line were close together, one of the reasons why the railway had been axed under the Beeching cuts of 1963, this stop was however, the shortest distance between stations on the railway line to Etongate.

Cliff was taken a little by surprise as the train came to a halt in the station. He got up and went to the carriage door and lowered the window to get a better view in case Charlotte decided to get off.

The platform was awash with steam and smoke, plus it was on the opposite side to the station building. There was only a guard and two men on the platform, who were walking towards the old steel footbridge which would take them over the tracks to the station on the other platform.

The adjacent platform walls were covered with lots of bright spring flowers in pots and baskets, it was obvious why the stations on route were used so often for TV and Films.

The guard blew his whistle, and then the locomotive whistle blew. The train again slowly started to pull out of the station, and as Cliff turned around he looked through the other window and saw a BMW M5 in the station car park next to the level crossing, where the gates were closed waiting for the train to move off.

He quickly moved across the carriage and lowered the window of the door to get a better look, it definitely looked like the BMW M5 that had visited Tate.

'Mmm, that's strange,' he thought, but then he thought again.

'Oh Shit,' realising he had potentially cocked up.

He quickly moved into the first-class carriage, which was a compartment type, he continued at pace along the companionway, looking into each compartment. Lots of people enjoying their day out, but no Charlotte. He got to the end and to the last carriage door on the left, he lowered the window and looked back. The platform was now a long way behind as the train was moving quite fast having picked up speed. He could now just about see Charlotte through the smoke and steam in her red coat, slowly walking towards the footbridge, and waving at him.

'Oh Fuck, the Governor's not going to be happy,' said Cliff to himself, thinking how he could have made such a school boy error.

He quickly pulled out his phone and rang Edee.

'Hi Cliff, how's it going, I hope you haven't lost Charlotte?' she laughingly joked.

'That's just it. I have.'

'What! You can't have done.'

'I have. Look Edee can you do me a favour and drive to Edendale Station, I think Charlotte may have met up with the driver of the BMW M5 that visited Tate. His car was at the station and that's where I lost her, I'll tell you how later,' Cliff said, rather despondently.

'Okay, I'll go now, but it's unlikely I'll get their before she will have left.'

'Edee, she's wearing a red rain coat, it's quite distinctive,' said Cliff, trying to assist his friend as much as possible.

'Okay Cliff, I'll keep you updated, bye,' said Edee, picking up her car keys and slipping on her jacket before making for the back door.

'Thanks Edee. You're a star, bye,' said Cliff, who was by now talking to himself, as the call had ended.

Edee, slammed the back door shut and locked it before quickly unlocking her car and climbing in. She started up the car and slipped the auto shift into drive, before setting off rather too quickly for the tight back streets of Yorksbey.

She kept looking regularly in the rear-view mirror, not wanting to be caught speeding as she sped through town at rather more than the speed limit. Unfortunately, every traffic light and pedestrian crossing conspired against her, and despite her best endeavours, eventually 12 minutes later she pulled into the small carpark of Edendale Station. As she had expected, no sign of any BMW M5, or any car for that matter, as the car park was empty, and also no sign of Charlotte.

She parked the car and thought she would just check if anyone had noticed Charlotte getting off the train. Not that she held out much luck with that, not considering how today was going.

She walked towards the station, a fine 19th Century stone building with grey slate roof typical of the era, and opened the main door. The building served as the ticket office, waiting room and a small buffet for visitors. It was quiet, despite a train having only been through about a quarter of an hour ago.

It was though, immaculately clean, and tidy and totally reminiscent of the steam age era.

Edee went up to the ticket office and rang the small bell on the counter.

Presently an elderly man came to the counter.

'Good morning, Miss, can I help you?' he asked.

'Good morning. I'm sorry to trouble you. I'm looking for my friend. I was supposed to pick her up from here, she was on the last train and I'm late. She's an attractive blonde lady in her thirties, probably wearing a red coat. I don't suppose you've seen her?'

'No. I haven't seen anyone like that. Perhaps if you try in the Buffet over there,' said the Ticket Officer, pointing across the Waiting Room Hall.

'Merci, Thanks,' said Edee, before turning and walking over towards the self-service buffet.

'Hello,' she said to the young girl at the till, before adding, 'I wonder if you can help me?'

As the young girl looked up, Edee was surprised at who it was. 'Oh. Hi Nancy. I didn't know you also worked here.'

'Hi there Madame Songe. Yes, I work here as a volunteer. Like everyone else, I try to do my bit for the Heritage Railway, it's such a good thing for the area, don't you agree?' she continued.

'It sure is,' added Edee. 'You are a busy one aren't you? I don't suppose you have seen Charlotte Tate here today have you?' asked Edee, without much hope or conviction.

'It's funny you should say that, but she was here not long ago. She got off the train from Yorksbey, she was rather rude though. I said hello, but she ignored me completely and went straight past me out into the car park, and she is normally so bubbly and nice,' said Nancy, in her usual helpful manner.

'Are we talking about the same Charlotte Tate?' thought Edee, before asking, 'I don't suppose you saw where she went, did you?'

'No, but I heard a car pull off rather quickly shortly after she left. Gravel went everywhere, made a right old din. I guess she was picked up by someone,' said Nancy, smiling at Edee.

'Merci, thanks Nancy. That's helpful, I think,' said Edee, wondering why Charlotte had met up with the BMW driver.

'You take care now. Au revoir, bye,' Edee added, before absentmindedly leaving.

'Bye,' said Nancy. Who went back to checking the till, without a care in the world.

Edee got back into her car and immediately called Cliff, who picked up on the first ring.

'Any luck?' Cliff asked desperately.

'Sorry Cliff. She was here, as you already know, but she's long gone, and I think she was picked up by your BMW driver. The car left shortly after Charlotte got to the station, and from what DS Jones had told me after he had looked at your photos, it was Peter Parker. Which seems rather odd to say the least,' said Edee, pondering her own statement and the likely possible implications.

CHAPTER 60 - WHAT'S IN THE SAFE?

Jones sat on one of the four bar stools in the Tate's kitchen drinking a mug of coffee, he was waiting for the Police Locksmith to open the safe in the study down the hall. He had been advised it shouldn't take long.

Opposite him on the other side of the marble top island sat Charlotte, still wearing sunglasses, but the bruise on her cheek was slowly fading, she was also drinking coffee from one of the £50 coffee mugs. She was quite stunning thought Jones, and he also couldn't see her murdering her husband, but he also knew that looks can be very deceiving and anything was possible.

Charlotte was looking at the headlines of the latest edition of the *Yorksbey News.*

He was woken from his thoughts as Charlotte suddenly spoke.

'Have you see me on the front page with OO7?'

'Sorry, Charlotte,' said Jones, not understanding her question.

'Here, on the front page,' said Charlotte as she passed him the newspaper.

Jones noticed the main headline first:-

"Local Business Man Found Dead at Golf Club"

Jones knew that DI Smith was not going to be happy about the case hitting the local news headlines, he had been hoping for a small mention hidden somewhere in the paper, but Jones also recognised the headline could have been far worse.

Jones eye though, was immediately drawn to the large picture of a stunning sexy looking Cat Woman, with her arms entwined with a dashing James Bond, with the caption:-

"OO7 Record Bid Secures Cat Woman"

'Oh, is that you Charlotte? You look…..stunning,' said Jones, struggling to find words that were suitable based upon the circumstances.

'Yes, I do rather don't I?' said Charlotte, looking at Jones for further compliments, which did not materialise. So added herself. ' £2000 bid, the highest ever for the Charity Ball Auction, can't beat that can you, pretty impressive?'

'You certainly can't, and you are,' said Jones, blushing slightly and hoping that Charlotte would change the subject, which fortunately for him she did.

'Bart's death also not surprisingly made the headlines. Oh, by the way did you arrest the delivery driver?' she asked, in a rather uncaring way.

'We did, Mrs Tate, but he has an alibi and I'm afraid he couldn't have been involved in the death of your husband. Also, his recollection of the encounter you mentioned was slightly different from yours, but I can see why you brought it to our attention,' said Jones, maintaining a calm manner.

'Oh,' said Charlotte, rather lost for words, but not particularly bothered either.

'I don't suppose you have thought of anyone that might have wanted to kill your husband?' added Jones casually.

'No, I'm afraid I haven't,' said Charlotte unconvincingly.

Just then Justin came into the kitchen.

'Oh, hello, you're back again. What is it this time? Have you found the killer?' he asked rather directly and then coloured up, realising he maybe shouldn't have spoken like that to a police detective.

'I'm afraid we haven't found the killer, and we are trying to open the safe. Ah, and here is the man with an update.'

'All sorted John. Rather straightforward if truth be known, these home digital safe's are designed just to stop your speculative burglar and to keep things from prying eyes,' said the specialist officer, who glanced at Charlotte in a rather knowing way.

'Okay thanks,' said Jones. 'Is there a gun in the safe?'

'No, no gun, but there was a small box of ammunition. It contained just the usual items, deeds, documents, some keys, that sort of thing, only other thing of note that you wouldn't find in your average home safe, is I would guess about £10k in used bank notes.'

'Well thanks again, I think you can go now,' said Jones. Who was not particularly moved by the news of the contents of the safe.

'I'll be off then. Goodbye, Sir, Madam, see you sometime John,' said the officer as he left.

'So, no gun in the safe. Do either of you know if he took it with him on the night of the Ball?' asked Jones.

'No, not that I'm aware of,' said Charlotte.

'No, me neither,' said Justin.

'I thought as much.' Jones bent down and opened his holdall that he had brought with him. He pulled out a plastic evidence bag which contained a hand gun.

'Justin, do you recognise this weapon?' Jones asked, as he held up the bag for them both to see.

'That's it, that's Dad's gun,' said Justin assuredly.

'How can you be so sure?' asked Jones enquiringly.

'Well, I can't. What I meant was that it sure looks like Dad's gun,' said Justin, clarifying his previous remark.

'Is that the gun that killed Dad?' asked Justin, as Jones placed the bag back in his holdall.

'Well, it was the gun that was at the crime scene,' said Jones, being careful of the words he used, before adding. 'Did either of you know that Mr Tate was planning to change his *Will*?'

'No, not me,' said Justin. 'I assumed that he would leave things to me and Charlotte, but I had never really considered it more than that, and never asked him'

'And you, Mrs Tate?'

'I'm not aware that he was planning any changes, I agree with Justin,' said Charlotte, not very convincingly. This left Jones wondering did she, or didn't she, know of the planned changes, he wasn't convinced either way.

'Thank you both again for your time. I'll just have a quick look in the safe and take a few photos, before I go if that's okay,' added Jones.

He left them, thinking what his boss would probably make of the latest developments.

CHAPTER 61 - WHITE AND PARKER

Smith was already in the car park of the Watermill Arms, leaning on the boot of the Insignia when Jones pulled up in his Astra.

'Good morning sir.'

'Morning Jones, well what have you got for me?'

'Well, something and nothing.'

'Go on.'

'No gun in the safe, but if I can believe Justin, the crime scene gun is Tate's, or at least one like it. Plus, neither of them knew about Tate changing his *Will*, or so they say.'

'Do you believe them?'

'Not sure, I'm keeping an open mind, just letting you know what they said.'

'With the gun potentially being Tate's that means that all our suspects now have the means of staging the suicide scene, so all still to play for.'

'Yes, but not getting us much further though,' said Jones, thinking who of the suspects now looked the most likely to have done the deed.

'Did they ask about Ledger?' continued Smith.

'Charlotte did but didn't look particularly surprised when I said he had an alibi.'

'Was that just a ploy originally to try and throw us of her?' thought Smith out loud.

'Could well be, if she did it, but did she do it?' answered Jones, with his question.

'Come on let's see if either White or Parker are here, it was good of Edee to put us onto them,' said Smith, marching off towards the pub.

Jones opened the pub door and held it open for his boss and Smith walked in to see Ted sat behind the bar, doing the crossword puzzle in the local newspaper.

'Mornin Ted, how are you this fine morning?' asked Smith cheerily.

'Mornin DI Smith, DS Jones, I'm fine, what do you think I've done now?' said Ted, laughing.

'Knowing you Ted it could be almost anything,' replied Jones smiling.

'Ted, sorry to trouble you, but we are checking on a Mr White and a Mr Parker, who we believe are or were staying here on the night of Oliver Tate's death,' said Smith, now in a more business-like manner.

'Aye, I was just reading the headline on that.' Ted closed the paper and passed it to Smith, who was clearly not happy at seeing the headline on the front page of the *Yorksbey News.*

'Sorry sir, I was going to tell you about that,' Jones said apologetically.

'Not your fault Jones, you don't write or print newspaper headlines.'

'I think most red-blooded men, and even some women, will gloss over the headline, I think their eyes will be drawn to Cat Woman, she looks rather sexy, don't you think?' Ted said smiling.

'I suppose so,' said Smith, realising that Ted was possibly right, and hoping maybe, he wouldn't get any more pressure from Peel for the headline.

'Ted, back to why we are here.'

'Yes, sure. Mr White and Mr Parker were both staying here that night, they had night keys and got back here about 1:30 am, after being out for most of the evening, I think at the *Ball*. They were both drinking as residents after the pub was closed, I left them to it when I turned in.'

'What time was that Ted?' asked Jones, keen to establish a timeline on the two suspects.

'It was getting late, must have been about 2 am, maybe a bit later. Is it important?'

'It could be Ted, it could be,' said Smith, clearly considering the implications of the suspects movements.

'Ted, I know this is a nice area, but do you have CCTV cameras?' asked Smith, now wanting to confirm his thoughts.

'We do, but really just of the carpark and the entrance.'

'How long do you keep the images or more to the point how often do you delete images,' asked Jones, latching onto his bosses thought process.

'Depends really, we aren't very security conscious here as you said, it's a nice area, so we usually delete the files once a week,' said Ted, trying to think when he had last wiped the files.

'If nothing's happened and I'm in the right mood I might even do it more frequently.'

Smith was hoping that Ted hadn't been too conscientious of late and asked, 'Have you deleted the files for last Friday night and Saturday?' fearing the worst.

'Funny you should ask that,' said Ted. 'But no, I haven't.'

'That's very positive, a bit of good news for a change, can we review the files then?' asked Smith, quite relieved at the sudden good fortune.

'You sure can,' said Ted, leading them through to his office where he let them view the CCTV images.

About ten minutes later they all emerged from the office.

'Thanks Ted, that's been very worthwhile,' said Smith, pleased with what he had seen, but not convinced the CCTV was fully conclusive, but urgently needed following up on.

'One more thing, are Mr White and Mr Parker still here, or have they checked out?'

'Mr Parker checked out on Saturday, and while Mr White was due to leave a few days ago, he extended his stay, but I haven't seen him for the last couple of days.'

'Did Parker provide his home address?' asked Jones, notebook at the ready.

'It will be in the register, you can have his details and also Mr White, albeit with data protection laws now, I'm not sure if you are supposed to get a warrant,' Ted said, trying to be helpful to his local law enforcement, but concerned he could potentially get into trouble for giving out the information without a warrant.

'Ted, you are correct, we do legally need a warrant, but it would save us some time if you could perhaps just let us have a quick look at your registration book.'

'Look, here it is, I won't say anything if you don't,' said Ted, winking at the officers.

'Thanks Ted, it will just save us a lot of grief, and one other thing, if you could give us a call when Mr White shows up that would be great,' said Jones, passing Ted one of his cards as he made a quick mental note of Parker's and White's home addresses.

'Jones, I think you need to get onto *Barnsley Nick,* ASAP and get them to see if Parker is at home, we need to talk to him, he needs to answer a few questions,' said Smith, who sensed that things might be slowly coming together at last.

CHAPTER 62 - INCRIMINATING EVIDENCE?

Smith and Jones drove the short distance from the Watermill Arms, up through Edendale to the golf club and they both parked up and made their way to the foyer. They were now seeking to get permission to look around the vicinity of the crime scene but were mindful of not upsetting Earl Hargrove or the Major, as they definitely didn't need Peel on their case.

'The CCTV information at the pub looks helpful,' said Jones.

'Yes, but not fully conclusive, while there is evidence that Parker left the Pub, we don't know for certain where he went. Also, they are both smart enough to get out and avoid being seen on the limited cameras,' said Smith. He was not totally convinced the CCTV images provided either alibis, or enough incriminating evidence against the two suspects, but they definitely needed to follow up on things, and speak to Parker and White.

As they entered the foyer they saw a young waitress with a tray of used breakfast making her way towards the restaurant and the kitchen.

'Good morning, do you know where the Major is?' asked Jones politely.

'If he's not in his office I think he's more than likely to be in the restaurant, I think he was in there earlier with Jarvis,' replied the waitress, being her usual helpful self.

'Thank you,' said Jones, smiling at the pretty young waitress.

'You're welcome.....Err, excuse me I hope you don't thing I'm speaking out of turn, but when Pat interviewed me, sorry PC Perfect, interviewed me, she said that if I remembered anything, to let her know.'

'Sorry, you are?' asked Smith, rather abruptly.

'I'm Nancy, I'm a waitress here.'

'Ah, yes, I think I remember you,' said Jones, looking at his note book. 'No, please feel free to talk with us, have you remembered something you think may be relevant to our enquiries?'

'Well, it's probably nothing, but I recall the Major and Earl Hargrove discussing the ballot for the Chairmen while I was serving them with drinks.'

'Go on,' said Jones encouragingly. 'When was this?'

'I think it was a couple of weeks ago, is the actual date important?'

'Maybe, maybe not, but go on,' said Jones cheerfully.

'Well, Earl Hargrove said something strange, well it seemed strange to me. That's why I remember it.....' continued Nancy, blushing slightly in embarrassment at potentially getting someone like Earl Hargrove into trouble.

'Please continue,' urged Smith, now in a rather more mollifying manner.

'....Earl Hargrove, said, "I think we need to ensure that the vote goes our way, Major, *do what you have too, and I mean do anything*, let's be clear Oliver Tate will not be the next Chairman, I will stake my life on it..... "or something like that,' said Nancy. Now wishing that perhaps she hadn't mentioned it.

'Thank you, young lady, you did the right thing in letting us know,' said Smith, in a sympathetic tone, seeing that the waitress was slightly over whelmed.

'Don't you worry anymore about it, but we'll follow up on your statement. It's okay, you can go now.'

'Okay, but I don't want to get anyone into trouble, I just thought I should let you know. I'll go then.' Nancy wandered off towards the restaurant, slightly reassured by the response she received, but still a little worried.

'Well Jones, I trust you have made a note of that, we'll follow up on that later.'

'You know me sir, all in my little black book.'

The two officers signed into the visitor's book and then walked along to the Major's office and Smith knocked on the door.

'Come,' said the Major in his normal brisk way.

'Ah, good morning Major, how are you today,' said Smith pleasantly.

The Major's office was like him, perfect in every detail. A place for everything and everything in its place. His desk in front of him had everything neatly located and positioned, it was a perfect example of how you would expect a former Major's office.

'Morning DI Smith, DS Jones, I was okay. I had been hoping that you two had concluded your business. What can I do for you?' said the Major, not bothering to offer the two officers a seat or a drink and was clearly in no great mood for pleasantries.

'Yes, I'm sure you had, we are sorry to trouble you, but we were wondering if we could re-visit the crime scene, we wanted to do this informally so as to not cause you and the members too much inconvenience,' added Smith, trying to be as ingratiating as possible in the circumstances.

'Well, that's good of you I suppose. Yes, you can, but try not to get in the way of play, some of the members can be rather.....awkward,' added the Major.

'Awkward? I can't believe that,' said Smith sarcastically, before adding, 'I can't see where they would get that from, but that would be most helpful.'

'Mmm,' replied the Major, not impressed with Smith's reply.

As the two officers turned to leave, Smith stopped and casually asked, 'I don't suppose you know if Earl Hargrove will be coming here this morning?'

'What's today. Ah, yes he's usually here about 11 am, shall I say you would like to see him?' asked the Major, curious as to why Smith was after Earl Hargrove.

'It's not important, but yes if you would let him know I would like a word, that would be most helpful. Oh, and one final thing Major, do you own a handgun? I know many ex-servicemen do.'

'A pistol, no I don't, any reason you ask?'

'No, just checking,' said Smith mischievously. With that the two officers left the office and made their way out and to the course leaving the Major contemplating why they wanted to speak to Earl Hargrove.

They walked down the now familiar path towards the 1st Tee and then the 4th Green, both officers looking out for potential murder weapons, but the golf course was kept immaculately, and no obvious items were apparent, just an oasis of grass and wonderful mature trees.

Luckily by the time they got to the 4th Green there was no one playing that hole. They looked around the immediate vicinity and close by, but there were clearly no objects that looked out of place, only lots of open spaces and wonderfully manicured greens and finely cut fairways. The 4th Green though, was also close to the railway embankment on one side with the potential for a weapon to have be discarded and not readily seen, so the two detectives split up and walked along the base of the embankment in opposite directions. They both walked about one hundred metres but neither found anything that remotely looked like a potential murder weapon. About thirty minutes later they both decided to give up and turned around and they walked back towards one another.

As they met up, Smith asked, 'Anything?' not expecting any positive news.

'No, what about you?'

'No, nothing. It's not looking hopeful, is it?'

'Certainly isn't,' answered Jones, before he added, 'Shall we just ask Pat, I mean, PC Perfect, to do one final recce along both sides of the embankment, it's about all we can do, but to be honest I'm not hopeful of finding anything.'

'Yes, okay, get Perfect to walk the full length, it's the only likely area on the course where something could have been discarded, or thrown,' said Smith, before adding. 'Come on let's go back and see if we can see Earl Hargrove.'

As they made their way back towards the club house, and under the railway bridge, they were fortunate to see Earl Hargrove and his prospective playing partner walking towards them, both with electric golf trollies, the two of them wearing quite traditional golf attire, and nothing too outrageous.

'Good morning DI Smith, DS Jones, I gather from the Major you wanted a word. If you could be quick I would appreciate it, I'm just about to start my round.'

'Good morning Earl Hargrove, Sir,' said Smith, nodding to the Earl's playing partner, who nodded in return. 'Yes, just a quick question, but it might be more appropriate in private.'

'Mmm, yes, see what you mean. Gerald, would you mind, I'll catch you up shortly at the first if that's okay,' said the Earl, in more of a statement than a request.

'No, that's fine David.' With that, the Earl's friend and playing partner carried on walking.

'Thank you. Sorry about this My Lord, just a couple of points that we would like you to clarify, the first is do you own a handgun?'

'No, I have a shot gun and licence all properly certified and locked up, but no revolver, never had the need.'

'Very good, and one final point, it's just that a witness has relayed to us something they overheard, while you were talking to the Major, a couple of weeks ago and we just wanted your take on it,' said Smith, in the most friendly and unassuming manner he could muster.

'Sounds like tittle tattle to me, who was it? but go on,' said Earl Hargrove, clearly concerned about what was coming.

'Well actually, it was a waitress in the club, apparently they heard you say; "…..we need to ensure that the vote goes our way Major, *do what you have too, and I mean do anything*, Tate will not be the next Chairman, I'll stake my life on it…..."

'Smith, I don't know what you're implying?' said Earl Hargrove, in a very stern manner, looking Smith directly in the eye and holding his stare.

'My Lord, I'm not implying anything, it's just something that we need you to clarify, having been given the testimony, we have to follow up on it. I'm sure you understand.'

'Mmm, I suppose so, what has the Major said?' asked Earl Hargrove. Mindful that the club secretary, could back him up, or hang him out to dry.

'Well, what the Major said is currently a matter for the record,' said Smith, bluffing and hoping he didn't have to say anything further.

'Look Smith, you know how things are often said in the heat of battle, don't you agree?'

'I understand My Lord, but did you say it?'

'I may have said something along those lines, but as I said, things are often said when discussing matters, it sounds worse though, than it really was.'

'Oh does it?' added Smith, revelling slightly in the Earl's discomfort.

'It was more a matter of speech, no more than that. I was asking the Major to canvas as many members as possible, and you know, encourage them by any *legitimate* means to vote for Graham Brook,'

'Was it now?'

'Yes, it was. You can't think I meant anything more sinister,' added the Earl, nearly pleading with the inspector to see his point of view. 'I have a position to uphold.'

'I think, I know what you meant, and you have clarified matters from your perspective My Lord, I thank you for that.'

'Will you be taking it any further Inspector?' asked Earl Hargrove, clearly seeking a positive response.

'Jones has made a note of your clarification and it will be added to the other evidence, but unless you were the killer, you don't really have anything to worry about, do you?' said Smith, with a twinkle in his eye and a slight grin.

'No, No I don't,' said Earl Hargrove, before adding. 'Right, I'll go and find my partner, goodbye,' as he marched off, not quite sure what to make of the encounter.

'No more than you expected?' asked Jones.

'No, not really,'

'You were a little previous about the Major, we haven't even said anything to him.'

'No, but he didn't know that did he,' said Smith, smiling broadly.

'Do you think he did it?' asked Jones without conviction.

'Nah, I would be really surprised, but then again, he did have, means, motive, and opportunity, albeit with his wife as an alibi,' concluded Smith, as the two officers continued on their way back towards the golf club and their cars.

CHAPTER 63 - DINNER DATES

'It wasn't Cliff's fault he lost Charlotte, it could have happened to anyone,' said Edee, defending Cliff as she always did.

CJ and Edee were sat in CJ's office around the coffee table, both drinking a cappuccino while contemplating recent events including Smith and Jones olive branch, and request to help solve the ongoing crime(s).

'I realise that Edee, it's just a bit frustrating. What is Charlotte doing being involved with a low life like Parker?'

'I know, something doesn't add up, unless the two of them were involved with Tate's death.'

'If what Jones has told you is correct, then it is possible Parker made his way from the Watermill Arms along the 8th (Par 4 - 435 Yards) 16th (Par 4 - 450 Yards) and 5th (Par 5 – 540 Yards) Fairways to the 4th Green. It's only about a mile, so fifteen minutes at a fast walk, less if he ran, so definitely doable,' said CJ, reconciling in his head the likelihood of that occurring.

'But from what you have learnt, it was Parker that told Tate of Charlotte's adultery, and she called him a liar,' said Edee, also annoyed that Charlotte had said she'd had sex with *Lawrence of Arabia* on the night of the *Ball*.

'Yes, but that may just have been a ploy to distract us,' said CJ, trying to resolve all the available facts.

'On another subject, how was your trip to London?' asked Edee.

'It was satisfactory, all went to plan at Hatton Garden as I had hoped, very rewarding,' said CJ, but still being rather non-committal.

Just then there was a knock at the front door and a newspaper was pushed through the letter box, Oscar was there in a flash, and he grabbed the paper in his mouth and ran to CJ and placed it at his feet.

'Good boy, thanks Oscar,' said CJ, rubbing Oscar's ear, before abruptly stopping, as he picked up the Yorksbey News, seeing the front-page headline and *the picture*. He quickly closed it up and threw it onto the table, rear page uppermost.

'What's the headline?' asked Edee. 'Anything interesting?'

CJ was now caught in a dilemma, tell the truth, or try and bluff out a lie.

Edee solved the quandary for him, as she picked up the paper and opened it up.

'I can see why you didn't want to look at it or say anything,' she said laughing.

'Nice picture of you though OO7, whose that Cat Woman, do I know her?' said Edee, teasing CJ.

'Okay, don't rub it in, I know I cocked up,' said CJ, with a wry smile, before continuing, 'It reminds me, have you sorted your Charity Ball Dinner Date?' asked CJ, considering he had hoped to be taking Edee rather than Charlotte.

'It's odd, I have *Lawrence of Arabia's* phone number from the list in the golf club, but he hasn't divulged his name, albeit we think it's Mr White, based upon the photos taken by Cliff and his earlier encounter.'

'Well at least you now have the opportunity to dig a bit further into his involvement and how we are to implicate him in the smuggling. You can use your female charm over dinner,' replied CJ.

'That's my intention.'

'When are you meeting him?' asked CJ, feeling even more jealous as they discussed matters.

'It's tonight, I've agreed to pick him up from the Watermill Arms at 7:30 pm.'

'That's a coincidence, Charlotte has also asked to pick me up tonight.'

Suddenly it was Edee's turn to feel the sensation of envy creeping over her. She would have traded the dinner with Lawrence of Arabia in a heartbeat to be with CJ that evening.

'Oh,' said Edee, unsure what else to say in the circumstances.

'Not that I'm looking forward to it,' said CJ, making Edee feel slightly better, before he added. 'But like you, perhaps I will get the chance to find out a bit more about her involvement with Parker.'

'As you're with Charlotte this evening can I call Cliff and say he can take the night off, as he doesn't need to keep tabs on her?' asked Edee.

'Yes, I'm sure he would like a break from the boring observation job.'

CHAPTER 64 - THE NIGHT OUT

Charlotte pulled up her black Audi TT RS outside the front door of Overhear Manor as previously agreed with CJ, she had surprisingly offered to be chauffeur for the evening for some reason, unbeknownst to her guest. CJ walked down the steps, he looked smart in his dark grey double-breasted suit and open necked white shirt and black oxford shoes. He looked back at Oscar who was sat nose hard up to the glass window of the lounge, unsure as to why his master was leaving him, CJ smiled at the dog, and then turned back towards the car.

He was not particularly looking forward to the evening, but in the spirit of the charity event he would be courteous and polite to the flirtatious vamp who was his partner for the evening. He opened the car door and slid in beside Charlotte, he nearly choked on her expensive perfume which filled the confined air of the sports car,

'Good evening, Charlotte,' and he kissed her gently on the cheek, he had to admit she looked stunning in her *Little Black Dress*, perhaps a little too much for him, but she did scrub up well, perhaps the evening wasn't going to be as bad as he had first thought. The only remaining concern he did have was how she was going to drive the car in the killer Christian Louboutin stiletto shoes, which were her trade mark, the one thing she seemed to have in common with Edee.

'Good evening James, you look very dapper this evening, now hang onto your hat.'

Charlotte floored the accelerator and spun the car around the ornamental fountain, gravel flying in all directions, and they were off to Oak Hall......

.... having paid the bill with a generous tip, CJ had returned from the little boy's room and downed the last of the red wine from his glass, he suddenly felt rather light headed, and he didn't think he'd drunk that much.

Charlotte though, had proven to be quite an entertaining dinner guest, and he was rather surprised how relaxed she appeared considering her husband had died only a matter of days ago, but as she explained, if you have been accused of adultery and hit around your face, any remaining love or affection quickly fades

CJ however, remained open minded, although his impression of her had been changed slightly and to be honest for the better. She had enlightened him as to her tough upbringing and bullying father, also the things she enjoyed and those she didn't, plus the reasons around her marriage to Bart, and also why her marriage had deteriorated over the past few months. She also told him, one or two rather bawdy but funny jokes and anecdotes which made him laugh out loud.

He on the other hand had been his normal discreet and guarded self, he rarely let people into his inner feelings.

'I think it's time we left Charlotte, thank you for a most pleasant evening.'

As they stood, not for the first time that evening, he looked over towards Edee and Mr White. They had from what CJ could make out, also had a pleasant evening, they had been in intense discussion at times, but he had also heard them enjoying a laugh together. A knot tightened in his stomach at the jealousy he felt, and if it weren't for his own stupidity, he would have been the one enjoying Edee's company rather than the Emirati.

He knew however that she would get any useful information out of him far easier than he would in any normal conversation, her wily ways might just get him to drop his guard.

Edee, raised her hand slightly and waved to them, smiling serenely, her guest instantly turned his head towards them and smiled broadly at them both. CJ was convinced the gesture was purely aimed at his partner, as Charlotte raised her hand and winked while smiling back in return. CJ nodded an acknowledgement, as Charlotte linked arms with him and they walked arm in arm towards the exit and the car park, thanking the waiter and waitresses for a wonderful evening as they left the magnificent restaurant.

The cool night air hit him like a hammer, but he felt hot and sweaty, and suddenly rather uninhibited. Charlottes high heels slipped on the gravel car park, and she held him tight, as they reached her little black sports car.

She pulled him close, her hands entwined around his neck.

'What say we take this a bit further CJ, I can feel you would like to, and I would too, my pussy is aching for you.'

Charlotte reached up to kiss him, CJ leant forward in response to the affection shown, her sexy body in the *LBD* with her heady perfume momentarily catching him off guard.

He suddenly realised it was wrong, and was shot back to reality.

'What are you… we, doing?' he said.

He suddenly recognised the carnal lust he felt, and the immediate fulfilment he knew he would subsequently enjoy with the release and the filling of Charlottes hot sex, in unadulterated rampant intercourse, was not worth the guilt and burden his heart would forever feel, following a moments instant gratification.

'You can't blame a good woman for trying,' said Charlotte, smiling longingly at CJ as she remotely unlocked the car.

CJ opened the driver's door and Charlotte slid into the figure-hugging seat, he closed the door, the 2.5 litre turbocharged engine instantly roared into life, the window lowered, and Charlotte looked out and said, 'She's a very lucky woman, I hope she's worth it CJ, but if you ever need a hot cat to play with, you know where to find me.' With that she winked and blue him a kiss.

At that very moment he heard Edee and Mr White, they were at the top of the veranda steps, he suddenly wondered how long they had been there, and what had they seen. Fear filled him as his head again started to swim.

The Emirati bowed graciously and took Edee's hand and kissed it, just like the night of the ball, he appeared again to be a near perfect gentleman, she thanked him and gave him back his jacket that was draped around the shoulders of her *LBD*, he turned and coolly walked towards the Audi TT.

'Your carriage and partner await.' CJ bowed and opened the passenger door. 'I think you two are far more suited.'

Mr White nodded towards CJ, and he climbed into the car, and he kissed Charlotte on the cheek. CJ closed the door and the car instantly sped off, gravel and smoke left in its trail.

Edee started to cautiously walk down the steps in her trade mark high heels and CJ moved to meet her, he briefly lost his balance, his head spinning even more, she precariously ran down the last steps and caught him before he hit the hard stone.

'James. Are you okay?' she anxiously enquired.

'I think Charlotte may have spiked my drink,' he slurred, as she gently lowered him down and they both sat on the steps, CJ with his head in his hands.

Edee looked concerned but CJ appeared to have slightly regained his composure.

'Thanks Edee,... I do love you Eden Songe,' he incoherently garbled.

She smiled and replied, 'I love you too, CJ Gray,' as she recognised he was now quite confused.

The evening was slowly turning into a complete role reversal of the Charity Night Ball.

Fifteen minutes later the metallic blue BMW Z4, turned in towards the gates of Overhear Manor, the registration recognised by the Manors security system so Edee could always drive in, without having to request the gates be opened.

CJ was sound asleep, snoring softly in the front passenger seat and Edee was a little concerned, albeit she had previously seen the effects on other victims of *Date Rape Drugs* and other similar stimulates, to know that CJ would be fine after sleeping it off, he might however have a thick head and the need for some paracetamol in the morning.

The car pulled up outside the front door which instantly opened, light flooded the area and Oscar ran out seeking his master. Mrs Wembley stood at the top of the stone steps as Edee got out of the car, she greeted her with a broad smile, happy to see her with Master James.

'Good evening, Madame Edee, this is becoming a habit, I hadn't seen you for a while and then twice within a few days.'

Suddenly though, Mrs Wembley panicked as she could see CJ in the front seat, comatose, 'Is Master James alright?' she urgently enquired.

'I think he will be okay; I believe his drink has been spiked. Can you please give me a hand to get him inside?'

'Of course,' replied Mrs Wembley, as she raced down the steps.

The two women struggled, but eventually managed to manipulate the dead weight of CJ, Oscar running around wildly, not helping, unsure what was wrong with his master. They finally lowered CJ onto one of the large sofas in the lounge and they both collapsed exhausted next to him, Oscar jumping on top of CJ, who remained completely unresponsive.

Oscar licked him profusely with no affect, and he finally gave up and curled up in a ball at his feet, slightly confused but keeping guard of his master.

'Will he be okay?' Mrs Wembley enquired again.

'He'll be fine after a good night's sleep,' Edee reassured her.

'I'll go and get him a blanket; will you take off his jacket and shoes, I'll then go and make up your old room in the South Wing Guest Room.'

Edee tucked CJ up lovingly in the blanket provided by Mrs Wembley, as he unknowingly whispered. 'I do love you; you know?'

'And I love you,' she whispered. She gently kissed the top of his head and stroked the loyal dog who was remaining on guard. 'Look after him for me Oscar.'

She turned off the lights, and quietly left, closing the double doors and made her way up the stairs to her old room, considering as she went, the nights events.

As she climbed the stairs she also realised how much she missed the old place, but knew she had one more task to do that evening and she pulled out her phone and typed the following message:

'White with CT, not sure where though.'

She pressed send and the messaged winged its way to the recipient.

CHAPTER 65 - BACK TO MY PLACE

Charlotte, turned briefly towards her passenger before ensuring her eyes were back on the road, with the speed she was driving all her concentration was really required to ensure the car remained on the tight narrow lanes from Oak Hall.

'Well Saheed, back to my place, I fancy some passionate love making, what say you?'

'I think I can oblige you in that regard Charlie,' he replied smiling.

Charlotte took her hand from the gear lever and gently caressed his crotch.

'Oh, I think you certainly can,' she said, relishing the thought of what lay in store, as he involuntarily breathed in at her touch.

'How was your evening Charlie?' he asked curiously.

'It was okay actually, but CJ Gray is rather a closed book, but the meal was wonderful as always, excellent restaurant and I wasn't paying. How about you?'

'Madame Songe is rather a charming woman, she has many stories and anecdotes to tell, but I find her rather enigmatic, I prefer my women to be, shall we say, more obvious,' he replied, turning, and smiling knowingly at Charlotte.

'Oh, I know what you mean,' said Charlotte, briefly turning to him and kissing him on the cheek.

He quickly grabbed the steering wheel to ensure the car didn't hit the verge, 'Eyes on the road, hands on the wheel I think, I would like to see the night out.'

He then gently pulled up her LBD and caressed her clitoris which was free of any panties.

'Oh, that is nice,' sighed Charlotte, momentarily closing her eyes and relishing his touch. 'But if you continue I think you will definitely end up in the ditch.'

He removed his hand and licked his fingers.

'Your sex tastes good, I think we are in for some fun!'

She looked across and said, 'I do hope so,' while smiling and giving him one of her infamous winks.

Charlotte pulled up at the gates to Tate House and lowered the window and punched in the code on the security gate keypad.

She looked up towards the house as the gate slid open, the light was on in Justin's room, but she was not overly concerned at her step son's opinion of her, bringing someone home so soon after his father's death, she knew that Justin respected his dad purely because of his money, nothing more.

His morals and principles were no better than her own.

Having driven up the long sweeping driveway, she parked the car next to Justin's BMW M4. She leant across and gently bit on the Arabs ear lobe, before whispering, 'Come on Tiger, let's go and enjoy ourselves.'

She opened the door of the small sports car and slid out, grateful that there were no photographers or onlookers to witness the view her spreadeagled legs offered.

He followed suit and the two of them met at the front of the car, where Charlotte placed her arms around his neck, while he pulled her towards him, his hands firmly around her sexy bottom and the two of them kissed passionately, as though their lives depended on it.

Her tongue searched for his and instantly found the target, he gently caressed her flesh, grinding his body against hers, she responded fervently.

He loosened his grip with his right hand and began caressing her breasts as she gently moaned while still ardently kissing him.

She pulled her lips away from his to take a breath and said, 'Not here, upstairs,' before kissing him again and then gently biting his lower lip.

She removed her hands from his neck and grabbed his hand and led him towards the front door, 'You're in for a treat, come on, follow me.'

CHAPTER 66 - THE MORNING AFTER

CJ's sleep had been disturbed, his vivid dreams were mixed with the real events of the previous evening, until he was unsure what was real and what was fantasy.

The drug had messed with his subconscious. His manhood had seemed at times in the still of night, to throb and ache at the visions of him having wild sex with Charlotte one moment, while making sensual love to the PVC Cat Woman the next. He fell into and out of deep sleep all night, until he suddenly woke, just before he was about to orgasm having sex with Edee on the bonnet of Charlottes Audi TT in the middle of the 18th Fairway.

His eyes suddenly open and awake. He looked around, it was pitch dark, Oscar quickly jumped up and lay his head on his masters, seeking a fondly ear scratch, CJ though, was alone and still fully clothed, his head thumping like a robber's dog. He then fell back into what was a restless but fortunately, a dreamless sleep.

Edee had risen early, her sleep had been at times slightly unsettled as she had worried about CJ, but after a refreshing shower she felt better. She took a towelling robe from the guest en-suite, and she strolled downstairs and checked in on CJ, who was still snoring loudly. Oscar though took the opportunity to nip out and get a fond rub around the ears from his favourite lady.

They both strolled through to the kitchen where Mrs Wembley was making coffee.

'Good morning Mrs Wembley, how are you today?'

The sun was already shining, but the sky looked a little threatening like rain was due, but still it was a good day to be alive.

'I'm fine dear, did you sleep well? I checked Master James earlier and he was still sound asleep, I hope he will be okay?'

'The bed was wonderful as usual, yes I also checked on James, I think he'll be fine.'

'Excuse me Mrs Wembley, has Jemima left any clothes here? I only have my dress and heels from last night with me,' Edee enquired.

'Of course dear, Miss Jemima has lots of things here, in case she stays over unexpectantly, let's go and have a look in her room after I've fed Oscar.'

CJ finally woke, the late morning light was streaming through the lounge windows, the curtains hadn't been drawn as they rarely were in the Manor.

He felt dreadful, he pulled the blanket from him and gingerly pulled himself into a sitting position.

'Oh Fuck!' That's not good.

No Oscar, that was also strange.

He was still in shirt, trousers, and socks, but no shoes or jacket. He couldn't remember anything after going to the men's room at Oak Hall, other than the vivid dreams of his at times hallucinogenic sleep.

He dragged himself to his feet and looked down at the Long Drive towards the River Meadows, even in his current state, it still looked pretty damn good.

He slowly walked out and up the stairs to his bedroom, where he undressed and left his clothes, unlike him, scattered on the floor. He then went to the medicine cabinet in the en-suite and took out two paracetamol and two ibuprofen and threw them into his mouth, and washed them down with a glass of water.

'Kill or Cure,' he thought.

Following a quick shave, he spent the next twenty minutes in the walk-in plunge shower, alternating between hot and cold water in an attempt to drag his mind and body into something resembling life.

He had become used to the extremes of showers during his military career, sometimes the extremes were potentially life threatening or alternatively life giving, depending on where he had been and what the water temperature. He had witnessed water, hot enough that it felt it could strip you skin, while he had also faced the other extreme of being cold enough to freeze a young polar bear's arse.

He finally felt a little better, and he turned the powerful head of water off, regrettably his head was still as thick as fog, he pulled a fluffy towel from the rail and vigorously dried himself.

He walked over, still naked to the North window overlooking the 10th Green, there was luckily currently no one playing the 9th or 10th. He stretched his arms over his head and yawned, just then, he noticed Edee coming through the garden gate with Oscar racing back and forth.

As always, she looked wonderful, tight beige riding jodhpurs and riding boots with a black skinny rib turtle neck jumper, she looked just like Jemima did when she went horse riding. He then suddenly wondered what she was doing there, and what was she doing in Jemima's clothes. It suddenly dawned on him that he also didn't know how he got home last night.

Was it his partner for the evening, the flirtatious Charlotte, or by the look of it, was it most probably Edee, who got him home, he needed to find out because his mind was currently a complete blank.

He smiled and waved to Edee, who looked up and waved back laughing, as CJ quickly covered his modesty, and also started laughing.

Presently, having got dressed into black chinos, dark grey tee shirt and brown brogues, he ventured warily down stairs to the kitchen.

Mrs Wembley was preparing food at the large island, while Edee was sat at the far end on a tall bar stool, chatting easily with the convivial House Keeper.

'Here he is at last Mrs Wembley,' Edee teased.

'Good morning Master James, are we feeling any better?' Mrs Wembley enquired.

'I feel slightly better, but not 100%. What happened?'

'It's a bit of a long story, but I fetched some Baguettes and Pain au Chocolat from the bakers to go with your Cappuccino. French fare you like, let's find a comfy seat and I'll fill you in,' Edee suggested, as they linked arms, and strolled off to the orangery.

Chapter 67 - We have a warrant

Charlotte lay on the super king-sized bed, looking at a man she admired, or thought she admired, rather than the normal one that used to lay there that she despised, but had reluctantly slept with for the past two years, who was now dead. She was contemplating where the recent events left her and what she truly wanted from life.

Was the rugged good-looking Emirati what she truly wanted, or was it something that she currently just needed, a stepping stone on her ongoing journey through life, she wasn't really sure.

Last night had been great, the sex once again was wonderful, possibly the best it had been with him, but was that what she really desired, while lust and sex were instantly gratifying, her conversations over dinner with CJ Gray had perhaps opened her mind to other things in life, she had surprisingly enjoyed the conversation and interaction, something she hadn't felt before.

Was she now looking for true love, or was that just a dream of impressionable young girls, and was the road she currently trod, a more sensible and realistic way of life for her. Was being married to a man that could provide her with the material things in life she required, while snatching moments of fulfilling sex with willing and undemanding partners, her true path.

She was dragged from her day dreaming by Justin.

'Charlotte, we are going now, I'll let you know when I'll be back, I might spend a few day's at Mum's,' he shouted out from downstairs.

Charlotte slipped off the bed and wrapped her silk robe around her and opened the bedroom door and then closed it quietly behind her and walked to the top of the stairs.

'No worries, you take care Justin, I'll see you some time,' she said, so only he could hear.

'Are you okay Charlotte? you sound,…… I don't know, different.'

'I'm fine, you take care of yourself Justin…..
Goodbye.'

'Goodbye Charlotte,' said Justin, closing the front door, thinking that life was perhaps changing for both of them.

She walked back to the bedroom and quietly opened the door, but her lover wasn't there, but she could hear the shower in the en-suite and realised she must have woken him.

She walked to the doorway and looked at him, so athletic and muscular.

'Sorry I woke you, is there room for a little one?' she asked, letting the robe fall from her shoulders onto the tiled floor.

'It's a good job you did, I've overslept; I really need to get going,' he replied resolutely, turning off the shower and wiping the excess water from his arms, legs and body and running his hands through his hair.

'Oh,' said Charlotte, surprised at being turned down by a man. That was a first!

'Okay, I'll get a shower now you've done. Help yourself to some breakfast, there's plenty of food in the kitchen, plus fruit juice and coffee,' she continued, slightly downcast.

He turned and picked a towel off the rail and started drying himself.

'Thanks Charlie,' he said as he absentmindedly kissed her on the cheek as she passed him.

Another first, she thought, perhaps he's not really….. the one.

Charlotte turned on the shower and relished the powerful spray which fleetingly invigorated her.

She quickly washed and as she turned off the shower she called out.

'What are your plans then?'

But there was no answer. She wandered into the bedroom, drying herself as she went, but the room was empty. Good job he's not that quick making love, she idly thought.

She quickly got dressed. Tight fitting silk blouse and skinny fit jeans, with her trade mark heels in the form of over the knee black boots, which she considered suitable, having looked out of the window at the rain starting to fall, the early morning sun and clear blue sky having given way, to grey leaden clouds.

She sat at the dressing table, looked at the reflection, and smiled weakly, she suddenly felt down, which was unusual.

She put on the slightest of makeup, with some neutral lip gloss, giving her the most natural look she could ever remember having, and tied her damp hair in a bun.

'Charlie. Charlie.' She heard her name being called.

'Coming.'

She quickly threw the quilt over the bed and made an attempt to make it look at least reasonable, before marching out.

'Charlie,' he called, now more urgently.

'Yes,' she said, rather coldly as she reached the top of the stairs and looked down.

'Where are the garage door keys?'

'What.'

'The garage door keys where are they? I need them now.'

Charlotte was not impressed, the normally polite and charming Saheed, was suddenly acting like many of the other men she had known, selfish, boring, and demanding.

'They're on the key rack in the utility room near the back door. Why do you ask?'

'I'm taking the Aston Martin.'

'Whoa there, what do you mean?'

'Your husband stole my diamonds, and I can't find them, so I'm taking the car in fair exchange. Like it or lump it.'

'Diamonds, what are you talking about diamonds?'

'Look Charlie, I'm taking the car, end of story.'

Charlotte suddenly realised this was a battle she couldn't win, but what did she care, the car was for someone else, she knew that, let him have it.

'Okay Saheed, take it, it's not mine.'

'Charlie are you coming?' he asked, more in expectation, rather than a question.

Charlotte was suddenly torn, twenty minutes ago she would have driven off with him in a flash, now she wasn't so sure.

'No, I think I'll pass,' she said, in a faint voice, tears pricking her eyes.

'Your choice Charlie, I'm off, I'll see you again sometime, I hope.' And with that he stormed off towards the utility room.

Charlotte, sat on the top step of the wide marble stairs, contemplating what was happening, had she done the right thing, tears welling in her eyes

She then heard the Aston Martin pull up outside the front door as it stopped, and she heard the door slam.

Suddenly the front door opened, and there he stood, so strong and purposeful.

'Are you coming or not?' he asked, still in a demanding, but slightly more conciliatory manner.

'Hang on,' she called, as she ran back and picked up her red rain coat from the walk-in wardrobe and quickly put it on, as she ran down the stairs and flung her arms around him and kissed him passionately, 'Oh Saheed, I don't know.'

The gate buzzer suddenly rang, then again and again.

'Let me get this. Please wait, let's talk.'

She looked into his eyes imploring him to at least stay for a while.

Charlotte pressed the intercom.

'Yes, who is it?' she asked, clearly annoyed.

'Police, we have a warrant to search the premises, we are looking for Sabeed Alham, aka, Mr White.'

'What!, What do you mean?' said Charlotte looking at Saheed and shrugging her shoulders. 'Who's Mr White?'

Mr White pulled a Glock from his belt, and pointed it at Charlotte threateningly.

'Charlie, do what I say, and you won't get hurt, don't and you will. Clear?'

Charlotte looked at him, suddenly with far different eyes and rather frightened. She slowly nodded her head.

'You're coming with me, please don't make a fuss,' he said.

'Release the front gate and get in the Aston Martin. NOW,' he continued, in a voice that meant exactly how it sounded.

Charlotte pressed the gate button and she quickly moved, Mr White grabbing her upper arm, forcibly moving her outside.

'Ow, that hursts,' she said, but he ignored her completely.

The gate was slowly sliding open, beyond it were three cars, two unmarked and one marked police car.

'Get in, quickly,' demanded Mr White, as he pulled open the passenger door.

Charlotte got in and Mr White slammed the door shut, he swiftly ran around the car and got in starting the engine which roared into life.

The three police cars started driving up the narrow sweeping driveway, and once they were about halfway to the house, Mr White slammed the car into gear and floored the accelerator, the rear wheels struggled to find grip as the gravel spewed out behind them, but as they did, he swung the wheel, and the car cut a path across the finely manicured lawn, directly towards the gate, leaving deep tyre marks in the fine green carpet.

Charlotte struggling to put her seatbelt on, shouted, 'The grass. The grass,' as huge wheel marks were left in the cars wake.

'Sod the fucking grass, now shut up,' said Mr White angrily.

Smith in the first of the police cars, and Jones behind, both suddenly realised what was going on, but couldn't go back because of the marked police car behind, so they had to keep going up towards the house.

Mr White struggled to keep the car in a straight line as he turned the wheel and the car oversteered dramatically, but he eased back slightly on the accelerator and regained control with a power slide onto the drive, and out of the gate.

He came to an abrupt stop and shouted at Charlotte.

'Open the fucking window.' As she did and the gate closed behind them he aimed his gun and fired at the intercom keypad.

'That should hold them for a while,' he said, as he floored the accelerator and drove out onto Edendale Lane.

Chapter 68 - Are you feeling better?

The Baguettes, Pain au Chocolat and Cappuccino were slowly having some positive effect, CJ's stomach felt better, his head though, was still not 100%, but it was becoming tolerable.

Edee had brought CJ up to speed on the evenings events from the point he could remember, and they were now considering them, and where that left the sting and who had killed Bart.

'I'm rather disappointed with Charlotte, we had quite a pleasant evening and I've seen another side to her, so for her to drug me like that, is pretty despicable.'

'Maybe she just wanted sex with you that bad,' said Edee, smiling at CJ.

'Very funny, I don't think.'

'She's a bit too obvious for me, I prefer my women, more subtle and enigmatic, you know that,' as he gently touched her hand and looked into her eyes. 'Thanks again, for looking after me last night,' he added.

Edee looked lovingly back at him, pleased that her efforts were appreciated.

Suddenly thinking of the night's events, she remembered something.

'You do know it may not have been her?'

'What do you mean?' said CJ questioning his *friend*.

'When you went to the little boy's room, White went over to talk with her. He had an opportunity to spike your drink.'

'I can't quite believe you are defending her, but you might be right, anyhow, it's all water under the bridge, there doesn't appear to be any long-term effects, albeit my dreams last night were very weird to say the least.'

'While Charlotte may be self-centred, I'd like to think she wouldn't stoop that low, but then again perhaps she might. Whoever did it though, did they think you were getting too close to the truth about Tate's death?' said Edee.

'Maybe, maybe not, but I take it your evening was okay, how was White or should I say Sabeed Alham?'

'He is rather handsome, and he was a gentleman, but to be honest not really my type. Albeit we had a pleasant evening, but he didn't let anything slip that we didn't already know.'

CJ was pleased that Edee had an enjoyable time, but was content her affections were not snatched from his grasp by the good-looking Emirati, but he already knew that White's extensive criminal dealings would not sit well with her.

'It was clear though from my gentle digging that he was clearly not Saheed Alham, but the identical twin brother of the man that runs Alham Industries, and as we knew, he is the master criminal known as Mr White, wanted by Interpol.'

'Yes, Cliff's visit had been very worthwhile and once we knew the connection between the twin brothers, setting things up was easier than I thought it would be.'

'I let Simon know that White and Charlotte left together last night, I'm not sure what they will do with the information, but at least they have an idea where he may be now.'

'Well done Edee that was good thinking.'

'Do you think he's involved in the murder?' asked Edee.

'No, I don't, I'm pretty sure I know who did it though, but I need to check our security cameras for the 9th Green, I'm just hoping if my hunch is right, the images will verify my theory. Come on let's go and check,' said CJ getting to his feet.

'Oh, so you think it may be Parker?' said Edee, suddenly latching onto CJ's thought process.

'I think he's involved, that is for certain.' And the two of them went to the study to check the Manor's hi-tech surveillance system.

Five minutes later they had the information they needed; the CCTV images were not brilliant, but the infrared technology showed that Parker had actually left the Watermill Arms, but that he didn't go to the golf club, he met an accomplice at the 9th Green at 2.30 am, and briefly discussed things, rather animatedly, but not reaching any sort of agreement. The two then went their own ways back to where they had both come from, Parker back towards the pub, and the likely killer back towards the clubhouse.

'That shows your theory still holds up James, but how are we going to prove it?' asked Edee curiously.

'I think I have an idea, but it will depend on a few things and the Aston Martin may still be key to flushing out the culprit. I think we need to go and speak with Smith and Jones about Parker, and where he is, as a matter of urgency.'

'Oscar are you coming?' said CJ. Which was rather a rhetorical question as he was instantly leading them to the front door.

'Edee, I think we'll take my car, as trying to get me and Oscar in your two-seater would be a bit of a tight squeeze.'

'Agreed, I'll come back later to pick it up,' said Edee, rather pleased, as it meant she would have an opportunity to be with CJ later in the day and possibly the evening.

With that they made their way to the garages and the Audi, having both picked up waterproof jackets as the rain was now falling quite heavily.

CHAPTER 69 - THE CHASE IS ON

CJ fired up the Audi and the powerful car pulled out of the garages, and along the drive, through the gates and onto Church Lane, the beautiful early spring sunshine having turned into a typical dull English day, but CJ was pleased to be alive, with Edee next to him and Oscar in the back, what could be better.

'I think we need Cliff to help flush out our killer,' said CJ, scrolling through the phone numbers on the dashboard screen before pressing *Cliff*. The phone rang twice and then he answered.

'Morning Governor, How are you?' he cheerily answered.

'Morning Cliff, I'm good, how are you?'

'You know another day, same shit, what can I do for you today sir?'

'Cliff can you please make your way to the Golf Club House, I would like you to help flush out our prospective killer, when you get their let me know and I'll let you know the plan.'

'Okay, we'll speak soon, bye.'

They continued on over the river bridge and onto Edendale Lane, under the viaduct in its usual splendour, up towards the golf club, the windscreen wipers now operating constantly due to the heavy rain.

Suddenly up ahead they saw a silver Aston Martin DB5, pull out of Tate House, clearly in a hurry.

'Is that what I think it is,' said Edee.

'It sure is, it's my DB5, I think we should follow, what say you?'

'I think your right, I wonder who's in it?'

As they continued up the road at just over the legal 40 mph, it was suddenly obvious the DB5 was in a hurry, it was moving ahead at great speed and was already turning left towards Etongate.

'Whoever's driving isn't hanging about,' said Edee.

'They sure aren't.'

CJ floored the accelerator, and the powerful car was soon doing 80 mph.

As they passed Tate House's gate they saw that police cars, with blue's and two's blaring, were coming down the driveway but were stopped by the security gate, which surprisingly remained closed.

'Hello, looks like Smith and Jones followed up on your message Edee.'

'Yep, but they appear to be somewhat stymied, looks like we had better follow that car,' she said smiling. 'Stop messing about James and get after it.'

The DB5 was already screaming up the road towards Etongate as the Audi approached the tee junction, and turned left.

White floored the accelerator and the back end of the DB5 slid out as he turned the wheel fully left onto Edendale lane, but he quickly increased the power and turned into the potential spin, regaining control and he quickly changed gears and the car was soon doing over 80 mph.

He looked in the rear mirror, 'Shit.'

'What is it?' asked Charlotte. Now quite frightened, who was this man she thought she knew.

'We've got company,' looks like Gray and Madame Songe are on our tail.'

Charlotte looked over her shoulder, 'Yes it sure looks like it. What are you going to do?'

'Well, I'm not stopping am I.'

As the car approached the tee junction he braked hard, changed down to 2nd, and pulled on the handbrake as he controlled the rear end, which broke away on the wet tarmac, with a perfect handbrake turn, before accelerating hard.

As they fast approached the next left junction ahead they were doing nearly 90 mph, but White new that Gray's car was far more powerful than the car he was driving, he couldn't out run them, not on the main roads.

'Where does the next left go Charlie?'

'Towards the train station at Edendale and then back towards Yorksbey along country lanes the long way around.'

He looked in the mirror, no sight of them, he again hit the brakes hard at the last minute and performed another near perfect handbrake turn, the tyres screaming as they tried to maintain grip on the wet road.

Luckily, there was no car coming the other way as the car slid sideways as they turned, taking up the whole width of the road.

'Come on old girl what have you got under the bonnet,' said White, as he again pushed the engine to its limits, the rev counter well into the red before he change gear.

They hit 60 mph in about 8 seconds and were again doing nearly 100 mph, 20 seconds later.

'Please slow down, you'll kill us both,' said Charlotte. Who was now quite fearful of what was happening, and for her life.

'Sorry Charlie, that's not happening.'

'Who are you? you look just like Saheed.'

'I'm Sabeed Alham. Saheed is my identical twin brother, he's the nice, honest one, I'm the ruthless black sheep of the family, but most people I deal with know me as Mr White, for obvious reasons.' He smiled, in some way pleased that his secret was out as far as Charlotte was concerned.

'Oh,' said Charlotte, trying to take it all in.

The RS6 traction control was fighting the power that CJ was seeking to transfer through the 4-wheel drive system and the tyres to the tarmac, they were soon driving at 100 mph, but the DB5 was nowhere to be seen.

'What the fuck,' said CJ. Unsure why he couldn't see the DB5 up the long straight ahead. While the Aston was quite quick for its age, its engine was based on technology that was nearly 60 years old, it only had 300 bhp, nothing compared with the Audi. 'Where had it gone?'

'Take the next left,' said Edee. 'I think they have turned off back towards Edendale Station.'

'Of course they have,' said CJ, thinking why he hadn't considered that.

As they approached the turning, Edee suddenly shouted, 'Look out!'

A lorry pulled out in front of them, CJ slammed on the brakes, the antilock system struggling to prevent a skid and failing dramatically.

'Fuck. Hang on,' shouted CJ, fearing the worst.

Edee grabbed onto the roof handle and braced herself for the impact.

CJ yanked the wheel hard left, the car slipped sideways, and came to a halt just millimetres from the lorry.

The lorry driver looked down from the cab and mouthed. 'Sorry.'

'Move it,' shouted CJ, as he gesticulated at the driver who obviously, and luckily, couldn't hear a word he was saying, but knew that CJ was far from pleased, albeit if you do 100 mph on normal roads you are potentially putting yourself and others at risk.

'You okay?' asked CJ.

'Yes, but my heart rate has just gone through the roof,' replied a thankful smiling Edee.

The lorry slowly moved on and the driver waved acknowledging his error in pulling out. CJ, selected drive and floored the accelerator again, but the road ahead was clear, no sign of the DB5.

The Audi quickly got back up to speed, and CJ was driving at times near to 100 mph, which for the narrow lane, he knew he was potentially pushing his luck.

'Do you think they turned back down towards Edendale, or straight onto the station?' he asked Edee.

'Who knows, it's a 50 / 50 toss up,' she replied, not helping CJ make up his mind.

He decided to keep going straight on towards the station, but there was still no sign of the DB5.

Shortly they could see the level crossing at Edendale Station, the gates were closed, and a train was pulling into the station on its way to Yorksbey, but no DB5 in sight.

'Bollocks, they have either beaten us to the crossing or gone the other way, it looks like no matter what, they have got away,' said a despondent CJ.

As they slowed to wait for the train to move off and the level crossing gates open, Edee looked to her left towards the station and the carpark.

'James, look it's the DB5, it's in the car park.'

CJ quickly turned the Audi into the carpark and the car slid to a stop on the loose gravel next to the empty Aston Martin.

'It looks like whoever it is, has abandoned the car and is going to get the train,' said CJ, before adding, 'Edee, check the boot just in case.'

They both quickly got out of the car and Oscar leapt after them, CJ running towards the station pulling open the doors to the ticket hall, but Oscar was now in front of him, sniffing for a trail.

No one in sight.

CJ looked around but there was no one, he looked towards the buffet area, the girl behind the till, pointed towards the platform, and the train that was about to leave.

CJ pulled open the door to the platform and again looked right, to only see the train guard as he blew his whistle and waved his flag.

He looked left, and there they were, Mr White with Charlotte being forcibly dragged along as they made their way towards the end of the platform, and the adjoining viaduct.

CJ ran towards them; Edee now close behind, having nearly caught up, luckily not having her usual stiletto heels, but the borrowed flat riding boots.

White and Charlotte were now on the viaduct as the train slowly started to pull out, smoke and steam filling the air.

'Stop there Gray, don't come any closer, I'll kill her.' said White, with malice, pulling Charlotte towards him, holding her tightly and pointing the Glock at her neck. 'I mean it.'

'Please CJ,' begged Charlotte. 'I think he really means it.'

'White, you can't get away with it, just let Charlotte go, she's done nothing to you,' pleaded CJ.

'I mean it, I'll kill her, don't come any closer.'

In the distance police sirens could be heard, Smith and Jones, having finally got through the security gate were now also in pursuit, but clearly too late to be of any help.

'Shit. He's going to jump onto the train at the last minute,' said CJ, trying to think how he could stop them. He then suddenly thought of something.

'Oscar. Go find.' The dog ran towards White and Charlotte and immediately sat down in front of Charlotte, nose in the air.

'Nice dog Gray, still so very obedient. You're a good boy aren't you,' said White, smiling at the dog. 'Like your master needs to be.' The rear of the train now slowly coming towards them.

'Please don't kill me?' pleaded Charlotte, now desperate and crying.

'Charlie I wouldn't do that.' Mr White pushed her to the ground, and he looked to leap onto the train from the narrow stone footpath that reached out along the long viaduct.

'White,' shouted CJ, seeking to distract him. Which it momentarily did, as White looked back as he was about to run for the guards van at the back of the last carriage.

'Oscar. Hup,' shouted CJ, as loud as he could over the steam, smoke and noise of the steam engine which was now building up speed.

Oscar leapt up.

His paws hitting White squarely on the top of his shoulders and his chest.

White was taken completely unawares, and lost his balance and footing, slipping on the wet mossy stone path and he fell backwards. His legs hit the low steel handrail which provided no security in the circumstances, but caught him at the top of his thigh, the momentum of his upper body, forcing him over the rail, and he screamed in the realisation that he was going to fall.

'NOOOOO!' Screamed Charlotte, as she saw White fall the 90 feet to the rocks in the river bed below.

She ran to the edge of the viaduct, and looked down at Whites dead body laying prostate in the river, his black soulless eyes, staring back at her. Oscar joined her also looking down at the lifeless body and then expectantly back to Charlotte.

She turned just as CJ reached her, he wrapped his arms around her, and he said, 'Come on Charlotte this way, nothing you can do now,' as he gently led her away.

'Are you okay Charlotte,' asked Edee. genuinely concerned.

'I think so,' said Charlotte, but clearly not, as she struggled to catch her breath, and tears flooded down her cheeks.

'Thank you Oscar,' she said, with clear gratitude and affection, realising the dog had most probably saved her life.

'Come with me,' said Edee, encouraging Charlotte and taking control, leading her back towards the station.

Smith and Jones, both breathless from running had finally caught up and now looked down from the viaduct at Whites body far below.

'Well, that will save Interpol deciding where to hold the trial, and they no longer have a master criminal at large,' said Smith sardonically. 'Well done Gray, and you too Oscar.'

'I gather Mr White was wanted for smuggling on three continents,' said CJ knowingly.

'Yes, he used his base in Dubai to predominately smuggle drugs, but almost anything. Diamonds, fire arms, people trafficking, gold, you name it, he had a finger in it,' replied Jones.

'He also blackmailed his brother at times, to use his legitimate business for the smuggling as you found out Gray. Interpol were after him for crimes in the Middle East, Europe and North America, and your assistance with Edee's in stopping him is very much appreciated,' Smith added, with gratitude.

'Bringing his criminal days to an end, might also just give us some extra brownie points with Peel,' said Jones smiling. 'What say you sir.'

'It might Jones, it just might.'

CHAPTER 70 - WHERE'S THE CAR?

'Gray, we will need a statement from both you and Edee at some point, not urgent but if you could come down to the station in Yorksbey later that would be good,' said Smith, recognising that the loose ends just needed tying up for Interpol.

'No problem, we'll be down later if that's okay.'

With that, the three of them walked back towards the railway station, but saw Edee approaching looking rather anxious.

'It's gone, the DB5, it's gone,' she said, looking astounded.

'Your joking,' said CJ. 'Just when we'd got it back.'

'Someone has taken it but who?' said Jones, with no idea, whatsoever.

'Edee, when you checked the boot, was there anything in it, say a bag or holdall?' asked CJ, rather expectantly.

'There was. How did you know that?' said Edee, looking quizzically at CJ, before adding. 'There was a blue holdall, and do you know what was in it?'

'I could guess, most likely money.'

'Yes,' said Edee. 'Lots of money.'

'Do you have any idea who took the car?' asked Smith.

'Yes I do,' replied CJ. 'But more to the point I think I know where they're going.'

'Well, are you going to enlighten us,' said Smith. 'Or is it your plan to single handily try and solve another crime?'

'I think we should re-convene at the golf club, and if Charlotte is well enough, I suggest you bring her along,' said CJ, looking at Smith and Jones, before adding.

'Oscar, I'm not sure your work for the day is done either.'

With that they made their way to their respective cars, with Charlotte going with PC Perfect, and they all set off, turning right out of the carpark, back towards the golf club.

Smith took the opportunity to call HQ to get a forensics team, and uniform officers, to check on White's body, just in case some unsuspecting walker found him, and had a potential heart attack. Dead bodies were not usually that common in Edendale, but there had now been two there, within less than a week.

'Well done boy,' said CJ, while giving Oscar a treat as he sat on the middle of the back seat. Which while driving is not the easiest of tasks, especially while rubbing his ear affectionately.

'He was brilliant,' added Edee. Also rubbing his other ear. 'You are a very clever and obedient dog.' To which, Oscar licked her ear in return.

CJ led the way in the Audi, with Smith, Jones and Perfect, following close behind, in their own cars.

'You know what's happened don't you?' said Edee, smiling at CJ and touching his hand which was resting on the armrest. 'Your theory still stands up doesn't it?'

'I think it does Edee,' as he again dialled Cliff's number, which was answered immediately.

'Governor, the DB5, it's here at the golf club.'

'Yes, we thought as much, keep an eye on the driver.'

'No problem.'

'Oh, and one other thing, perhaps make it difficult for the car to be moved, but don't actually stop anyone, and if Parker takes the car, follow him discretely and keep me informed.'

'No worri.....,' but suddenly the phone call went dead.

'That doesn't sound good, the quicker we get there the better,' said CJ, concerned for his friend and colleague, as he floored the accelerator. They shortly turned right into Oak Hall Lane and sped down the narrow road towards Edendale, passing on the way the luxury Oak Hall Hotel and Restaurant they had been dining at only yesterday.

Meanwhile the police cars went straight on, back the route they had come, making sure that if the driver of the DB5 was to try and make a run for it, they could cut it off, no matter which route they took.

The Audi now free from police observation, picked up speed and quickly dropped down the hill and under the viaduct and to the junction with Edendale Lane, a quick check to make sure no cars were coming, and CJ turned left. Within a minute they were at the golf club entrance, and he swung the Audi right into the carpark and looked to bring the car to a halt outside the club house.

Edee saw him first, Cliff lying unconscious close to the parked up DB5, and she had the passenger door open before the car screeched to a standstill. She was out and running towards Cliff before CJ even had time to switch off the engine and release his seat belt.

She knelt beside him and felt for a pulse, which she was relieved to eventually find.

'Are you okay Cliff?' she asked, more in hope than expectation at getting a response.

'Huh,' came the reply.

Smith and Jones cars arrived, pulling into the car park, with blue lights flashing.

Parker though, suddenly opened the driver's door of the DB5 and leapt out, catching Edee by surprise, her back to him.

Parker forcibly pulled her upright, his left arm around her neck, the Glock in his right hand pointed at her cheek.

Smith and Jones were now out of their cars, but stopped immediately, as had CJ, having seen that Parker had taken Edee hostage.

'Now don't do anything silly,' said Parker, threateningly. 'Just all back off.'

'Okay Parker, but don't you do anything stupid either,' said Smith, concerned that Parker had previous, and a reputation for armed assault.

'Shut the fuck up. I'm in charge here and this is what you are all going to do. You can all back off and lay on the ground, face down and let me take the French Tart and the Aston Martin.' With that he pointed the gun at them and fired a warning shot over their heads.

The two police officers ducked, and immediately got down on the ground.

CJ though, remained calmly standing and said, 'I suggest you take the sensible route Parker, currently you are not really in much trouble, but this could easily get out of hand.'

'I suggest you also get down now, whoever you fucking are, or your girlfriend gets it, do you understand?' shouted Parker, pointing the gun back at Edee's cheek.

'Parker, currently you are only going to be charged with possession of class A drugs and a stolen car. Even you know, that's not worth killing for?' said CJ evenly, still coolly standing in front of Parker.

'Gray, do as he says,' said Smith, pleading with him not to antagonise Parker.

Just then PC Perfect's marked car came into the carpark and pulled up next to the others.

'That's right Gray, get down on the floor, like the others. Be a good little boy now,' said Parker.

'You hurt Edee and it won't be a prison cell for you. It will be *hell*, I'll see to it,' said CJ, in a tone that Parker recognised and fully understood.

'Just, shut the fuck up and get down,' said Parker. Who fired another shot, this time above CJ's head, to which CJ, again ignored.

'Parker, better men than you have tried to kill me, you haven't the balls.'

'I think he's right,' said Edee very calmly, not a bit like Charlotte had been earlier, before she added, 'Little men like you, need your toys to prove your worth, don't you?'

'You can shut up as well,' said Parker, now pushing the gun firmly into her cheek and holding her tighter around the neck.

CJ suddenly decided to take charge of the situation.

'Oscar. Go find.' The dog ran towards Edee, stopped in front of her, and sat down obediently nose in the air, smelling the residue of drugs on Parker.

'Good boy Oscar,' said Edee, quite quietly, and then suddenly going very limp.

'What,' said Parker, unexpectedly confused and taken off guard.

Swiftly Edee snapped into action, simultaneously she stamped on the top of Parkers right foot, breaking his toes, while smashing her head back violently and breaking his nose and thrusting her elbow into his stomach, knocking the wind out of him.

Before he could react, she then grabbed his right wrist that held the gun and pulled it down, around, and up, forcing him to the ground, continuing to pull the arm back up behind his back as she forced her knee into his shoulder blades, and as she knelt on him, kicked away the gun that he had dropped on the ground.

'Oh Peter, don't take women for granted, or ever call me a French Tart,' said Edee, mockingly, smiling at the prostate Parker, as Oscar started licking the blood from Parker's nose.

'Oh Oscar, don't do that, it's disgusting,' said Edee laughing.

'She's *bloken* my *dose*,' said Parker, clearly in distress, hurting and struggling to speak clearly.

CJ, Smith, and Jones, all quickly ran towards Edee.

'Edee, I momentarily forgot you were a black belt in karate,' said CJ, looking at her admiringly, before adding. 'You were brilliant, as were you Oscar,' as he rubbed the dogs ear affectionately. 'Good boy.'

'Jones, cuff him, and read him his rights,' said Smith firmly.

Jones took over from Edee and dragged Parker up from the ground, and put handcuffs on him, his hands behind his back.

'Peter Parker, I'm arresting you for the possession of Class A Drugs with intent to supply; possession of a stolen vehicle; possession of and discharging an unauthorised firearm; attempted kidnap; and the suspected murder of Oliver Tate, *"You do not have to say anything. But it may harm your defence if you do not mention when questioned something which you later rely on in court. Anything you do say may be given in evidence."* Do you understand?' said Jones, while blood was still pouring from Parker's broken nose.

CJ put his arms around Edee, grabbing her tightly

'Are you okay?' he said. Then looking into her deep brown eyes, he unexpectedly kissed her passionately, realizing how much he really loved her.

She was briefly taken by surprise at his sudden show of affection, but melted in his arms and kissed him back passionately.

CJ, suddenly realising everyone was looking at them, especially a very jealous Smith, let Edee go, and he looked up, extremely self-conscious.

'I didn't kill Oliver Tate,' shouted a limping Parker, as Jones led him slowly towards Perfect's marked police car, Parker was virtually pleading with the policeman. 'Possession of drugs and a stolen car yes, but murder. No!'

'Just come quietly,' said Jones. 'You'll get your say when we get to the station.'

'But I didn't do it! It was her! That blonde over there, the one in the red coat!' said Parker, pointing towards

Charlotte, who was slowly walking away from him towards the Club House.

'But you would say that, wouldn't you,' said Jones, apparently disregarding Parker's accusation, and putting him in the back of the car.

CHAPTER 71 – THE PLAN

CJ and Edee went to check on Cliff who was now on his feet, a little confused and slightly concussed, but otherwise okay.

'Do you need to go to hospital to be checked out?' asked Edee, concerned for her friend.

'Nah, taken worst blows than that, haven't we Governor?' said Cliff smiling, slightly groggy but speaking the truth.

'Yes, I think we have Cliff, but are you sure you're okay?'

'Yes, stop fussing.'

'Did you see who knocked you out?' asked Edee. Still anxious for her friend, as Smith joined them

'No, it could have been anyone, but I suspect it was Parker, when he saw me looking around the DB5,' said Cliff.

'Mr Ledger, we will want a statement from you at some point, and I'm afraid another one from you two please,' said Smith, rather wryly. 'But it's not urgent.'

'Smith, I think you should check the boot of the DB5, either for the holdall with the money, or the spare tyre with the cocaine,' said CJ. 'Also perhaps check Parker's own car.'

'Thank you Gray, I do know my job,' said Smith sarcastically, but added more sympathetically. 'But thanks again for your help, you have both been a godsend today and also Oscar of course.'

'We're happy to oblige as always Simon,' added Edee, sensing again she needed to calm down the two alpha males.

'Cliff, if you are feeling up to it, I've got another task for you, and I think you may find Oscar useful,' said CJ earnestly.

'Sure, I'll be fine, what is it?'

CJ quickly explained what he wanted, and Cliff wandered off towards the Golf Shop with Oscar on his lead, who was wondering what he had done wrong to be shackled, and away from his master.

CJ and Edee wandered over to Smith who was looking in the boot of the DB5.

'No holdall, but the spare wheel and drugs are here,' said Smith. 'So at least we have Parker on a number of charges, Barnsley Nick will be pleased he's off the streets at least for a while, and a lot longer if we prove he murdered Tate.'

'On that subject Smith, I don't think he did it,' CJ said firmly.

'No, neither do I Simon,' said Edee. 'James has a theory, and we would like your help and assistance to try and flush out the killer.'

'You don't, and you do,' said Smith, rather taken back by the turn of events, but because of Edee's support of CJ, was curious as to what they wanted.

'I think all the potential suspects and protagonists will be at the club, and I would like you to go along with me, as I explain what I think happened, and who killed Bart,' said CJ, far more in hope than expectation, but was pleasantly surprised by the reply.

'Ah, a Miss Marple in the making have we?' said Smith jovially, laughing at his own joke.

'Well actually, more a Poirot and Miss Marple tag team, but yes,' said a smiling Edee.

'Okay, we'll try it, but if it's not going well, or not helping the investigation, I may stop you.'

'That's seems reasonable,' said CJ, as he explained what he planned, while they walked towards the golf club and the lounge bar.

CHAPTER 72 - WAS THIS HOW IT HAPPENED?

Smith, CJ, and Edee walked into the Lounge bar, they were pleased to see, that most of the suspects that Smith and Jones had been considering were there, and Smith sort to gain their interest.

'Excuse me, I wonder if I could have your attention.' All those in the room looked up from what they were doing or stopped and looked at him.

'I think you all know me, I'm DI Smith, and you have been interviewed by myself or DS Jones at some point since the body of Oliver Tate was found on the 4th Green, and I thought I would update you all on certain recent events that have affected our investigation.'

In the room were the following, Earl Hargrove sitting in his usual chair sipping a glass of his customary tipple of Louis Treis, and next to him sat the Major, looking rather annoyed at the imposition of being summoned, with his arms firmly folded.

Charlotte sat on one of the brown leather chesterfield sofas, still wearing sun glasses to hide the bloodshot eyes she had, following her tearful encounter with Mr White, next to her, was Ian Westbank, who had heard about her recent ordeal and was seeking to comfort her.

Justin sat at the bar on a high stool talking idly to Nancy, who had been asked to remain there to serve drinks to those that required them. Jarvis was behind the bar in his usual position taking stock and reviewing the lunch time takings. The only potential suspect not there was Carol Tate, but CJ had told Smith her presence wasn't required, albeit she may possibly need to be questioned later for a statement.

'Well get on with it,' said the Major, venting his growing impatience.

'Thank you Major, this is a serious matter, which I hope you hadn't forgotten.'

'Yes, sorry,' said the Major, suddenly rather more conciliatory.

'Thank you,' and Smith continued. 'Many of you won't be aware, but a criminal wanted by Interpol was here from Dubai, and had been a suspect in the murder, and earlier today he kidnapped Charlotte Tate, but he was subsequently involved in a tragic accident, and has unfortunately lost his life.'

The majority of those in the room seemed unmoved and at a loss as to the significance, except for Charlotte who let out a muffled sob, Justin though, looked across at his step mother, rather more anxious at the news.

'Are you okay Charlotte?' he said, in a concerned voice, as after he left this morning he knew she was not her usual self. Charlotte looked at him and nodded and smiled weakly, while Westbank consoled her by putting his arm around her and also holding her hands, which had the most expensive false fingernails possible.

'Also, just a short time ago, Peter Parker, a criminal from Barnsley and a known associate of Tate's, was arrested for being in possession of cocaine, an unauthorised firearm, a stolen Aston Martin and more importantly suspicion of assisting in the murder of Oliver Tate.'

This fact did cause a stir, Earl Hargrove who up to now had been sitting rather indifferent to events, suddenly looked up, as the car he had purchased was being discussed. Also, Justin looked rather sheepish as he also knew what was or had been in the car, while Charlotte looked rather relieved, as did the Major.

Earl Hargrove downed his drink and called out, 'Nancy, another of my usuals, please.' At which the young waitress turned to Jarvis, who was already pouring the cognac.

'Now, you all know CJ Gray and Madame Eden Songe, they have been assisting North Yorkshire Police in bringing to justice these two criminals and because of their involvement Mr Gray has a theory as to what occurred on the night of the murder. He is going to convey this too you, and seek your assistance, as all of you he believes are involved, some more than others. Gray the floor is yours.'

'Thank you DI Smith,' said CJ easily, he was well versed in speaking to large numbers of people. He looked at all the suspects one at a time and finally said, 'Thank you all for being prepared to assist the police, and to go along with my thoughts, as I think it is in all your interests to establish the true events relating to Oliver Tate's death. If only so it eliminates the rest of you, and we can then get back to doing what we all enjoy, playing golf.'

'Here, Here,' said the Major and Earl Hargrove, who were desperate for club affairs to return to normal.

'I will start by telling you how I believe Oliver Tate died and what went on at the Charity Ball and immediately afterwards, including Bart's potential thought processes. I will also provide my opinion as to how you are all involved in this unfortunate crime.'

'So, you don't believe it was murder?' asked Justin. Before regretting having spoken and drawing attention to himself.

'I am currently unsure, but I am positive that things will become clearer with *all* your assistance,' said CJ, before continuing.

'The police had quickly established that everyone here, and the two criminals just mentioned now by DI Smith, had a motive to kill Bart, some stronger than others, but all of you had a motive.'

'That's a bit strong,' said Earl Hargrove rather indignantly.

'I'm sorry if I have offended you Earl Hargrove, but I'm afraid it is a fact, and you will all know that, even you,' said CJ evenly. With that, he then continued without waiting for a reply.

'The police also established that you all had the opportunity, that is obvious to anyone considering the case, but the issue that has given DI Smith and DS Jones the biggest headache has been the *means,* and this is where my theory comes to the fore.

'I will however prior to disclosing that, just give everyone a little background as to the events leading to the death.'

'We are aware that Bart and Charlotte had an altercation as the ball drew to a conclusion, but there were events that occurred during the evening which the *Suspect* as I will call them, overheard or became aware of, either by stealth or good, or bad fortune depending upon your point of view.'

CJ now had everybody's interest, and they were all very attentive.

'Bart had previously been threatened by our two criminals because of his involvement in the smuggling of drugs in the Aston Martin imported from Dubai, and the apparent double crossing of them both. They both wanted back what Oliver Tate had apparently taken from them, and they made it clear that if he didn't quickly produce the goods, they would kill him. Not a good place to be.'

'He had also accused his wife of adultery with one of the criminals, with evidence provided by the other, what a tangle web.'

CJ, paused for a moment to let the statement sink in, before continuing.

'I now give you my take on the *means*. After the *Ball* had ended and with Bart's adrenaline flowing, he was still on a high and in need of time to think, so he decided to go and hit some golf balls by the clear moonlit evening. He obtained his car keys from the Night Porter and went to his car and pulled out his five iron from his bag in the boot and for good measure took his Glock revolver from the glove box, as he felt the need for reassurance just in case he was threatened again. He returned the car keys to the night porter and made his way down to the 1st Tee, having picked up a basket of range balls that were lying by the golf shop.

'Bart, albeit rather worse for drink and a reason he probably did what he did, then started to hit golf balls from the first tee, which is bathed in light from the bridge street lamps. As I said, either in frustration, or to help him think, or vent his anger or annoyance, who knows, but hit some balls he did.'

At which point, the Major interrupted,

'That surely seems a bit farfetched. How have you come to this unusual conclusion?'

'Major, please don't call me *Shirley*,' said CJ dryly, before continuing. But I know, because I spoke with Tom, the head groundsman, who confirmed that range golf balls were found on the 1st Fairway, at about 150 to 160 metres from the tee, on the morning after the Charity Ball. Also, Tate's 5 iron is missing from his golf bag. Shall I continue Major?'

'Yes, I suppose so,' said the Major, now feeling rather foolish for butting in.

CJ continued. 'The *Suspect* had as I said previously, overheard a number of things that would potentially be to their advantage, and armed with the information either followed Bart or came across him and took the opportunity to try and blackmail him.

'An altercation took place, tempers became frayed, but the result was that Bart was hit with the 5 Iron and he fell and hit his head on one of the large stone markers that identify the Tee and Hole Number, killing him instantly.

'The Post Mortem Report identifies that the cause of death was by blunt force trauma, and a further review of the 1st Tee stone and the wound, will I believe, verify the impact of the stone caused the death.'

CJ, again paused for dramatic effect, but also to allow the audience to digest his opinion, before continuing.

'The *Suspect* initially panicked, but what was fortunate for them was that Bart had his gun on him. The quick-thinking *Suspect* dragged the body to the adjacent 4th Green, away from the stone and positioned the body to look like a suicide. They shot Bart in the mouth, wiped the gun clean of their finger prints and put the gun in his right hand.

'The *Suspect then* picked up the 5 iron, the empty basket of balls, Bart's mobile phone and made their escape, hoping that the police would think it was suicide,' said CJ. Before Smith added.

'Well that certainly fits with the Post Mortem, that's for certain, so we now have the *means,* but how does this help find the *Suspect*?' asked Smith.

Who was pleased to have a means, but was concerned that it didn't particularly fit with the person currently arrested.

'Quite so DI Smith, if you let James continue, I think things will potentially become clearer,' said Edee, who was now sat on a bar stool, observing everyone's reaction to CJ's theory.

'Thank you Edee,' said CJ, before continuing again. 'The issue then, now that the means has been established, is who actually did it?'

'Well, the evidence led the police to believe Parker did it, but recent evidence and my observations lead me to believe it wasn't any of you men here, but a woman is the *Suspect.* especially as Parker believes a Blonde Woman in a Red Coat is the guilty person.'

With that, everyone in the room looked at Charlotte, the blonde in the red coat, which she was still wearing.

'You can't be serious CJ, I didn't do it,' said Charlotte, clearly taking aback by the revelation. 'I went straight home after the Ball, Ian took me, didn't you?' as she looked to Ian for support.

'Yes. I did,' said Ian, but without the conviction Charlotte had expected.

'The thing is Charlotte, there is much to incriminate you, and Parker's accusation does add weight to your guilt,' said CJ, toying slightly with Charlotte's emotions.

'But I've never met him,' said Charlotte, clearly now rather distressed.

'Surely that's not true,' said CJ. 'Only this week Cliff Ledger, followed a blonde woman in a red coat onto the train at Yorksbey, and by all accounts they met up with Parker at the station at Edendale and drove off with him.'

'That wasn't me, it wasn't me,' said Charlotte, who was starting to sob as Ian tried to comfort her.

'Gray, can't you see your upsetting her, she didn't do it, the evidence is not conclusive,' said Ian, now seeking to support his lover.

'The problem is though that today, Edee and I established categorically that Parker did actually meet a blonde with a red coat on the night of the murder,' said CJ.

'Well, it wasn't me,' said Charlotte, now pleading with CJ to believe her.

'How did you establish that,' said Smith, now also very much intrigued.

'The security system at Overhear Manor is pretty sophisticated, as you know, and I have cameras that monitor the 9th Green and 10th Tee at the bottom of the garden. We checked them for activity on the night of the murder, and Parker met with a blonde woman at 2.15 am. Parker then returned to the Watermill Arms, and the woman walked back over the bridge towards the golf club.'

'So, it wasn't Parker that murdered Tate,' said Smith, realising the error they had made arresting him for suspicion of murder.

'No, it wasn't, it was possibly a very clever and manipulative woman,' said CJ decisively.

'You see, on the morning after Tate's death, there were footprints in the dew. Large and small footprints on the 1st Tee but only small footprints on the 4th Green, those of a woman, and there was evidence the body had been dragged from the 1st Tee to the 4th Green,

'Well, it wasn't me,' said Charlotte, before adding. 'Not that I'm not clever or manip…..,' but stopped short thinking how her words were starting to sound.

'No Charlotte it wasn't you, you were wearing stiletto heels, and as Edee demonstrated on the morning after, walking in stiletto heels on the grass is near impossible, it needed someone who was wearing flatter shoes, those worn by people working long hours on their feet.'

'It also couldn't be you Charlotte, because you knew Bart was left-handed, but the *Suspect* didn't. They put the gun in his right hand, something Bart wouldn't do if it were suicide, nor would you have done, but you did, didn't you Nancy?'

'What, what are you talking about,' said Nancy, rather astounded at the sudden developments. 'Why are you asking me?

'Because you killed Bart, and have been trying to mislead everyone for a while,' said CJ, looking Nancy straight in the eye, seeking some weakness, but none was forthcoming.

'It can't be me, I'm not a blonde, I'm a brunette, you can all see that,' said Nancy, nonchalantly, dismissing CJ's theory.

'Yes Gray, she's a brunette, it can't be her,' said Justin, but as usual regretting speaking and colouring up as he was suddenly the centre of attention.

'Come on CJ, I think you have gone a bit too far now,' said Jarvis. 'Nancy is such a nice girl, she couldn't do it, she is nothing but kind and helpful, even though she hasn't been here that long.'

'That's all true, but nonetheless, I'm afraid that Nancy is the *Suspect* and the killer.'

'Don't be silly Mr Gray,' said Nancy, rather coyly. 'I'm just a simple waitress.'

'A waitress, yes, simple no. Let me try and convey what I think has occurred,' said CJ, setting off again with his theory, everyone now even more attentive than before.

'I think that having overheard the argument between Batman and Spiderman at the Ball, you saw an opportunity to potentially blackmail Bart, to put right the wrong of 19 years ago.'

Nancy remained quiet, looking straight back at CJ, and unmoved.

'What do you mean Gray? The wrong of 19 years ago?' said Smith, struggling himself to understand what was happening.

'Would you like to expand on this Justin?' said CJ, looking cooly at him. 'I think you know the story.' But the young man kept his head down and his mouth shut.

'Perhaps if I explain,' said Edee, sensing that her feminine ways might encourage a better response, before continuing. 'I checked with the Barnsley registrar, to establish who Nancy's parents were. Now registrars can sometimes be less than helpful, but he finally gave me the information I was looking for.'

'Yes, you see Edee is quite the charmer when she needs to be, a bit like you Nancy,' said CJ, but not getting the waitress to open up.

'Your father is, or was, Oliver Tate. Wasn't he?' said Edee, looking at Nancy, seeking confirmation, or acknowledgement of the fact, but still none was forthcoming.

'The thing is, we think you have only just found this out, because your mother died only recently, didn't she?'

'I don't know what this has to do with Mr Tate's death,' said Nancy, very calmly, sensing that people expected a response, before adding. 'And, as I said, you can all see, I'm not a blonde.'

'No, you're not Nancy, but the thing is, you were a blonde on the night of the ball,' said CJ accusingly.

'What are you talking about Gray,' said Justin, but realising he may well be making things worse.

'On the night of the ball, all the staff were also in fancy dress, and Nancy had chosen Goldilocks as her character for the Ball, and she had a wonderful *blonde* wig, not to dissimilar to Charlottes hair. The other thing is that on the night of the Ball, Charlotte was Cat Woman, and wore a black wig, so Parker never saw Charlotte as a blonde, but only you Nancy.'

Everyone, and they had all been at the ball, suddenly turned as one and looked at Nancy, and they now quickly realised who Goldilocks had been, and how she had been so innocuous at the ball.

'After the ball had ended, you met up with Parker at the 9th Green, I can only assume you thought that you could cut a deal with him, there was the drugs, the money and the DB5, all potentially on offer, but I don't think he was bothered about partnering with you, he wanted it all, and from the CCTV images I think he told you to do one.

'So, you forlornly walked off, back to the club house, but on your way back you came across your father, Oliver Tate, amazingly hitting some golf balls.

'We all know my thoughts about what tragically happened after that,' added CJ solemnly.

'Mr Gray this is all very interesting, but I didn't do it, it's a fanciful theory, nothing more,' said Nancy incredulously.

'Perhaps, but the thing is, you then tried to implement Charlotte and anyone else, to throw the police off your scent, because your plan for the death to be considered as suicide was not washing with the pathologist or the police.'

'You tried to implement Earl Hargrove with the discussion he had with the Major.'

'So, it was you. You little…..' said Earl Hargrove, deeply hurt that his reputation had been brought into question.

'You then lured my *Fixer,* Cliff Ledger on a wild goose chase to implement Charlotte with Parker. You wore the wig again and red coat, plus sun glasses, which Charlotte had taken to wearing, because of the bruise to her cheek. Once you were looking like that, Cliff just assumed it was Charlotte, especially when Justin drove you to the station.'

Justin now looked extremely uncomfortable, and was as bright as a beetroot.

'You see, I think Justin, was sympathetic to your predicament Nancy. The fact that your father hadn't contributed to your upbringing, Justin felt as any half-brother would, the need to help right the wrong, and so he assisted you.'

'When you lost Cliff at Edendale station, you were just going to the buffet and to do your voluntary work, all very worthy, but you had previously arranged to meet Parker there and that's what Cliff saw, his car. Plus, when Edee finally arrived, you had removed the wig, sunglasses, and coat, and boldly misdirected her, telling her that Charlotte had driven off with Parker.'

Nancy was now not looking quite so easy, but still holding her nerve.

'All theory, hypothetical conjecture, nothing more, where's your evidence Mr Gray?'

'That's true Gray, where's your evidence?' said Smith, giving Nancy some unexpected support.

'That is the issue. This is my theory, my take on things, what I believe happened, but where is the evidence? said CJ paradoxically. 'That is the question.'

CHAPTER 73 - THE EVIDENCE

CJ turned away slightly forlornly, and looked towards the door as Nancy smiled, suddenly looking slightly relieved.

'CJ, you're telling me it's just a hunch, a theory,' said Charlotte, now concerned that the actual evidence implemented her and Parker. 'Tell me you have more. Please,' she begged.

'So that's it,' said Justin. Also, now rather relieved and looking rather more self-assured. 'You have no evidence?'

Suddenly the door opened, and in rushed Oscar, followed directly by Cliff, who was holding a Blue Holdall, a Red Coat, a Blonde Wig, a 5 Iron and a mobile phone, behind him was DS Jones.

'Ah, here is the evidence,' said CJ wryly. 'Thank you Cliff, Oscar. and DS Jones.'

Nancy and Justin suddenly looked totally crest fallen, the wind taken from their sails, but Nancy rallied quickly.

'So you have some props, what links them to me? they could be anyone's.' said Nancy, but not now, so self-assured.

'True they could, but I guess DS Jones will tell us where they were found.'

'Hello everyone,' said DS Jones. 'The items here were all found, just now, in Nancy's locker in the staff canteen. Oscar and Cliff found them having earlier been tipped off by CJ.'

The room as one suddenly gasped, except for Nancy and Justin.

'So what! Someone else could have planted them. She could have!' said Nancy, pointing dramatically at Charlotte, but desperately clutching at straws for a get out of what was starting to look like a completely hopeless situation.

'Maybe,' said CJ. 'But I don't think so. Cliff, just let Oscar sniff those things your holding. There's a good boy.' Oscar proceeded to sniff all the items.

'My trained tracker dog, Oscar, will now smell the scent of the person who has recently worn or touched these items and seek them out,' said CJ, looking directly at Nancy.

'Right Oscar. Go find.'

Oscar immediately ran across the room, and sat bolt upright in front of Nancy, who instantly looked a beaten woman.

'So, you dog can do tricks, so what,' said Nancy, with one final throw of the dice, trying to convince everyone of her innocence.

'Nancy, I think the games up,' said CJ. 'Plus, I have my final piece of the jigsaw here,' and CJ held up a beautiful earing.

'This, I believe is yours. You will remember at breakfast on the morning after the ball, I commented on your beautiful and unique earing. At the time I initially thought it was a single earing you were wearing, but by the way you reacted at the time, and you held your ear, it made me subsequently think it probably wasn't,' said CJ, seeking a reaction from Nancy.

At that moment Nancy, involuntarily held her ear, and on it was the identical earing that matched the one in CJ's fingers.

'You see Nancy, I found this the morning after Bart's death and more importantly, I found it where he died, on the 1st Tee.'

With that Nancy, put her hands to her head.

'Enough,' she said. 'Enough, I can't do this anymore. Yes it was me, I'm so sorry.' She fell to her knees crying, with Oscar licking her profusely, in apparent sympathy for the young waitress.

Edee walked across and helped Nancy to her feet and hugged her.

'Would you like to tell us your side of events,' said Edee, compassionately, recognising that Nancy possibly didn't intentionally kill her father, Oliver Tate.

Nancy presently composed herself and the others listened intently.

'Mr Gray, you're a clever man, and I believe compassionate and tolerant. I do hope the courts are equally understanding of my plight.'

To which CJ nodded graciously, acknowledging her statement.

'Your theory is actually very accurate and close to reality.

'However, I just want you to now understand that I didn't mean to kill the father I didn't know.

'But I'm not sorry he's dead.

'You see he got my mother pregnant, and then disowned her. He never provided any help for her or me, and my mother never wanted me to have anything to do with the heartless bastard, that was my biological father.

'My mother, all my life, just told me that my father didn't offer to support her or me and she wouldn't tell me his name, not until on her dying deathbed when she finally did.

'Oliver Tate was the reason my mother died so young, at just 42 she drank herself to death, and when I found out who my father was, I vowed to get some recompense.

'I initially latched onto Justin, as just a means to get to my father, but I grew to like him, and he has supported me like the brother I didn't know I had. He has been kind and sympathetic, and he felt that our father should have contributed to my upbringing, so he tried to help me.'

At that point, Nancy broke down crying, and Justin went to her side and held her tight.

'Oh Nancy, I'm so sorry it hasn't turned out as we hoped,' said Justin, before continuing. 'Once the Aston Martin was delivered with the drugs and money, we looked to get something by hook or by crook, but it didn't work out as expected.'

Thankful of Justin's intervention, Nancy then felt strong enough to continue.

'I did meet Parker, and hoped he would do a deal of some sort, he'd perhaps take the car, it was worth far more than the drugs were. Justin the drugs and me the money, but he wasn't having any of it, well not until I killed my father.

'But I didn't do it deliberately, please believe me.

'On my way back from our meeting on the course, Batman was hitting golf balls, worse the wear for drink. I approached him and said who I was, and that I would like to get to know him, but he wasn't having any of it. He called my mother a cheap whore, well actually far worse than that, but I'm not going to repeat what he said.

He started swearing at me and telling me to go away and leave him alone and never try to see him again. I pleaded with him to just listen, and help be a part of my life.'

Nancy started to cry again, and she struggled to speak.

'Are you okay Nancy, do you want a drink?' asked Edee sensitively.

'No thank you Madame Songe, you are so kind though,' said Nancy, sincerely, before going on.

'He then hit me, like he hit Charlotte at the *Ball*, it really hurt, no one had ever done that too me before, I was so angry.

'Angry, that he had hit me.

'Angry, that he had also dismissed my mother when she also needed him.

'Angry, that he didn't support my mother or me.

'Angry, that he didn't want anything to do with me.

'So I picked up the golf club and hit him, and surprisingly he went down.

'I shouted. *"Get up you bastard,"* but he didn't, he had hit his head on the stone as he fell, and he was dead.

'The rest you all know.'

With that she turned to Justin and grabbed him tight, 'I'm sorry Justin, please forgive me for killing your dad.'

'I forgive you, he has always been a heartless bastard, I'm not sure he ever loved me, and I have never loved him, but I will always love you.'

Smith nodded to Jones, before saying, 'Thank you Nancy for providing your side of events, I'm sure that the courts will take this information and your admission into consideration.'

'Nancy Williams, I'm arresting you for the Manslaughter of Oliver Tate and for perverting the course of justice, *"You do not have to say anything. But it may harm your defence if you do not mention when questioned something which you later rely on in court. Anything you do say may be given in evidence."* Do you understand?'

With that PC Perfect led her away, as Jones continued.

'Justin Tate, I'm arresting you on suspicion of perverting the course of justice, *"You do not have to say anything. But it may harm your defence if you do not mention when questioned something which you later rely on in court. Anything you do say may be given in evidence."* Do you understand?'

Jones then also led him away, following PC Perfect and Nancy.

Edee wandered over to Charlotte.

'Are you okay? I guess it's been a long day for you and a lot to take in.'

'I'll be okay, plus I get half of Bart's fortune,' Charlotte said sardonically. 'I'm made of strong stuff. CJ may have told you a few things I let him know the other evening. It'll take more than today's events to break me,' added Charlotte, smiling weakly but feeling very down and near to tears.

Edee, embraced her and said,' Come on let's get Ian to buy you a drink, I think you deserve one.'

'You know your very lucky don't you,' said Charlotte, with feeling.

'What do you mean?'

'To have a fella like CJ, that loves you so much,' said Charlotte as she looked over towards CJ, who was stroking Oscar.

Edee's eyes followed.

'I guess so,' said Edee, quietly, not quite sure how to respond.

'Of course he does, you only have to see how he looks at you. Make sure you don't lose him, he's a keeper that one, and if you don't, I'll be after him in a flash,' said Charlotte, smiling at Edee and hugging her tight.

Chapter 74 - All's well that ends well

DI Smith, strolled over to CJ, Cliff and Oscar as Edee joined them.

'Well, you three, sorry you four, thank you for your assistance, it has been very helpful,' said Smith earnestly.

'You're welcome,' they all said together, and Oscar gave a short bark.

'I also now see how the DB5 got here,' said Smith, as he continued. 'While we were all preoccupied at the viaduct, Nancy took the opportunity to take the car and the money.'

'Yes she had been working again at the station buffet,' said CJ, 'and seeing her chance to finally get some recompense, called Parker to do one last deal which he agree too. He agreed to take the car and drugs, and she would take the money.'

'The problem was that Cliff was nosing about,' said Edee. 'Parker knocked Cliff out, but then we all turned up, so Nancy only had time to put the money, with all the other things in her locker, hoping to move them later when no one was about.'

'She is quite smart and bright for a young girl,' CJ said, 'it's such a shame she got involved so tragically with Bart.'

'Yes, but I suspect the judge may be lenient with her, when it comes to sentencing,' said Smith, also feeling rather sorry for the young woman.

'I do hope so,' said Edee, sincerely.

'Right then,' said Smith. 'Despite everything, I would like to think we would have got there in the end without your help, but to be honest I'm not so sure, and especially with the top brass wanting the case closing as a suicide.'

'Sometime a little help is all you need,' said CJ, smiling, and for once being courteous to Smith.

'Are you feeling okay James?' asked Edee ironically. 'It's not like you to be so reasonable with Simon.'

'You would think he had the bang on the head, not me,' said Cliff, also ribbing the CJ.

'Okay, enoughs enough,' said CJ, taking the jesting in good humour.

'Simon, when do you think you will be done with the DB5?' asked CJ, politely changing the subject.

'Forensics need to do the once over, but not long, I'll give you or Edee a call if that's okay,' replied Smith.

'That's fine and understood.'

'If you could all come down the station to complete *all* your statements, as soon as possible, that would also be good, and once again thanks for your help, it is very much appreciated.'

Smith then picked up the bagged evidence and made his way out.

Earl Hargrove and the Major then joined them.

'Well done, CJ, Madame Songe, jolly good work,' said Earl Hargrove. 'And you too, Cliff isn't it, you have all been wonderful in bringing this saga to a close. Thank you, most sincerely.'

'Don't forget Oscar,' said the Major, rubbing Oscar's ear, and showing him rather unusual affection.

'No, we definitely can't forget Oscar, and all that he has done,' said Earl Hargrove, laughing.

'CJ, I'll be in touch about the delivery, I've arranged the payment to the British Legion as we discussed, all sorted,' continued Earl Hargrove. With that, he shook everyone's hand before starting to walk off, with the Major close behind.

'Oh, by the way Major,' said CJ curiously,' if Bart had become chairman, what would you have done?'

'Never would have happened, wrong sort altogether,' replied the Major smiling at CJ, with a twinkle in his eye, as he continued walking.

'Right, you lot, time for home I think,' said CJ. 'Cliff do you want a room for the night or are you off, back down to Suffolk?'

'I think I'll get off home if that's okay Governor, it's been a while since I crossed the threshold,' said Cliff dryly.

'No worries, thanks again. I couldn't do things without you,' said CJ, most sincerely and touched his forehead with his right forefinger, in salute to his friend.

Edee grabbed her friend and kissed him on the cheek, 'Merci. Thanks Cliff, you take care now and a safe trip.'

'Bye all, see you soon, and you too Oscar.'

And Cliff marched out to find his motor bike for the trip home.

'Then there were three,' said CJ, looking fondly into Edee's eyes. 'Shall we go and get your car and maybe some dinner?'

'I'd like that,' said Edee, and they strolled off arm in arm, with Oscar leading the way as usual.

Ten minutes later the two of them walked into the hallway of Overhear Manor.

'Mrs Wembley! We're home! Edee's staying for dinner if that's okay,' shouted CJ warmly.

Mrs Wembley walked through from the kitchen, in her usual cheerful manner, and was very pleased to see Madame Edee holding onto Master James arm.

'You both look happy with yourselves, have you had a good day?'

'Well, I think you would call it eventful Mrs Wembley. What say you Edee?' said CJ, looking longingly at her.

'I think that probably sums it up, but also rewarding and eye-opening,' replied Edee.

'Oh, very good,' said Mrs Wembley, not prying further as was her way, before continuing. 'And will Madame Edee be stopping the night?'

'Will I?' said Edee hopefully, looking deeply at CJ.

'Yes she will,' said CJ firmly.

'Oh. That's wonderful,' said Mrs Wembley, before wandering off back to the kitchen, pleased that Master James and Madame Edee were at last getting on so well, she had always known they eventually would.

'Well Edee, shall we go to bed then?' asked CJ evenly and rather unexpectantly.

'It's a bit early for sleeping isn't it? and we haven't had dinner,' said Edee, looking and sounding rather confused.

'Who said anything about sleeping,' said CJ, smiling and kissing Edee longingly before lifting her off her feet and marching her off up the stairs.

'Oscar, go find Mrs W, there's no place for three, not with what I have planned,' said a smiling CJ, before again passionately kissing Edee, happy to have his true love in his arms at last.

EPILOGUE

'……..you knew we were bringing the imported car to Overhear Manor to swap it with the one Grandad bought back in 1965, we only needed some false plates and the Police and HMRC were happy to go along with our sting, especially as the car we used was that on the paperwork, which really annoyed Bart, but you reap what you sow,' said CJ, clarifying recent events to Jemima.

'So have you got Grandads Aston Martin back yet from the police, and when are you delivering the imported DB5 to Earl Hargrove?' asked Jemima.

Father and Daughter were catching up on the recent events with a long overdue telephone conversation, it must have been all of 5 days since they had last spoken!

'Smith rang me yesterday and said your grandad's DB5 can be picked up today, and now Earl Hargrove has given £2m to the British Legion, I plan to deliver the DB5 that's been stored in our garages since the exchange tomorrow. With Alham Industries, also having been paid in full, and Earl Hargrove expecting to have to pay another £3m to Tate, I thought this was a good way out for all, and fortunately he agreed, a win win.'

'Yes, I think it's a great deal all around, it helps service veterans, which is close to your heart, but I still don't get how you found the diamonds though.'

'Well, Oscar did his thing as expected, initially he found where Tate's drugs were hidden, they were in the spare tyre. Smith passed those to HMRC and the Drug squad. The £5k of drugs Cliff bought from Mr White were swapped for them, and they were the ones Parker was charged with possessing, that were in the spare wheel of the DB5 delivered to Tate.'

'Stop waffling Dad it doesn't suit you,' joked Jemima, teasing him.

'Okay, so I digressed. Well, when the drugs were initially removed, Oscar was still not happy, he kept sniffing about and when we investigated further we found a bag of diamonds behind the carburettors. We assumed these were what Mr White was smuggling and removed them, which was potentially a risky strategy as it put Bart in danger, but it didn't matter in the end with both him and White not making it. Two men not particularly missed by anyone and with them not around, no one else in the UK really knew or cared about the diamonds.'

'You mean you didn't tell the police?' interrupted Jemima. 'Will you get into trouble?'

'Not really, I sort of forgot to mention it to the police and HMRC and what they don't know won't hurt them. Alham's also not bothered, he's just pleased his twin brother is no longer forcing him to smuggle, so he's not planning to say anything.'

'Edee Cliff and I, then agreed we should put them to good use, and an *old friend* took them off my hands, after I visited him in Hatton Garden London. The million pounds he offered for them, has now been given to the Armed Forces *Charity (Help for Heroes) SSAFA*. Another win for our brave and glorious former servicemen and women.'

'Oh, that is really wonderful, you must be pleased?'

'Yes, I think everything worked out okay in the end regarding our sting, the only downside is that poor Nancy, will end up in prison for just trying to bond with the father she didn't know.'

'Oh that's such a shame.'

'Smith tells me that for manslaughter the sentence is between two and ten years, but because of the circumstances, Nancy might get away with something nearer the lower term, so hopefully she can set up a new life after serving her time, she might be out within 12 to 24 months with a bit of luck.'

'I do hope so,' said Jemima sincerely, before adding, 'and what about Justin?'

'I get the feeling that Smith may not pursue the charge in the circumstances,' replied CJ.

'Now then, more to the point, how are you getting on with Edee, she sounded very happy when I briefly spoke with her earlier.'

'Why. What did she say?'

'Nothing really, should she have? she just sounded, well, happy and content.'

There was a pause before CJ continued.

Jem, I hope you don't mind, but I need to ask you something.'

'Go on,' said Jemima, sounding rather worried.

'I love Edee, and she loves me,' said CJ, seeking his daughters approval of his developing relationship with the woman he loved.

'Oh dad, that's wonderful. I couldn't be happier for you, and mum would be really happy you have finally moved on. She would want you to enjoy life.'

'You think so?'

'Yes of course.'

'Thanks Jem, I feel so much better now. Sorry though, I've got to go now. I can hear Edee coming down the stairs, you can hear her heels anywhere, and I've got a proposal for her.'

'Now don't go spoiling things by rushing anything.'

'I won't, you take care, love you. Bye Jem.'

'Love you too. Bye Dad.'

CJ ended the call, and he wandered out into the hall, with Oscar following close behind, and he looked up at Edee gracefully coming down the stairs.

He couldn't have felt better, the love making last night had been tender but passionate, she was a wonderful lover. He felt like a young man again, and she looked stunning and elegant as always, he was so happy.

Happier than he had been for years.

As she reached the bottom stair he met her and pulled her to him, he gently chucked her under the chin and he kissed her and she kissed him back passionately, her arms entwined around his neck. She was also feeling the happiest woman in the world.

The kiss reminded her of the night of the Charity Ball, but this time she knew they both shared a love for one another, and would remember it for the rest of their lives.

CJ broke away from their embrace, and he gently held her hands.

He looked intensely into her deep brown eyes.

'I love you Edee.'

'I love you too James,' she solemnly replied

CJ then paused for dramatic effect, he looked at her longingly.

Oscar sat down next to them, he also sensed something big was about to happen.

'Madame Songe, would you do me the honour......'

Edee's heart was suddenly racing, this was all too quick, she had just committed to loving CJ, she loved James with all her heart, but she now wanted their relationship to develop, with courtship, country walks, candlelit dinners, she wanted wooing. Marriage was surely far too quick, but was she just being selfish, she did want something more, she truly loved him,..... but was this all too soon...'

A big grin appeared on CJ's face, and he continued.

'...........of please having dinner with me at Oak Hall at 7 pm this evening.'

'Oh James, you teaser, mon amour. I would really like that. Merci. Oh, yes please,' said a relieved, but oh so happy Edee.

She suddenly realised the first part of the rest of her life was just beginning.

The two of them kissed again, with Oscar sensing life was only going to get better, as he barked at the pair, but he was slightly worried, that he was also no longer the sole centre of his masters universe.

THE END OF THE BEGINNING

CJ Meads

EDENDALE GOLF COURSE

1st	Par 4 - 405 yards	
2nd	Par 4 – 425 yards	
3rd	Par 5 – 510 yards	
4th	Par 3 – 195 yards	
5th	Par 5 – 540 yards	
6th	Par 4 – 300 yards	
7th	Par 3 – 186 yards	
8th	Par 4 – 435 yards	
9th	Par 3 – 175 yards	
10th	Par 5 – 495 yards	
11th	Par 4 – 415 yards	
12th	Par 4 – 385 yards	
13th	Par 4 – 420 yards	
14th	Par 4 – 412 yards	
15th	Par 4 – 375 yards	
16th	Par 4 – 450 yards	
17th	Par 4 – 385 yards	
18th	Par 4 – 465 yards	

Par 72 – 6973 yards

CJ Meads

JAMES BOND GOLDFINGER – ASTON MARTIN DB5

For those of you unable or unwilling to check out on *Google* what really happened to the original DB5 from the film, I'll just give you a little pocket synopsis of one of the most iconic car's in history.

An original standard Aston Martin DB5, is now worth about £500k, but could be worth well more at auction, having cost £4,248 including tax in 1964. The same cost as a semi-detached house back then.

There were four DB5's used during filming of *Goldfinger,* but only one had all the gadgets. This was Chassis Number DP/2161/1.

A second DB5 was used for driving shots and two others for publicity purposes.

The original, with all the gadgets, was purchased by Anthony Pugliese 111 for $250k, but it went missing from the Florida Boca Raton Airport in 1997. It is believed that the insurers paid out for the theft, and the original, allegedly has never been seen since.

If it were to go to auction today, it would likely make at least £20m

Aston Martin made eight replica cars for the 2019 film *No Time to Die,* and the DB5 seen in the high-speed chase at the start of the film sold for £2.92 m at a charity auction in 2019.

Earl Hargrove I feel got a good deal when all said and done, a true replica for under £6m, but probably priceless……..

CJ Meads

ACKNOWLEDGEMENTS

Well, where do I start, I don't have the usual people to thank because there aren't really any, albeit Sharon and James at least took the time to read the novel, and they quite liked it so, to them a big thank you.

I do understand that many of you, don't have the time in your busy lives for reading, but I hope you, the reader enjoyed the little bit of escapism.

The Literary Agents I contacted didn't like the book, or chose to disregard my requests as they possibly had enough clients, whatever the reason, there was no one looking at my attempt at a novel, and saying well, I like that, lets run with it.

So, I resorted to self-publishing, and Kindle Direct Publishing (KDP) gave me the opportunity to put my work out into the world, and to them I am rather grateful.

Now this way to market doesn't suit everyone, as you need to decide who is going to be you sounding board and your proof reader etc. Well, I chose to just do it myself and hopefully all the errors were removed, but I'm not fully convinced, even now.

I just hope that someone who has bought the book quite likes the story, I do, but then again I wrote it, and it is based upon things I enjoy, or know something about.

Having retired. I felt that having written technical documents and business letters all my working life, I would try writing a novel, mainly because I have always felt that everyone has at least one in them.

So, this is my effort, and to be honest it is the type of book I like, short chapters, entwined story, an easy read whodunnit plot, with a bit of love interest, and some humour to boot. I would like to think there are no plot holes, not like some novels, and if you solved who the killer was before the reveal, then my work is complete.

I hope you got to the end, and also liked it, but I fully understand if you didn't.

I really enjoyed writing the book, and having set a target of 3 months minimum, and a maximum of 6 months to write it, I cracked it out in 10 weeks, albeit proof reading, took just as long.

If enough interest is shown, then the sequel is already floating around in my head, with the plot written down and ready to be fully developed, as you will see in the new title, "It Wasn't Me."

I would just like to know that there is at least one reader who would like to hear more about CJ Gray Mysteries, if there is, I will write it, and send a copy to them for free.

If not, then I will seek to do something else with my endless holiday's now I am retired.

So, I am just left with thanking you dear reader, for deciding to buy a copy, for that I am truly grateful, albeit earning a living from writing is not really my aim, but I do enjoy writing and if someone else also likes my style, then we will continue on our journey together.

The Next CJ Gray Mystery

It wasn't Me?

When Charlotte Tate is found holding the murder weapon while standing over a dead body, the game finally looks up for the stunning Femme Fatale, but she knows who will help her?

CJ Gray, his enigmatic side kick Eden Songe, and his loyal dog Oscar, are drawn into another adventure of murder, blackmail, greed, corruption, kidnapping, lust, and romance.

There are the usual twists and turns in this adventure with the usual red herrings that attempt to throw you off the scent.

Set around the stunning Golf Club in the picturesque North Yorkshire village of Edendale, the story again takes you from the sunny metropolis of Dubai to the glorious Yorkshire Dales.

The story provides an opportunity for everyone to enjoy the escapism, with the expected twists in the next adventure in Edendale, with CJ Gray and the gang.

CJ Gray, Edee, and Oscar are back
Edendale is a village to die for
Another easy-read Whodunnit Mystery

Follow CJ Meads at :-

https://the-world-according-to-spiel.com/

Contact:

email:- cj.meads@btinternet.com